BRIGHT YOUNG THINGS

BRIGHT YOUNG THINGS

Scarlett Thomas

Hodder & Stoughton

Copyright © 2001 by Scarlett Thomas

First published in Great Britain in 2001 by Hodder and Stoughton
A division of Hodder Headline

A Flame Trade Paperback

The right of Scarlett Thomas to be identified as the Author of the Work has been
asserted by her in accordance with the Copyright, Designs and Patents Act 1988.

10 9 8 7 6 5 4 3 2 1

A CIP catalogue record for this title is available
from the British Library.

ISBN 0 340 76781 2

Typeset by Palimpsest Book Production Limited,
Polmont, Stirlingshire
Printed and bound in Great Britain by
Mackays of Chatham plc, Chatham, Kent

Hodder and Stoughton
A division of Hodder Headline
338 Euston Road
London NW1 3BH

For Tom

Thanks. . .

Francesca Ashurst, Sam Ashurst, Hari Ashurst-Venn, Couze Venn, Tom Fraser, Jason Kennedy, Alyss Thomas, Matt Thorne, Nicholas Blincoe, Rebbecca Ray, Simon Trewin, Sarah Ballard, Kirsty Fowkes.

Part One

Bright Young Things

Bright Young Things wanted for big project.
SAE to PO Box 2300 Edinburgh.

The room contains a desk, a woman and two large stacks of paper.

On the right-hand side of the desk, in a uniform pile, are the blank application forms, ready to be sent out. On the other are the stamped addressed envelopes, a haphazard stack, sent in by people wanting further information about the Bright Young Things job. The woman, Jackie, doesn't look at the handwriting on each envelope, except to note the colour. She has been instructed to put application forms only into those envelopes addressed in blue or black. The ones with the small red capitals, the big green swirls, they go in the corner of the room: Discard Pile A. The colour thing doesn't strike her as odd. All her jobs have some weird aspect to them. She just does what she's told.

Jackie is a professional envelope-filler. Occasionally she works from home, but with the kids screaming and chewing up all the envelopes, it isn't ideal. More often she takes jobs like this, in a small room in a damp, empty block. All she has to do is put the forms in the envelopes and note how many she has done. Everything is provided for her; she just has to turn up and do what a machine can't do. You need a brain for this, and eyes, and hands. Some of the envelopes have no stamps; some are already stuck down. These must be discarded.

She's up to number 105, and in a good rhythm now. Like a robot, her left hand pulls an envelope from the stack, scans the colour and either retains or throws it. A discarded envelope is dealt with in two seconds – look and discard, no need to waste time on those. The ones with blue or black writing are opened and filled with a form from the pile. A right-handed movement – into the envelope, tear off the strip and seal. This takes a total of five seconds. The envelopes without strips – the licking ones – Jackie throws on to a pile she's invented: Discard Pile B. For three-sixty an hour she's not going to lick anything. People should think about that when they send SAEs.

In a minute she averages forty-five envelopes. In an hour she can do 2,700. By the end of the day she'll have processed over fifteen thousand.

When the envelopes are stuffed, she will go home and forget about them. Almost thirty per cent of the people who sent off their SAEs will send back the application form, to a different address this time. A man will sit in his office and read them all. And from the two thousand or so he reads, he will select six.

Anne

The 747 lurches in the sky. One more time, and Anne's going to be sick.

'Is it supposed to do this?' she asks the man next to her.

'This is nothing,' he says. 'One time I was on a flight and the plane just dropped two thousand feet.'

'Two thousand?' Anne tries to remain composed.

'Uh-huh. They have to keep on either odd or even numbers depending on which way they're going. You can't drop just one thousand in case you have a head-on with a plane going the other way.'

Anne processes this information. On the large screen at the front of the cabin is a map showing the plane's progress. Anne finds the little graphics of the world and the plane comforting. They abstract the whole experience. Right now the pretend-plane is somewhere over the Atlantic, a couple of hours from Heathrow. After it lands, she's never flying again, Anne decides.

'She sat on a rescue boat for eleven hours,' says the woman on Anne's other side.

'Who?'

'My mother.'

'Sorry?'

'When she was rescued from the *Titanic*, dear.'

On the runway at LA, Anne had mentioned to her neighbours that she was a nervous passenger. The old woman said her mother had been afraid of flying. Then Anne said she was OK on boats, and the old woman had started telling her about the *Titanic*. The woman has slept for most of the flight, but every hour or so she wakes up and continues the conversation.

'I inherited the gift from her.'

'The gift?'

'For reading cards.'

'What, Tarot?'

'Yes, dear. Her cards told her it was a bad week for travelling.'

She nods back off to sleep and Anne opens her book again. She can't get into it. Picking up her walkman from the fold-down table, she inserts the small headphones in her ears. She's on her third REM tape, doing what she always does: fixating on one track and playing it over and over again. For take-off at LA it was 'Losing my Religion'. For a few hours over the Atlantic it was 'Tongue'. Now it's 'Daysleeper'. Over and over again. Her mother would call it obsessive.

As a child, Anne never did anything in half-measures. At Sunday School, some girl once told her that if she ever lied she would go to hell. For a month Anne didn't speak, because she was afraid she would lie by accident. She couldn't even answer a question like *Where are the cornflakes?* with a simple *I don't know*, because maybe she did know and had just forgotten. In Anne's six-year-old mind, the devil would count that as a lie. So she just stopped speaking.

Her mother took her to a child psychologist who had bad breath and wet armpits. Anne continued with her silence, but blushed as he asked her increasingly embarrassing questions about 'inappropriate behaviour', and whether anyone she knew had touched her in ways that had made her feel uncomfortable. The trip to see him did cure her silence in the end, especially when Anne was told she'd have to go back again unless there was an improvement. Between the psychologist and the devil, she chose the devil.

After that, words became Anne's only friends. Diary after diary explained why she couldn't fit in at school; why the other kids thought she was weird. Eventually her parents sent her to a special school, complaining relentlessly about the expense. Once there, Anne was told she was too clever and was sent to a room to read Judy Blume books by herself, to try and bring her down to the level of the other children. She was twelve.

Teen fiction soon became an obsession. Anne read every Judy Blume (her favourite was *Forever*), and then started on Paul Zindel, feasting on his seminal *Pigman* and then *The Pigman's Legacy*. After that it was anything she could get her hands on. American kids — fat or lonely or abused, she had to know more about them. Anne could have been an agony aunt. She knew about *issues*. About bullying, suicide, divorce, pregnancy and sex. Any time one of the other kids had a problem, she knew what to do. Any time one of the other kids was depressed, she lent them her copy of *Are You There God? It's Me, Margaret*.

There were no rules at the special school, and no home-work. When she was twelve and a half, Anne started writing poetry. The poems helped her through what the school called 'learning time', which consisted of non-compulsory lessons. At break times she held court in the playground or in an unused classroom, talking about contraception or religion, firing off rounds of teen angst to bewildered pre-teens who would never quite allow her into their group. Out of school she spent her time at the library. She was a loner, and although no one would have called her a well-adjusted child, she wasn't unhappy.

During her four years at the special school she wrote seven hundred poems and attended no classes. The school thought she would get bored eventually, but she never did. The policy of boring a child into submission had worked on every other pupil who had ever attended, each one drifting into the non-compulsory lessons eventually. But it didn't work on Anne. She simply never got bored.

There didn't seem to be much point in Anne sitting her GCSEs, since she had never attended a class, but the school registered her anyway, hoping for at least a pass in English. She started with the biology exam. The first question was about contraception; the second was about the menstrual cycle. Since these subjects had been more than adequately covered in Anne's teen fiction, she got an A. She also got As in English Language, History, Geography, Religious Studies and Art, for which she just turned up in the exam room and drew an abstract of a penis – not that she'd ever seen one. These marks were enough to get her into a grammer school for her A levels, and finally to Sussex University to read English and Philosophy.

Her parents paid for her flat on Brighton seafront, and for her car, although she hadn't asked them to. They also provided her with a generous allowance, which she spent on books, magazines and sushi, the only food she would eat. Anne's first year was spent thinking about nothing, and her resulting dissertation – on the subject of zero – won her acclaim from everyone except her parents, who decided at the beginning of Anne's second year to withdraw the flat and the car and the allowance, feeling that she had been overindulged.

They had hoped that Anne would be forced into student life, but not being one to be forced into anything, Anne found a bed-sit, worked as a cleaner and read Sartre for a year. At the end of the year she staged her own suicide. Her thesis was a dossier of papers relating to her death: a diary of events leading up to it and the suicide note itself. Her stunt made national news. Her parents reinstated the flat, the car and the allowance, and organised therapy.

In her third year, Anne read Baudrillard and listened to Radiohead. She'd never been into indie music before, preferring saccharine pop and seventies disco, but this was the year she discovered MTV. The new groups fascinated her, and their lyrics were like a kind of poetry: surreal, bubblegum poetry, as meaningless and alienating as anything she'd ever encountered. For her third year project Anne invented a videogame called 'Life'. She graduated with a First.

Anne has never had a best friend or a boyfriend. She's still a virgin.

The trip to America was a last-ditch attempt by her parents to encourage her to get a life. But all she has done in the last two months is think about the end of the world. The aunt she was staying with had to go up to San Francisco to see a sick friend, so Anne was left in the house on her own. She ate lots of potato chips, cheese and alfalfa sandwiches and microwaveable french fries. She discovered chat shows: Geraldo, Ricki, Sally Jesse Raphael, Jerry Springer. And she didn't leave the house — except to visit the twenty-four-hour supermarket — at all during the two months she was there.

The atmosphere on the plane changes as land appears below. The turbulence has gone and everyone's relaxed.

'Looks like we might live after all,' says the man next to Anne.

'Yeah.' She smiles at him.

'I could have told you everything would be all right,' says the old woman, waking up again.

'How?' Anne asks.

'The cards. I did them this morning.'

'Why didn't you tell me that before?'

'You wouldn't have believed me. People only believe in predictions after they've come true. That's how Mother ended up on the *Titanic*. She didn't believe it was a bad week for travelling until the ship started going down.'

The man in the next seat presses a finger to his temple and twists it back and forth, implying the old woman is mad. Anne starts putting her walkman and her book in her rucksack.

✳   ✳   ✳

Anne has a McDonald's at Heathrow before taking the tube back to Islington.

Her parents' flat is empty when she arrives home; she remembers that they are still at the villa in Tuscany. A copy of the *Guardian* lies on the kitchen table, open at the Media Appointments section. On top of it is a note reminding Anne it's time she found a job, and that her allowance runs out in September. Anne's mother has already circled in red the jobs that she thinks would suit her daughter. They are all PR or charity related.

Anne pours a glass of Coke and sits down with the paper. For some reason it is suddenly important that she finds a job from *this* paper. Today. Without meaning to be rebellious, she sets about looking for the most inappropriate job description, but in the end settles for the most vague: *Bright Young Things wanted for big project.*

She doesn't apply for anything else.

Jamie

Some days there seem to be numbers everywhere. Jamie Grant hates numbers. They just can't leave him alone. He hates the number 42 bus, his home telephone number and his inside leg measurement. He once saw a programme where born-again Christians played with barcodes on consumer items, making the number 666 every time. They said consumerism was the work of the devil because you could turn barcodes into the number 666. Jamie laughed when he saw that. Christ, you can turn any number into 666 if you really want to. No, consumerism is not the problem; numbers are.

In a lot of ways he is normal. His parents are divorced, but they both still love him. Last week he attended his first funeral, for a relative he'd never met. He's twenty-two and he's ordinary. Except for one thing. He's just graduated from Cambridge University with a First in Pure Mathematics.

He has a girlfriend he doesn't love and a best friend who is too tall and as a result drinks too much. Jamie masturbates precisely (how he hates that word) twice a day – when he gets up and before he goes to bed. If Carla is around he does it in the bathroom, in secret, and then pretends to be too tired to do it with her. She doesn't mind. She doesn't really like sex, and anyway, she chose him as a husband, not a fuck. In Jamie's circle that's fairly ordinary. No. In *Carla's* circle that's ordinary.

Jamie remembers that he doesn't have a circle; he just orbits other people's.

As he cycles up Mill Road, Jamie plays his favourite game: listing all the things he could do that would really surprise everyone. He could get contact lenses to replace his swotty glasses; maybe green ones. Then, with his new green eyes he could start a band and become like Damon or Liam ... no, definitely Damon. He could dump Carla and shag groupies. Perhaps go around the world. That would surprise everyone. Or maybe he could just get married, have kids and go on the dole. What he really doesn't want to be is a mathematician. Because that's what everyone expects.

His favourite fantasy is to be a pilot and fly a plane. If everyone would get off his back, he'd just fly his own plane around the world and have adventures. He imagines finding strange lands and looking for secrets, like Indiana Jones or Lara Croft. He likes Lara Croft. He likes pop music. He likes motorbikes. So why the hell does everyone see him as such a geek? It's those fucking numbers, that's why. Because he knows what they do. Because he can work out the square root of things. That makes him a geek. What's the square root of everything? Nothing.

In a worse mood than when he went out (to get rid of his mood), he returns and lets himself into the small terraced house he shares with Carla and Nick. He wishes they'd do something interesting. He always makes an effort to come home slightly earlier than he is expected, hoping he will find them fucking. The thought turns him on in a peculiar way. Not that he'd really want to see Carla fucking Nick, just that it would set him free. If only he could hate them, he would be free. He could stop looking after Nick and dump Carla. All he needs is a *reason*. And tomorrow he will be twenty-three. Things will have to change.

He's bought the *Guardian* and a packet of Marlboro from the shop at the end of the road. He hasn't smoked since he was about ten. He goes up to his room and puts both items on the bed.

His bedroom is the only room in the house with a TV. Carla never watches it because she prefers the radio, and Nick just reads, when he's in. Carla says that TV is for the working classes, to keep them entertained and to stop them having any revolutions. What stops this theory being interesting is that she actually thinks this is a good idea, and she's proud to be part of the class that makes TV, rather than the class that consumes it. God, he hates her. He checks his watch: six o'clock. She'll be at choir practice right now.

He flicks the TV to Sky One and watches *The Simpsons*. It's an episode he's seen before: Lisa falls in love with her teacher and nobody understands her. He cries during the scene when the teacher reads out a bit of *Charlotte's Web*, Jamie's favourite childhood book. He cries when the teacher leaves town at the end. This is another thing: he has to stop crying all the time.

Carla comes in at about seven. Her choir practice is over and she's looking for an argument. She walks into Jamie's room wearing M&S cream trousers and a cotton blouse. He wishes she would wear something nylon for once. Lycra, or whatever. For a moment he imagines her dressed in whore's clothes: a mini skirt, high heels and a boob-tube. Is that right? They don't wear boob-tubes now, surely? Too seventies. Maybe just a little vest top with no bra. And she'd have to swear. Not that this really turns him on – quite the contrary – but it cheapens her. And she's so fucking expensive that she really needs a price cut.

While Jamie's been thinking, she's been talking.

'Are you listening to me?' she demands, her voice clipped and precious.

Cunt, thinks Jamie. Are you listening to me, *cunt*?

'Sorry?' he says.

'I thought we might go to that concert tomorrow.'

'Did you?'

'It's your birthday.'

13

'I'm aware of that.'

'It's a recital.'

'I thought so.'

Jamie stares at the TV screen. *Don't be mean. Don't be mean.* Give her another chance. Give her . . . a challenge.

'I want to go clubbing,' he says.

'Sorry?'

'Clubbing? It's what young people do.'

'It's what plebs do. God, Jamie, what's got into you?'

He stays silent, watching the images on screen.

'Could you turn that thing off?' she says, pissed off.

He doesn't move. He doesn't want to hurt her, but he can't help it. On reflection, she probably isn't hurt, just confused. He wonders how you would actually hurt Carla. She sighs and leaves the room, slamming the door behind her. Jamie still doesn't move.

Later, he hears her on the telephone, talking to some other public school bimbo.

'He's just changed *so* much.' Pause for commiseration. The other girl probably asks for details, over-stressing at least one word in every sentence. They all do it.

'He's been playing computer games and watching *TV*.' Maybe the friend tells her that's normal. 'Yes, I know, but all the *time*? And he's so *distant*. Earlier on he said he wanted to go *clubbing*.' She giggles conspiratorially. 'I *know*. It *could* be quite good fun, I suppose. But I think he wants to do it *seriously*. Last week he told me he wanted to go to a *rock* concert. Sorry? Blah, I *think*.'

Another pause.

'Blah, that's right.'

She's trying to say Blur but she can't even manage that.

Jamie's got a copy of *The Face* hidden under the bed. He pulls it out and looks at the clothes and the people. Maybe this is what he could have been, had he not been so bright. He hates that word. It's what people have always said about him, from his junior school – in the days when he still had an accent – to his grammar school. *Jamie, he's so bright.* And they always sighed at the end of the sentence, as if his brightness made them tired, because it was just too dazzling.

As far as everyone here is concerned, his background is just a blip, an aberration. He's bright and he's escaped.

Well, now he wants to go back.

He remembers loving his primary school and all his friends. But just before the Eleven Plus he was put in a special class, with the other bright boys and girls. They were taught by the headmaster and kept out of ordinary classes. From that moment, Jamie's best friend, Mark, and girlfriend, Gemma, disappeared from his life. At the time he didn't even notice.

Last summer he spent his holidays in Taunton with his mother and her new boyfriend. Walking around his home town was a surreal experience. Sometimes, in the bank or in the record shop, he'd see a familiar face, but not be able to give it a name. He'd tried to track down Mark and Gemma once and found they'd got married – to each other. They hadn't invited him to the wedding. Why would they? He was never really one of them. While Gemma and Mark struggled with long division, he was doing algebra with the headmaster. He was just too fucking bright.

The people in *The Face* look like they're on drugs. They look like they're having fun in their dressed-down clothes; in their avant-garde photo shoots. Could he have been like that? Maybe he would have been if it wasn't for the numbers. Maybe he could still be something interesting, even with the stupid numbers. With all his numbers he'd be qualified to deal drugs, maybe; 28 grams in an ounce, 3.5 in an eighth. That's how they sell drugs, isn't it? He doesn't really know. But the people in this magazine aren't that. They're artists and pop stars and underground rebels. They're not the losers that Carla and her friends think they are. They're probably just really nice people.

He looks at his clothes: chinos from The Gap; white T-shirt bought by his mother about five years ago. It's greyed in the wash. Is that good or bad? He has a lot to learn. Worse, he has a lot to unlearn. He pulls one of the Marlboros out of the packet and lights it. He remembers smoking years ago in Taunton town centre, with Gemma breathing cold smoke in his ear, telling him she would always love him.

Picking up his newspaper and the rest of the cigarettes, he struts out of the bedroom and down the stairs. Carla wrinkles her nose as soon as she sees him and places her small white hand over the telephone receiver.

'God, Jamie, what are you doing?' she half-says, half-mouths.

'I'm going down the pub.'

'Sorry?'

'You heard.'

She rolls her eyes and speaks into the receiver. 'I'll call you back.'

Jamie stands defiant, enjoying the smoke.

'Are you dumbing down?' asks Carla eventually.

'Dumbing down?'

'Yes.'

'Dumbing down?'

'That's what I said.'

Jamie laughs. 'Where did you get that from?'

She flicks her fringe to one side. '*The Telegraph Magazine*.'

'You haven't got a clue, have you?'

'*Me?* Jamie, you need help.'

'Whatever.'

The pub is brown and quiet. Jamie hasn't been in here before, but he likes the calm, contemplative atmosphere of men with nowhere to go. He orders a pint and sits on his own at a table near the dartboard. What Jamie needs, what he really needs, is to strike out on his own. His degree is over and he has no reason to stay in Cambridge. Just because they all want him to be a mathematician doesn't mean he has to be one. Anyway, it's only his ex-tutors and Carla who really care.

He browses the Appointments section of the newspaper, looking for something to get him out of all this. Something far away – further than London, if possible. He's not qualified for any of the creative, arty jobs he'd really like. But then he sees something that intrigues him. *Bright Young Things wanted for big project*. The address is in Edinburgh. Bingo. He sends an SAE on the way home, scared that he'll lose his nerve otherwise. He doesn't tell anyone that he's applied, because when he disappears, he doesn't want anyone to know where he's gone.

Thea

'Push it back in, dear.'

'Sorry?'

'Push it back in.'

Thea considers the situation. She's in a small toilet in an old people's home, with an old woman, Mabel Wells, bent over and waiting to be wiped. Blocking her way to the door is a big wheelchair, reminding her of her previous dilemma: how to actually get the woman on the toilet. She has never taken anyone to the toilet before; never even pushed a wheelchair. Her whole right side still hurts from being squashed against the wall by the substantial weight of the old lady, after the struggle to get her out of the chair. Now Mabel is balanced precariously, leaning on Thea's left shoulder, and there is a big red turnip-shaped thing hanging out of her anus. It looks like an internal organ.

Thea sweats, steadying herself on the silver hand-rail.

'Push it back in, dear.'

Mabel has a voice like a witch.

'Push it back in?'

'Yes, that's right, Veronica.'

'It's, um, *Thea.*'

Mabel squints, wiggling her large bottom.

'The-a,' she says, pretending to struggle with the word. 'What a peculiar name.'

Thea doesn't say anything.

'Are you new?'

'Yes.'

'I like Veronica.'

'I'm sure you do. She's back on tomorrow morning.'

Mabel shifts her hand on Thea's shoulder, grunts, and says, 'It's a prolapse, dear.'

'What, you mean that's your bowel?'

'Yes.'

'And you're sure I should push it back in?'

'Yes, dear.'

'Won't it hurt?'

'Just get on with it. There's a horrible draft.'

Thea scans the room for some plastic gloves. Those things are like gold dust in here, although it's supposedly Rule 1: *Always Use Gloves*. But there are none. Taking a deep breath, she leans over and gets behind Mabel, scanning the prolapse briefly. After counting to three in her head (a habit picked up as a child as a strategy for pulling off plasters), she cups it in her right hand and pushes. It glows purple and wobbles around like a jelly. It's like trying to push a jelly through a straw.

'It won't go,' she says.

'Push harder, dear. It won't hurt me.'

Yeah, thinks Thea, *but what if it explodes?* She says nothing and pushes harder. Eventually it sucks itself back up. Thea wipes the perspiration from her head with her left hand.

'Now take me back,' squeaks Mabel impatiently. '*Big Break* is on.'

'You just finished watching it.'

'Really?' She sighs. 'Oh dear.'

The day room is full at this time of the evening. The TV is on, but not many people are watching it. The current programme is some kind of thriller, the sort that is shown in two parts over a weekend. On screen a young woman walks down an alleyway, unaware of the man following her. He catches up and pushes her against the wall, pressing a knife to her throat. You can't see his face. Thea turns away; the scene makes her uncomfortable. She'd change the channel, but Rule 17 says that the TV must always stay on BBC1, except for half an hour on each weekday when the old people watch *Countdown*.

Thea wonders why she doesn't find the day room depressing. Normal people find this kind of thing depressing. Her problem, or perhaps her advantage, is that she sees things through a camera in her head. And because her camera is objective, things are neither happy nor sad, they just are. She assesses the material in this room. Over in the corner is an old lady, senile, with only one breast. These facts should be introduced by a voiceover, Thea decides, mentally storyboarding the scene for her imaginary documentary: *Almost Dead*.

The woman is supposed to be doing a jigsaw, but she's trying to eat one of the pieces. The jigsaw was her daughter's idea. She visited earlier, but has gone now. Thea's camera zooms in on the chunky wooden piece as the woman forces it into her mouth. It's too big for a child to swallow, but the woman has a greater chance of managing it. Her false teeth are on the table next to her, and Thea mentally edits in a shot of them before cutting back to the woman as she begins to chew, her mouth full of gums and wood.

'What the hell is she doing?' demands Matron, sweeping into the room.

'Sorry?' says Thea, pausing her imaginary camera.

Matron is a devout Christian, and Rule 5 is that no one must blaspheme in the residential home at any time. So far today she has said 'God' twice, and 'hell' three times. Now she briskly walks over to the woman with the jigsaw and rips the wooden piece out of her mouth. The woman starts to moo like a cow. Camera back on, Thea pans from the mooing woman to Matron, who's walking back towards her, waving the square of wet jigsaw.

'This,' she hisses, 'could kill her. Where did she get it?'

'Her daughter.'

'Stupid bloody woman. Jesus Christ.' Blasphemy six, seven and eight. Although, does *bloody* count?

Thea focuses on the piece of wood as it dances in front of her face. It's a fragment of Thomas the Tank Engine, his little furnace and chimney.

Cut from swearing matron to CU on jigsaw piece.

'Are you listening to me?' says Matron tiredly.

'Of course. What should I do next?'

'Have they all been toiletted?'

'Yes,' Thea lies.

'Very good. Just keep an eye on them, then. See if they need anything – but don't give them anything to eat or drink because then they'll all have to *go* again, and the night girls won't be happy if they have to toilet them twice. I'll come round with the medication in about half an hour.'

'OK.'

As soon as Matron leaves the room they start complaining. One woman wants a biscuit, another wants sherry. The other part-time girl, Louise, comes bustling around from the laundry room and explains to Thea that the old people only have sherry at twelve forty-five on weekdays. Thea composes a shot around Louise. She's about seventeen, plain like a scone, and fat.

'You coming for a fag?' she asks.

'Yeah,' Thea says. As they leave the room she notices a puddle forming under the chair of one of the old people. She turns her head guiltily and pretends she hasn't seen it. They walk along the dim corridor to the staff room. Brenda and Lucy are already there, with a pot of tea and fags on the go.

'How are you getting on?' Brenda asks Thea as they sit down.

'OK,' says Thea, lighting a cigarette.

'You're a student, aren't you?' asks Lucy.

'Just finished my degree.'

'Where were you?'

'Bristol.'

'And now you're living in Brighton?'

'Yeah. I'm staying with my foster parents for a bit while . . .'

'My Luke's just got a place at university,' interrupts Brenda proudly.

'Really?' says Lucy. 'You must be so pleased.'

'Yeah, well, my Bill still wants him to go in the army like he did.'

'What does Luke want to do?' Lucy asks.

'He wants to be a DJ.'

'That's cool,' Thea says.

'Not when he's living under my roof,' Brenda snorts.

Lucy pulls a magazine out of her bag and flicks through it. She starts talking to Brenda about some plate she wants to buy and hang on her wall. Then Brenda takes out her false teeth and talks about denture cream. Thea composes a shot or two around them, but they are unsatisfactory subjects. There are a few old Sunday supplements and a couple of newspapers on the table. Thea picks up the last Monday's *Guardian* and opens it to the job section.

By the time Thea leaves the nursing home it's gone eight. That means there's only a couple of hours before Leisure 2000 shuts. This is the arcade in which Thea has spent all of her free time since she finished university. She used to hang around in here sometimes as a child, addicted to Space Invaders. Now she'll shoot anything that moves, fly anything that flies and stalk dinosaurs until the arcade closes. She loves the hazy hours away from everything; they feel stolen, and therefore delicious. It's like the feeling of having a big jar of sweets and being able to eat them all, or perhaps the feeling you get before you have bad sex. You know you'll feel sick afterwards, but it doesn't stop you doing it. The thing is, as long as Thea's sitting in a miniature cockpit or standing behind a big gun, she's not making films, and although it makes her hate herself, she can't really help it. It's all the fault of that Cardiff MA admission person.

The thing is, until the Cardiff interview, Thea had never failed at anything in her entire life. She was one of those ten-grade-A GCSE girls, whose picture appeared in the local paper alongside snaps of Abby and Nicky, school friends she doesn't see any more. After GCSEs, Thea stayed at the girls' grammar school she already attended and took three A levels. She got two As and a U. The U was contested and later Thea was given a third A. By that time it was too late to take up the university place she'd been offered, so she went travelling for a few months. Then, eventually, she did do the course she wanted, with most of her classmates a year younger than her and lacking any of the experience she'd gained from travelling. When she returned from university with VD and a First, she had nothing to do for the summer except sit in the arcade and play games. She even succeeded at the games she played; that was part of their allure. She always took top score, always finished right to the credits.

Cardiff was the only thing she ever failed. The MA was full by the time she applied.

Bryn

The *Guardian* is on the dashboard of the MG, along with the *Sun*, the *Daily Mail* and *Loot*. The guy behind the wheel doesn't touch them, doesn't move, because if he moves he will be seen. He can't be seen. He smokes slowly, his arm propped on the window frame. The car smells sweet with skunk weed, smoke melting out of the open window.

Number 37 looks quiet today, like yesterday, but she's got to come out some time, right? Doesn't she need milk, or fags, or whatever? Bryn could do without this today, but Tank needs his cash this afternoon. Jesus. It shouldn't be this fucking difficult. Wait for her to come our snap, snap, snap, and go home. Out of this gyppo council estate.

The radio's on low, playing a remix of Inner City's *Good Life*. The tune lifts in the wrong place and goes all Latino. The original never did that. Bryn presses the button for the local station. An old Whitney Houston tune. Sorted.

The early August sun trips in the window, hotter than yesterday. Whitney's singing about her married lover, about waiting for him to come round and fuck her. Outside the car a couple of blokes from the pub walk past, then Tank's mate Gilbert, on his own with his kid. He's probably had his kid down the pub again, giving it blowbacks in the garden to send it to sleep. Someone should tell Social Services, but they never will. Around here, child abuse is a conspiracy. Everyone does it. You don't tell.

Bryn looks away. Gilbert's the local fuck-up. He got put into care when he was twelve after getting in with a local paedophile ring, giving the old men blow-jobs for Mars Bars. All the other kids called him Cadbury, old enough to make up the nickname, but too young to bother with the fact that Cadbury never made Mars Bars. At fifteen, Gilbert got kicked out of care and moved in with some bloke called Tracey. When Gilbert didn't pay the rent, Tracey threatened – seriously – to saw off Gilbert's head with one of his chainsaws, so he went and worked on some fishing boat.

When he came back he blew all his savings on a bet down the pub. Then Tank put him in touch with some Bosnian bloke whose sister wanted British nationality and Gilbert married her. He got paid five hundred for the wedding and was due another five hundred for the divorce. But before the divorce could come through, Gilbert got busted by the Home Office. About five minutes after the man in the suit had knocked on the door, a journalist from the *Sun* turned up. No one knew how they'd all found out about Gilbert.

No one except Bryn.

Gilbert was inside for two years after some other stuff was taken into consideration, but Bryn didn't feel bad.

Bryn's always been pretty shit at everything, but he's good with a camera. When he was twenty, he did a BTEC National Diploma in photography at the South-East Essex College. After that he went to London to try to get a job in the music press, but he didn't have any contacts and no one wanted to know him. He came back to Southend and now he deals drugs, trying to get the odd bit of freelance photography work on the side. Every so often he supplies his contact at the *Sun* with stories, like the one about Tank's housing benefit scam, but it never goes any further. They usually pay him for the tip-off and send one of their own photographers, without even looking at Bryn's shots.

The job he's doing now is for a man he met down the pub. Bryn doesn't know why he wants pictures of Fiona.

He sits and waits. Nothing.

At about four he packs it in and goes round to Tank's.

'Bryn, my man,' says Tank, holding out his fist as a welcome, pretending to be black. His fingers still have the letters 'l o v e' and 'h a t e' tattooed on them from when he was whatever he was before he decided he was black. Tank is about forty, has three kids he never sees (Ketamine, Jasmine and Marley), and long dreadlocks, which are naturally blond. He's wearing beige combats, a black short-sleeved shirt with a Japanese pattern on it, and Adidas sandals. Bryn isn't sure about the sandals.

They walk into Tank's sitting room, where an audience of seven people watches as Bryn explains to Tank why he hasn't got the money today and negotiates another half-ounce bag of weed for the time being. Afterwards, Tank takes out his special bag and gives Bryn a spliff's worth of some draw that's supposed to taste a bit like chocolate. It's solid, though, which Bryn doesn't smoke that often, and can't sell down the Reggae Club either. He thanks Tank and checks his weed. It looks unfamiliar. Tank explains that it's Purple Sensi from Amsterdam, where they grow it under ultra-violet. He shows everyone the big purple buds, then goes on about female flowers and all that shit. Bryn's heard it before. Everyone's heard it before.

There's some porn film playing on the TV. Next to the TV is a stack of VCRs, all recording the porn film. If you ask Tank he'll tell you how he's not into porn and disrespecting women, which is a load of shit. But still, the pirating gear isn't his. It belongs to Wilf, the bloke from upstairs. The others start talking about the latest drug-bust on the house. Some of them were here on the day it took place so they're comparing stories, like war veterans. Tank goes back into the kitchen.

On the TV screen a Japanese girl is taking her clothes off for a much older man. She looks about thirteen. All the girls in the room are deliberately not watching. 'Mad' Mike is looking, and Bryn, but that's all. Bryn's not embarrassed. This counts as work, for two reasons. Firstly, because it's only a matter of time before he lets the *Sun* know about Wilf, and also, because Bryn is interested in pictures. It's his job. And if the pictures move, he isn't bothered.

He finishes skinning up his joint and sparks it up, passing it straight to a girl he's never seen before. This is the way it always is. You come round Tank's to score, and then you have to stay and have a spliff. If you didn't, Tank would bitch to all the others who come round, and tell them how you're rude or disrespectful or whatever that week's word for cunt is. Tank would make an example of you and go on about how you only use him for his contacts, his cheap drugs and free entry to Uno's on the seafront. Yeah, right. But you've still got to play the game.

'Hey, Bryn,' calls Tank from the kitchen.

The Japanese girl lies down on a small bed. The older man climbs on top of her.

'What?' Bryn calls back.

'Come in here, mate. I've got something for you.'

'Yeah, coming.'

He walks slowly into the kitchen. Tank's got his big mirror out on the work surface. There's a line of white powder on it and the remains of one that Tank's obviously just done. He's shaking his head a little, his Medusa hair snaking over his shoulders.

'Nice,' he splutters. 'Top gear, mate.'

'Charlie?' says Bryn.

'Here,' Tank says, handing him a rolled up twenty.

'Cheers,' says Bryn. He hovers over the line, noting the way Tank has left it fat in the middle. He wants to smooth it out a bit, play with it, like you do. But that would be disrespectful. This is a gift. Aware that he owes Tank money, he says, 'Are you sure?'

'Fucking hell, man, it's only a bit of charlie. Anyway, I'm road-testing it for Colombian Pete.'

Colombian Pete is from Birmingham.

'Anyway,' adds Tank, 'we're brothers, man. I know you appreciate this. You know the score. I wouldn't get it out in *there*,' he gestures towards the sitting room, 'with all those vultures. That's why they're here. Sitting around waiting for free samples. That blonde bird's been here for a week.'

Bryn leans down and snorts the line.

'You fucked her then?'

Tank laughs. 'Oral.'

Bryn laughs. 'Yeah, mate.'

His throat is bitter with the taste of the powder. He recalls the time that Tank, wanting to impress Colombian Pete, stitched up Gilbert and put him in casualty. He'd come around uninvited and kept caning all Tank's charlie, taking when it wasn't offered, and so on. When Gilbert went for a piss, Tank set out a line of Ajax. When he came back he said he'd reserved it especially for him. That was the week before Tank became a Rastafarian.

By the time Bryn leaves it's almost seven. He nips in the pub for a half and then round to his mum's for a sandwich, which he can't eat. She's still on at him to get a proper job. He promises to check out all the job supplements she got him. Tells her they're in the car.

At the Reggae Club, Bernie's DJing, playing all his old dancehall tunes. Drum and bass hasn't happened in Bernie's world. It's all straight Cutty Ranks and Daddy Freddy; no unnecessary remixes. Daddy Freddy's singing '*We are the champions*', and a couple of girls are trying to move their hips on the dancefloor but looking ridiculous, like they've barely graduated from the youth club. Bernie's skinning up on one of his massive speakers. Bryn goes over and sorts him out with his weed and then leaves. All this shit does his head in.

He goes down to the seafront and hangs around one of the arcades waiting for a bloke to show up. After that he goes in the White Horse, which has three fruit machines. Bryn sticks all Bernie's money in one of them without really noticing what he's doing. A girl he fucked a couple of weeks ago comes over. She's wearing cheap perfume and a white T-shirt Bryn recognises; it's his.

'All right?' she says, leaning against the fruit machine.

Bryn nods at her. He can see her mate sitting at the bar, watching. These girls always come in twos, he realises. A fat one and the one you fuck. He tries to remember what she was like, but he can't. On the machine, he's just got two cherries.

'Remember me?' she says. 'My name's Julie. We slept together.'

'Yeah.' He's distracted by the possibility of a third cherry. 'Give us a minute.'

'OK. Do you want a drink?'

'Yeah, if you're buying.'

'A pint of lager?' She smiles, like she's clever because she knows what he drinks.

'Nah. Get us a vodka and lime.'

Her smile thins. 'OK.'

He sticks his last quid in the machine and waits while Julie stands at the bar, trying to get served. Eventually she comes back with his green drink. He downs it in one and checks his watch.

'I've got to go down the Reggae Club,' he says.

'Thought you'd just been there.'

'Are you stalking me or something?'

'Don't flatter yourself. I had to see Cliff. Saw you walk in as I was going out.'

'Cliff?' The student dealer.

She nods. 'Do you want to see what I got?'

'You what?' says Bryn, but it's too late. She's pulling a small white wrap out of her pocket and opening it. She places it on the fruit machine. The powder inside is baby-gro pink: speed. There's not much there. Maybe a tenner's worth.

'Shit. Get that off there.'

She moves it on to the windowsill. Everyone can still see.

'Do you want a dab?' she offers.

Bryn stares at her. She's got blonde hair with a couple of red streaks in it, and blue eyes. He still can't remember what she was like. She's about eighteen or nineteen. Maybe she's a student. He can't remember.

'Put it away,' he urges.

She scowls. 'All right, keep your pants on. I'm just going to have a dab.' In full view of the barman and just about anyone who's looking, she licks her finger and presses it into the powder. Then she sticks it in her mouth, trying not to make a face with the bitterness. Bryn wonders if she's trying to impress him. As far as he can remember, she wasn't into powder a couple of weeks ago, just spliff.

'I'm going to have to go in a minute,' he says.

'Where?'

'The Reggae Club. I told you.'

'I'll walk over there with you if you want.'

'What about your mate?'

'She'll be all right.'

Fat Girl smiles and winks at her friend as Bryn pulls on his jacket.

'Why do you want to go to the Reggae Club if you've already been there?' he asks.

'Why do *you?*'

'I've got to go and see Bernie. Who've you got to see?'

'No one. I just want to have a little chat.'

He sighs. 'Come on then.'

Outside, it's started to rain.

All is not well at the Reggae Club. There's been a bust, and everyone's in the street outside, waiting for the police to go away.

Bernie's kicking a stone across the road.

'Fucking Babylon,' he moans.

Bryn laughs. 'Where's your weed, mate?'

'On the floor in there where I dropped it.'

'You going back in to get it?'

'Yeah. When this lot PISS OFF,' he says, raising his voice as a policeman walks past. A police dog stops to sniff Julie and she strokes and pets it before the policeman calls it to heel.

'Who's this?' asks Bernie.

'Julie. Look, I'm going back down the seafront. It's a bit dodgy here.'

'Check you later then.'

Julie's still hanging around.

'Where are you going now?' she asks, as they set off.

'Seafront.'

'Is this all you do?'

'What?'

'Walk backwards and forwards like this?'

Bryn looks at his feet. 'Pretty much.'

Emily

It all started as a joke. Just another art school irony.

Emily's standing in the flat in Battersea, looking at her reflection. She is tall, thin and pretty. But not tall enough to be a model, not thin enough to get the attention she's always wanted (she gave up anorexia a couple of years ago, but she misses it now), and not quite pretty enough to attract Lenny, the MA student she has coveted for two years. Emily wonders what he's doing right now. She doesn't even have an address for him.

Emily is a graduate; a bright young thing. She has no ties, no responsibilities and no commitments. Some people would bask in the freedom, but it makes Emily nervous. She's going nowhere. She's been out of college for almost three months and no one's approached her about a job. She's filled in form after form at graduate fairs – nothing. And she was stupid enough to think she would be headhunted a week after finishing. What a joke. But here's the real joke: Emily, in a short black cocktail dress and high heels, wearing red lipstick and false eyelashes. And this is the girl who only shops at Diesel and Slam City Skates.

When her flatmate Lucy suggested joining the escort agency, Emily had laughed and made some crack about it being the biggest ex-art student cliché. Lucy had pointed out that since they'd been at St Martin's they were a cliché anyway, thanks to

Jarvis Cocker. Emily had seen her point. So they'd gone to see a woman called Tina, who had examined them and written their names on little Rolodex cards, on which Lucy had seen her add: *gay, publishing, ART.* That was a couple of weeks ago.

Last night Lucy accompanied an elderly investment banker to the launch of his ex-wife's kiss-and-tell novel. He'd turned out to be very camp and undemanding, and Lucy had earned £200 just for standing next to him, looking pretty. Emily is hoping for something similar tonight.

She leaves the house at seven and cabs it over the river to Chelsea. David is already sitting in the small wine bar when she arrives. She gives him the once-over: mid-thirties, dark hair, dark eyes. Clean. She looks for a wedding ring. There isn't one. He briefs her on the night ahead. She hears the words: Annabel, party, drinks, canapés and dancing.

'Cool,' she says.

'Have you done this before?'

'Oh yes,' she lies.

The party is taking place a couple of streets away. David and Emily walk there. He's obviously thinking about holding her hand, and it feels awkward, like a first date. He asks her about herself, and she tells him as little as possible. He speaks slowly to her, as if she's having trouble understanding him. Emily grits her teeth and smiles, just thinking about the money. Why should she care what he thinks of her? And why would he assume she's educated? Well, *duh*. The accent could give it away, but David's not that bright himself. It turns out he's some sort of sales rep, selling new-age books for some unknown publishing house in the South-West. Emily laughs when he tells her. She likes the idea of combining hard-sell with woo-woo.

The problem with David being in publishing is that Emily knows half the people at the party. She's lucky her sister, a publicist at Penguin, isn't there. Even Annabel turns out to be the girlfriend of Lucy's brother's best friend. Jesus. London's so big, but the world is so very small. Emily drinks a lot without meaning to and mingles like a pro. David hovers around the edges of the party, not quite taking the plunge, and Emily regrets the fact that she's paid to be here with him. True, it adds a certain *frisson* to the evening, but ultimately it's boring having to do what you're told. The only fun she has is wondering what they would all say if they knew what she was really doing here.

A couple of hours later she and David are standing in the lobby of a hotel. The night has gone well, but David doesn't want to leave it there.

'I don't really know how to say this,' he begins.

'Say what?'

'You must have been in this situation before.'

'What situation?'

'Well, here we are, we've had a fantastic night and I was wondering . . .' He grins coyly and looks at the floor. 'Do you do any, um, extras?'

Emily smiles. 'You're not in a massage parlour.'

'OK, then.' He drops his voice. 'Well, how much extra for a fuck?'

Most girls would like to think that at this point they would smile politely and explain that their body isn't for sale. How hard would that be? Emily's already earned £200 just for being this guy's date. Which of course leads her to speculate: just how much *could* she charge for a fuck?

She's pissed enough to sound bold.

'Another two hundred,' she says. 'Cash.'

David points at the lift. 'Let's go, then.'

They don't speak all the way up to the room. Emily's wondering if David is a psychopath. Do new-age book reps have it in them to bludgeon someone to death? She thinks not. Anyway, she reminds herself, any one of the men she's slept with in the past could have been a psycho. The only difference between them and David is that he's paying for it. She's been alone, naked, in strange places with thirty other men before. Why should this one be any different?

The hotel room is big and comfortably furnished. Emily walks over to the bed and slips off her high heels. Her feet immediately feel better and she starts to relax. She notices how drunk she really is. And although she hasn't realised before, she's also dead tired. Will he expect her to leave afterwards? Or will she be able to crash out in this big, comfortable bed?

'Drink?' offers David, opening the mini bar.

'Vodka. Thanks.'

He passes Emily a small bottle of vodka.

'Orange, Coke or tonic?' he asks, scanning the bar for a mixer.

'Coke, thanks.'

He passes her a can of Coke and a glass. He selects a small bottle of Scotch and drinks it straight from the bottle. He's shaking a bit, like he's nervous.

'Do you want to take a shower?' asks Emily, remembering some dialogue from an episode of *The Bill* she saw last week.

'No,' says David. 'Do you?'

She shrugs. 'Not really.'

'Good.'

He sits next to her on the bed, and starts rubbing her leg with his hand. His breathing is heavy, his eyes fixed on the wall in front of them. Emily sips her drink and lights a cigarette. She offers one to David and he takes it. She wonders what should happen next, whether things will happen naturally, or whether she'll have to initiate the actual sex. For a moment she considers – with some hope – the possibility that he's one of those 'talkers' you hear about who don't actually want penetrative sex.

Then he takes his hand off her leg.

'Strip,' he says.

'Sorry?'

He blushes. 'Can you take your clothes off, please?'

Emily stands up nervously. She pulls off her stockings one

by one, trying to make each movement fluid and seductive. David stares. She can't tell whether he's impressed or not. When the stockings are off, she removes her knickers, and dangles them from one finger momentarily, before dropping them on the floor. She almost laughs, imagining what she'll tell Lucy. The funny thing is, she's almost getting into this. She's tried to have dirty sex with boyfriends in the past, done the whole stripping thing for some of them. But at the end of the day it's always just your boyfriend sitting there. This time it's for real. If only David was a bit less of a dickhead, this could be a total turn-on.

Emily peels her dress over her head, and there she is, naked. She hasn't noticed before, but David's got his cock out. It's small and stubby, not very erect. He's pulling at it distractedly. Not wanking, maybe just trying to get himself aroused. Surely he would be aroused by now, though? She's just stripped for him, for God's sake. Maybe he's a New Man.

He puts out his cigarette. 'Come here,' he says.

Afterwards he cries, and Emily just sits there smoking, sore and slightly hypnotised. The whole thing has taken just under three hours. He hasn't asked for anything kinky. He hasn't even asked for a blow job. All he has done is push his little cock into her, relentlessly, for almost three hours, like some kind of sewing machine. For the first hour Emily did all the things that usually work: moaning, thrusting, that pelvic floor muscle thing. For the second hour she planned an exhibition. For the last (and it was like being rubbed with sandpaper) she recited William Blake's 'London' in her head, over and over again.

So now he's crying. Why the hell is he crying? She's the one who should be crying, for God's sake. But she's actually too tired to care. When she asks if she can stay for the night, David accepts, and then clings to her all night. All in all, Emily isn't a very good prostitute. She's kissed, she's stayed the night and she didn't even insist on a condom. *The Bill* hadn't prepared her for all these details.

In the morning David mumbles something about the hotel bill already being covered by his credit card, and then leaves. Emily dozes until about ten and then sits up in bed and orders breakfast and a newspaper. The curtains are already open. (Did he do that? How quaint.) The sun is intense, falling on her face as she lights a cigarette and reviews her night. On the bedside table is the money. She counts it and finds two hundred and ten pounds. A tip. How generous. But her bravado is melting away in the sunlight. Somehow, what she's done doesn't seem so funny any more.

Her stomach churns. What the hell is she doing here? With no friends to laugh with and no irony to find, the situation just seems tragic. She was a child, then an art student, and now she's a hooker. All in the space of what seems like five minutes. Emily tries to find the rewind button, but she can't. The one thing she forgot last night was that the difference between just having sex and charging for it is that charging for it makes you a prostitute.

Of course, last night it was a laugh being an escort. Emily's always been the rebellious one (ask anyone at college) and the thought that someone at the party might find out . . . It had been kind of thrilling. But now? How can she defend what she's done? She fucked a stranger for two hundred quid. She thinks back to the last thing she bought for that amount. A pair of *sunglasses*. Jesus. She's fucked a man for a pair of sunglasses. No heroin habit, no kids, no debts. Those are reasons to become a prostitute. But for a pair of sunglasses?

Emily needs a holiday. She wants to go far away for a very long time.

Breakfast arrives in about fifteen minutes. Emily discards it, gagging on the smell of hotel bacon and eggs, suddenly not hungry. She pours a cup of coffee and opens the *Guardian Weekend*. Reading some news (well, Julie Burchill, the Style section and

Dulcie Domum) puts her experience in perspective a little. In fact, with the smallest of smiles on her face, Emily realises she's learnt something from the experience. It's time to find a real job.

Paul

Paul's been on the Internet for seventy-two hours and is beginning to develop eye strain. He's already fucked up the company that fired him, what . . . seventy-four hours ago? Yeah. Wednesday morning, that was when he cleared his desk. He's already undone the whole accounts system, changed everyone's passwords and deleted 16,000 e-mails from the company's server. That took up the first twenty-four hours. Since then he's been planning something big.

In the gaps (waiting for text to load, waiting to crack a password, whatever), he's gone for twenty-three pisses, had five pizzas delivered, had Internet sex with a girl called Vicky, and thought a lot about the number 23. It's no accident that he's been for twenty-three pisses. No accident that he's had five pizzas. Two plus three equals five. Two and three. Always the number 23. Rebecca was twenty-three.

Rebecca, in an indirect way, was the one who got Paul fired. Her and Daniel, of course. Paul's never met Rebecca, but he tried to help her, once. It was one Friday in May when she rang up the support line and got Paul.

'My e-mail's fucked,' she said.

He cleared his throat. 'And?'

'And can you fix it?'

Her voice was little-girl-on-speed.

'Maybe,' he said. 'What's wrong with it?'

'None of my messages are coming through. Well, I mean, I've had no messages for about three days now but that's just not right. My, uh, friend Dan always e-mails me like twenty times a day, so I thought there must be something wrong at your end.'

'Did you?'

'Yeah.'

'Why?'

'Hello? Techno boy? I haven't got any e-mails. I was expecting e-mails. Something's fucked.'

'Good logic,' says Paul.

'And you are technical support, right?'

'I am.'

'Are you trying to stall me?'

Paul laughed then. 'Yeah. Probably. What's your login name?'

He wasn't trying to chat her up; his motives were higher than sex. He was just trying to keep her on the line for as long as possible, because that cost the company money.

She paused. 'Um . . .'

'Take your time.'

'It's, um . . . this is really embarrassing.'

'We have all the time in the—'

'*Wetpussy.*'

'Sorry?'

'You heard.'

'Wetpussy?'

'Yeah.'

'Can you spell that?'

'Of course I can spell it.'

'No, I mean can you spell it out?'

'Why?'

'*Why?*'

After half an hour or so, Paul had solved Rebecca's problem.

Stuck in the company's cache were the missing e-mails, about twenty-three of them, all from this guy Daniel. *What are you wearing right now?* the first one said. Then: *Where are you?* Then: *Maybe you're out. I'm just going to keep sending these. Hope you're not ignoring me. I'd really like to see you naked right now.*

These were interesting enough for Paul to want to look at Rebecca's entire e-mail history, which he did, forwarding all those to or from Daniel to his home e-mail address. And from then on, he decided to become their God. His target list (other people had 'to do' lists) had a new objective. Before, it had said: *Waste time. Cost the company money. Give free stuff to customers.* Now there was a new item on the list: *Make Rebecca fall in love with Daniel.* It was like a random act of kindness. And random acts were dada. This was definitely dada. And that was cool.

For the first few weeks Paul just observed. He set up his work system to forward all Rebecca's e-mails to his home, so he could study her in comfort. She and Daniel were both actors. She had just graduated from Dartington, and Daniel was in the middle of his training at RADA. They had met at a mutual friend's party and swapped e-mail addresses, but hadn't met since. It was obvious to Paul that they were in love, but with Dan's playful sexual aggression, and Rebecca's playful teasing/frigidity, they were getting nowhere. Paul's input was clearly going to be needed here.

Inspired by kiddie divorce films (the ones where the parents get back together after the cute kid and the blossoming next door neighbour trick them into it), Paul started adding and subtracting from the e-mails. At first he just added the odd word here and there. But before too long, he was composing whole messages all by himself.

So one night, Rebecca never got the e-mail that asked what she was wearing; instead she got a message of love. And Daniel finally got what he wanted: an incredibly pornographic description of what Rebecca was wearing – or rather, what Paul imagined she was wearing. His instinct had been right. In response to Rebecca's titillating honesty, Dan sent her a genuine message of love; and in response to his message of love, Rebecca really did send him something dirty – a detailed description of when and how she would give him a blow job. They arranged to meet the following week.

Daniel eventually proposed to Rebecca in an e-mail. She said yes. Paul had stopped tampering by this point, but he was still observing, of course. Unfortunately, they'd worked out that someone had been tampering (which made them kind of grateful, but also pissed off about their lack of privacy), and had contacted the ISP. After an investigation, Paul was found out. It wasn't just the cupid stuff either. Paul's boss discovered that everyone with the same initials as Paul were not paying for their e-mail accounts; that all elderly users were actually being paid by the company each time they sent an e-mail; that the local cat home was entirely run from anonymous company donations, and that although Paul could have increased his salary by any amount he chose, all he'd taken for himself was software and unlimited e-mail accounts.

It was a shit job anyway, Paul reasons. And when he's eighty, he'll be more proud of what he did for Rebecca and Dan than of some stupid job. But all this has unsettled him. He was stimulated by what he did. The customers were his friends. In this new, empty world, he has no friends, not real ones.

He rubs his eyes and stares into the screen. His community is right here, in this box, talking on the Pavement chat room, or posting on alt.hackers.malicious. Paul hasn't had real sex for six years. He has a girlfriend, but he's never met her. She wants to meet, but Paul hasn't got time. His project needs a lot more work.

His new project is his only passion. It's a virus, of course, planned for release exactly twenty-three days after the Millennium. That's the random element; it can't be on 1 January 2000, because he doesn't want to be upstaged by that stupid bug. He wants the world to settle down and get back to normal before

MoneyBaby (the name of his virus) hits. Of course, there's nothing evil about Paul's virus, his hero being the infamous *rtm:* Robert Tappan Morris, the inventor of the first computer virus, or *worm*, as people called it then. Paul's virus is good. Well, it'll make some teenagers rich anyway. Paul's virus will infect banks and give them such a fever they won't even realise that they're giving out money to seemingly random suburban teenagers. Paul didn't want to make the teenagers totally random, preferring to choose those who seemed interesting or needy or clever. They have to be clever, because the sooner they tell someone what's happened, the less damage the virus will be able to do.

Take Freddy in Arizona, still mourning the death of Kurt Cobain. He wouldn't tell anyone if he received a million dollar windfall. He'd spend it on CDs, slushies and bomb-making equipment. Kim in China would spend it on travel, and Jane in Bath might spend it on that creative writing course she always wanted to take. Zak in Iceland might stop his plans to poison everyone at his school, and Cherry in Buffalo will be able to fund her heroin habit without starring in teen porn films. Paul's totally into the idea of the great teen conspiracy, and how long the mass secret will exist.

For some reason though, Paul's project is not exciting him today. He's lost his context, his reason to rebel. He's lost the job he hated, and that sucks. It's like the idea of having a girlfriend. Being attached gives you something to fight against. What Paul really needs is another job to get fired from, and then another and then another. Because without it, he may as well slit his wrists.

He sends off for a few application forms. They arrive. And the one he likes best is the one with the section asking about his greatest fear.

Part Two

Chapter One

'Where the hell are we?'
    'What the fuck are we doing here?'
    'Who brought us here?'
    'Can you remember anything?'
    'Is this some kind of island?'
    'This is totally fucked up.'
    'Please tell me I'm dreaming.'
    'I still feel sleepy.'
    Anne stays silent, the voices distorting in her ears. Sunlight falls on her face and hair, making her feel hot and dirty. This is some kind of island, that's pretty obvious. There is salt in the air, a small breeze, and sea all around. She counts five other people. They look kind of familiar. No one knows how they all got here. They're freaking out, although they seem as dazed as she feels.
    Four of them are taking out their mobile phones and trying to dial out, with no luck. Anne's brain hurts. When she tries to make it go backwards she gets that feeling like she's coming down with flu. She vaguely remembers an argument with her mother, a train to Edinburgh, a cheap hotel and then waiting for a job interview that she didn't even want to attend. That was what the argument had been about. She can't remember beyond the waiting – some non-airconditioned room in some

sticky building in the suburbs. The interviewer giving her coffee. She looks at the others. They were all there too. Weird.

The island is quiet and still. It has one house, one shed which is next to the house, an orchard, an empty washing line and a load of rough grass with pale flowers. It has the feel of a wintry place, although it is quite hot, just like it was in Edinburgh. Almost completely round, and about half a mile in diameter, it's the most unlikely place Anne's ever seen. It seems like the kind of thing you'd imagine or draw, not somewhere you'd actually be. Apart from the house and shed, the only structure on the island is something that looks like a child's toy windmill stuck on the top of a big wooden pole. It's taller than the house. There's a mist out to sea, and it's impossible to see any mainland. Anne turns and stares at the house. It looks like a holiday home. She's not sure why. It seems empty, too, although she hasn't been inside.

It was just outside the front door of the house that they all came to, about fifteen minutes ago. They were all lying next to each other, like a row of dead bodies, with their belongings (two bags, a couple of rucksacks and a folder) beside them. The sign on the door is still there. It says: PLEASE MAKE YOURSELVES AT HOME.

Anne sits down on the grass and picks a daisy, focusing on it so she doesn't have to focus on this situation. Penetrating the stalk with her thumbnail, she makes a perfect hole, then picks another daisy and threads it through the first one's stalk. Everything feels very slow. The coffee is the last thing she can remember before waking up here. It must have been drugged. She picks another daisy. She's never taken drugs before.

When the daisy chain is complete, she binds it around her wrist. The dark-haired guy watches her do this and smiles. He's been almost as quiet as Anne so far, just watching the others. There is a skinny bloke with dreadlocks, swearing a lot and talking nonsense to a tall, fair-haired guy who just looks dazed. The other two girls are talking. Well, the dark one is sniffling a lot and the blonde one is talking. Anne is intrigued by the blonde one. She's like a girl from a pop group manufactured specifically to seem cool and unmanufactured. She's wearing silver sunglasses which prevent Anne from looking at her eyes. She bets they're brown and her hair is dyed. Her hair is up in two kids'-TV-presenter bunches, tied with seventies-style bobble bands. Anne has some of those herself, although she prefers the ones with little animals on.

The girl with short dark hair looks serious. She vomited as soon as she woke up, and now she's crying, her blue-green eyes all red around the edges. She's the most sensibly dressed of everyone wearing a long skirt, plain vest top, suit jacket and a small silver necklace. Anne didn't bother dressing up for the interview. Well, you don't nowadays, do you, especially if you don't want the job. She's wearing a short combat skirt, a Pokémon T-shirt, a snowboarding-style fleece jacket (yes, it's summer, but it's a cool jacket) and a child's plastic necklace with matching bracelets, all in candy colours. Her straight brown hair is down, and she's wearing no make-up except for pink cherry-flavour lip-gloss and black mascara.

She takes off her trainers and starts making a daisy chain for her ankle.

It's too hot out here. The quiet is freaking Anne out. Where are the cars? Where are the people? Where is the bustle? All she can hear is the waves against the cliffs and a few sea birds. It smells and sounds like the villa in Tuscany, not that she's been there since she was about twelve. This was so not what she expected when she got up this morning.

The fair-haired guy says he's going to walk around the circumference of the island. This won't take him more than ten minutes. A couple of the others call to him to be careful. The island is high above sea level, and Anne can't see if there's any way down or not. Falling would be a pretty good way to get down, she thinks. As he sets off towards the cliff edge, Anne pretends this is a videogame and she's controlling this guy. He's a bit like Duke Nukem, but without the porn or the guns or the muscles. She presses forward on her imaginary direction pad and circles him around the island. He returns and reports what she could have predicted. There's no way down. As if someone would drug them, bring them here, and then just let them walk – or swim – away.

'Shall we go inside, then?' asks Pop Girl. 'It's too weird out here.'

The good-looking dark-haired guy is the first to get up.

Inside, the house is dark and cold. It smells a bit of something that could be mothballs. It's dusty, too. The front hall is big and square, with a red tiled floor and a staircase leading to a balcony upstairs. There are no carpets, just huge rugs everywhere. A large painting of the earth is hung at the top of the stairs, all blues and greens and swirls of sea. Anne wonders if this island is on the picture somewhere, and if so, where.

'What's in here?' the dark guy asks Vomit Girl. She came inside briefly for a glass of water, Anne remembers, just after she was sick.

'A sitting room off there,' she says, pointing to the left. 'A library thing down at the end and a kitchen around the back.' She smiles weakly. 'I'm Thea, by the way.'

'Paul,' says the dark guy, smiling back.

Anne can't remember if they spoke at all at the place in Edinburgh. She thinks not.

'Shall we all have a look around?' suggests Duke. 'Get the lay of the land.'

Pop Girl giggles. 'Yeah, let's get the *lay of the land*,' she repeats. He blushes and a couple of the others shift around. Then everyone drifts down the corridor. Nothing about this seems very real. Anne's wondering who's going to panic first, but no one seems to know how to react.

'Is there anyone else on this island?' asks Dreadlocks. 'Or is it just us?'

'If there is anyone else here, they're being very quiet,' says Paul.

'There's no one in here,' says Thea.

'There was no one outside,' says Duke.

The house is pretty much as Thea described. The sitting room off to the left is big, and looks weird without a TV. There are no electronic devices of any kind in the room, just a couple of big brown sofas and a large Indian rug on the bare, unvarnished floorboards. There's also an open fire, a mantelpiece with nothing on it, a bureau and a single table, pushed to the side of the room. It's cold and dusty and Thea's shoes make an echoey, clicking sound on the tiles. Anne's legs feel heavy and she wishes she could go back to sleep.

Upstairs there are six bedrooms, three to the right and three to the left. Each door has one of their names on it. Whoever planned this intended the boys to be along the right, the girls along the left.

'Hot Christ,' says Paul as they walk, dazed, from room to room.

The bedrooms are identical. They are all white: white linen, white towels, white walls.

'It's just like a hospital,' says Pop Girl, yawning.

'What kind of hospitals do you go to?' asks Thea. 'It's more like a hotel.'

'What kind of hotels do *you* go to?' asks Pop Girl, raising her eyebrows.

They both laugh sleepily. They seem to have established that it's not like a hospital or a hotel.

'Whatever,' says Paul. 'It's still fucked up. Hot Christ.'

'Can you stop saying that?' asks Thea.

'Saying what?' asks Paul.

Each of the rooms also contains a blank, white notebook, and some white clothes.

Anne's stomach does a kind of flip, but she doesn't say anything.

'What is going on here?' asks Thea quietly.

A small staircase leads to an attic room, but the door is locked.

'Kitchen?' suggests Pop Girl. 'I'm really thirsty.'

'We need to work out what's going on here,' says Duke.

As they walk down to the kitchen, it strikes Anne that this place was probably used as some sort of hotel or guest house once. Otherwise why would all the bedrooms have bathrooms?

'Does anyone else feel sick?' asks Pop Girl. She's made it to the kitchen table and is sitting slumped over it, heaving about, being dramatic. Everyone else is sitting at the table as well, except for Paul, who is trying to put the kettle on, but has found that the electric stove doesn't work. He finds a small camping stove in the end, with a full gas cylinder, and uses that. He doesn't seem to have any trouble filling it, and water comes straight out of the tap. There's running water here, at least, then, although Anne's not sure where it comes from.

'Yeah,' says U-rated Duke Nukem. 'I feel queasy.'

'I've got bad gut rot,' says Dreadlocks.

'I'm OK,' says Anne quietly.

'You look pale,' says Duke.

'You do actually,' says Paul.

'Everyone says that,' she replies. 'It's normal. Don't worry.'

'You should get a sun bed or something,' says Pop Girl.

Anne doesn't say anything. She likes being pale. It suits her.

'I feel better now I've puked,' says Thea. 'What are your names, by the way?'

'Emily,' says Pop Girl.

'Anne,' says Anne.

'Er, what, me?' asks Dreadlocks. 'Er, Bryn.'

'Jamie,' says Duke.

'Paul,' says Paul again. He's going through the cupboards.

'What are you doing?' asks Thea.

'Trying to find some cups.'

'Do you think we're supposed to . . .' begins Bryn.

'What?' says Emily sarcastically. '"Make ourselves at home"? Of course we're supposed to. Or – I know – maybe we could just not drink anything until we all collapse and die. Then I guess we won't get into any trouble.'

Bryn seems offended. 'Sorry,' he says huffily.

'I think we're already in trouble,' says Thea.

Paul looks over at Bryn. 'I think we should go ahead and do what we want, just like the note said. For Christ's sake, we didn't exactly ask to come here.'

Bryn looks pissed off. He lights one of Emily's cigarettes. Thea lights one too.

Anne's thinking about those TV programmes where members of the public get duped by some trick or other, sometimes involving throwing puppies off a bridge (not *really!*) or giving someone something to hold and then running away. The joke is always that trusting passers-by will be happy to stop and help without realising that they are being set up for a joke, or will try to stop the 'comedian' from throwing the puppies over the bridge, without realising that there are no puppies, without realising that the *joke* is that there are no puppies. By trying to stop the comedian from throwing them over the bridge, the passers-by seem stupid, because the comedian and the audience know that there are no puppies.

'So who wants coffee?' asks Paul, having found some cups.

Everyone says *me* or grunts, except Anne, who doesn't like tea or coffee.

'What do you think they gave us?' asks Jamie.

'Downers?' suggests Bryn. 'They sometimes make me feel sick,' he adds.

'I don't feel right at all,' says Jamie, shaking his head. 'I'm still all woozy.'

'The coffee might make you feel better,' says Thea. She looks like shit.

Paul opens the fridge to get some milk. Anne's wondering what the chances are of there actually being any in there. After all, this is an island in the middle of nowhere. She's as surprised as everyone else when the fridge turns out to be packed full of stuff, and that it's actually cold. The fridge is plugged into some sort of rechargeable battery, which no one but Anne seems to notice.

'Shit,' says Paul. 'Look at all this.'

He starts poking around. Anne can see milk, cheese, meat, several bottles of white wine, mineral water, lemonade, orange-ade, butter, eggs and salad cream. It's all from Sainsbury's. So they're still in the UK then.

Anne pours a glass of Evian.

Paul starts going through the cupboards. There are tins of fruit, Spam, corned beef and soup. One large cupboard contains only baked beans — about three hundred cans. Another has only packets of rice and beans. There's also a kitchen store full of bottled water, more beans, more canned food, matches, red wine — about a case full — and other miscellaneous items in multi-pack slabs. Whoever lives here won't starve in a hurry, or run out of matches. There's so much stuff in the kitchen store that it's hard to see everything. Who knows what supplies are at the back or on the top shelves? It looks as if someone's stocked up for the end of the world or something.

'We have, like, been kidnapped, haven't we?' asks Bryn suddenly.

'Yep,' says Paul, handing out the coffees. He frowns, but doesn't say anything else.

'I think maybe we're supposed to care,' says Thea.

Anne thinks Thea would probably try to save the non-puppies.

Paul looks at Thea. 'I do care. Anyway, it's all right here. It's cool.'

'Cool?' says Thea. 'You *are* joking.'

'There's more food in the fridge here than in my flat,' he replies.

'Same here,' says Bryn. 'This is like a holiday place or something.'

'Hello?' says Emily. 'This totally sucks. Get with the programme. Fucking hell.'

'We were *drugged*, remember,' says Thea.

'We don't even know where in the world we are,' says Emily.

'We're still in the UK,' says Anne quietly. 'Or close, anyway.'

'What?' asks Jamie. 'How do you know that?'

'Sainsbury's,' she says. 'Unless our kidnappers do an international weekly shop.'

Paul laughs.

'This is *so* not funny,' says Emily.

'It is, though,' says Paul. 'I can't wait to see what happens next.'

'I was just going to go home and argue with my mother,' says Anne. 'So I'd rather be executed, which, let's face it, is probably what happens next.'

There's a pause. A cold feeling in the room.

'Look, it's probably just a mistake,' says Bryn.

'What, like a computer error?' says Paul, laughing.

'Maybe it's a trick,' says Jamie uncertainly. 'We should just wait and see.'

'It's not like there's any other choice,' says Thea, getting up and going to the window.

'I've got to be back in London,' says Emily. 'I've got stuff to do.'

'This is totally out of order,' sighs Thea. 'We didn't agree to this.'

'We *so* didn't agree to this,' agrees Emily.

'Shit!' says Bryn suddenly, looking at everyone. 'You were all at that interview.'

'Well done,' mutters Anne.

'*That's* where I've seen you all before,' says Emily.

'Didn't you realise?' says Jamie, sounding surprised.

'I still feel all drugged,' says Emily. 'But yeah, obviously I realise now.'

'That odd little office,' says Paul.

'That horrible coffee,' says Bryn.

'Shit. We have actually been kidnapped,' says Thea, making it official.

'You're quick,' says Anne.

Chapter Two

Jamie can't believe this girl's being so cool. She's intriguing.

'So we all applied for that Bright Young Things job,' he says.

'Weird shit, man,' says Bryn.

'Is that office the last thing everyone remembers?' asks Paul.

Everyone nods. They all look tired and slightly confused.

'The coffee,' says Thea. 'I took a sip of the coffee and then woke up here.'

'The coffee's the last thing I remember, too,' says Jamie.

'Same,' says Emily.

Jamie looks at the coffee he's drinking now. Maybe a sip of this will take him back.

'I don't even drink coffee,' says Anne. 'I only drank a little bit to be polite.'

'No one asked us if we wanted it, did they?' remembers Jamie.

'That's right,' says Paul. 'Usually they ask if you want tea or coffee.'

'That weird guy just sort of gave them to us all, didn't he?' says Emily.

'There wasn't any receptionist either,' says Paul. 'Just that buzzer thing.'

Jamie remembers not being able to find the place for ages. He had the right street he just couldn't find that right number. It had eventually turned out to be a small office above a betting shop, with a grey, rusting intercom and a pile of mail inside the door. Jamie remembers being disappointed that this wasn't a cool media place, that it was more a place for dull old things than bright young ones. He'd felt a lump in his throat as he was buzzed upstairs, knowing this had been his one chance of adventure. He'd suddenly realised that you really shouldn't respond to those vague job ads, and you certainly shouldn't go all the way to Edinburgh for an interview for a job you know nothing about.

He remembers how excited he felt when the application from came back to him in the envelope he'd addressed to himself. There'd been the extra thrill of hiding the envelope from Carla; getting up early every day for weeks to intercept the mail. He's aware that the interview seemed more exciting because he'd *made* it seem more exciting. Because he was applying for the job in secret it had started to feel more like an affair or a drug habit or something glamorous, and he'd had a purpose every day, sneaking around, feeling increasingly distant from Carla. Maybe that was his whole purpose, he suddenly thinks; to distance himself from Carla without actually telling her he didn't love her.

The application form had seemed extra-thrilling because of all the questions Jamie hadn't expected. There was the one about his greatest fear, his favourite book, and there were even a couple of those ink-blot pictures where you have to say what you think they look like. The form had led Jamie to believe he was applying for something at a big company that was interested in people, not some small, smelly outfit that may or may not have just kidnapped him.

'Maybe it was the receptionist's day off,' suggests Anne, smiling.

'It was a horrible place,' says Paul distantly. 'Reminded me of my flat.'

Everyone's quiet for a moment.

'So we all get there for ten o'clock,' says Emily.

'It said ten on my letter,' says Jamie.

'And mine,' says Thea, sitting back down at the table, looking scared.

Everyone else nods.

'That was pretty much all it said,' says Jamie. 'Just the time and place and stuff.'

Everyone nods again.

'Yep. We all got the same letter,' confirms Paul.

'And there's just this guy there handing out coffee in a dingy office,' continues Emily.

'Not saying anything,' adds Bryn.

'Didn't he speak at all?' asks Jamie, trying to remember.

'Yeah, he did,' says Thea. 'Didn't he say, "I'll be with you in a minute", or something?'

Paul frowns. 'Yeah, something like that. I think he said "someone" rather than him.'

'Maybe *he* was the receptionist,' suggests Emily.

'There must have been more than one person there,' says Jamie. 'The application form seemed too detailed. I thought it was a big company. I was sure they'd have a panel, or at least a couple of people.'

'I thought so too,' says Bryn. 'I thought it seemed well professional.'

'We weren't really there long enough to find out,' says Paul.

'Did the guy have an accent?' asks Jamie.

'Can't remember,' says Anne. 'Did he?'

No one else seems able to remember whether he did or not.

'Then he left us to drink the coffee,' says Emily. 'Then we wake up here.'

'Must have been full of downers,' says Bryn again.

'Can anyone remember anything else?' asks Emily.

'There were those roadworks outside,' says Jamie. 'It was noisy.'

'And hot,' adds Bryn. 'Hotter than here.'

'The room we were in seemed all dark and dusty,' says Jamie.

'We should still be sitting in that room,' says Thea tearfully. 'We shouldn't be here.'

'Shhh,' says Emily, patting her shoulder. 'It'll be OK.'

'It won't, though, will it?' she says. 'We don't even know where we are. Or why.'

'Or how we got here,' adds Jamie.

'Well, we didn't walk,' says Paul, smiling.

'We must have been flown here,' says Anne, with a shiver. 'I hate flying.'

Jamie's never really met people like this before. The girls seem nice, although Thea's all stressed and Anne's all weird. Emily's gorgeous, of course. The guys are different. With Paul, it's hard to put your finger on what's unsettling about him, but something is. With Bryn, it's obvious. All that matted hair and his stained teeth. He looks rough. Good-looking, but rough. Jamie's seen pictures of people like him in *The Face*, although not often. Is it even fashionable to do that with your hair any more? Jamie's not sure.

'Why would anyone want to kidnap us?' he asks the others.

'Yeah, you'd think they'd choose some important people,' says Anne.

Thea's been looking at the kitchen door every couple of seconds.

'Expecting someone?' asks Paul, the next time she does it.

'I'm scared,' she says. 'What if they just turn up and kill us?'

'We'll hear them coming,' says Paul. 'Don't worry, we'll have good warning.'

Jamie wishes he'd thought of that.

'They haven't brought us here to kill us anyway,' Paul says.

'Like you'd know,' says Emily.

'They wouldn't leave us food if they were going to kill us.'

Bryn gulps down his coffee. 'Maybe we're worth more alive.'

Anne giggles. '*They were worth more alive,*' she repeats, in a film-trailer voice.

Jamie doesn't really know what's serious and what isn't right now. How can she joke? What the hell is this place? And who are these people? Mind you, although Jamie doesn't really understand why Anne's being so tongue-in-cheek about being abandoned on an island with a load of strangers, he's not actually that freaked out either. He is trying to be scared about the situation, but all he keeps doing is running through scenarios in his head. He sees himself telling people back home what happened, and how he engineered the dramatic escape. He imagines himself on talk shows, selling the book of his experiences, never having to worry about numbers again, except for the staggering sales figures.

He has briefly considered that being kidnapped might not be fun, and that this could (as the book jacket will suggest) end in tragedy, but even that outcome seems better than his actual life. He remembers how adventurous he felt going up to Edinburgh on the sleeper, fantasising about a Bond Girl mysteriously popping into his compartment and asking for his help. This situation is real, but it's more like Jamie's fantasy world than reality ever has been before. Being held hostage on a remote island is just so much more exciting than what he expected: boring interview, train home, Carla demanding what the hell he thought he was doing, rejection letter. And after all, it doesn't seem as though they're in any immediate danger.

Thea's making some kind of fear-noise. Like a sob with no tears.

'Oh, God,' she says.

'Calm down,' says Emily. 'It's all right.'

'Who's scared?' asks Paul, in a who's-having-fun kind of way.

'Shut up,' says Thea.

'I think we're *all* scared,' says Emily.

'I'm not,' says Anne.

'Me neither,' says Paul.

'I'm not that scared,' says Bryn. 'This is better than the hotel I stayed in last night.'

'Well, you're scared, aren't you?' Emily asks Jamie.

Everyone looks at him.

'Not really,' he says. 'I'm finding it quite relaxing in a weird sort of way.'

'That'll be the drugs, mate,' laughs Bryn.

'Are *you* actually scared?' Anne asks Emily.

'If I was on my own I'd be shitting myself,' she says.

'But . . . ?' prompts Anne.

'But, well, with you lot here it's not very scary, if you know what I mean.'

'Am I the only one who's scared then?' asks Thea.

'I'm sure we will feel scared,' says Jamie. 'You know, when they come.'

'Maybe no one will come,' suggests Anne.

'Will you shut up,' says Thea. 'For God's sake. This isn't a joke.'

'I wasn't joking,' says Anne.

Jamie's trying to work out what it is about this place. It shouldn't be relaxing, but it is. Accepting the fact that they are all trapped here, and that there are no shops or other people or any of that normality, then it sort of seems like a retreat or a health farm or something. And even the trapped feeling isn't that intense, because they're not properly imprisoned, and they have the run of this big house and the island. Jamie rubs his legs and tries to stand up. He feels wobbly from the drugs.

Once on his feet, his legs feel too heavy to sit back down, so he walks over to the window.

Bryn's smoking another cigarette, holding his head as if it hurts.

'Can one of you come with me to the toilet?' Emily asks Anne and Thea.

Paul laughs. 'You need someone to go to the toilet with you?'

'I'm not going upstairs on my own,' she says.

Thea goes with her.

Outside it looks bright, and it's probably still hot, although it's hard to tell with it being so cool inside. There is a small orchard just beyond the window. The apples seem ripe. In fact, Jamie can see that some of them are too ripe and are rotting on the trees. He turns away from the window, crosses the kitchen and walks out into the hall.

'Where's he going?' Bryn asks.

'Dunno,' says Paul.

Jamie had noticed a door before, under the stairs, and now he wonders if it's a cellar door. Maybe there's something down there, some clue as to what they're all doing here. The door actually looked like it could be for a cupboard, but Jamie's house in Cambridge has the same kind of door, and although visitors think it's a cupboard, it's a cellar. The door is on a small catch, which Jamie pushes up with his finger. Sure enough, the door opens and there are stairs leading down. It's dark, and smells damp. Suddenly he's scared. Maybe the others should come too. He walks back down the hall.

Paul, Anne and Bryn are still in the kitchen. There's no sign of Emily and Thea.

Jamie clears his throat. 'There's a cellar under the stairs,' he says.

'A basement?' says Bryn.

'Yeah,' says Jamie. 'Shall we have a look?'

'You know what they say about not going into the basement,' jokes Bryn.

No one laughs. Maybe they think the *Scream* stuff is outdated. Or maybe they're just more scared than they're admitting.

It's impossible to see what's down there. There's a light switch at the bottom of the basement stairs, which Anne flicks up and down several times. The clicking sound echoes in the cold room. The light doesn't come on.

'It's busted,' says Bryn.

'Must need a new bulb,' says Jamie.

'I don't think it's going to come on,' Paul says to Anne, who's still flicking the switch.

'There must be some candles somewhere,' says Anne.

'Shall I go and have a look?' offers Jamie.

'Good idea,' says Paul.

Jamie doesn't know where to find candles. He tries the kitchen first, assuming practical things would be kept in there. Then he goes through all the upstairs rooms. Emily and Thea are in one of the bathrooms. Jamie can hear them talking. He's scared by the idea of two girls talking in a room, but he doesn't know why. Eventually he finds a box of six candles in the bureau in the sitting room.

Back in the dark basement, Anne is singing something. It's some pop song Jamie recognises; something he thought was marketed at teens and gay men. He lights one of the candles. He can just see Anne wiggling her small hips, still humming the bassline of the song. What the hell is the name of it? It's by that American girl, the one in a gymslip. Jamie's masturbated over pictures of her for God's sake; you'd think he'd remember her name.

Anne's voice echoes. Jamie holds up the candle.

'Are there any more of those?' asks Paul.

'What?'

'Candles.'

'Yes. There are six.' Jamie takes the box out of his pocket to show them.

'Cool,' says Anne. 'Can I have one?'

'I don't think we should use them all up,' he says. 'We might need them.'

'For what?' asks Bryn, taking a candle from the box and lighting it.

When Jamie was about twelve, he went through a phase of reading what he called 'island books'. The story was always basically the same: via a plane crash or a boating accident, a group of people would end up on an uninhabited island, having to survive against the odds. Someone would make a play for the role of leader — usually the coarsest, brashest person — but the heroic, quiet guy whom everyone respected would challenge him and ultimately lead everyone to victory over whatever obstacle was in the way.

Jamie wishes this was more like that.

Bryn's gone on ahead with candle number two.

'Hey, look at this,' he calls.

The other three walk to where he is, by the far wall. The two candles illuminate a single bed. It's rather more basic than the beds upstairs. It has a metal frame, a thin, dirty mattress, and no sheets or pillows.

'Nice guest room,' says Anne, wrinkling her nose.

'This is horrible,' agrees Paul. 'Let's go back upstairs.'

'It stinks of piss down here. What are you doing?'

Jamie jumps. Emily has emerged from the shadows like a ghost. She's obviously back from the toilet.

Paul's walking away from the small bed.

'What are you doing?' Bryn asks him.

'Going back up,' he says.

* * *

The kitchen has become like a base camp, which is good. Jamie wants to suggest sealing the door or something, and formulating a defence strategy for when the kidnappers appear. All everyone else seems to want to do is just sit here. Well, everyone except Anne. She's gone outside and Jamie can see her through the window. She's just picked an apple, bitten into it once and thrown it away. Now she's wandering towards the cliffs.

'I'm just popping outside,' he says to the others.

They ignore him. Emily's giving Thea a pep talk on the importance of not behaving like a victim. Thea's pointing out that for once she is a victim – specifically a *kidnap* victim – and therefore has every right to act like one. Jamie gets up and walks out of the back door, noticing that no one even looks up. This upsets him. His mother always told him not to worry about what other people think, but he always does.

Anne is sitting cross-legged on the grass.

'Hello,' he says, walking towards her.

'Hey,' she replies, without looking round.

He sits down next to her.

'You like the company then?' he says.

'Sorry?'

'That lot back there. Were they annoying you?'

Anne shakes her head. 'No. They're all right.'

'Are you feeling scared?' he asks.

'Yeah, terrified,' says Anne sarcastically.

'So . . . ?'

She fiddles with her daisy chain. 'What?'

'What are you doing out here?' Jamie asks.

'Nothing. What about you?'

'I'm, uh . . .'

'They're pissing *you* off, right?'

'Not really,' he says.

'So you came out here to try to seduce me?'

Jamie blushes. 'Of course not! How can you say that?'

Anne laughs. 'I'm a virgin. We have special powers.'

'You're ... Oh, never mind.'

As if a girl like Anne would be a virgin.

He pulls a packet of Marlboro out of his pocket. 'Do you want a cigarette?'

'No.'

'Do you smoke?'

'No.'

'Do you hate me?'

She looks at him with her big brown eyes. 'Of course not. Why would I?'

'Because I'm a geek.'

She laughs. 'A geek? What do you mean?'

Jamie sighs. 'Never mind.'

'Seriously. Are you into computers and stuff?'

'No. I did maths at university.'

'That's cool. But really that makes you a nerd rather than a geek.'

'Thanks,' he says.

'There's nothing wrong with being a nerd.'

'Yeah, right.'

'I love nerds.'

'Do you?'

She wrinkles her nose, as if giving the question a lot of thought. 'Not really.'

'Oh.'

She smiles. 'I suppose they're OK.'

'Thanks.'

She studies him. 'So, maths is pretty cool, right?'

'Are you taking the—'

'No.' She shakes her head. 'I love numbers,' she explains.

'I don't.'

'What?' she asks.

'Love numbers. I hate them.'

'But you're a mathematician.'

'Yes, well, kind of.'

'And you hate numbers?'

'Yes.'

'Wow,' she says. 'That is the coolest thing I've heard all day.'

'What, hating what you do?'

'No, I guess . . . just working with something as abstract as numbers but secretly hating them. Or even having the capacity to hate something like a number. I bet all the other nerds love them.'

'I suppose they do.'

'It's like being an astronomer and hating planets.'

'Mmm.' He's not that sure where she's coming from.

They sit there for a few moments, watching the sea crash about below them.

Jamie's still trying to feel like he's been kidnapped. The weird basement helped.

'So do you think zero is a number?' asks Anne suddenly.

'Sorry?'

'Zero. Is it a number?'

'Yes and no.' Jamie rubs his legs. 'You can say it is, because you use it as a number within number systems. Or at least, you use it in the same way as a number. For example, in the number 507, the zero acts like a number. It signifies that there aren't any tens in the number, just hundreds and units. On the other hand, because the whole concept of zero is for it to indicate the absence of a number, it can't really be one.'

'Don't you want to know what I think?'

'Um, yeah, OK, if you find it that interesting.'

'I think that zero isn't a number.'

'Great.' He'd rather talk about something else, like escaping.

'Do you want to know why?'

'OK.'

Anne smiles. 'People say that zero is the opposite of one, right?'

Jamie nods. 'I suppose so.'

'Because one is presence and zero is absence.'

'That's the idea,' he says.

'But it's really minus one, though, isn't it?'

'What is?'

'The opposite of one. If the opposite of something is its absolute reverse, like its image in a mirror or whatever, then the opposite of one must be minus one. Zero just sits between them both and gives them meaning. So I think that zero isn't a number. I think zero is God.'

'What did you do at university?' Jamie asks.

'English and philosophy,' says Anne.

He smiles. 'So I expect zero has a philosophical application?'

'Yeah, in psychoanalysis, where the self is represented by one, and the other by minus one. The zero is the mirroring point and therefore the point of separation. It is also the point of identification, alienation and otherness.'

'Where did you read that?'

'I didn't. I made it up.' She smiles. 'Do you still hate numbers?'

'Of course,' says Jamie.

'What about zero?'

'Zero's all right,' he concedes. 'But then, it isn't really a number.'

Chapter Three

When Thea was in the Lower Sixth, there was a group of kids in the Upper Sixth who were really cool. They had these parties that you only got invited to if you were a real somebody, and although they knew the whole Lower Sixth because they all shared the sixth-form common room, only six or seven of them ever got invited. It was always the same lot: the corrupt Form President, the girl with the schizophrenic mother, the guy who always smoked dope in the common room, the girl who was admitted to hospital for overdosing on Pro Plus, and so on.

Thea never got invited. Maybe that was why she hated them.

Or maybe it was their sense of humour. Two guys in particular – Henry and Kenickie (Grease fan – how cool and ironic) – always upset her, however hard she tried not to let them get to her. She'd try to be friendly towards them, but conversations always went the same way. Thea would say something like, 'All right?', and they'd say, 'Yeah, cool,' or something like that. Then she'd ask if they'd seen Sasha or Mary or whoever she was trying to find. Thea remembers that sixth form was all about trying to find someone. You never went around on your own; you were always trying to find someone.

'Haven't you heard?' they'd say.

'What?'

'Sasha was in an accident this morning.'

'Seriously?' Thea would say, even though she knew they were winding her up.

'Yeah,' they'd reply. 'Haven't you heard? She's dead.'

And then Thea wouldn't know what to say. If she laughed and acknowledged it was a joke, there was always the chance they were telling the truth, in which case she'd be committing an awful act by laughing. But if she acted shocked and upset, she'd seem like a fool because of course they were only joking. It's like what's going on here with this kidnapping. No one's getting upset because it might be a joke. On the other hand, no one's really laughing just in case it isn't.

Jamie and Anne come in from outside and sit down at the kitchen table with the others. Jamie pours himself a glass of wine from the half-empty bottle on the table. Thea's already had a glass and she feels slightly better. She hadn't been sure about drinking the wine at first, but Emily had persuaded her that drinking was probably the best thing to do in this situation. Anne looks at the wine suspiciously, then pours a glass of lemonade. She starts freaking out when she tastes artificial sweeteners in it and tips it down the sink. Instead, she pours herself a glass of milk from the fridge, and somehow manages to find a box of strawberry Nesquik in one of the cupboards. Then, in one of the drawers, she finds some straws. Everyone watches as she rejects the blue, yellow and green ones in favour of a pink one, presumably to go with her milkshake. Thea doesn't know why everyone else finds this so interesting. OK, she's doing it with that infuriating innocence – which just has to be put on – but Thea won't be sucked into it. As far as she's concerned this girl needs to grow up.

'Skin up,' says Bryn to Emily.

'What?' she says.

'You must have some draw,' he says.

'Why must I have some draw?'

'Girls like you always do.'

'Oh,' she almost blushes. 'Well, I've got a little bit . . .'

She rummages around in her rucksack and eventually pulls out a small lump.

'Give me that,' says Bryn.

'What?'

'*I'll* build one up.'

Emily shrugs. 'OK.'

Bryn pulls some tattered-looking small green skins from one of his pockets. The front of the packet has been entirely ripped away. He produces a joint in about thirty seconds and shares it with Emily and Thea. Jamie, Paul and Anne all say no. Anne's slurping on her milkshake. Jamie's writing something on a piece of paper. Paul's watching Anne. Thea wonders where Jamie got the paper and pen.

'Where did you get that?' she asks.

'Sitting room,' he says. 'In the bureau.'

'Oh.'

'I'm planning our defence shelter,' he says. 'For when the kidnappers come.'

Anne smiles. 'I always wanted to meet a Boy Scout.'

'Do you think the kidnappers will come?' asks Emily.

'If they are kidnappers,' says Paul. 'It could just be a load of situationists for all we know. Or even some of our friends.'

'For fuck's sake,' says Thea. 'If this is a joke or a situationist prank or a dada statement or whatever else, it isn't very funny – or interesting.'

'I think it's funny *and* interesting,' says Anne.

'Shut up,' sayd Thea.

'Stop telling me to shut up,' says Anne. 'It's just what I think.'

'What do you think then?' Bryn asks Thea. 'Why do you think we're here?'

'Me? Um . . . Maybe it's just a really weird job interview.'

'What do you mean?' says Emily.

'Well, all this could be some kind of test.'

Her words sound weak, because she doesn't believe in what she's saying. Thea's already decided that when the kidnappers appear, which they will, she's going to bolt and hide on her own, maybe down by the cliffs. The way she's feeling, if all the others get murdered sitting in their *defence shelter*, then that's just fine with her. Of course, if they weren't being so blasé she'd be happy to work with them, but for the time being she's going to listen to what they have to say, assess their theories and be polite. And when the shit hits the fan, Thea's going to be looking out for herself. For now, she's going to keep worrying about her stomach cramps. What a time to have your period. Emily lent her a tampon upstairs before, but said it was her last one. Tomorrow – if Thea makes it that far – she's going to have to use bog roll.

The others are more convinced by her job interview idea than she is.

'What, you mean that this is the interview?' asks Anne.

Thea says nothing.

'It would make sense,' says Paul.

Emily laughs. 'Yeah, like that totally makes sense. Please.'

'No, I see what he means,' says Jamie. 'We went for a job interview, and the last thing we all remember is drinking coffee and waiting to be shown into the interview room. What if this is the interview room?'

'Fucked up, man,' says Bryn.

'So if this is the interview, then there's no need to be scared,' says Emily cheerfully.

'Yeah, whatever you reckon,' says Paul sarcastically.

'This is the scariest job interview I've ever been to,' says Thea.

'It must be illegal,' says Jamie.

People look at him strangely, like he's just said the sky is blue.

'So where's the interviewer, then?' asks Anne.

'Maybe there is no interviewer,' suggests Paul mysteriously.

'Yeah, it could be a bonding exercise,' suggests Emily. 'You know, a wild men in the woods kind of thing. See if we end up working as a team.'

'Wild men in the woods?' says Bryn. 'Oh, you mean where everyone goes into the woods and bangs drums and seeks their inner man? They did that on *Home and Away.*'

Anne looks up. 'Yeah. Alf Stewart and Donald Fisher went.'

'Is Alf still in it?' asks Emily.

'Of course,' says Anne.

'And Ailsa,' adds Bryn.

'Ailsa's in a coma right now though,' says Anne.

'I only watch it round my mate's house,' says Bryn. 'His mum has it on all the time.'

'What about Bobby?' asks Paul. 'I fancied her.'

'Dead,' says Anne. 'Ages ago.'

'Sophie?'

'Left Summer Bay with her love-child.'

'Shannon?'

'Living with a lesbian in Paris and attending the Sorbonne.'

'For God's sake,' Thea says, sighing.

'Do you watch *Neighbours* as well?' Emily asks Anne.

Anne nods. 'It's not as good as *Home and Away* but . . .'

Emily laughs. 'You're taking the piss, right? By "good" you mean really bad. Like, you watch it in an ironic way.'

'No.'

'Seriously?' Emily doesn't seem sure if Anne's joking or not.

'Yeah, seriously. Here's an example. About ten years ago there was this plot where Bobby Simpson, Pippa's out-of-control foster daughter, starts seeing the local headmaster Donald Fisher's son Alan. At around the same time, this woman called Morag has come to Summer Bay and she's living in this really big Gothic house generally being evil. It comes out that Fisher had an affair with her a long time ago and that Bobby was the resulting love-child. Meanwhile, Bobby's getting on really well with Alan, who is obviously her half-brother, although neither of them knows that. Morag and Fisher don't want to reveal the truth to Bobby for the time being, but they can't have her sleeping with her own brother, so the whole situation gets a bit complicated. Just as they start to intervene, Fisher's son collapses on the beach, is taken into hospital and later dies.

Fisher then comes clean with Bobby. She dies too, several years later. I think she drowned, but that was during my No TV experiment. Anyway, ten years on, the book Alan wrote about his difficult relationship with his father, *On the Crest of a Wave*, is put on the HSC curriculum. It also gets picked up by a film company. So right now, there's this film crew in Summer Bay trying to get to grips with all the characters who are still there, because Alan based the book on real life. And there's this actress character walking around trying to get into the part of Bobby, about eight years after the original character actually left the series, and the best thing is, all the plot from right back then is still consistent with now.'

'Wow,' says Emily. 'You really know your soaps.'

'Only that one,' says Anne. 'And *Neighbours*, I guess. People say that Australian soaps are silly and fluffy. But *Home and Away* always has the best, most interesting psychopaths, the most well-drawn characters and the most imaginative plots. You know, like Joey's dad being a cult leader and then Joey becoming schizophrenic and seeing his dad appear in his computer screen – after his dad was shot by Terry Garner, the slaggy local cop. Or when they wanted to tackle racism. Instead of just having some black characters come along and have everyone be nice to them, they had a plot where the leader of this right-wing political party came to do a rally in Summer Bay. It showed how lots of the locals got taken in by her ideas, and demonstrated that although the "anti-foreigner" ideas are morally wrong, they are quite logical. There was a lot of debate between the characters, which was much more effective than all that crap they do on *Eastenders* or whatever. The black teenagers started thinking about their identity as well. Then they had this Aboriginal teacher who came and . . .'

'Don't you like *Eastenders?*' interrupts Emily. 'It's so good at the moment.'

'No,' says Anne. 'I think it's the worst thing on TV.'

'It's a bit depressing,' agrees Jamie.

'And the acting is appalling,' says Anne.

'Do you think so?' asks Emily. 'I thought it was all right.'

'No. The acting in *Home and Away* is fantastic, though.'

'Seriously?'

'Yeah. It's good on *Neighbours* as well. Susan and Carl are great comic actors.'

Thea can't believe they're going on and on about this crap.

'Do you watch *Heartbreak High?*' asks Paul.

'Of course,' says Anne.

'I like that,' says Emily. 'I fancy Drasick.'

'You'll never guess who's in *Home and Away* at the moment about to play the part of Bobby in the film, then,' says Anne.

'Who?' asks Paul.

'Anita from *Heartbreak High*. How cool is that?'

It doesn't make too much of an impact on anyone else, although this is the most animated Anne has been since they all got here. Thea sighs. Typical for it to be about something as irrelevant as soap operas. *Australian* soap operas.

'Don't you like any English stuff?' asks Thea.

'Not really,' says Anne. 'Not on TV. I like English books and magazines, but for TV and movies it's got to be Australia or America. You wouldn't want to get me started on *Beverly Hills 90210* or *Savannah*.'

'*Savannah?*' says Emily.

'Aaron Spelling's finest hour,' prompts Anne.

'Apart from *Sunset Beach*, of course,' says Emily, smiling.

Anne laughs. 'Channel Five's all fuzzy on my TV.'

'What's that film with the lawnmower?' says Emily.

'*Lawnmower Man?*' suggests Anne.

'No, the zombie film.'

'*Braindead,*' say Paul and Anne together.

'That's Australian isn't it?' says Emily.

'New Zealand,' says Paul.

Thea just can't believe this. It takes nothing to get this lot started talking about rubbish. If they are going to talk about the world outside, why not talk about something interesting?

'I'm lost,' she says. 'Weren't we talking about wild men in the woods or something. What's all that about?'

'It's a bonding thing,' explains Emily. 'Getting back to nature. Blokes do it. You know those weekends they send marketing executives on where they have to hunt treasure or something?'

'Yeah,' says Thea.

'And all work together and whatever?'

'Yeah.'

'Well, it's like that.'

'Oh. I still don't get how that's connected to this.'

Emily sighs. 'Look, they've put us in an extreme situation and they're waiting to see how we cope.'

'Oh, what, you mean like how we collect food and water?' says Jamie.

Thea looks at the fridge. 'It's not exactly a survival situation,' she points out.

'So it's unlikely to be that, then,' says Bryn, sighing.

'Anyway, let's get this straight,' says Emily. 'Paul thinks it's a prank.'

'Maybe,' says Paul. 'Although I'm into the interview idea as well. Maybe they're going to wait and see which one of us survives.'

'What?' says Thea.

'You know, when we all start killing each other.'

'We're not going to start killing each other,' says Emily.

'They do in the films,' says Paul.

'Right. And you,' Emily points to Thea, 'think it's a bonding exercise?'

'Have you seen *SFW*?' interrupts Anne.

'What?' says Jamie. '*SFW*? What's that?'

'*So Fucking What*. It's a film. It's about kidnap, a hostage thing.'

No one else has seen it.

'Anyway, no,' says Thea, answering Emily's question. 'I don't think it's a bonding exercise.'

'You suggested it though,' says Bryn.

'No, I just said maybe this is a job interview after all, but I'm not sure about that now.'

'What do you think now, then?' asks Paul.

'That we've been kidnapped. That's it.'

'You think we've been kidnapped as well, don't you?' Emily asks Anne.

'Not really,' says Anne.

'So what *do* you think?'

'Nothing. Maybe we're all in the same dream.'

'What?' asks Emily.

'Astral projection.' She nods. 'Yeah. That's my theory.'

Paul laughs. 'I like that better than mine.'

'I just wish she'd grow up,' hisses Thea to Emily. 'This is serious.'

'I'm not the one under the influence of drugs and alcohol,' says Anne.

'You don't need it,' mutters Bryn.

Jamie goes back to writing on his piece of paper.

Chapter Four

There's nowhere near enough drugs here. Bryn could really do with feeling normal right now. It was cool that the blonde girl had a spliff's worth, but why the hell didn't she bring any more? Bryn allows for the fact that no one knew they were going to be taken hostage on a remote island, but still.

Someone once told Bryn not to lie. It was probably his mum. That's not the thing that's going through his mind right now, though. He's thinking about some other piece of advice given to him, this time by some A-level student he was fucking for a while before he became impotent again last year. *Be careful what you wish for*, she'd said. *You might just get it.* At the time Bryn had thought she was just talking shit. But now he gets it. Yeah, he lied on his application form. He lied so that he could get the kind of job that would mean spending days on end with people like this. So he wished for it and now it's come true. Cheers. Thanks a lot.

He doesn't get any of this. He doesn't get why these people like soap operas and pop music and stuff for teenagers and kids. Why would they? They've obviously all been to university. He understands why Tank's mum likes *Home and Away*. She's dying of emphysema and likes watching 'all the young people'. And of course Bryn watches it when he's round there because Tank's mum's so depressing. You'd watch anything, wouldn't you? And the way these people talk. They're all bad, but particularly the weird girl, Anne. They are English, but they use American words. Maybe they learnt to do it at university. Maybe it's even correct. Bryn wouldn't know.

'What do you think, Bryn?' asks Emily.

'About what?' he says.

'Why do you think we're here?'

Why is she asking him?

'Uh, maybe it's an experiment,' he suggests.

'An experiment,' repeats Emily.

'I like that,' says Paul. 'What kind of experiment?'

'I don't know,' says Bryn. 'But my mate's sister got paid about three thousand quid for being in these drug experiments. She's in Warley Hospital now.'

'Seriously?' says Emily. 'Drug experiments? I've never heard of that.'

'I looked into it once,' says Thea. 'Loads of students do it. I was going to do a sleep one, where they keep you awake and see what effect it has on your reaction times and whatever. It wasn't strictly drugs, but I could have chosen an anti-depressant trial instead.'

'Marie, my mate's sister, she did the lot,' says Bryn. 'Drugs, sleep, food additives. She's a bit stupid, though, you know — wrong in the head — and it all got fucked up.'

'What happened?' asks Anne.

'They used some diet pills on her. Marie's massive, so she was well up for it. She got a rash though, soon after, and started pissing all the time, like, without realising, but the fee they gave her paid off her washing machine and she thought the pissing would stop. Then she did Roofies, you know that date-rape drug? Well, anyway, this psychologist gave her these Roofies and had a whole conversation with her to see how much of it she could remember afterwards. That was all right, except when she left the experiment, the drug hadn't quite worn off and she ended up on Canvey Island being fucked by these two blokes and she couldn't remember how she got there or how to get home. Then she did a clothes dye, but that made both her arms go purple; then she tested that stuff they put in food to stop you absorbing fat, but that made her leak shit all the time; then they gave her more slimming pills which didn't do anything; then an epilepsy drug which gave her reduced sight in one eye; a sleeping pill that put her to sleep for ten days; and artificial sweeteners which gave her a brain tumour.'

Anne starts laughing.

'It's not funny,' says Thea.

'No, I know it's not,' says Anne, still giggling. 'It's just the way he tells it.'

'Is she all right now?' asks Thea.

'No, I told you, she's in Warley Hospital.'

'What's that?'

'A mental hospital,' explains Bryn. 'In Brentwood,' he adds.

'So what's that got to do with us being here?' asks Emily.

'Well, maybe they're going to experiment on us,' he suggests. 'And this way they don't have to pay us. They could put something in the water. I don't know. It's just an idea.'

'It would have cost so much more to set all this up, though,' says Thea. 'Definitely more than paying us to do it in the outside world. I mean, you're talking money for the ad, whatever they drugged us with, the plane or however they got us here, the use of this island, the time of whoever selected us from all the applicants . . .'

'Unless whatever they're testing is illegal,' mumbles Bryn.

'I wonder why we were chosen from all the applicants,' says Emily.

Bryn frowns. 'Are you saying we were picked on purpose for this?'

'How else would we have got here?' asks Emily.

Everyone nods.

'Lots of people must have applied for the job,' says Jamie.

'I wonder if we were the best or the worst of them,' muses Anne.

'I've got an idea,' says Emily. 'Why don't we all say the most ridiculous reason we can think of for why we're here, completely off the top of our heads.'

'Why?' asks Thea. 'Haven't we just done that?'

'It's a good way of coming up with solutions,' says Emily. 'My dad always makes me do this stuff. He's always saying that to enable original thinking, you have to include ideas you'd usually dismiss as ridiculous. It's like you have to count what you'd usually automatically discount, and often that frees up your thinking or sometimes even provides a solution in itself. Once I was going to this party and I couldn't think what to wear, and Dad said, "Why don't you get all the most inappropriate things out and stick them all on your bed, and try to make an outfit from them. It'll give you some ideas." Anyway, I did, and I ended up wearing some of it to the party, and everyone thought I was some style icon.'

'What does your dad do?' asks Jamie.

'He's a management consultant,' giggles Emily.

'So what did you wear?' asks Anne.

'Jeans and a T-shirt,' she replies.

Everyone looks confused.

Emily smiles. 'You see, my friend works in fashion, and it was this big after-show party and everyone was going in Versace and Moschino, which were very cool at the time. It was meant to be really smart, and so by just turning up in jeans, I got loads of attention. There's no way I would have even considered doing it, but the more I looked at them lying there on my bed, the more I realised that this was the only way to make a real statement. I got laid as well.'

'You're a genuine bimbo,' says Paul, sounding shocked.

Bryn doesn't know if he's joking or not.

Jamie's writing something. His defence shelter design lies in a ball on the table. No one said anything when he screwed it up and threw it away. Bryn would actually feel better if they were all nailing the doors shut, rather than just sitting about drinking wine, but no one's come to murder them yet. It occurs to him that these people have probably never felt real danger before. OK, maybe one of them almost ran their BMW into something once, or flicked a light switch with wet hands, but nothing more than that. Maybe they just don't know how to act scared. Well, Thea's pretty good at it, but then you get the impression she'd be just as scared in the Ghost House of her local funfair.

The kitchen table is a mess of ashtray-saucers, cigarette butts and bottles. Bryn can't shake off the feeling that whoever owns this house will be pissed off if they make too much mess. Stupid, eh?

'Maybe they're going to breed us with aliens,' says Anne.

'What?' says Thea nastily.

Anne looks hurt, although it's a fair guess she isn't.

'Calm down. It's my ridiculous suggestion,' she says.

Thea sighs and lights a cigarette.

'Your turn,' Emily says to Bryn.

'I can't think of anything,' he says.

'Come on,' prompts Emily. 'Just the most stupid thing you can think of.'

'All right. What about a trampolining competition?' he says.

'A trampolining competition,' repeats Emily.

'Yeah, that's why they've brought us here.'

'But that's stupid,' says Emily.

'No,' corrects Anne. 'It's ridiculous. I think it's cool.'

Girls like Anne don't usually say Bryn's cool.

'Well, what's yours then?' Paul asks Emily.

'Porn,' she says. 'They're going to film us having sex.'

'Who?' says Thea. 'I'm not having sex.'

'I will be,' says Emily enigmatically, looking from Paul to Bryn and back.

'Well, then it's not ridiculous,' says Thea, sounding confused.

'You said it, sweetie,' Emily returns.

'We're here to farm sheep,' says Jamie, and giggles. No one else laughs.

'Let's hear Paul's,' says Anne.

'Nuclear testing,' says Paul.

'Is that it?' says Thea.

'What's yours then?' he asks.

'We've been brought here to fall in love,' she says.

'You cynic,' says Emily. 'That's not ridiculous. Love's cool.'

Outside it's starting to get dark. A minute ago the light was yellow. Now it's blue.

Bryn feels itchy all over. Maybe he's allergic to these people. Thea's right. There isn't going to be any romance here. Not that Bryn knows too much about romance, of course. He knows about sex (not enough, though — he's shit at it) and how to get girls to have sex with him, but romance ... that's way too embarrassing. He feels uncomfortable because it now looks like sex could be on the cards with the blonde girl. Bryn's not so sure about blondes. He's a Posh Spice sort of bloke. He reminds himself that this girl would probably be a right goer. The thought doesn't excite him, though, it just makes him itch more.

'What are you doing?' Anne asks Jamie. He's been writing things on the bit of paper for hours now, or that's what it feels like.

'I'm writing a list,' he says.

'Of?' demands Emily.

'Suspects,' he replies. 'For the kidnapping.'

'Cool,' says Anne. 'Can I see?'

She tries to grab the piece of paper but Jamie holds it out of her reach.

'What's wrong?' she says. 'I just want to have a look.'

'Hang on,' he says. 'I've just got to . . .'

He chews his pen for a moment, looks at the sheet of paper and then writes something else on it. There are several more pieces of paper underneath it and Jamie pockets all except the one he's just written on. This gets a raised eyebrow from everyone but Emily, who's now examining the electric blue polish on her toe-nails.

'What are they?' asks Thea.

'What?' says Jamie.

'Those bits of paper you've just hidden.'

'Not important,' he says.

'Don't you want us to see your list?' she says.

'Yeah.' Jamie points at the single sheet in front of him. 'This is the list. The other stuff's private.'

'Fuck the list,' says Paul. 'I want to see the private stuff.'

Anne smirks. 'Come on, Jamie. Pleeeease?'

He frowns. 'Why are you all so interested in me all of a sudden?'

'Because you're doing something secret,' says Emily, looking up from her feet.

'And that makes me interesting?'

'I think so,' says Emily. 'Isn't that what makes most people interesting?'

'What?' says Thea. 'Having something to hide?'

'I think it's better if people are upfront,' says Bryn. The last thing somebody hid from him was genital warts.

'No,' says Emily. 'Think about it. People who are easy to read are usually the most boring people. It's always the mysterious people who are cool. You know if you're on the tube or something, and everyone's reading the *Evening Standard*, but there's one person reading a private letter or writing on a notepad or something? That person will seem more interesting because they're doing something private. It's like if someone's having a conversation on their mobile in a really loud voice, it really pisses you off, but if they are whispering and trying not to be heard, you want to know what they are saying.'

'So I'm interesting because I've got some bits of paper in my pocket?' says Jamie.

'Sounds a bit mad to me,' says Thea. 'But she is sort of right.'

'Does this mean I wasn't interesting before?' he asks.

'Of course you were,' gushes Emily. Thea gives her a look.

'Anyway, can we see them now?' asks Anne.

'No!' says Jamie.

'Leave him alone,' says Thea.

'Can we at least see the list of suspects?' asks Emily.

'Of course,' he says. 'But I haven't got very far with it.'

'Are we going to make this defence shelter or not?' asks Bryn, more interested in doing something physical.

'It's getting a bit dark,' says Thea. 'Can someone put the light on?'

Chapter Five

The light doesn't work.

'The one in the cellar didn't work either,' says Jamie.

'Maybe all the bulbs have gone,' suggests Bryn.

Emily yawns. She still feels incredibly tired. Thea gets up and leaves the room.

'There's no electricity in the house,' she says when she returns one minute later.

'How do you know?' Emily asks sleepily.

'Well, none of the lights work, and there's no meter.'

'There must be electricity,' says Jamie.

The light's fading fast now.

'Well you try to find some sign of it, then,' says Thea.

'There are three in here,' says Jamie. 'Three signs, I mean.'

'A riddle,' comments Paul.

'What are you on about?' says Thea.

'It's a riddle,' repeats Paul.

'Not you,' says Thea. 'How can there be electricity?' she asks Jamie.

'I told you, there are three signs,' he says.

He's being quite sweet, Emily thinks. She doesn't know anyone else who's quite this arrogant without being in any way cool. Maybe that's part of his charm. But who's she kidding? He doesn't have much charm; the other two are much more sexy. Of course, they have their drawbacks as well. Paul's kind of mean. He's the type of guy who makes you feel nervous all the time, like you might be a fraud and he's going to expose you. Emily's aware that pretty much everyone is a fraud, and has bullshit conversations all the time, but there's always that unspoken agreement that if you don't say the other person's bullshitting, they won't say you are either. Paul clearly doesn't play that game. He's the kind of guy who'd point out you were two years old at the peak of the now-trendy TV show you're claiming to have adored as a young child, but really only discovered when you were about twenty, after *Sky Magazine* or *The Face* did a feature.

Emily decides that Bryn doesn't have too much going for him personality-wise, but he is, nonetheless, good-looking, and he probably has a huge cock. But Jamie? He's all blond and ruffled and smokes his cigarettes nervously, as if it's a habit he's only just picked up. He's from a totally different world. So is Bryn, but while Bryn's world is probably like Ibiza, Jamie's is more Prague, or some other worthy place that students go to. Emily's more of an Ibiza girl really, or at least, given that choice she would be.

'I can see three as well,' says Anne. 'Plus one more.'

'What are they then?' demands Thea.

'It's pretty obvious,' says Paul. 'Unless you're retarded,' he adds.

'Don't play stupid games,' says Thea. 'What are these signs?'

'Well, there's the toaster,' says Paul.

Everyone looks at the toaster. It's plugged in by the stove.

'And the fact that there are light sockets and bulbs,' says Anne.

'And these,' says Jamie, pulling a packet of 13 amp fuses from the drawer. 'You wouldn't have these without having plugs to fit them in, and you wouldn't need to change them anyway unless there was electricity to blow them in the first place.'

'Maybe whoever owns the house got cut off,' says Bryn.

'Well there weren't any letters on the mat,' says Thea. 'As well as there being no meter,' she adds.

'What?' says Jamie, looking confused.

'No letters on the mat. Come to think of it, there was no post when we walked in here. Unless whoever owns this place removed it recently, you'd expect there to be all sorts of utility bills, junk mail and everything. And if the electricity had been cut off, then there'd be disconnection notices lying there.'

'Do postmen come to places like this?' says Jamie slowly. 'I don't think they do.'

'*Duh,*' says Emily. Suddenly she can't believe everyone's being so thick.

'What?' says Bryn.

'Well, where exactly would this electricity come from? I don't remember seeing any big pylons or cables outside. We are on a remote island, you know.'

'There was that windmill thing,' says Anne.

'But it wasn't connected to anything,' Thea points out.

It's almost completely dark now. Bryn has lit another of the candles.

'There must be some kind of generator,' says Jamie, thoughtfully.

'A what?' asks Bryn.

'A generator. They run on diesel. It's probably outside somewhere.'

'How do you know about generators?' asks Emily.

'One of my friends' grandparents had one at their holiday home,' he says.

'We can't go poking around outside now,' Thea says. 'It's dark.'

Emily walks over to the window. Sure enough, all she can see is her own face reflected in it. And when she presses her face to the cold pane, to cut out the small light from the candle, it's as if she's staring into nothing. There are some sounds. Mainly the wind and the sea. The wind's actually whistling. Emily's only read about that in books.

'Can't we take a candle out there?' she says.

'You can try,' says Jamie, 'but it'll get blown out.'

'Oh,' she says.

'I'm cold,' says Thea.

The temperature has dropped along with the light.

'It was hot before,' says Emily. 'Why's it so cold?'

'We must be somewhere north,' says Paul. 'Hot in the day but cold at night.'

'Isn't there an open fire in the lounge?' asks Bryn.

'Shit,' says Jamie.

'What?' asks Thea.

'If we hadn't been so busy drinking wine and talking crap we could have found the generator *and* got some logs for the fire.'

'I don't remember you talking much crap, Mr Silent,' says Emily.

'Oh yeah. The list,' says Anne. 'Let's see it.'

Jamie glares at her. 'Hadn't we better sort out the light and heat problem first?'

It's seriously cold. Emily's nipples are hard.

'We should move through to the sitting room,' says Thea. 'It'll be warmer in there with the carpet and everything.'

'It's still not going to be very warm,' comments Emily.

Ten minutes later they're in the sitting room. The situation has turned into some kind of sleepover. Jamie suggested getting all the duvets from upstairs and sleeping under them together, to keep warm through body heat. The duvets are in the centre of the room now, being arranged by Thea.

'I guess if I'm going to lose my virginity I might as well do it Jerry Springer style,' says Anne.

'You're not a virgin really,' says Emily. 'Are you?'

Anne says nothing.

There are two whole candles left. Two burned away completely in the kitchen. Two are burning now. Emily has never seen a candle burn away as quickly as that before, when it actually matters. The only times she's used candles have been either for masturbating – in which case you don't actually light them – or to provide nice lighting for baths, dinner parties and sex. And when you get bored of dim, sexy light, you just switch the real light back on. Emily gets nervous when she thinks of the possibility of there being no real light here at all. She got a sense for what it would be like before, when the others went to get the duvets and took the candles with them. She couldn't see anything at all. Her eyes never adjusted to the dark, or whatever's supposed to happen; she just sat there with Anne, commenting on how black it was, while Anne went on about the house probably being haunted.

'What time is it?' asks Jamie.

'Almost eleven,' says Emily, holding the candle up to her solid silver Accurist watch. She wishes it had a little light on it. But modern watches aren't like that. There's no reason for them to be. Well, except maybe under these circumstances. But it's not every day you find yourself kidnapped and abandoned on some dark, remote, cold island. Accurist weren't to know. Emily feels as if she might cry. It's like she's at a party she's had enough of, and now she just wants to get a cab home.

'How long have we been here?' asks Jamie.

Paul shrugs. 'About five or six hours,' he says.

'We must have been unconscious for a long time.'

'I don't know why I still feel tired,' says Emily. 'If we were out for that long.'

'Maybe it's your body clock telling you it's time for bed,' suggests Jamie.

'It's still early, though' says Bryn.

'What time do you usually go to bed?' asks Jamie.

'About two,' says Bryn.

'God,' says Jamie.

'Same,' says Anne. 'About two or three.'

'I usually stay up until four or five,' says Paul. 'I'm allergic to sunlight.'

'Are you?' says Thea.

'No,' he says. 'But then I wouldn't know, since I don't see much of it.'

'Don't you work?' she asks.

'Not any more,' he says. 'And when I did it was the nightshift.'

Everyone starts getting under the duvets. There's a bit of politics about who ends up next to whom, and in the end, the *girl boy girl boy* dinner-party style seems to be the least embarrassing, particularly for the boys, who really didn't want to be next to one another. It's still embarrassing, of course, but not cold. Emily is tired, but doesn't want to go to sleep because she's scared. After all, last time she went to sleep she woke up on a scary island. Maybe she's developing a phobia. She considers suggesting that everyone should take it in turns to stay awake and play lookout in case the kidnappers turn up, but doesn't want to appear too panicked, especially after her whole 'don't be a victim' thing from before, plus the fact that she didn't admit to being scared when they asked her. Instead, after lying thinking for a bit with the others still fiddling around having last cigarettes and whispered conversations about nothing, she gets up.

'Where are you going?' asks Jamie.

'To block off the door. Give me a hand.'

Jamie gets up to help, and he and Emily drag the heavy bureau over to the door.

'Now *there's* a fire hazard,' comments Paul.

'Shut up,' says Emily, her voice breathy.

'What are you doing?' asks Anne, looking over.

'Blocking off the door,' says Emily again.

'Someone could still get in,' Anne observes.

'That's not the point,' says Emily.

She takes a couple of breakable items from the room:

a vase and an empty wine bottle, and balances them on the bureau.

'There,' she says.

'What's that all about?' asks Bryn.

Emily sighs and gets back under the duvets.

'It's to wake us up, silly. If someone comes.'

'And then what?' asks Jamie. 'What'll we do if they do come?'

'We'll kick the shit out of them,' says Bryn.

Emily has settled between Jamie and Bryn; Anne is between Paul and Jamie; Thea is between Paul and Bryn. There is silence for about half a minute.

'Do you think we're still somewhere near Scotland?' asks Thea.

'Must be,' says Bryn. 'Like Anne said, the shopping's from the UK.'

'What are those islands called?' asks Emily.

Paul yawns. 'Which ones?'

'You know. The ones off to the left.'

'The Shetland Isles?' suggests Jamie.

'No, they're the ones at the top,' says Paul.

'It's weird, not knowing where we are,' says Anne. 'It's interesting. Alienating.'

'I thought alienation was a bad thing,' Thea points out.

'Maybe,' says Anne. 'Sartre and Camus may not agree.'

'Oh, please, not sixth-form existentialism,' she retorts.

'What are the ones on the left called?' asks Emily again.

Paul shrugs. 'The Hebrides?' he suggests. 'Who knows?'

'Is anyone here from Scotland?' asks Jamie.

No one is.

'So we all came up from the South, then,' says Paul. 'That's interesting.'

'Maybe we were chosen with that in mind,' suggests Jamie.

'Hmmm,' says Paul. 'Maybe.'

'Are you all from London?' Jamie asks.

'I am,' says Emily.

'Me too,' says Anne.

'I'm from Bristol,' says Paul.

'Brighton,' says Thea.

'Essex,' says Bryn.

'Oh. I'm from Cambridge,' says Jamie. 'Well, that's where I live at the—'

'Where's this suspect list, then?' Anne interrupts suddenly.

'It's here,' says Jamie, pulling out his bit of paper. 'Shall I read it out?' He pauses, and then carries on. 'OK, these are my suspects for the kidnapping. Right. There's my mum; my flatmate Nick; my girlfriend Carla, although she wouldn't ever do anything this radical, so I've crossed her off; my university tutor; and another student from my course – Julian Chan. I beat him by one point in our finals and now he hates me. That's it.'

Pretty much everyone is laughing.

'Your mum,' says Anne. 'That's classic.'

'I'd like to know why your mum would want to kidnap me,' says Paul.

'Well, that's the thing,' says Jamie. 'You all have to write your own lists, and then we'll see if we've got anyone in common. You know, like say Julian turned out to be Thea's brother and Anne's ex-boyfriend or something? Do you see what I mean?'

'I haven't got a brother,' says Thea.

'I've never had a boyfriend,' says Anne.

'You know what I mean,' says Jamie.

'We know what you mean,' says Emily, nicely.

'Does it have to be people we know?' asks Thea.

'I'm putting the Government at the top of my list,' says Paul.

'Right,' says Thea. 'That would be no, then.'

'Whatever . . .' starts Jamie. 'Whatever you think.'

'Can't we do it in the morning?' says Anne.

'Yeah, I'm fucked,' says Bryn.

'I thought you said it was early,' says Thea.

'Yeah, well being kidnapped probably made me more tired,' he says.

Everyone settles down again after that, getting warm under the covers.

Emily wonders if Thea feels self-conscious because of her period.

For no reason at all the tune from 'Up Where We Belong' by Joe Cocker and Jennifer Warnes enters her head and will not leave.

Chapter Six

Paul wishes he could check his e-mail. It's not like he's expecting anything in particular, but it's a habit. He wishes he'd picked up that magazine at Kings Cross, then he could be reading about 'Final Fantasy VIII' right now, rather than having to talk to this lot. He wishes he could have a hot bath. But nevertheless, he's finding this whole experience interesting, and he's determined not to lose his cool. Paul knows that whoever's fucking with them will have won as soon as they all lose it, and he also knows that if this is some sort of test, then the least stressed-out person will win. Paul is planning to be that person.

'What's your favourite film?' asks Thea.

'Who are you asking?' says Jamie.

The candles have almost completely burnt out now.

'Anyone,' says Thea.

'All the Kevin Smith films, but particularly *Mallrats*,' says Emily.

The candles both die. 'It's very dark,' says Jamie.

'What, *Mallrats*?' jokes Emily.

'No,' he says. 'In here.'

The darkness feels nice, like this is a campfire rather than a kidnap situation.

'Duh,' Emily says. 'What's yours?'

'*Tetsuo*,' he says.

'*Tetsuo*,' says Paul. 'Hmmm.'

'What's that supposed to mean?' says Emily.

He doesn't reply.

'*You* like Tetsuo?' Thea says to Jamie.

'Yeah,' he replies. 'It was on BBC2 really late one night a few years ago and I thought the write-up in the paper made it sound like it was worth watching. I thought it was brilliant. I bought the video and I've seen it loads of times now.'

'*Tetsuo* is cool,' says Anne.

'Doesn't the cyborg get fucked by a vacuum cleaner?' says Emily.

'Yeah,' says Thea. 'That scene was hilarious.'

Paul doesn't know if she's attempting irony.

'My favourite film is *Babe: Pig in the City*,' says Anne.

'You're such a kid,' laughs Emily.

'That film is not for children,' says Anne seriously.

'What's yours, Thea?' asks Jamie.

'*The Last Seduction*,' she says. 'John Dahl is my favourite director.'

'Cool,' says Emily. 'Paul?'

'What?'

'Favourite film?'

Paul wants to say *Chasing Amy*. But there are two reasons not to. Firstly, it really is his favourite film and it made him cry. Secondly, Emily obviously likes Kevin Smith. How could she? The man's a genius and she fucking likes him.

'*The Curious Dr Hump*,' he says instead.

'Who?'

Paul summarises: 'Mad scientist kidnaps people and forces them to have sex so he can extract some kind of love enzyme from them while zombies stand around banging tambourines.'

'I read a book like that,' says Emily. 'About some scientist taking—'

'Maybe that's why we're here,' interrupts Anne.

'Sorry?' says Emily.

'To have our organs harvested.'

'Don't be stupid,' says Jamie.

'Yeah, thanks Anne,' says Thea. 'I'm going to have great dreams now.'

'Sorry,' Anne says huffily.

'Bryn?' says Emily.

'What?'

'Favourite film?'

'*War Games*,' he says.

'*War Games*?' says Emily. The one with the—'

'Two kids and the computer,' says Thea. 'I remember that.'

'We are now at DEFCON four,' booms Paul.

'Isn't that, like, a bit too retro?' asks Emily. Paul imagines her frowning, trying to understand why anyone would choose what is basically an uncool film.

Bryn is silent for a moment.

It's too dark to see anyone's expression.

'It was the last film my dad took me to see before he died,' he says eventually.

Now everyone is silent. How do you follow that?

'But apart from that, I like *True Lies*,' he adds.

Everyone breathes a sigh of relief.

'Action film classic,' starts Thea. 'Great, oxymoronic title—'

'How did your dad die?' interrupts Anne.

'Anne!' says Emily.

'He was run over,' answers Bryn. 'By a pizza delivery bike.'

Paul can hear Anne trying not to laugh.

'One of those mopeds?' he says, to cover the choking sound coming from his right.

'Yeah. My uncle Dave was driving it at the time. They had a feud. He finished it.'

Paul wonders what it's like when your life is basically a black comedy.

✻   ✻   ✻

The dark room doesn't seem so cold any more. The thing that worries Paul is the silence. He likes it when people are talking, because then he doesn't have to listen to the nothingness. Irrationally, he wishes a bus would pass, or a plane would fly over, or someone going past the window would laugh, just out of the pub. He misses the electric whirr of his flat and the flats of everyone he knows; the noise of fridges, freezers, computers, TVs. There is the odd sound here and there, but they are exactly that – odd. They're countryside noises, the kind of thing Paul's only ever heard on holiday: crickets, night insects and the occasional moth hitting the windows.

The favourites game continues. Paul's playing a game of his own, trying to second guess everyone's choices. And of course he's going to pick the most ridiculous thing he can in each section. For music he chooses 5ive. Trouble is, both Anne and Emily instantly start raving about how cool they are. Emily's obviously being ironic, but Anne? Paul's not sure if she's being ridiculous for the sake of it, like him, or if he's misjudged her and she's just like Emily. Or maybe she actually likes 5ive. In a way, Paul quite likes then, too. Particularly now Anne's jiggling up and down next to him singing 'Everybody Get Up'. This is too confusing.

Emily chooses Take That.

'But which one was your favourite?' asks Anne, still bouncing up and down.

'Robbie, of course,' she replies.

'Passé!' squeals Anne. 'And Robbie's way too obvious.'

'Which one did you like, then?'

'Mark Owen,' says Anne. 'I would have fucked him.'

For some reason her words sound shocking, as if a seven year old has said them.

Thea chooses Blur. As soon as she does, Emily tries to unchoose Take That and claim them for herself. Clearly the ironic choice wasn't the one to go for this time. They start to bicker about which single came out in which year, when they bought each one, which is the best album (*The Great Escape* vs 13) and who's met Damon. They're neck and neck until Thea scores a point with a rare Japanese import.

'Well, I've still got the issue of *The Face* with the Union Jack cover and the first *ever* Blur feature,' Emily says.

'Like I care,' says Thea wearily, clearly tiring of this.

'I love Blur,' says Jamie. 'But if I had to choose something different, it would be um ... in second place, Prince, but in first place, definitely Pavement.'

'Pavement?' says Emily. 'Isn't the lead singer really sexy?'

'Stephen Malkmus,' says Jamie. 'Yeah. He is.'

'He looks a bit like Paul,' says Anne.

'Thank you,' says Paul. 'I'll take that as a compliment.'

'I love Pavement,' says Anne. 'But my choice has to be Billie.'

Paul's certain she's playing the same game as him now.

'Delakota remixed "Honey to the Bee",' says Bryn. 'Cool tune.'

'Oh, I love Delakota,' says Emily to Bryn. 'What other stuff are you into?'

'You know, mainly DJs like David Morales, Richie Rich, Frankie Knuckles, Norman Jay,' he says. 'And some of the lot who used to DJ at The Edge in Coventry, like Randall and whoever.'

No one says anything. He lights a fag, his unhealthy-looking face orange in the black.

'Apart from that, I'm into Chicago house, happy house, handbag, happy hardcore, ordinary hardcore — although not what people call hardcore now; that's what we all used to call *dark* and it's shit — a bit of R&B, although not with all those fat girls singing about love and all that when-you-walked-out-that-door bollocks. TLC are all right, and I liked Eternal before Louise left. Mariah Carey. Ragga. Bit of jungle. I don't like drum and bass much. Some people reckon it's the same as jungle but it isn't. I think they're calling it UK garage or speed garage or whatever now. Fuck knows, though. I stopped following all the new stuff when it became really shit a few years ago.'

'I don't like current house music much,' says Thea. 'I know what you mean.'

Bryn sighs. 'There was a time when Kiss FM had only just started, and you could get it in Essex if you were lucky. They had really cool stuff on late at night, and sometimes guest DJs like Cold Cut and Norman Jay. And during the day they had Dave Pierce, you know, that Radio One DJ? Right, he used to be called—'

'*Dangerous* Dave Pierce,' says Emily. 'I met him in a club recently.'

'Right,' continues Bryn. 'When he was at Kiss his show was really sorted. I don't know what's happened to him since then. Of course, in those days most people thought Radio One was bollocks, but it was all right really, because the house scene was still quite new and they got people in who really knew about it and played top tunes, and because it was still sort of underground no one really bothered about being, you know, *popular*. They certainly didn't have any of that phone-in jukebox crap where Tracey calls in with a big fucking shout out to all the hardcore crew in Ingatestone and requests whatever her and her mates have heard while some bloke from Liverpool's been fucking them up the arse in some Ibiza toilet. I quite like Danny Rampling, but all the other tossers on there at the moment are total wankers. All the tunes are fucking mong-out dark shit. I'd rather listen to my mum nagging me than listen to Radio One at any time from six on Friday until Sunday morning. It's fucked. But the worst thing is that now you've got all these eighteen year olds who don't remember anything about 1988 — they haven't even heard of A Guy Called Gerald or anything that started it all off. You say A Guy Called Gerald to them kids and they'll go, "Who?". I don't even know what they're really into. Yes I do. Fucking Moloko, and those stupid fucking Ibiza albums with all that trance shit on. Have you seen *Top of the Pops* recently? It's full of stuff like Alice Deejay, ATB ... all that crap. I like Phats and Small, though,' he concedes. 'And Faithless.'

'What's the name of that bloke from Radio One who got shot?' asks Thea.

'They should have finished the job,' says Bryn.

'I think he's nice,' says Emily.

'What is his name, though?' says Thea. 'It's on the tip of my tongue.'

There is a moment of thought, but it comes to no one.

'I like the *Evening Session*,' says Jamie. 'And John Peel.'

It's warm now, under all the duvets. Paul, for reasons he doesn't totally understand, wants to move closer to Anne. It's nothing sexual. He just wants a human touch. He doesn't know why.

'TV programmes,' says Anne.

'*Friends*,' says Emily instantly. 'I've got all the videos.'

'I hate *Friends*,' says Thea. 'With a passion.'

'How can you hate *Friends*?' asks Emily. 'It's so good.'

'It's stupid,' says Thea. 'No one is actually like that.'

'I like "Chums",' says Anne. 'On *SM:TV*.'

'I like that,' says Jamie.

Paul has trouble imagining Jamie tuning in to Saturday morning TV, unless it was for a wank-fest over Britney Spears and the girls (or possibly H) from Steps.

'Oh, and Jerry Springer,' says Emily. 'I adore Jerry.'

'This gets worse,' says Thea. 'How can you like that stuff?'

'Come on,' says Emily. 'Jerry's cool. I've got the book with all the show titles in it.'

'Weird,' says Thea, shaking her head.

'What do you like, then?' asks Jamie.

'I don't watch much TV,' she says. 'I quite like *League of Gentlemen*.'

'That's cool,' says Emily. 'Do you like the *Fast Show* as well?'

'No,' says Thea.

'It is pretty stupid,' agrees Anne.

'What's yours then?' Emily asks her.

'*Home and Away*, of course,' she says.

'Bryn?' asks Thea.

'I like News 24,' he says. 'And the Discovery Channel.'

'What?' says Emily. 'Don't you find that stuff boring?'

'Nah,' he says. 'I like knowing what goes on in the world.'

'I like *The Simpsons*,' says Jamie. 'And *South Park*.'

'I just saw the *South Park* movie,' says Emily.

'Now that's a good film,' says Paul, and he means it.

'What about you?' Emily asks Paul. 'What's your favourite TV programme?'

'*Who Wants to be a Millionaire?*' he says, randomly.

'Don't get me started on that,' says Emily. 'I've phoned every single time . . .'

'Computer games next, then,' says Jamie.

'Videogames,' corrects Emily.

'What?' says Jamie.

'Videogames is the correct term,' she says.

'Don't bicker,' says Anne. 'Although Emily is right.'

There's a faint orange glow in the room where two or three people are smoking.

'Emily first then,' says Jamie. 'Since she's the *expert*.'

'Me?' she says. 'God, no. I'm out too often. I barely even get the chance to watch TV. I've played "Sonic" and "Ecco the Dolphin". One of my ex-boyfriends had a Megadrive. But that's it really. Oh, and I've played "Mortal Kombat" once, although I couldn't really get the hang of it.'

'I like "Tomb Raider",' says Jamie.

'What format?' asks Paul.

'Sorry?' says Jamie.

'Have you got a PlayStation?'

'PC,' says Jamie.

'Cool,' says Paul.

'I wish I had my Gameboy,' says Anne. 'Then I could play "Pokémon".'

'You've got "Pokémon"?' asks Emily. 'That's like, supposed to be the next big thing, but I thought you could only get it in America and Japan.'

'Import,' says Anne wistfully.

'They had a Gameboy in *The Beach*,' comments Jamie.

'Yeah, well we're not in *The Beach*, are we?' says Anne. 'And even if we were I wouldn't have "Pokémon". They had "Tetris", didn't they? Or some boring game, anyway.'

'What beach?' asks Bryn.

'Never mind,' says Emily.

'What else do you like apart from "Pokémon"?' asks Paul.

'Every "Mario" title – especially the second one where you can play as Princess Daisy, although I suppose the third one is my real favourite – the original "Streetfighter" series, the "Tempest" games, but mainly "Tempest 2000", "Duke Nukem" – particularly the second one, "Time to Kill", which is fantastic – "GTA", "Zelda", "Theme Park", "Theme Hospital", "Rayman", "Broken Sword" . . . I enjoyed "Metal Gear Solid" at the time, but then I discovered the "Final Fantasy" series and it seemed a bit shit. It's worth it though just to hear Liquid Snake's stupid accent: "The Genome soldiers are our—"'

'Don't give the plot away,' says Paul, laughing. '"Final Fantasy VII" *is* the best game in the world, though.'

'Absolutely,' says Anne. 'Along with "Pokémon", of course.'

'I'm looking forward to that,' says Paul.

'I thought you'd be more into "Doom" and "Quake" and everything,' says Anne.

'Nah,' says Paul. 'I'm a vegetarian.'

'What's so great about "Final Fantasy"?' asks Thea. 'It's a platform game, right?'

'No,' says Anne.

'It's an RPG isn't it?' says Jamie uncertainly.

'Yeah,' says Anne.

'I remember when it first came out,' Paul says. 'Me and two of my friends all got the game on the day of its release. We decided we'd have a competition to see who could finish it first. It was one of those things where the rules of the challenge weren't made entirely clear, so I just thought we'd compare the hours racked up on our memory cards when we all finished. I'd heard it took about seventy hours to complete, and I reckoned I could do it in about fifty, although I saved my "fast" game on one block of memory card and then kept another one going so I could explore the world without knocking back my hour score.'

'Do you play on a PlayStation?' asks Jamie.

'Yeah,' says Paul. 'I work on a PC, so I don't really play many games on it. I also like collecting consoles. I've got a few old Ataris, a NES, a Master System, a SNES, a Megadrive, a Jaguar, a Saturn, an N64 and the PlayStation. I've got an old Spectrum as well, although it's fucked, so I use a Spectrum Emulator on my computer.'

'Snap,' says Anne. 'Except I never got a Saturn, and I don't have any Ataris.'

He's beginning to really like this girl. 'Have you got a working Spectrum?' he asks.

'Oh, yeah,' she says. 'And a load of old tapes. It was the first machine I had.'

'What's your favourite Spectrum game?' asks Paul.

'"Automania",' she says. 'You know, the one with Wally Week in it.'

'Cool,' says Paul.

'And "Ms Pacman",' she adds. 'Because it's so ridiculous.'

'I know,' he says. 'They just put a hair ribbon on Pacman.' They both laugh.

'It's good you did the fast and slow version thing on "Final Fantasy VII",' Anne says, getting back to the subject, 'because all the Chocobo racing and breeding takes up loads of time. I spent about a week just in the Gold Saucer.'

'What are you talking about?' asks Emily.

'Chocobos are these magic birds, a bit like ostriches, that you can ride across the World Map,' explains Anne. 'And the Gold Saucer is kind of a Las Vegas thing – a game, or really several games, within a game. You can go there for a laugh, or to save up GP to buy special items. They have Chocobo races there. You can bet on the races or even ride in them.'

'I'm even more lost now,' says Emily. 'You can buy stuff?'

'Yeah,' says Paul. 'I bought a villa in the Costa Del Sol.'

'What's the premise for the game?' asks Jamie.

'You start off as this character called Cloud,' explains Paul. 'The "world" in the game – which is made up of this big city called Midgar, and then various villages over several continents – is controlled by a corporation called Shinra, who are corrupt, and who drain all the magic Mako energy from the planet. They do evil experiments and generally use magic for evil and whatever. It's the usual Japanese narrative set-up. Cloud is a mercenary who's been hired by a revolutionary organisation called Avalanche. Once Cloud has helped blow up a Mako reactor, he joins the group – or rather, they join him – and he sets off on his life's crusade, which is to defeat Sephiroth, the ultimate evil force in the game.'

Anne continues: 'As you go through the game you pick up items and magic. It's a lot more complicated than "Mario", where you just power-up with mushrooms and flowers, or even "Tomb Raider", where you can keep a few Medi Packs in your rucksack. In "FF7" you can carry unlimited items, and you have weapons and armour which you can equip with particular types of magic. You can cast bad spells on enemies, good spells on yourself, summon Gods and Goddesses to help you in battles, or use magic to increase your strength. You also win money and points in every battle you have. You can use the money to buy items in towns. It's so cool, there are shops everywhere, and really cool subplots in the towns and stuff . . .'

'So what happened with this competition with your friends?' Thea asks Paul.

'Well,' he says. 'The problem is that the game really gives you the feeling of being in another world. My two friends, Nick and Tony, shared a flat and they became totally absorbed in the experience, and also in the competition between them. But the worst thing they did was to decide to do their competition in real time. Instead of comparing memory card times, they were just going to see who finished first. It was a big mistake. For two days and three nights, they didn't move from their PlayStations. They both believed they were Cloud. They both loved the same female character. The trouble is that one of the themes of the whole game is the idea of the split between good and evil, not just in the world but within people. Even the good characters have weaknesses they have to overcome, and some of the bad characters have interesting motivations that aren't entirely evil. Anyway, the main good character, Cloud, is linked to the main bad character, Sephiroth. In a way they are two halves of the same thing; a living dialectic. Only by the fusion of Sephiroth's desire for evil and Cloud's desire for good can the world be changed and ultimately saved. Anyway, in the game there are scenes where Cloud becomes confused and is almost controlled by Sephiroth. At about the time that this was happening in the plot of the game, Tony started to become a bit unhinged. He'd been up for about forty-eight hours by this point; his vision had long gone and his brain was starting to go a bit messy. On all games it says you're supposed to take breaks every hour or so, or at least look at something other than the screen for a few minutes. But Tony never looked away from the screen in all that time.'

'What about Nick?' asks Emily.

'The same, but he wasn't as mad as Tony.'

'What do you mean?' asks Thea. 'Why was Tony mad?'

'He started believing that Nick was Sephiroth. At the point in the game where you're supposed to go into the North Cave and face Sephiroth for the last time, Tony abandoned the game and decided to invade Nick's bedroom instead. Nick had put up this joke sign saying "North Cave — abandon hope all ye who enter here", which Tony may have taken literally. They both kept ornamental Samurai swords in the house, and Tony had already decided that this would be his best choice of weapon. So he burst into what he clearly thought was the North Cave, to defeat Sephiroth with his sword. Forced to defend himself, Nick grabbed his own sword. They both swung at each other at exactly the same moment. The police found their two headless bodies one week later, when people started missing them and their corpses started to smell.'

There are a couple of moments of silence.

'Is that true?' asks Thea

'Of course not,' says Paul. 'I don't have any friends. Brilliant game though.'

Chapter Seven

Anne is woken by the sound of Jamie swearing. She yawns and turns. She's now facing Paul, although he's facing Thea. The whole group looks like a party that's just passed out mid-conga. She props herself up on her elbow. Bright sunlight picks out little bits of ash on the carpet, some pairs of shoes and socks. It's a warm morning, a complete contrast with the cold night. Everyone seems to be stirring. It looks like Jamie woke them all up.

'What time is it?' asks Thea sleepily.

'Ten,' says Jamie.

There are yawning sounds and a lot of stretching.

'I had the strangest dream,' says Anne sleepily. 'I was skiing down this slope and—'

Paul laughs. Emily giggles sleepily.

'Very funny, Anne. We all know the joke,' says Thea.

'I don't,' says Bryn.

Emily sighs. 'You must know it. It's the one where these two blokes and a girl are in a hotel, and for whatever reason, like the hotel's full or something, they all end up having to share a bed — and of course the girl goes in the middle, between the two blokes. In the morning, the first guy says he's had this amazing dream that he was being wanked off by a beautiful woman. The second guy says, "God, that's a coincidence, I had exactly the same dream," and the girl says, "Men are so typical. I had a nice innocent dream about skiing down a lovely snowy slope." Or whatever. I'm shit at telling jokes.'

Bryn thinks for a minute, then laughs. 'I get it,' he says.

Anne quite likes Bryn.

'What's wrong with you?' Emily asks Jamie.

He's taking his nerd thing a bit far this morning, sweating over more bits of paper. He makes Anne think of an antique computer, slowly and painfully creating data because it just can't do anything else. She looks over his shoulder. He's making notes on his list from last night.

'What are you doing?' she asks.

'Still trying to work this mess out,' he says.

'Why?' asks Anne.

'Because we're still here.'

Half an hour later, everyone except Thea is in the kitchen. She's washing the duvet covers in cold water in one of the upstairs bathrooms, which seems stupid to Anne, since they've only slept in them for one night. Maybe Thea's got OCD or something. Anne read a book about that once.

Getting up turned out to be a slow, leisurely affair. Some people are still complaining of sore backs from sleeping on the floor; others are commenting on the peace and quiet. For some reason Anne starts thinking about her parents at the flat in Islington. They'll both be at work now, sweating in the London heat, probably trying to conduct extra-marital affairs as well as fitting in too many clients and too many lunches. They'll work all week and barely see each other. The cleaner will come every other weekday. There'll be the usual Chattering Class discussions about art and politics and literature and restaurants and gardening and which play they'll see on Saturday. They'll accumulate about six newspapers between them by the end of each day, which Anne's mother will recycle every Sunday morning. On a Sunday afternoon she'll play tennis and Anne's father will play golf. The whole of London, including them, will not stop. People will be hurrying to work or to enjoy themselves or just to nowhere, caught in the slipstream of everyone else's hurry. But on the island everything is perfectly still and calm and no one is hurrying, because no one has anything particularly important to do.

Emily's cooking breakfast, loudly frying bacon, sausages, eggs, mushrooms, bread and tomatoes. Jamie, Paul and Bryn are sitting at the table. Jamie's still doing something with his stupid list. Bryn's smoking. Paul's trying to make a two-way radio out of everyone's mobile phones. Or at least that's what Anne assumes he's doing. Unless he's just taking them all apart for fun, which isn't that unlikely.

'Do you think it might be revenge?' suggests Emily.

'What?' says Jamie.

'Being here, dummy. Do you think someone's trying to teach us a lesson?'

'Eureka,' mumbles Paul, as he drops a rubber keypad under the table.

Anne's already considered the revenge thing, and rejected it.

Jamie's getting excited. 'We have to make our lists or we'll never find out.'

Emily walks over and opens the back door. Some fresh air comes in, but not much.

'What, you mean like we all bullied the same kid at school?' says Paul.

'And he died during the initiation ceremony for our gang,' adds Anne.

'In a grey scene in a forest in winter,' says Paul.

'With the sound of children's laughter carried on the cold wind . . .' giggles Anne.

'And now it's the anniversary of his death and *someone's* having a party.'

'Will you two stop being so cynical,' says Jamie.

'We're not,' says Anne defensively. 'We were just saying.'

Bryn flicks his fag end out of the back door.

'Wouldn't we remember if we'd all bullied some kid at school?' he says.

'Maybe we've forgotten,' suggests Jamie.

'Right,' says Bryn. 'Anyone else go to school in Southend?'

Everyone shakes their heads.

'Bit unlikely, then, isn't it?' he says.

Thea comes into the kitchen and sits down.

'What's going on?' she asks.

'We're going to do our lists,' says Emily.

'Oh,' says Thea. 'I thought we were doing that anyway.'

'Well we're including our pasts now,' says Emily.

'She thinks it might be revenge,' says Anne.

Jamie's counting out six fresh sheets of paper.

'Right,' he says. 'I want everyone to write down the following: date of birth, place of birth, mother's maiden name, schools attended, towns lived in other than your home town, names and details of siblings, and names and details of partners or ex-partners.'

'Why?' asks Thea.

'It's so we can see who or what we've got in common,' explains Paul.

'We could all have shagged the same person or something, you see,' says Emily. 'And we wouldn't even know we've got them in common.'

'I get it,' says Thea.

'I don't think that's going to be the answer,' says Anne. 'Considering that I haven't ever shagged anybody.'

'Get over yourself,' says Thea.

'I think she's telling the truth,' says Paul.

'What about holiday destinations?' says Thea, ignoring Paul. 'Maybe we all pissed off the same beach bum or something.'

'Cool,' says Emily.

'What about jobs?' says Bryn. 'Maybe we all worked for the same boss.'

'There are lots of possibilities,' admits Jamie.

Anne wonders if this task is going to be a bit big. She gets what they're doing, but, you know, maybe they were all in the same nightclub one night and didn't help someone who was ill, or maybe they all inadvertently saw something they shouldn't have seen, or bought a traced product. Hey, maybe they were just in the wrong place at the wrong time – like at a job interview on Monday 6 September 1999. In any case, if they want to be scientific about this and find an actual connection, it's basically going to take feeding everyone's entire lives into a database and then doing a really sophisticated search. Anne starts writing the program in her head for just such a database, and then she embarks on a pleasant fantasy about her system being used in international espionage and possibly detective work. Her sheet of paper remains blank.

Emily's serving the fried breakfasts.

'How do you stay so thin eating stuff like this?' asks Thea.

'I don't eat it,' she says. 'I just cook it.'

Breakfast is quiet, since everyone's writing their lists. Soon people start to ask for another sheet of paper, and then another. Anne wonders why Jamie's not freaking out about paper supplies. After eating most of her breakfast she gets up and leaves the room. The frying smell's getting to her, and this enforced task is completely pissing her off. She doesn't like enforced tasks. She heads for the library.

'Where's she going?' asks Jamie.

'Who cares,' says Thea.

The library is soothing, which is why Anne goes there. No one goes into libraries really, certainly not cool people, or people who want to get laid. Anne's good at using the cool conspiracy for her own purposes. If you convince people something isn't cool, at least you can enjoy it on your own. If people are convinced that somewhere isn't cool, you can go there on your own and cry.

She doesn't really know why she's crying now. Maybe it's just habit, the thing she always does when she leaves a room full of people. Who knows? Maybe she doesn't like being held on this island against her will. But when she tries to think of the things she really misses, there isn't much worth mentioning: *Home and Away*, Superdrug cherry hair conditioner, her dog hairband with the little bell, her things. She misses her evening walk across London a bit, and her thoughts. Maybe she's just naturally tearful. She doesn't even really hate the people here. They're all fairly nice, except Thea, and she seems like she could be nice if she tried.

There are four copies of *The Tempest* in the library. All in English. Anne wipes her eyes. While the others are still playing exam room in the kitchen, she's actually learning something about whoever brought them here, or at least, the person who owns this house. This person is clearly an English speaker, probably a university graduate – unless there's some other demographic Anne's forgotten whose members are likely to own four copies of *The Tempest*. *The Tempest*s are in what must be the 'Literature' section of the library. Other noticeable sections include Philosophy, Religion, Psychology, The Environment, Politics and Utopias. The Utopia section is bigger than Anne would have expected, and includes obscure sci-fi novels as well as theoretical works.

Anne wonders who put this library together and why. The books don't seem as dusty and old as books you'd get in a natural collection built up over time. She checks the inside jackets of some of the classics and finds that they are mostly modern reprints. There are several books on renewable energy. Anne is surprised to see that one of their covers has an image of a pylon-windmill structure like the one outside. A quick read of the dust jacket confirms that it is a wind-powering device for a renewable energy system.

*   *   *

Back in the kitchen, Jamie seems to be interpreting data, reading all the sheets of paper the others have fed to him. Anne sits down at the table.

'Where's your list?' Jamie asks her.

'I don't have one,' she replies.

'Why not?' asks Emily.

'Couldn't be bothered,' she says, and makes a strawberry milkshake.

Jamie sighs. 'Paul and Thea have a Bristol connection,' he says. 'Paul was born in Bristol and Thea went to university there. But according to the other lists, no one else has even been to Bristol.'

'I went to Bristol once,' says Bryn.

'Why didn't you put it on your list, then?' says Jamie.

'Forgot,' says Bryn. 'It was only for the day. I was five.'

'I've never been to Bristol,' says Anne.

'This isn't going to work,' says Thea. 'There's too much human error.'

'Three of us have sisters called Sarah,' says Jamie.

'So?' says Thea.

'Just thought it was interesting, that's all. Anyway, there isn't much else.'

He lights a cigarette and sits back in his chair.

The kitchen is a mess. The sink is now full of dishes. There's so much debris on the table that Paul has been forced to move on to the floor by the back door, where he seems to be continuing his electronics research, apparently unconcerned about everything else. The sun falls on his head, making his dark hair shine. Maybe he feels Anne's stare, because he looks up and half-smiles at her. She looks into her glass and blows some pink bubbles in the froth of the milkshake.

'I know something we all have in common,' says Bryn.

'What?' says Emily.

'Well, the job interview. Maybe it's just that.'

Anne's intrigued that no one's doing the survival thing yet. No one's talked about escape. No one's made a play for leader. She's not a real weirdo and Jamie's not a real nerd. This isn't the way it's supposed to be. No one here has any *va va voom*.

'So, are you going to sabotage the generator as well?' Thea asks Anne.

'What, as well as your stupid research—' begins Anne.

'All right,' interrupts Emily. 'I think me and Anne are going to go upstairs.'

'Why?' says Anne.

'You can help me, uh, organise the bedrooms,' says Emily.

'Well, I'm going to go and find the generator,' says Thea. 'Anyone going to help?'

'Yeah,' says Bryn. 'I'll come. I'll chop some wood for the fire as well.'

'I thought we should have a talk,' says Emily once they get upstairs. She's multi-tasking, taking on the oh-so-important job of bringing Anne into line, and combining it with the equally urgent job of plucking her eyebrows. God knows where she found tweezers, but this girl could be Jamie's new model army all by herself with these survival skills.

'OK,' says Anne. 'What do you want to talk about?'

Emily's eyebrows are dark. So are her roots, which Anne can see now she's put her hair up. She's already beginning to get a rash where she's plucked and she's mumbling something about needing witch hazel.

'You want to talk about witch hazel?' says Anne.

'No. Just . . . Look. Could you chill out a bit?'

'Me?' says Anne. 'What did I do?'

Emily's right eyebrow is now completely red, so she starts on the left one.

Chapter Eight

Jamie's thinking about Jerry Springer. And Bryn.

He can't believe that they're back on to that whole 'interview' thing. As if this is a job interview. Where's the panel? The questions? The reason Jamie's thinking about Jerry Springer is because he feels that Bryn would be better off as a guest on his show than as a man in a crisis. Jamie might not know all the names of the shows like Emily, but he saw the one called *Honey, I'm really a man*. Maybe Bryn's could be called *Honey, I'm really stupid — don't listen to my screwed up logic*. Jamie is also severely pissed off that no one asked him to go and chop wood or find the generator. He's so pissed off that he doesn't even feel like himself. He's not usually bitchy, for God's sake. Not even in his head.

Paul's finishing off the washing up.

'Why are you doing that?' asks Jamie.

Paul shrugs. 'I hate mess,' he says.

All the junked up mobile phones are on the cleared table in pieces. Jamie's glad he didn't have a mobile, although none of the others seem to mind Paul completely taking theirs apart. Paul dries his hands and sits down. He seems to have made coffee, and places a mug in front of Jamie.

'Thanks,' says Jamie.

'No problem.'

'So what's all this?' Jamie asks, pointing to the heap of electronics on the table.

'What, the phones?'

'I mean, what are you making?'

'What have I made, you mean,' says Paul, smiling. He picks up a concoction of wires, LED displays and numeric keypads. 'Look.'

Jamie looks. He sees nothing.

'It's "Ultimate Snake",' explains Paul.

'"Ultimate Snake"?'

'Yeah. You know "Snake", the computer game you have on your mobile?'

'I don't have a mobile.'

'But you know some of them have little games programmed into them?'

Jamie nods. He sort of wanted to get one, but Carla disapproved.

'Well, the best one is "Snake". The object is to move this snake-shaped thing around the screen, guiding it to little bits of food. You're not supposed to let the snake touch the edges of the screen, or its own tail. The thing is, as it eats the food, it gets bigger, and it's harder to stop it touching its own tail.'

'So what's "Ultimate Snake"?' asks Jamie.

'I've made it two-player,' says Paul. 'Look.'

He hands Jamie a numeric pad from one of the phones. Seems like this is going to act as some kind of joypad. The pad is attached to a small LED screen, which has another pad attached to it, which is what Paul's holding. He presses a few keys.

'Right. You can see there are two snakes on the screen now,' he says. 'That one's you and that one's me. We're both going for the same bit of food, which is that dot in the far left-hand corner at the moment. And we're trying not to touch our own tails, the edges of the screen or each other. Amazingly improved, I'd say.'

There is a little bleep and Jamie's dead.

'What are the controls?' he asks.

An hour later the score is Paul fourteen, Jamie eight.

'Didn't you tell the others you were making some kind of radio transmitter?' Jamie asks, furiously hitting the number 2 on the pad to try to get his snake up to the piece of food faster than Paul's.

'Yeah, but wait till they see this,' says Paul.

Eventually, the battery starts to run down. Jamie lights a cigarette.

'More coffee?' asks Paul.

'Sure,' says Jamie.

Paul gets up and finds some clean mugs. 'What do you think of this whole *it's a really weird job interview* notion?' he asks.

'Crap,' says Jamie. 'What about you?'

'Dunno,' says Paul. 'Could still be, I guess.'

They sip coffee.

'Where are you from again?' asks Jamie.

'Bristol,' says Paul. 'Well, just outside Bristol. You?'

'Taunton,' he says, lighting a cigarette. 'You did art at university, didn't you?'

Paul laughs.

'Why are you laughing?'

'You're still acting all polite,' he says. 'It's sweet.'

'Sweet?'

'Yeah, sweet. It's not an insult. You're not trying to be cool like the others.'

Jamie doesn't know if Paul's being nice or not. He sticks to his original question. 'It *was* art, wasn't it?'

'Yeah,' says Paul. 'How about you?'

Jamie tells him about his maths, and he's as impressed as Anne was. What is it with these arty people who think numbers are so romantic? He's still trying to locate the part of Paul's past that taught him how to fuse together four mobile phones, and also the part that made him opt to create 'Ultimate Snake' rather than a more useful device (like an escape pod — they'd do it on *The A Team*). Trouble is, Paul's not keen to talk about himself. Jamie establishes that he did some kind of postgraduate cross-over and now works with computers. Other than that, Paul leaves him in the dark.

'So you're a geek then?' Jamie asks, smiling.

'What?' says Paul, laughing.

'I'm a nerd, according to Anne's classification,' he explains, noting the way Paul's eyes change colour slightly when he says the word *Anne*. 'But you should be a *bona fide* geek since you work with computers and everything.'

'Hmm. I never go out,' says Paul. 'But I do play a lot of games. That makes me an Otaku.'

'What's that?'

'It's a Japanese geek.'

'And they never go out?'

'Not really. The word just means that you're so into your hobby that you stay in and do it all the time. Have you ever played "Metal Gear Solid"?'

Jamie shakes his head. 'No.'

'There's a character in it called Otakon. He's a Japanese geek.'

'What's his hobby?'

'Manga.'

'What's yours?'

'The same. Oh, and visiting places I'm not wanted.'

'Without going out?'

'Yep. Via computer.'

This doesn't make a lot of sense to Jamie. Maybe Paul's a hacker.

'What do you think of "Tomb Raider"?' Paul asks.

'It's OK. Easier than I expected.'

'Than you expected?'

'Well, I'd never played a videogame before, and I'd heard they were hard.'

'Yeah. "Tomb Raider" is pretty easy,' says Paul. 'You should try "Metal Gear Solid".'

'Why?'

'It's all about stealth and silent killing. I'm sure you'd be into that.'

'Thanks,' says Jamie.

Paul laughs. 'You know what I mean. I bet you love all that strategy stuff.'

'I suppose so,' says Jamie. 'You don't sound much like you do, though.'

'What?'

'Like all that stuff.'

'I do. I'm just not a big fan of "MGS", that's all,' says Paul.

'Why not?'

'It's too Americanised. There aren't any real manga characters in it.'

'I thought that about *Akira*,' says Jamie.

Paul looks surprised.

'I thought you didn't know anything about manga and anime,' he says.

Jamie gets the impression he's said the right thing without meaning to.

'I don't,' he says.

'But you watched *Akira*?'

'Well, I liked *Tetsuo* so much I thought I'd try some other Japanese classics.'

'Oh, yeah. I forgot about *Tetsuo*. But you didn't like *Akira*?'

Jamie shakes his head. 'Nope.'

'That's cool,' says Paul. 'You're not really supposed to say you don't like it, because it's such a classic. It's a bit like saying *Blade Runner*'s shit or something.'

Jamie doesn't like *Blade Runner* either, but thinks it best not to go into that.

'I agree, though,' says Paul. 'So why didn't you like *Akira?*'

'I didn't like the drawings that much, and the American adaptation was stupid.'

'How do you know about adaptations and drawing?'

'I don't,' says Jamie. 'It's just what I think.'

'Did you watch any more anime?'

Jamie's confused, as always, by these terms. 'What exactly is anime?'

'Manga that moves.'

'And manga is . . . ?'

'Japanese comics. So did you?'

'What?'

'Get into any more stuff?'

'No. I just like *Tetsuo*.'

Jamie doesn't mention the one time he looked up *hentai anime* on the Internet. He knows more or less what *hentai* means. There were so many sites to choose from: monster sex, extreme bondage, machine sex . . . all in little cartoons. Jamie loved the style of the drawing, and the extreme nature of the porn. Because they were cartoons, the women could be stretched into the most ridiculous positions, their tiny waists contrasting with everything else in the picture, their big eyes dripping with innocence. And no one got hurt. Jamie's fantasies always feature artificial women in some sense or other. When he first masturbated, he tried thinking about a girl he knew at school, but he couldn't even get an erection. Then he tried thinking about his favourite teacher, but there was still something too soft and real about her. Later, as he got older, he realised that it was far more pleasurable to think about unreal women: women with lots of make-up and stilettos and short skirts. It was all right to think about doing really dirty things to those women, because they were deliberately putting themselves on display, making themselves consumable, making you able to own them. Recently Jamie's become interested in breast implants – not in real life of course, but in his fantasy world. To him, breast implants create breasts which are made only for sex. They are no longer symbols of motherhood or childhood; no longer *nice*. You could do anything to breasts like that, and treat the owner of them exactly how you wanted.

'What do you think the others are doing?' he asks eventually.

Paul shrugs. 'No idea.'

Jamie has another cigarette while Paul attaches a new battery to 'Ultimate Snake'. Jamie looks over his list again, and the lists made by everyone except Anne. They really do have nothing in common on paper, these people and him. But yet there are so many common reference points; even some unexpected ones. For example, Jamie finds it weird that they've all seen *Tetsuo* — well, all except Bryn. They all watch TV, they all want to be cool. And they're all scared, but no good at showing it.

Maybe that's the only part of this that their lives prepared them for. Let's face it, none of them knows how to light a fire or gather food (not that they have to, but still). None of them knows how to construct a compass, use ropes or carve crude instruments. But they all know how to act cool. After all, life's pretty scary most of the time. And the number one skill you need in the world out there is how to show no fear. If you see a dog in the street, don't act scared. If you see a dodgy bloke with a bulge in his jacket pocket, don't act scared. Stay calm. Don't let people see that you're shy or nervous. If you watch a horror film, remember to laugh. If someone else seems scared, laugh at them. In the real world, danger is either fantasy, in which case you laugh, or too real, in which case you ignore it. People die on the roads, in trains, on buses and in planes. People die from carbon monoxide in their rented flats, from food poisoning and from terrorist bombs. There's never any warning. Jamie and the others come from a culture in which a fire alarm doesn't mean fire; it just means you get to go and stand outside and giggle for a while. But a prawn or a peanut could still kill you.

'Do you want another game?' asks Paul.

Chapter Nine

Thea doesn't have any sunglasses, and the brightness is making her squint. It's hot again and the sea is calmer than yesterday, but the waves are still over three metres high. They'd be great for surfing if they broke on some sort of beach. But there's no beach here; the waves smash directly into the cliffs.

It took Thea two minutes to find the generator in the shed at the back of the house about an hour or so ago, after she'd hung the wet sheets and duvet covers on the line. There was a book lying next to it, with a picture of a big, tall windmill on the front. Since it is exactly the same as the one in the picture, Thea now realises that the structure by the front of the house is for collecting wind energy. At the back of the house, near the shed and facing the direction the sun seems to be in at midday, are two portable solar panels. They look like the little panels you get on solar-powered calculators, only much bigger. From what Thea can now see, the 'generator' isn't really a generator at all, but what looks like a big car battery. On closer inspection, she sees it is actually a series of batteries connected to what the book describes as an 'inverter' – a white box on the wall which collects the DC current from the solar panels and the wind turbine and converts it into the AC current used by the house. Whatever the house uses is automatically converted, and whatever is left over is saved, not exactly for a rainy day, but for one with neither sun nor wind.

The book is very general, but inside the front cover is a letter from the company which supplied the system. It doesn't mention where the island is, but does explain that the wind and solar levels here are sufficient, in combination, to provide power for the house. It also states that hydro power would be possible here, but very expensive to install.

The letter, dated April 1999, also explains the effectiveness of the rainwater tank, now positioned just outside the back door. Again, without revealing the exact area of the island, the company assures their customer (referred to only as 'Dear Sir') that local levels of rainfall will be sufficient for a family of four to use for regular washing, cooking and flushing toilets. It also explains the ecologically-friendly sewage management system connected to each of the toilets. It doesn't say who this family of four is supposed to be, or what kidnappers would want with an eco-friendly house. Mind you, Thea imagines that this renewable power is less to do with the environment and more to do with not being able to get power from anywhere else.

While she's reading, she's half-watching Bryn chop down one of the apple trees with the axe they found in the shed next to the manual. This morning she found her period had finally stopped, which was a relief. Unfortunately, her period always gets heavier just before it stops, and it was awful when she woke up to discover that she'd bled through Emily's tampon on to the duvets and her normal underwear. All of the bedding is still soaking in soapy (rain)water upstairs, and Thea's now wearing some of the clothes she found in one of the bedrooms. She quite likes them: a long raw cotton skirt and short-sleeved cotton top, both white. There was a white jumper as well, but it's too hot for that out here, so she's wearing it tied around her waist. It feels nice to be wearing clean clothes, and it's gorgeous out here.

Thea pulls up her skirt to sun her legs. Bryn's chopping at the base of the tree.

'Can I help?' she asks.

'No,' he says. 'Almost there now.'

Bryn's tied his long blond dreadlocks back with an elastic band, and taken off his shirt. Thea can see that he has a tattoo on his right arm, but she can't see what it is. Each time he swings the axe at the tree a few leaves flutter off. Eventually the tree falls, scattering apples and leaves everywhere. Bryn walks over and sits next to Thea. He's sweating.

'Time for a break,' he says.

He seems to have caught the sun on his back, and a couple more freckles have come out on his face. He takes a swig from the bottle of lemonade Thea brought out with her, and lights one of her cigarettes. It's nice not to feel so frightened, she thinks. When they first came outside, all Thea could think about was how to escape if someone came. Now she feels more relaxed.

'What are you thinking about?' she asks Bryn.

'Canvey,' he says.

'What?'

'Canvey Island. It's nothing like this.'

Thea switches on her imaginary camera. Time to interview Bryn.

'Do you live there?' she asks.

'No,' he says.

'Is it near where you live?'

'Yeah. Don't you know about Canvey?'

Thea shakes her head. It's important to speak as little as possible when you're interviewing a subject, to encourage them to talk independently of you. That way, when you edit the video, it seems like they're performing a monologue.

'You can see it from Southend, sitting in the estuary. It's like Gotham City up there at night, and some sort of toxic dump in the day.' He pauses. 'It's completely beautiful.'

'Beautiful?'

Bryn looks embarrassed. 'I don't want to go on and on about it.'

'I want you to,' says Thea.

'Oh. I'm only interested in it because I'm doing, like, a project ...'

'A project?'

He lowers his head. 'Yeah. It's a bit stupid.'

'Yeah, right. I bet it's not,' says Thea.

'It's no big deal.'

'So tell me then.'

'It's just a photographic thing. Essex Gothic. Stupid name really.'

'I think it's a great name,' says Thea.

'No, it's stupid.'

'So it's pictures of Canvey Island?' she asks.

'Yeah. It's a bit shit really, so I don't know why I'm even bothering telling you about it. I was just thinking, you know, that if I'd brought my camera here, it would have been a good, like, contrast.'

'What sort of camera have you got?'

'Just a second-hand 35mm,' he says.

'Same,' says Thea.

'What, you into it as well?' he asks.

She nods. 'Yeah. More films now, though.'

'Films?' Bryn looks impressed.

She smiles. 'Yeah. Documentaries. How did you get into photography?' she asks, zooming out from Bryn's face.

'Did a BTEC at South-East Essex College,' he says.

'Did you like it?'

'Oh yeah. It was wicked. Didn't exactly walk out into a career, though.'

'Who does?' says Thea. 'What did you want to do, ideally?'

'Music press, tabloids. At least that's what I wanted when I first started the course. But then I got into, you know, like, the more artistic side of it. But you've still got to make a living, and that was the bit that was hard. All the other kids off my course went to university to do art and photography or whatever, but I thought I could make it in the real world. I'm still trying.'

Thea wants to talk more, but Bryn's got up again and is now chopping the tree into logs. Without meaning to, she wonders what it would be like to kiss him.

She rolls over on to her front to get some sun on the backs of her legs. All of a sudden she feels self-conscious doing this. What if Bryn thinks she's doing it for his benefit? Showing off her body for him? Yuck. Thea could never be accused of showing off her body to any man. Once she punched someone who made a crack about her nurse's uniform in the arcade. Everyone left her alone after that. At university she was known for looking like a tomboy. Of course, she got wasted on snakebites in the bar like everyone else, and had her share of pissed-up one night stands with skinny Student Union boys. But wherever she went, the same phrases followed her: *You wouldn't know she had legs. Why don't you ever wear a skirt? You'd look really nice with more make-up.* Usually this stuff came from girls like Emily, trying to give her advice. But the point about Thea is that she's strictly a behind-the-camera girl. She wants to see, not be seen. No one's really ever understood that about her. And for a few moments she fantasises that Bryn might.

'I'm going for a walk,' she tells him, sitting up.

'Whatever,' he says.

There's a path in front of the house that leads straight to the cliffs. The path is yellow and sandy, the only genuine desert island feature on this wannabe desert island. Thea walks slowly down this path, heading for the cliffs. Looking out to sea, she notices that there are no boats, no other islands, not even any seagulls. There are some screeching noises, so there must be seabirds out there; Thea just can't see them. There is a whole world out there, but the sea mist prevents any of it from being seen. Thea's not sure what scares her more: the thought that their kidnapper is going to turn up here, or the thought that he never will.

The yellow path leads to a headland, with a cliff ledge underneath it. Thea's fairly sure Jamie didn't come down this far when he searched the island yesterday. She drops on to the ledge and sees that the way to the left is blocked by some kind of prickly bush which looks like it goes on forever. The other way is blocked by rocks, which are worryingly damp and mossy, giving the impression that the sea sometimes makes it up this far. Trying not to look down, Thea scrambles over the first rock. But on the other side of it, the path is so narrow and overgrown that it's going to be impossible to pick through it without some kind of scythe. But it *is* possible to get down there. And if you could get down there with a boat ... Maybe this island isn't totally inescapable after all.

When Thea gets back to the orchard, Bryn's just about finished cutting up the small tree for logs. He's also made a pile of apples.

'Apple pie,' he says as Thea approaches. 'Got a fag?'

They sit and smoke for a few minutes.

'You know what?' says Bryn.

'What?'

He moves closer and touches her face. 'You're gorgeous,' he says.

She smiles. 'Thanks.'

'Seriously,' he says. 'I'd really love to, you know, when we get out of here ... I'd love to take some photographs of you.'

Chapter Ten

Bryn doesn't know what he's said wrong, but then he doesn't know too much about women. In any case, Thea's done a runner into the house. And she looked well fucked off. He only said he wanted to take pictures of her.

It's so quiet out here. Bryn's been trying to work out what it is that's been disturbing him, and that's it. There is a constant crash of waves, and the low buzz of late-summer insects, but that's pretty much it. There are no birds singing, no radios blaring, no cars, no vans, no DSS women screaming at Kylie or Liam to pack it in. Bryn remembers reading something once about the noise that exists in towns, that doesn't really come from anything, but sort of comes from everything. He likes that idea. He likes the fact that even if everyone shut up in a town, there'd still be all that noise. Stuff you can't see: the hum from a distant nuclear reactor, the whir from roadworks on the other side of town, the taxis and factories and ten million radios and five million arguments and two million fucks and a thousand nervous coughs and a girl humming in a field somewhere, far away.

And all that noise goes up. Bryn read that somewhere as well, years ago. All the sound made on earth travels up and out into space in shimmering waves. He told some girl about this once and she got really into it, wondering if distant aliens were listening to Elvis, or closer ones were listening to Five Star. The whole thought makes Bryn a bit freaked out, though. Nothing ever goes away. Not sound, or rubbish, or nuclear waste, or beer bottles, or anything liquid or solid or gas. It all just stays around in the universe, pissing you off, when all you ever wanted to do was get rid of it. He wonders if your thoughts actually disappear, or if, when you die, they leak out of your brain into the soil, get eaten by worms and stay in the food chain for ever.

Tired from all the woodcutting, Bryn lies back in the sunshine and drops off.

Chapter Eleven

At the moment, Anne's in the lead, but Emily could soon close the gap in the 'Ultimate Snake' Championship. If only she could take out Paul, she'd be dead set for second place. Jamie's keeping score, of course, and talking part half-heartedly, having designed the round robin format for the whole contest.

Emily's wondering if anyone's missing her yet. She remembers making some joke to Lucy about not coming back if she got the job. And although she still didn't really mean it, it wouldn't have been out of character for her to mean it. She's been depressed recently. Losing the job in the art gallery sucked, and even the dates from the agency fizzled out after David grassed her up to the owner and said she overcharged for sex. Like, *duh*. Didn't he know that she wasn't even supposed to offer sex — like, it was supposed to be discreet? This island's great because none of Emily's history is here. She's never going to bump into any ex-shags, or walk past the restaurant in which some guy told her she wasn't 'beautiful' like his normal model girlfriends, or see a Chelsea girl sneer at her, noticing her cellulite (in summer) or her moustache (bleached) or her overplucked eyebrows (the pain is like an addiction). Emily hates girls and what they notice. But in some weird way she hates men more, because they don't notice, because second-best is always good enough for them, because even when it comes to having their cock sucked any mouth will do.

When Emily was about sixteen, she thought that men chose her because they could see there was something special about her. She fucked guys with whom she shared a love of art, or who were also Blur fans, or liked the same clubs as her and felt part of the 'scene'. After they'd fucked her, she soon became aware that as far as art-appreciation went, they only liked Pink Floyd album covers, or maybe The Scream; they thought Blur were OK but preferred New Order, and that they only said all this stuff, and went on the club scene in the first place, to get a shag. Emily is painfully aware that she is easy; that she is the stock-in-trade of those 'uncovered' programmes set in Ibiza or Greece or wherever, where all the girls go topless for a laugh and take three blokes a night in club toilets.

There seems to have been a recent vogue for American teeny-pop stars to put out drippy tunes about not being ready for sex yet. Their lyrics take the concept of virginity seriously, either urging boyfriends to wait, or thanking them for waiting, or telling them to fuck off if they won't wait. Emily can't listen to any of these songs. She switches the radio off whenever they come on. It's like that stupid *Dawson's Creek* programme she's watched a few times. She's a total Jen, but she wishes she were a Joey.

'Ha!' says Anne, having beaten Paul once more.

Bollocks. This means Anne's definitely going to take first place in the tournament. Emily just has to play Paul now. A score of forty-five or more will give her second place – as long as it's a winning score – but if she loses or gets less than that, it's curtains for her 'Ultimate Snake' Championship challenge.

'We could have some away fixtures in the sitting room after this,' says Jamie. 'These scores could go on aggregate.'

'Or we could just start again,' says Emily, beating Paul to the first piece of food.

'Fuck,' says Paul.

Thea comes in through the back door.

'What's wrong with you?' asks Emily.

'Nothing,' says Thea, but she's crying. She walks through the room, out into the hall, then, going on the banging sound that follows, up the stairs.

'Wow,' says Paul.

'Drama,' says Anne.

Jamie immediately rushes out of the kitchen after Thea.

Which leaves Emily with only one option: to go and find out what happened from Bryn.

He's asleep when she gets outside, looking kind of sexy with his shirt off and an apple in his hand. On his right is a pile of logs. On his left is a pile of apples. There's a bottle of lemonade, but it's all warm from being left in the sun. Emily takes a swig anyway. It's horrible.

She touches Bryn's chest and he wakes immediately.

'Mum?' he says.

Emily laughs. 'Silly, it's Emily.'

'Where's Thea?' asks Bryn, sitting up and stretching.

'She ran in the house a few minutes ago. She seemed to be crying.'

'Oh.'

'So what made her cry?' asks Emily, taking out her box of Silk Cut.

'Cry?' says Bryn.

'Do you want one of these?'

He takes a cigarette. 'Cheers.'

'So . . . ?' She's flirting.

'What?'

'The goss,' she says. 'Tell me what happened to make Thea cry.'

'Oh, that,' says Bryn. 'I didn't know she was, uh . . .'

'So tell me what happened.'

Bryn starts telling some um-and-ah tale of him woodcutting and Thea sunbathing. There's even a hint that there was some attraction between them — or at least from Bryn's side anyway.

'I thought she'd want me to kiss her,' he explains. 'It was one of those, you know, *moments*, when you just know that something's going to happen. Anyway, then I told her she was gorgeous and just before I went to kiss her, I said I'd like to take some pictures of her.'

Emily starts laughing, rolling around on the grass.

'What?' says Bryn.

'You total perv!'

'I didn't mean it like that, though, did I?'

'You *so* did. God, men are all the same.'

Paul and Anne are still sitting in the kitchen. They don't seem to be doing anything, just sitting staring at each other. Oh well, maybe they don't have much to say. Emily heads straight through the door and upstairs to clean her teeth. The lemonade has left an aftertaste.

Emily's room is next to Thea's. And it's a complete accident, but as Emily's cleaning her teeth, she realises she can hear everything going on in the next room. At first it's all sobs and shushing noises. Then some quiet, then the sound of a nose being blown, then some more quiet.

Then voices.

'Why are you so upset?' says Jamie, his voice muffled by the wall.

'I hate it here,' says Thea.

There are more sobbing sounds for a couple of minutes. Emily washes her face.

'Come on,' says Jamie soothingly. 'You can talk to me.'

'About what?' Thea says petulantly.

'Whatever it is that's made you so upset.'

'Just being here makes me upset.'

'None of us wants to be here,' he reminds her.

'No? You all seem to be having fun.'

'We're just making the best of it,' says Jamie.

There's a pause. Emily lowers herself to the floor and gets comfortable.

'I feel so stupid,' says Thea.

Emily makes a face. Get to the point, girl.

'Don't,' says Jamie. 'This is a difficult situation.'

'You don't seem to find it difficult,' she says.

'Well, I'm a survivor,' says Jamie.

Emily puts her fist in her mouth. *I'm a survivor*. God, he's sweet but ridiculous.

'I found the generator, by the way,' says Thea.

'Brilliant. We'll have to power it up before it gets dark.'

There are sounds of movement. Jamie must be getting up.

'What, now?' says Thea.

'Come on, you'll feel better if you come and do something.'

'But I can't . . .'

'What?' asks Jamie.

'I can't face *him*.'

'Bryn?'

'Yes,' she says.

'Why? What happened out there?'

'Nothing. It was stupid.'

'So what's the problem?' asks Jamie.

'I think I may have overreacted a bit.'

You can say that again, thinks Emily.

'Did he make a move on you?' asks Jamie.

'I don't know. I think I wanted him to, anyway. It wasn't that.'

'So what's the problem?'

'Just something he said.'

'What?' Jamie asks.

'You wouldn't understand.'

'You could try me.'

'He said he wanted to take pictures of me.'

'Oh, I see. What a bastard.'

'No!' protests Thea. 'I don't think he meant that.'

'Well what else could he mean?'

'He's a photographer. He likes taking pictures of buildings and whatever. I think he thought I'd take it as a compliment. I mean, we'd both been talking about photography, so it wasn't a completely out-of-place thing to say. That's why I feel so bad for overreacting.'

'So where's the problem?'

'What problem?' she says.

'Come on. You're so upset.'

Emily wonders if this is ever going to get interesting.

'It's just that I can't have my picture taken,' Thea says. 'Ever,' she adds.

'Why not?'

'I just can't.'

'Aren't there some religions that—'

'What? Believe that a photograph takes your soul away? Well, they're right. It does. It completely takes your soul away.'

'I don't understand,' says Jamie.

There's a long pause. Then Thea's voice, softer now.

'When I was twelve I found out that my uncle had hidden a camera in my bedroom.'

'What do you mean?'

'He used to record me getting undressed. He had hours and hours of video tape of me in my socks and knickers, or just my knickers, or completely naked. Apparently the ones of me in my socks and knickers were the most popular.'

'Shit!' says Jamie. 'Are you serious?'

'Yeah. He used to keep the videos for himself and his friends, and print off stills to sell to some specialist dealer in Soho.'

'What, like a . . .'

'A paedophile. Yeah.'

'Jesus. No wonder you—'

'He did it for two years, starting when I was ten. I found the camera when I was looking for secret passageways. You know, you do that kind of thing when you're a kid. It took me ages to work out what it was for. When I did, my mum was pretty upset, but in the end she said there was no reason for me to take it further, because it wasn't like he'd touched me or anything. I don't think my dad thought it was a big deal, although I'd expected him to go mental. They didn't want any trouble, I suppose. It was that sort of family.'

'Gosh. What did you do?'

'I went to the police. There was some talk at school about what to do if a grown up makes you feel uncomfortable. You know the kind of thing. I told a teacher and she took me to the police.'

'That's amazingly brave.'

'When they investigated Uncle David, they found a lot of nasty stuff.'

'What kind of nasty stuff?'

'You don't want to know.'

I do, thinks Emily. But Jamie doesn't press her.

'What happened to him?' he asks instead.

'He went to prison. He's still there, in fact.'

Emily does a quick calculation. Thea said she was twenty-two. Must have been some pretty fucked up shit if this guy's been in prison for almost ten years.

'What about you? What happened to you?'

'I got fostered by these really nice people in Brighton. End of story.'

'But what about your real folks?'

'I haven't spoken to them for ten years.'

'Really?'

'Yeah. They were trailer trash anyway. Didn't give a shit about me.'

'God.'

The conversation seems to be over.

'Please don't tell anyone what I told you,' Thea says.

'Of course,' says Jamie.

There's some shuffling, the sound of a door banging and they're gone.

Chapter Twelve

There's sexual tension in the kitchen.

'What are you two doing?' asks Jamie, as he walks past with Thea.

'Nothing,' says Paul. 'What are you doing?'

'Going to sort out the electricity,' says Jamie.

'Are you feeling better?' Anne asks Thea.

'Yes thanks,' she replies acidly.

Then they are gone. Paul goes back to looking at Anne. He smiles. She smiles back.

'What?' she asks.

'What?' he replies.

This has been going on for the last half an hour. She's got some book from the library which she's reading, and he's just looking at her, and tinkering with some other bits of phone. Every so often she looks up and smiles. He smiles back, they both get embarrassed, ask each other what, and then Anne returns to her reading.

There isn't a word for Anne. Paul's been trying to think of one all day. Maybe it's because he's never been faced with a girl like this, who makes him think these kind of thoughts. Maybe that's why he doesn't have the word. As far as he's always been concerned, women fall into two general categories: the girlfriends that you rebel against – strange Bridget Jones women who just want to trap you, marry you and then get fat in comfort – and the girls you mess around with while you're rebelling against them. He doesn't want to have sex with any of them. He's certainly not interested in sleeping with Bridgets. They always want the lights off, and they moan about their cellulite, the bastards who've used them and all the clichéd things you've ever heard. And the other girls, the ones who don't even have names, they worry about all the same things, but just haven't reached the self-esteem high of Bridget, who doesn't have particularly high self-esteem anyway. They'll fuck anyone, do any drugs and abuse themselves, until they eventually find a man or a religion or a self-help manual that'll turn them into a Bridget, and then they'll get married and fat as well.

Paul doesn't have a problem with sex in theory, he just doesn't want to actually put his penis inside people like *that*. It's so false: the moans, the positions. Why do they all do that? It's not because they enjoy it. Usually it's because it hurts, and they enjoy that in a low self-esteem kind of way.

Anne looks up from her book.

Paul smiles. She smiles back.

'What?' he asks.

'What?' she repeats.

She goes back to the book.

He knows there are women out there who are different, but he's never met any. It makes him angry that he only ever meets the fucked up ones. Why make love to someone who hates their body? What the hell is the point of that? Why share an intimate experience with someone you can never get close to, who is shielded by dyed hair and false, painted nails and horrible make-up that stains your pillow? Why share an experience with someone for whom that very experience is their essential hang-up? Why share an act of love with someone who's just going to cry afterwards, or want to get married, or talk about all the pain in their life? That's why Paul thinks that sex must really hurt for these women; they always end up in so much *pain* afterwards.

This is why he doesn't have sex. He is never going to have children, never going to have a 'partner'. He can watch other people do all that stuff, but he can't do it himself. The only woman he's ever been in love with was a character in a videogame: Aeris. And now she's in the Life Stream. Paul's interested in various things: dada; the number 23 (Anne's twenty-three, he heard her telling Emily); games; communication networks; animals; the environment. But so far he's never been interested in love, because, honestly, it just hasn't seemed that relevant.

He's tinkering with a resistor and a small LED bulb as he thinks, making a miniature circuit. Anne looks up from what she's reading. She smiles at him. This time she holds his gaze a bit longer than usual.

'Paul,' she begins.

The kitchen door opens and Emily walks in.

'What are you two doing?' she asks.

'It's funny,' says Anne. 'Jamie asked us the exact same thing, but it's quite obvious that I'm reading and Paul's building a plane to get us out of here.'

Paul smiles at Anne.

'Calm down,' says Emily. 'I didn't suggest you were having sex or anything.'

Anne goes pink. Paul feels himself get a little hot.

'You're both going red,' says Emily. 'Kinky.'

'Shut up,' says Paul.

'Coffee?' asks Emily, fiddling with the kettle.

'Whatever,' says Paul.

'Yuck,' says Anne. 'I'll have some milkshake.'

'Where's Bryn?' asks Emily.

'Don't know,' says Anne. 'Still outside, I think.'

'Jamie and Thea have gone to—' begins Paul. At that moment things start to whir and the kitchen light comes on.

'—sort out the electricity,' finishes Anne.

'Cool,' says Emily. She finishes making the coffee on the electric stove.

'Thanks,' says Paul, when she gives it to him.

Emily sits down, looking thoughtful. No one says anything.

The back door opens and Bryn comes in, carrying logs.

'Don't put yourselves out,' he says, panting and sweating.

'What?' says Paul.

'I think he means we've got to help,' says Emily. 'I'll go and give him a hand.'

She gets up and hurries out of the back door. Bryn staggers through towards the sitting room. Paul and Anne stay where they are.

'What?' says Paul, responding to the funny look Anne's giving him.

'What?' she replies.

Here we go again.

'Aren't you going to help with the logs?' asks Paul.

'No.'

'Why not?'

'I don't do manual labour,' she says.

'What do you do?' Paul asks.

'Nothing,' she replies.

Probably realising that she's going to get sucked into helping with something if she stays around here, Anne disappears upstairs.

Paul brings in the apples.

Gradually the day disappears and the orange glow from the electric lights in the house becomes more and more comforting.

'Right. Apple pie.'

Emily's in the kitchen, looking homely.

'Apple pie,' says Paul. 'Yum.'

'You can help if you want,' says Emily, smiling at him.

'I think I'll just watch, thanks.'

'Suit yourself. Where are the others?'

Paul shrugs. 'I think Jamie and Bryn are lighting the fire.'
It's dark outside now.

'Is everyone inside?' she asks.

'I think so,' says Paul. 'Anne's upstairs. I don't know what
Thea's doing.'

'What are *you* doing?' Emily asks.

'Watching you.'

'Oh.' The word is fluttery, like she's embarrassed. 'I'm not
that interesting.'

'You beat the whole *Sacred Manhood* thing going on in the
other room.'

'Thanks.'

'You're welcome.'

'What about Anne?' asks Emily playfully.

'What about her?'

'Everyone knows you've got the hots for her.'

'Do they? How?'

'I think it's just a vibe people are getting.'

'Which people?' he asks.

'The rest of us.'

'You're so clever,' he says.

'Fuck off,' says Emily.

He laughs. 'I fancy you much more than I fancy Anne.'

'No you don't.' She's obviously not going to be taken
in by that.

'Maybe not.'

'Why did you say it then?'

'Just wanted to see how fast you'd get your knickers
off,' he says.

'What?'

'Well, you're obviously pretty easy.'

'Why are you being so mean?' she asks, in a much smaller
voice this time.

He looks down at the table.

'Sorry,' he says. 'I just don't like it when people make assumptions.'

She looks really pissed off. 'Obviously.'

'Sorry,' he says again.

'I was only teasing you.'

Paul smiles. 'I've never been very good at being teased.'

She smiles too. 'I bet you were a fucking annoying child.'

'I was, actually.'

'Did you dissect animals and pull the wings off things?'

She's found various ingredients now and is mixing them in a bowl.

'No,' says Paul. 'Never animals. Only technology.'

'Very tame.'

'Not really. And I was against dissecting animals, in fact.' He laughs.

She raises an eyebrow. 'What's funny?'

'I just remembered something. Sonia.' He's laughing more now.

'Who's Sonia?'

'One of the school lab mice.'

'What happened?'

'He was already dead when I did this, but—'

'He? I thought you said it was called Sonia.'

'Yeah. I named him after this girl in my class. He looked just like her.'

'Uh huh. So what did you do to this dead mouse?'

'I animated him.'

'You *animated* him?'

'Yeah. I made him a little circuit, and put a small battery in his stomach. When the teacher made the first incision into him and completed the circuit I'd set up, Sonia started moving his legs about like mad, you know, as if he was alive and was in pain being cut up like that.'

'What did the teacher do?'

'She was quite cool. She pulled out the circuit, said something like "very clever", and then got on with the dissection. They did actually ban dissection in the school a while after that — I mean, not as a result of my terrorist tactics, but a couple of years later when the Vegetarian Society did a petition.'

'Did your classmates freak out when they saw the mouse move?'

'One boy — Wesley — he sort of screamed. That's it, really.'

'Oh.' She looks disappointed.

Paul knows he shouldn't really have bothered telling her anything about himself. She's the kind of girl who takes part in those ridiculous discussions where you have to provide a punchline at the end of everything you say, every anecdote you tell. If anything ordinary happens, or sad, or tame, it's just not good enough. The end always has to be funny. Paul wonders if the end of all this will be funny, or if, like most things in life, it'll just be disappointing.

Chapter Thirteen

The house seems a bit friendlier now all the lights work. Anne knows all the lights work, because in the couple of hours since the electricity was turned on, all the lights have been switched on – and left on. Everyone's dads would be furious. Anne wonders how long the wind-and-solar-powered batteries will last.

Her bedroom is bare like the others', except for all the Utopia books she's been taking out of the library all day. They're made very interesting reading, but now she's got that feeling like she's tired, but not. This means she's turned on, and once the idea to masturbate comes to her, it's something she can't leave alone. She's been reading on the bed, so she slips under the covers and turns off the bright overhead light.

It's over in about two minutes. Maybe this island thing is quite sexy after all.

Anne's fingers smell like plasticine afterwards. She likes it. Humming something by Another Level, she wanders downstairs.

'Hi,' she says, walking into the kitchen. 'What's happening?'

'Emily's baking cakes,' says Paul.

'Apple pie,' Emily corrects.

'Where's everyone else?'

'In the sitting room, I think,' says Emily.

✻   ✻   ✻

There is smoke coming from the sitting room.

'For fuck's sake!' Bryn's voice.

'Just … hang on … don't!' Jamie's voice, urgent and a bit panicked.

Anne walks in and coughs.

'Jesus,' she says. 'What's going on in here?'

The room is full of smoke.

'We're trying to light this fire,' says Jamie.

'But the wind keeps blowing the smoke back into the room,' says Bryn.

'It's because it's not lit properly,' Jamie says, this time to Bryn.

Anne gets the impression they've already had this conversation.

There's a bottle of vodka by the fire. Bryn pours some of it over the logs.

'Why are you doing that?' asks Anne.

'Alcohol burns. It's like a barbecue,' he explains.

Jamie sighs. 'It's just making the logs wet.'

'Now I see why you have smoke,' says Anne, coughing some more.

'Fucking hell,' says Emily, coming in through the door.

The boys look pissed off.

'Are you trying to light a fire?' she asks.

'What do you reckon?' says Bryn sarcastically.

'All right,' she says. 'Me and Anne are going to take over now.'

'You what?' says Bryn.

Jamie starts protesting as well, but Emily shoos him and Bryn out of the room. She makes them take their wet logs with them.

'Bring in some dry ones,' she says. 'And then don't bother us.'

'Fine,' sighs Jamie.

'Right,' says Emily. 'I *think* I know how to do this.'

'I thought you definitely knew,' says Anne.

'I know how to set fire to things.'

'Does that include logs?'

Emily wrinkles her nose.

'Hi,' says Thea, peering in through the door. 'Has Bryn gone?'

'Yeah,' says Emily. 'Why are you bothered about Bryn?'

'No reason,' says Thea defensively, walking in and sitting down.

There's something going on here, but Anne's not sure what.

'Do you know how to light a fire?' Anne asks Thea.

'Yeah,' she says. 'Do you have any newspaper?'

Anne looks around. The boys had been using twigs for kindling. Maybe they already looked for newspaper and didn't find any. After all, there aren't too many news-agents around.

Emily's poking around the room.

'I don't think there is any,' she says.

'There must be something to light the fire with,' says Thea. 'I mean, there's all this other stuff lying around; all the food and wine and other supplies. And since there's no central heating, whoever brought us here must have considered that we'd need to use the fire.'

'Unless we're supposed to freeze to death,' says Anne.

Thea glares at her. 'I'm so sick of—'

'All right,' Emily cuts in. 'We need to think of where we'd find paper.'

'What's that smell?' asks Thea.

'*Vodka*,' Anne and Emily say together.

'It's disgusting,' says Thea. 'Where did it come from?'

'The boys poured it on the logs,' explains Emily. 'Like, *duh*.'

'Books,' says Thea suddenly.

'What?' says Emily.

'We can use pages from the books to light the fire.'

'You can't do that!' squeals Emily. 'You can't burn *books*.'

'Well, what do you suggest?'

'We could at least have a look around for something else first.'

Five minutes later the three girls come back with a box of firelighters from the kitchen store. There were about two hundred other boxes, so it doesn't seem as if getting warm is going to be too much of a problem for a while. There were loads of boxes of candles as well, stacked behind the red wine.

'Someone's gone to a hell of a lot of trouble to set this up,' says Thea.

The fire's really catching now. Emily's doing the pious Victorian child thing on her knees in front of it. Anne and Thea are sitting on opposite sofas, facing each other and at right angles to the fire. Anne notices for the first time that Thea has changed out of her original clothes and is now completely dressed in stuff from the house. She quite suits the long skirt look. Maybe the short hair helps. Anne doesn't know what she's going to do when she has to change clothes. All that floaty hippy stuff really isn't her.

'My foster mum's going to be so worried,' says Thea.

'My parents won't care,' says Anne.

'They will really, won't they?' says Emily.

Anne shrugs. 'Maybe. Oh, I guess so. What about your parents?'

'They won't even know anything's happened to me,' says Emily. 'I don't talk to them much, maybe once a month or so. I'm just so busy all the time with work and going out and everything ...' She sighs. 'You mean to call them every week, but you never do. I used to tell my mum when I had job interviews, but I don't bother any more. I was going to tell them when I actually had a really good job, not when I was just going for one.'

'Will anyone have reported you missing?' asks Thea.

'Maybe my flatmate Lucy,' she says. 'But she'd leave it a while longer. I've gone off to places before and not come home for a while. She'll just assume I've met someone, or that I'm having a good time somewhere. She might get worried if she calls my mobile and can't get through, I suppose. But then again, she might not. She might just think I'm in a tunnel, or out of range. Will anyone have reported you?' Emily asks Anne.

'Who knows?' she says. 'My parents think I'm a bit weird, so they might give it a couple of days before reporting me missing. They did know I was going for a job, though. I had to get them off my back somehow.'

'So they have the address of the interview and everything?' says Thea hopefully.

'No,' says Anne sheepishly. 'I said the job was with a big PR firm.'

'Great,' hisses Thea.

'But you told your folks where you were going, right?' Emily asks Thea.

'My foster mum knew I was going for a job, but not which one. I don't live with her any more, so I don't tend to give her details about exactly where I'm going. I just told her I had three interviews this week, which I did, and she wished me luck.'

There's a pause while they consider this. Anne wonders how long it will be before the police take the disappearances seriously. Young people must go 'missing' all the time, and then turn up having just been out with mates, or having forgotten to phone or whatever. Anne knows from soap operas that people have to be missing for twenty-four hours before the police can even file a report, and then it takes them a while to actively look for the person. Anne wonders when they'll make the job interview connection, and what kind of trail the bogus job people have left behind. They must have been bogus, surely? Unless they were targeted too, by whoever it really was. She wonders if they'll be found before they've been killed, or afterwards.

'Oh well,' Emily says to Anne. 'At least you'll be able to get it on with Paul.'

'What are you talking about?' says Anne, feeling herself go red again.

'Duh,' says Emily. 'Come on, girl. He fancies the fuck out of you.'

'Me?' says Anne.

Thea sighs. 'Here comes the innocent act again.'

'Seriously,' says Anne. 'I don't think he does.'

'He told me,' says Emily. 'Well, more or less.'

'God,' says Anne. She thinks for a minute. 'No. You're winding me up.'

'Haven't you seen the way he looks at you?' asks Thea.

She doesn't say this like a friend. More the way you'd say it to a stupid person.

Anne doesn't get this situation. She's sitting here, kidnapped, on a deserted island in the middle of nowhere, with two girls she's never met before – one of whom despises her – and they are trying to give her relationship advice. Even without the kidnap and the island, this is still weird. Her friendships, few and intense, have always been about the other person relying on her; looking for her insights on a situation. No one has ever dared to offer Anne advice. After all, she's an expert in sex and love affairs and anorexia and bullying and pregnancy and death and abortion and religion. What would she need advice on? Anne would never approach someone else for advice or interpretation. There are two reasons for this. First of all, she isn't interested in anyone else's advice or interpretation. Secondly – and crucially – she never gets into situations that would require her to seek advice in the first place.

'No,' she says. 'You've got it wrong.'

'Whatever you say,' says Thea, obviously having tired of the subject.

The fire has started blazing and is making a comforting whooshing noise.

'It's very quiet,' comments Emily. 'Without traffic or anything.'

'When do you think we're going to get out of here?' asks Thea.

'Who knows?' says Emily. 'When they find us.'

'If they do,' says Anne. 'Which doesn't look likely now.'

'I'd like to punch whoever's responsible for us being here,' says Thea.

'Aren't we responsible for being here?' asks Emily, clearly trying to be profound.

'We didn't kidnap ourselves, did we?' says Thea. 'That would be the bad guy.'

'Or bad *guys*,' says Emily.

'Maybe it wasn't a bad guy who brought us here,' suggests Anne.

Thea looks at her as if she's gone crazy.

'Whatever,' she says.

Anne feels like she's on Ricki Lake. All Thea needs is the hand movements.

'What do you think the boys are doing?' asks Emily.

'Probably playing "Ultimate Snake",' says Anne.

'What's "Ultimate Snake"?' asks Thea.

Chapter Fourteen

So far today, Jamie's fucked up a lot of things. The only thing he didn't fuck up was being there for Thea, which is pretty cool considering Jamie's never been required to 'be there' for anyone before. Occasionally he's been relied on for *support*, which is something entirely different altogether. *Being there* for your friends sounds more campfire, somehow; more *Dawson's Creek*. Which is cool.

Jamie's had a fixation with Dawson Leary since Channel 4 began showing the first series a couple of years back. It's Jamie's all-time favourite TV programme, not that he'd tell the others of course; it would make him seem far too childish. Most romantic heroes these days are dark – in looks and theme – but Dawson being blond was just the first cool thing about him. He was kind of a nerd as well, staying in his room watching films and doing homework and planning projects. The only thing Jamie objected to was the way Dawson coveted Joey. He was much more in favour of Jen, not because of her alcohol-fuelled almost-threesomes and near-suicidal tantrums. It was the idea that she could change from all of that – change for Dawson, or sometimes, late at night, for Jamie.

He tries to think of this as something more than a total cliché. It's not like he wants a woman with a past so he can reform and own her. Maybe he likes the idea of exploring his own wild side, or maybe in some weird way he feels that he'd have more in common with a woman who's interested in experimenting with life a bit. If Jamie was ten years younger, Jen would be his perfect woman. Whatever anybody says, she's so much cooler than Joey. She comes from New York, for God's sake. She's cosmopolitan and cool. And that's what Jamie is going to be one day, with a cool girl like Jen; still wild enough to be fun, but settled enough to love only him.

Paul and Bryn are playing 'Ultimate Snake'. Jamie can't beat either of them, so he's just sitting at the kitchen table vaguely watching them, thinking, wondering if the girls have lit the fire yet, and when the kidnappers are going to come.

'Did we ever work out what we'll do when they come?' he asks.

'The kidnappers?' says Bryn. 'We'll kick their butts.'

'What if there are more of them than us?'

'We'll die,' says Paul. 'Unless we do the *Home Alone* thing.'

'That film was funny,' laughs Bryn. 'That little kid and all them gadgets.'

'I haven't seen it,' says Jamie.

'It's wicked,' Bryn assures him. He coughs. 'Has anyone got a fag?'

Jamie gives him the last but one Marlboro, and then lights the last one for himself. He's concerned that he's not getting the most out of this situation. As a child, Jamie always made sure he got the most out of things. Even now, as an adult, he won't leave a museum until he has seen everything in it; won't skip any exhibits in an art gallery. When Jamie was really little, his mother was very poor, and he always felt incredibly guilty for wasting anything that she had paid for. At the cinema he always tried not to blink too much, or get distracted, and if he got a new toy he played with it until it literally wore out. He'd finish every bag of sweets, no matter how sick he felt, and he always swallowed chewing gum rather than throwing it away. Any experience had to be savoured totally; initially so his mother knew he was grateful, but later, as it became a compulsion because Jamie didn't ever want to feel that he had missed something.

This experience is a variation of all the adventures that Jamie has always dreamed about. These adventures always start with the words: *Against all the odds.* Against all the odds, Jamie survives an expedition to Antarctica. Against all the odds, Jamie survives a plane crash in the jungle. Against all the odds, Jamie survives after being kidnapped and held on a remote island.

There are several reasons why he doesn't feel like he's getting the most out of this experience. First of all, the odds aren't really there. There are no odds to be up against, and surviving isn't that hard in a house well stocked with food and drink. Secondly, the experience is being ruined by the other-people factor. Bryn's already pissed Jamie off by chopping the logs himself, then ruined Jamie's fire by covering them in vodka. He's even better at 'Ultimate Snake' than Jamie. Paul seems to be operating on his own plane entirely. Already the kitchen is a mess of wires and LEDs and things which have become detached from other things, or attached to new things. Paul reminds Jamie of the evil boy in *Toy Story* (which he *has* seen), deconstructing everything and then putting it back together the wrong way.

For the last hour or so, the boys have been intrigued by the voices coming out of the sink. At first it was frightening, until they realised that they were actually hearing the girls talking in the sitting room. No one understands how this works. Paul explained it's probably a pipe. After the novelty wore off, and after they'd all finished laughing at Paul's supposed crush on Anne, the voices had become like a soothing radio programme. Now the girls' conversation has suddenly turned pornographic.

'Do *you* shave it?' Thea's saying.

'Me?' comes Emily's voice. 'Of course.'

'What, totally?'

'No. I leave a little bit at the top. Like porn stars.'

'Oh, I know what you mean,' says Anne.

'I don't look at porn,' says Thea. 'So I wouldn't know.'

'Shame,' comments Paul.

'Shut up,' says Jamie.

'Emily's probably been in it,' comments Bryn. 'That's how she knows.'

They listen to the voices again.

'Porn's cool,' says Anne.

'I thought you were a virgin,' says Thea.

'Doesn't mean I can't look at porn.'

'Doesn't it make you want to, you know, *do it*?' asks Emily.

'Yeah, of course,' says Anne. 'But there's nobody to do it with.'

Paul laughs. 'Hello?' he says to the sink. 'I'm over here.'

Jamie's got an erection. Not just from Anne, but from the way all the girls are talking.

They continue.

'So is that the only reason you haven't fucked anyone?' asks Emily.

'What?' says Anne.

'You think nobody wants to.'

There isn't any sound for a second. Maybe she nodded.

'That's stupid,' says Emily. 'Anyone would want to fuck you.'

'So how come I'm still a virgin?' asks Anne.

'Maybe they think you're too childish,' suggests Thea.

'Ouch,' says Paul. 'What a bitch.'

'She's all right,' says Jamie. 'She's probably only joking.'

'Oh shit!' comes Emily's voice.

'What?' says Anne.

There's the sound of one or more of them moving around.

'My apple pie,' says Emily. 'Shit, I've got to . . .'

There's the sound of a door opening and then someone running down the corridor. Emily bursts through the kitchen door and heads straight for the oven.

'Where's my apple pie?' she demands, when she finds it empty.

'I took it out,' says Paul. 'It was done.'

She gives him a big smile. 'Thank you.'

'It's on the side,' says Paul.

'Cool,' she says. 'Who wants some?'

'Me,' says Jamie.

'Me,' says Bryn.

'Me,' says Paul.

Someone coughs. It isn't anyone in the kitchen.

'What was that?' asks Emily.

'What?' says Paul.

'That cough. It sounded like Thea or Anne.'

'I didn't hear anything,' says Bryn.

'Weird pipes,' says Paul, adding, 'We heard everything you just said.'

'Oh,' she says, blushing. 'Well, anyway, shall we have apple pie in the other room?'

'Aren't you supposed to have befores before you have afters?' asks Bryn.

'What?' asks Emily.

'Well if this is, like, dessert, then have I missed something?'

'If you want anything else, you can get it yourself,' she says. 'I'm not your cook.'

'God,' he says. 'Touchy.'

'Fuck off,' she says.

'Is there any cream?' asks Paul.

'Yeah, there's some in the fridge, isn't there?' says Emily.

'I'll bring the bowls,' says Jamie.

With Emily carrying the apple pie and a knife to cut it, Jamie carrying six bowls and spoons, and Bryn carrying the cream and some red wine from the kitchen store, they all walk through to the sitting room. Bryn's been grumbling about there not being any lager or fags. No one imagines there'd be any cigarettes anywhere in the house, and so there's a panic breaking out among the smokers.

'Would there be any stashed anywhere, do you think?' he asks.

Emily shrugs. 'I said I didn't smoke on the form.'

'What form?' asks Bryn.

'The application form. There was a question asking if you smoke.'

'Oh, that,' he says.

'What did you say?'

He thinks back. 'I probably said I didn't.'

'Why would you say you don't smoke?' asks Paul.

'You never admit to smoking on application forms,' says Emily. 'Most offices have a no-smoking policy nowadays, so if you say you smoke, you're instantly telling your employer that you'd spend half the day standing outside wasting time. Anyone would much rather employ a non-smoker, so you just have to pretend you are one.'

'What did you say on your form?' Jamie asks Thea.

'The same,' she says. 'That I don't smoke.'

'Great,' says Jamie. 'We're fucked, then.'

'As if what we put on the form's going to make any difference,' says Thea.

'I said that I smoke,' says Anne.

'What?' says Jamie.

'On that form.'

'But you don't smoke,' says Emily.

'I know,' says Anne.

'Do you always lie on forms?' asks Paul.

'Yeah,' she says.

'I'll go and look in the kitchen,' says Emily. 'In that big larder thing.'

When she comes back, she's carrying 200 Silk Cut and 200 B&H.

'I could only find these,' she says, grinning.

'Cool,' says Bryn.

'Where were they?' asks Jamie.

'With the medical supplies,' she says. 'Behind the beans.'

'Medical supplies,' says Paul. 'Interesting.'

'And the seeds,' she adds mysteriously.

'What seeds?' asks Jamie.

'For growing things. Herbs and stuff. Food.'

'Weird,' says Thea.

'I'll try a B&H,' says Jamie, taking a packet out of the box.

'Let's have one of those, mate,' Bryn says to Jamie.

Jamie wonders why Bryn doesn't just take a whole packet for himself.

Thea takes a box of Silk Cut.

Everyone's happy.

Chapter Fifteen

It doesn't take long to finish the apple pie. Bryn's moaning about there not being any other food, although there's plenty in the kitchen. Thea's not saying anything very much, although Bryn seems to have forgotten about what happened between them earlier. Either that, or he doesn't care. Their special moment is now completely lost, though, for good or bad, and it looks as though Thea will just have to forget about the kiss she thought she might want.

The fire's made the room cosy and warm. The flames are giving everyone a costume-drama glow. People are watching other people when they think they're not looking, maybe searching for something in their faces. Who knows what they are seeing. Bryn and Emily are sitting together on one sofa, with Anne sitting on the floor in front of it. Thea's on the other sofa with Jamie, and Paul's on his way out of the door.

'Where are you going?' asks Emily.

'Kitchen,' he says. 'I'm going to bring "Ultimate Snake" in here.'

'Bring us something to eat,' says Bryn.

It's totally dark outside. But it seems cosier tonight with the fire and electric lights.

'That light's too bright,' says Bryn.

'Turn it off then,' says Emily.

'Won't it be too dark if we do that?' says Jamie.

'We should get the candles,' says Emily. 'It'll be nice.'

Anne's reading something.

'What about Anne?' says Jamie. 'She's reading.'

Anne puts the book to one side and yawns.

'I've finished,' she says. 'Candles would be cool.'

'What is that you've been reading?' asks Bryn.

'Nothing,' she says. 'Just some space-community utopia thing.'

'I'll go and get the candles,' says Thea.

Paul's sitting at the kitchen table, eating what looks like a cheese sandwich.

'What are you doing?' Thea asks him.

'Eating a cheese sandwich,' he says.

'Oh.'

'How are you feeling?' he asks her.

'What do you mean?'

'Are you still scared?'

'Yes, of course I am. Aren't you?'

'No.'

He takes a huge bite from the sandwich.

'Are you really a vegetarian?' she asks.

'Yeah. Why?'

'Me too,' she says, and smiles.

She sits down next to him.

'Do you want a bit?' he offers. She takes the second half of the sandwich.

'So why aren't you scared?' she asks.

'Death doesn't bother me,' he replies. 'That's it. If you believe that death's the worst thing that can happen to you, and you can make yourself not afraid of it, then there's nothing to be scared of.'

'That reminds me of a poster my old flatmate had in the

bathroom,' she says. 'Something about there being only two things to worry about ... Oh, I know, it goes, *There are only two things to worry about, either you are sick or you are healthy. If you are healthy, there is nothing to worry about. If you're sick, there are only two things to worry about, either you will live, or you will die. If you live, there is nothing to worry about* ... It ends up with you either happy in heaven, or happy in hell, shaking hands with your friends.'

'I know it,' says Paul. 'It's true. There is nothing to worry about.'

'But you worry all the time,' she says.

'How do you know?'

'I can see it in your face. You worry about loads of things.'

'Yeah,' he smiles. 'I do worry about normal things. I worry about GM food.'

'Why?' she asks.

'Because it will kill us all. That's why I'm not worried about death.'

'But you worry about it because it will kill us. That doesn't make sense.'

He smiles. 'I just mean it's inevitable.'

'It's inevitable that we'll all die one day. We don't have to like it.'

'Oh, I don't like it,' says Paul. 'I'm just not scared in a panicked way.'

'Right.' She finishes the sandwich, including the crusts, and lights a cigarette. 'Oh, I forgot to say,' she says.

'What?'

'I think there may be a way down the cliffs.'

'Didn't Jamie look all around there yesterday?'

'Not on this bit,' she says. 'You have to go over a rock, and then it seems as if you might be able to climb down. If we built a boat or something we could make an attempt at getting away from here.'

Paul looks less excited than she'd hoped.

'What's wrong?' she asks.

He shrugs. 'Nothing.'

'Don't you want to escape?'

'The water would be very cold.'

'You don't want to escape because the water might be cold?'

'I'm not sure. This is quite fun, don't you think?'

'No. Come on, Paul. We can't stay here forever.'

'Maybe.'

'I thought you liked making things,' she says.

'So?'

'You could make the boat.'

'I'll make the navigation system,' he offers. 'But I don't do woodwork.'

'No,' she sighs. 'I suppose you probably don't.'

'Why are you so desperate to escape?' he asks her.

'Why?'

'Yeah,' he says. 'Why?'

'You ask the weirdest questions.'

'I don't understand,' Paul says. 'What's weird about it?'

'Well, we've been kidnapped. Why wouldn't we try to escape?'

He smiles. 'That's what I'm asking you.'

'No, you're asking why we *would* try to escape.'

'Well?'

Thea frowns. 'I think it's the logical thing to do. Anyone who's trapped tries to escape. It's a natural reaction.'

'What have you got to go back to?' he asks.

Thea thinks about the old people's home: the banana purée, *Countdown* and diarrhoea. Then she thinks about the sweaty, smelly arcade and the elderly out-of-season tourists sitting at the one-armed bandits all day, waiting until it's their turn to go in an old people's home just like the one she works in, but not even near the seaside. She thinks of the arcade game she's just completed, and the one she was planning to start. She thinks of some friends she rarely sees, and the local film club she hasn't attended for over six months. She thinks of the aerobics class she went to only once, and the boyfriend who dumped her three months ago. She thinks of evenings alone with freezer food that she has to eat on the day she buys it because she has no freezer. She thinks about her favourite TV programmes, less cool than the others': *Newsnight*; *Modern Times*; *Late Review*. She thinks of her foster mother, dying of cancer, and her real mother who she hasn't spoken to in ten years.

'Loads,' she says defensively.

She can hear voices through the pipes. Everyone's talking about university.

'Shall we go through?' Paul asks.

'Sure. I'll just put some food together for the others.'

'OK. I'll see you in there,' he says.

Thea decides that a salad would be good; all this fresh stuff's going to go off soon. She boils some rice while she sets out a plate of cold meat. Then she makes a salad from the stuff in the fridge. It turns out well: spinach, lettuce, green beans, olives, little bits of celery, radishes, tomatoes, cucumber and onion. In a separate bowl, she mixes tuna, sweetcorn, onion, cucumber, diced tinned tomatoes and the rice. Then she butters the last of the fresh, crusty bread and arranges all this on a tray. Then she finds six plates and six forks.

All the while she's been listening to the conversation through the pipes. The others seem to be talking about some pretty sensible stuff now. The education thing has taken off as a topic. Now they're talking about their degrees. And it's funny, but from what they're saying, it seems that they all got Firsts. Thea finds the candles, then picks up the tray and takes it through to the sitting room. They're still talking.

'Cool,' says Bryn, seeing all the food.

'Yum,' says Emily. 'Cheers for doing this, Thea.'

'That's fine,' Thea replies. 'Help yourselves.'

They all do. She lights the candles herself, then switches off the light.

'I got a First as well,' she says.

'What was yours in?' asks Emily.

'Film Studies,' says Thea. 'What about everyone else?'

'Maths,' says Jamie. 'But you all knew that already.'

'Art,' says Emily.

'Art,' says Paul.

'English and Philosophy,' says Anne.

'What about you, Bryn?' asks Jamie.

He looks uncomfortable. 'Chemistry,' he says.

Thea can't imagine that this is true, or that he got a First, but she says nothing. Maybe it is true, but he certainly never mentioned it to her. In fact, from what he said to her, the highest educational qualification he's got is a BTEC.

'So we all got Firsts,' muses Thea. 'Any MAs?'

'Yeah,' says Paul.

'You've got an MA?'

'MSc actually,' he corrects.

'What in?'

'Computer Programming,' he says. 'Why?'

She doesn't say anything, but she can see a pattern emerging. She wonders why Jamie didn't spot this connection in his research earlier on.

'No one else with an MA?' Thea asks.

No one says anything.

'Why do you think it matters?' asks Jamie.

'We really are bright young things,' says Paul.

'Yeah,' agrees Thea. 'We are exactly what our kidnapper advertised for.'

'Which means?' says Bryn, through a mouthful of tuna salad.

'Maybe we weren't chosen for the reason we thought,' says Thea.

'What, revenge?' asks Emily.

'Or whatever,' says Anne.

'Mmm,' says Jamie. 'Interesting.'

'Are there any clues in the *house* as to why we're here?' asks Emily.

Everyone looks uncertain.

'All the survival food has to mean something,' says Anne.

'Yeah,' says Emily. 'It's like someone else's desert island fantasy.'

'All that Spam,' says Paul.

'Yuck,' says Thea.

'All that horrible lemonade,' says Anne.

'It could be worse,' says Jamie. 'There could be no food or drink.'

'At least there's lots of wine,' says Emily.

'It's as if the person who brought us here wants us to have a nice time,' says Paul.

'Yeah, maybe we won a holiday and didn't realise,' says Bryn sarcastically.

'Maybe we're in space,' suggests Anne.

'Nothing bad's happened yet,' says Emily, ignoring Anne. 'Not really bad.'

'Merely keeping us alive isn't like giving us a holiday,' Thea points out.

'There are all the challenges,' says Paul.

'What challenges?' asks Thea.

'The electricity, the logs, all that stuff,' he replies.

'That's true,' says Emily.

'Maybe the biggest challenge is how to escape,' says Jamie.

'Maybe someone wants to see how fast we do it,' says Paul.

'Yeah,' says Anne really slowly. 'Like a game.'

Something happens in the room. The word *game* suddenly doesn't seem fun; it seems scary. It's like when you have children singing in horror film soundtracks.

'We still need clues,' says Jamie.

'Yeah, Scooby,' laughs Paul.

Jamie gives him a look.

'Are there any really obvious things we haven't noticed?' asks Emily.

Everyone thinks.

'I can think of something,' says Paul.

'What?' says Jamie.

'Well, not something we haven't noticed, but something we haven't investigated.'

'What?' prompts Emily.

'That little attic room,' he says.

'It was locked, though,' says Thea.

'Well, we'll unlock it then,' says Paul.

'Let's go,' says Jamie.

Everyone gets up.

'God, we are *so* the Red Hand Gang,' says Emily.

Chapter Sixteen

It's a bit easier to see everything now the lights work, although the one at the top of the house isn't very bright.

'It's well dingy up here,' says Bryn.

'Scary,' adds Emily.

There's some giggling going on up above them.

Everyone's going up the thin attic staircase in single file. Bryn deliberately stayed back, and it looks as if Emily's done the same. The others seem excited.

Bryn's never been that thrilled by this sort of thing. He'd be interested only if it was something that mattered, like breaking and entering for real. It's not that he's not interested in sussing out why they're really here, but he just doesn't feel like one of the gang. He still feels like they're all little kids playing together, and he's from the only DSS family in the neighbourhood.

Just as he's thinking this, Emily tickles him and makes some sort of ghost noise.

'You're quiet,' she whispers to him.

'Mmm.'

'Are you scared?'

'No,' he says. 'Don't be stupid.'

Jamie's leading the expedition party, and they've already reached the top.

'How are we going to get in?' asks Thea.

'Got any plastic explosives?' asks Paul.

'Don't start,' says Thea. 'Seriously. Any ideas?'

'We could kick it in,' suggests Jamie.

Someone laughs.

'I could pick it,' offers Bryn. 'I'm good with locks.'

'Really?' says Jamie.

'Cool,' says Paul.

'Up you go, then,' says Emily.

As Bryn walks to the top of the stairs, he tries to remember if he has actually picked a real lock before. He thinks not. But regardless of this lack of knowledge, he's still offered to do it. He's an expert, right? No. But the reason he has claimed to be an expert lock-picker is because as far as the crew in Southend is concerned, he *is* an expert lock-picker. And it's just out of habit that he's opened his big mouth here.

The first time Bryn picked a lock, the door was actually unlocked at the time. No one knew this, not even Bryn. It was him, Tank, Gilbert and some bloke from Manchester called Craig, and they were trying to get into Gilbert's house after he'd locked himself out one Friday night. They hadn't even tried the door handle; Gilbert had been moaning all night that he'd lost his keys, so they'd just assumed it would be locked. Bryn had seen something on TV the night before in which someone picked a lock, and it was so cool that he fantasised that with a hairpin, or possibly a safety pin, and a bit of a wiggle, he could get in anywhere. And that night at Gilbert's was his chance to prove it.

It's hard to describe what goes through your mind when you actually believe you can do something you in fact can't do. Bryn's experienced the feeling several times, particularly when attempting any martial arts moves (too many Cynthia Rothrock and Bruce Lee films), intravenous drug use (*Trainspotting*) and tightrope walking (the circus on TV at Christmas). Each of these miscalculated attempts has left Bryn with a scar somewhere on his body, and put together have resulted in four hospital admissions, thirty-one stitches and a broken leg.

The problem is that the people who are actually experts always make whatever it is look so easy, and so you feel that all you have to do is attempt what they have done with the same I've-done-this-a-million-times-before attitude, the same smug expression and an identical air of expertise. That night at Gilbert's, Bryn had assumed exactly the right look and attitude, cool as a cucumber, and claimed he'd need something like a hairpin to do the job properly. Tank and Gilbert were both gobsmacked that Bryn had any idea how to do this, and they both helpfully scanned the alley next to the house for something similar. They managed to find a grubby yellow pipe-cleaner, which Bryn examined for a good minute and a half before proclaiming that, 'This might just do the trick.' After a few seconds of wiggling it around in the lock, he thought he heard a click. He tried the door handle, and the fucking thing opened! Gilbert was really grateful, and Tank thought it was the coolest thing ever. He told Bryn he hadn't known that he had those sorts of skills, and that some of his mates would be able to make use of them in some little plans they had brewing.

It was at that moment that Bryn realised he'd dropped the pipe-cleaner before he even started trying to pick the lock, and he was just so fucked (on about ten New Yorkers) that he hadn't realised he wasn't actually picking the lock at all. Gilbert and Tank never found out, of course, and after that it didn't take long for everyone in the pub to hear about Bryn's new skill. He got invited along on a couple of break and enters, the theory being that there'd be no actual breaking involved if Bryn picked the lock of whatever warehouse, factory or house whoever it was wanted to enter.

He felt like the fucking girl in Rumplestiltskin, required to keep turning straw into gold when he hadn't even done it for real in the first place. And there was no funny little bloke in a funny little hat to help him. He just had to blag it.

The first couple of times he made something up about the lock being the wrong type, and threw in a bit of made-up technical jargon to explain why. Then, before the biggest break-in, when one of the blokes had helpfully got the spec on the kind of lock used on the door, Bryn deliberately cut his hand on a broken pint glass so he could claim that the relevant tendon wasn't working properly. Each time he didn't pick a lock, his crew (or whichever crew he was supposedly helping out) would find an alternative way of getting in, usually by smashing a window. But because Bryn's descriptions of unpickable locks and strange security deterrents were so convincing, he ended up with even more of a reputation for being an expert lock-picker, without ever having picked any locks.

So that's why he's offered his services now. It's just habit. Trouble is, no one here is on drugs, and when he fucks it up, it'll be really obvious that he's fucked it up. At least when there are drugs involved, you can improvise a bit. And there's no way he can blag any technical bullshit with this lot. They're all boffins. It would be all right if it was just Emily here with him, he reckons. She's not really a boffin like the others. Of course, he'd most like to be here alone with Thea, although she's not talking to him any more. He'd probably tell her the truth about not being able to pick the lock. Or maybe not. Anyway, it's not very relaxing having all of them standing here looking at him like this. With all this pressure on him, and sweat starting to trickle down the back of his neck, he makes his way up to the door.

The first thing he does is fiddle with the handle.

Then he gets on his knees and puts his eye to the keyhole.

'Hmm,' he says. 'Difficult one, this.'

'What is it?' asks Jamie, bending down to help examine the lock.

'Has anyone got a hairpin?' asks Bryn.

This is something he's learnt. No one ever has a hairpin. And when no one has a hairpin, you can just tell them that it's a shame, but this type of lock really requires the precision of a hairpin.

'I've got one,' says Anne, pulling one out of her hair.

Bryn takes it from her and immediately drops it.

'Bollocks,' he says. 'I've lost it.'

Everyone looks at him.

'I can't do it without one,' he says.

'Here, then,' says Anne. 'Have another one.'

As she reaches up to her hair, he notices for the first time that she's wearing them in little criss-crosses. The first hairpin came from the first criss-cross; the second is also coming from the first criss-cross, which now isn't strictly a criss-cross any more. Bryn panics when he realises that since she's got one whole criss-cross left on the other side of her head, and one hairpin in her hand, he's got three more hairpins to lose. Reluctantly he takes the one she offers him, examines it for a few moments and then gets on his knees in front of the lock.

'Can you really do this?' asks Thea.

'Should be able to,' he says. 'Unless the lock's too stiff.'

'Too stiff?' says Paul.

'Yeah. If it's too stiff, the hairpin won't be strong enough.'

'I see,' says Paul. There's a laugh in his voice somewhere.

Bryn wiggles the hairpin around for about three or four minutes.

'Is it working?' asks Anne.

'Shhh,' says Emily. 'You'll put him off.'

Eventually, Bryn gets up. His legs hurt from kneeling.

'This is going to take a while,' he says. 'Shall I let you know when I've done it?'

There's a noise from inside the room. It's a tapping sound.

'Hello?' calls Jamie. 'Is there anyone in there?'

Emily laughs nervously. 'Like there'd be anyone in there, dummy.'

Bryn looks through the key-hole and sees nothing. There are no more sounds.

'It was probably a bat,' says Paul. 'You get bats in attics.'

'Euuugh,' says Thea. 'Can we go now?'

'It might have been birds on the roof,' suggests Anne. 'You know, if there's a nest.'

'Whatever,' says Thea. 'Shall we go back down?'

Bryn's pleased he doesn't have to pretend to pick the lock any more.

Chapter Seventeen

'Truth or Dare,' says Emily, once everyone's back in the sitting room.

No one seems to feel adventurous anymore.

'You what?' says Bryn.

'Is that the game where you have to tell the truth?' asks Thea.

'Yeah,' says Emily. 'Or take a dare.'

Emily's getting excited. Truth or Dare is her favourite game. It reminds her of teenage sleepovers, storms, new relationships, group holidays.

Jamie and Bryn have come via the kitchen store, so now there's coal on the fire. It's going to get very hot. There's wine, cigarettes, glasses, ashtrays (well, saucers) in the room. Everything's sorted. Emily's back on the sofa with Bryn, facing Thea and Jamie on the other sofa. Paul and Anne are both sitting on the floor; Anne's right in front of the fire, warming her hands, and Paul's sprawled next to Emily's sofa, propped up on one elbow, looking as if he might fall asleep.

'How do you play it?' asks Thea.

'Haven't you played before?' asks Emily.

'No. Well, maybe when I was in Isreal. I can't remember.'

'You went to Israel?' asks Bryn.

'Yeah. On a Kibbutz.'

'My mate did that,' he says.

Everyone waits for the story, but there doesn't seem to be one.

'Right,' says Emily. 'What happens is that someone goes first, say for example it was me. So then I choose the person who I want to ask, say for example Anne, and then she has to choose either truth or dare. If she chooses truth, then I ask her a question to which she has to give an honest answer. If she chooses dare, then I have to come up with a dare for her to do. Then it's her turn to choose the person she wants to ask, and they choose truth or dare, and so on. That's it.'

'What if the person doesn't want to answer the question?' says Jamie.

'They have to,' says Emily.

'What if they refuse, though?' says Thea.

'Then they have to take a dare,' says Emily. 'And if they pick truth and then lie – Paul, I hope you're paying attention to this bit – then they have to do the forfeit.'

'Forfeit? says Jamie. 'That sounds ominous.'

'Oh, it is,' says Emily. 'We'll choose it now. I think it should be to run around the island five times – naked.'

'Cool,' says Anne, giggling.

'You're not serious?' says Jamie. 'It's dark out there. Someone could fall.'

'We'd better tell the truth then,' says Paul, smiling.

'Are we all agreed?' asks Emily.

Everyone nods, apart from Thea, who's frowning.

'Can I just watch?' she says.

'No,' says Emily. 'It has to be everyone.'

'Why?'

'Well, if you watch, you'll get to hear all our secrets, but we won't get to hear any of yours. It won't be very fair.'

'Hang on,' says Bryn. 'What do you mean, secrets?'

'Duh. That's, like, the *point* of Truth or Dare,' says Emily.

'I thought the point of Truth or Dare was to get laid,' says Paul.

'That's Russian Post Office,' says Emily.

'*And* Truth or Dare,' says Anne.

'What would you know?' asks Bryn. 'It's not as if you get laid very often.'

'I still know,' she says. 'And I think I've played this more often than you.'

'So how come you haven't got laid then?' he asks.

'Because I never choose dare, silly,' she says.

'What's Russian Post Office?' asks Jamie, but no one answers.

'So, is everybody in?' asks Emily.

'Doesn't look like we have much choice,' grumbles Thea.

Jamie looks like he's going to take this very seriously.

Paul sits up and crosses his legs. Anne turns away from the fire to face everyone.

Emily's sitting forward, her elbows on her knees.

'Right, who's going first?' she says.

'You should, since you know how to play,' says Jamie.

'OK. Then I pick Paul.'

Paul tips his head back and smiles up at her. 'Fire away,' he says.

'All right. Do you want to fuck Anne?'

'Emily!' says Anne. 'You can't ask that.'

'Why not?'

'You never ask those questions first in Truth or Dare.'

'Hang on, what do you mean, *those* questions?' asks Thea.

'Never mind,' says Emily.

Anne's right. Sexual questions should be introduced slowly, later in the game.

'Do I have to answer?' asks Paul.

'No,' says Anne, picking fluff off the rug.

'I reckon Paul should start, then,' says Jamie, lighting a cigarette. Emily gives him a saucer from her ashtray pile. 'Cheers,' he says, balancing it on the edge of the sofa.

'Right,' says Paul. 'Emily, then.'

Emily smiles. 'Moi?'

'Truth or dare?'

'Truth.'

He thinks for a moment. 'Have you ever considered suicide?'

'Cheerful,' says Bryn.

'Yeah, what kind of question is that?' asks Thea. 'I thought this was supposed to be fun. I'd rather answer a sexual question that that.'

'You don't have to answer,' Jamie says to Emily.

'It's all right,' says Emily. 'We can't keep vetoing questions.'

She doesn't mind, she's just thinking about how to answer.

'I heard a story about this guy,' starts Anne, distractedly making a little pile of her bits of fluff. 'It was on TV. He was depressed, so he decided to kill himself. When he got home from work he took a load of painkillers and sleeping pills and went to bed. Four hours later he woke up, not dead. So then he decided to cut his wrists, so he ran a bath and lay in it, got a razor and slit both his wrists. But that didn't seem to be working either, so he tried to electrocute himself by dropping the toaster in the bath. When none of that worked, he called an ambulance and went to casualty.'

'I think I know that bloke,' says Bryn.

'You would,' comments Paul.

'Emily?' says Thea. 'Are you all right?'

'Yeah, I'm just thinking,' she says.

'Don't you know whether you've ever considered suicide?' asks Anne.

'Anne!' says Jamie.

'Sorry,' she says. 'But this game is a bit slow.'

'Yes, I have considered it,' Emily says eventually.

'Have you ever actually tried to kill yourself?' asks Paul.

'Now that would be another question,' says Emily. 'But yes, since you ask.'

'Gosh,' says Jamie. 'Why?'

'You know,' says Emily dismissively. 'Life was getting me down. I was a teenager.'

'Because you were a *teenager?*' says Jamie, shocked. 'I was a teenager, but I never . . .'

'Yes, well,' says Emily. 'It was just one of those things.'

Jamie looks like he could never understand this. He puts out his cigarette.

'I want to live forever,' says Paul. 'But I wouldn't mind dying now.'

Thea laughs. 'Is that some sort of dada statement?' she asks.

'It is now,' says Paul.

'I'd rather die now than live forever,' says Thea.

'Why?' says Emily, looking aghast. 'Wouldn't you want to live forever?'

'No,' says Thea. 'It would be awful. Give us a fag, Jamie.'

Jamie gives her one from the packet of Silk Cut they now seem to be sharing.

'Yeah, have you never seen *Highlander?*' asks Bryn. 'Fucked up, man.'

'That's a good point,' says Jamie. 'You wouldn't want to see everyone you loved die.'

'Unless they were immortal as well,' says Emily, pouring wine.

'If everyone was immortal that would be all right,' says Jamie. 'That would be cool.'

'It would be cool anyway,' says Paul. 'I'm planning to download my thoughts into some other place just before I die, if they've developed the technology in time, that is.'

'Be a bit of a fucker if they hadn't,' says Emily. 'Or if they developed it just after you died.' She laughs. 'How gutted would you be?'

'He wouldn't be gutted if he was dead,' Anne points out.

'What would you do?' Paul asks Anne.

'What would I do if what?' she asks.

'If you had to choose whether to die now or live forever?'

'Either of those would be OK,' she says.

'Don't be stupid,' says Emily. 'Both would suck. I thought we just said that.'

'No,' corrects Anne. 'What we have now sucks. I think anyone with half a brain would be desperate to either die now or live forever. That's why I understand people killing themselves. It's going to happen eventually, so why wait? That's the most fucked up thing about life. You know it's going to end. It *has* to end, but you never know when it's going to be. You could be knocked down by a car on the way to school age twelve, or you could live to be a hundred. You never know when your time's going to be up. *That* is what sucks. I never really plan what I'm doing tomorrow or the next day, because I know that there might not be a tomorrow or a next day. My house could catch fire while I'm asleep, or an axe-murderer could break in, or I could just have one of those twenty-something cot deaths. So if you knew you were going to live forever, life would be a whole load more fun, because you wouldn't be waiting for it to end all the time. At the moment, life's like sitting down to watch the only copy of a great film on a dodgy projector, not knowing if the projector's going to break halfway through. I'd kill myself if I had the guts, just to take the element of chance out of it. I mean, if you weren't sure you could watch the film all the way through, you wouldn't watch it, would you? You wouldn't want to risk being disappointed.'

People seem surprised at her outburst.

'I think living forever would rule,' says Bryn.

'We wouldn't be worried about being here then, would we?' says Paul.

'You're not worried now,' Thea reminds him.

'No, there is that,' he concedes. 'Anyway, whose turn is it?'

'Mine,' says Emily. 'I choose Anne.'

'Me?' says Anne.

'Yeah. Truth or dare.'

'Truth,' she says.

'All right. If you had to be stuck on a desert island—'

Everyone groans.

'Seriously,' she says. 'If you had to be stuck on a desert island with one other person, who would you choose?'

'I'm already stuck on a desert island with five other people,' Anne points out.

'Narrow it down to one person,' says Jamie.

She sighs. 'Does it have to be one of you lot?'

'No,' says Emily. 'Anyone in the world. Who would you choose?'

'Um, I'd probably choose to be by myself,' she says, after a few moments' thought.

'You wouldn't *really*, though,' says Emily. 'Would you?'

Anne thinks for a minute. 'Maybe,' she says. 'Well, I guess that would have been my answer before I came here. But maybe . . . Now I know what it's like, I probably wouldn't want to be left here alone. And if I had to pick one person, it probably would be one of you lot, since I don't have any other friends. Probably Paul, Jamie or Emily. No offence Bryn and Thea, but neither of you like me, so I wouldn't choose you.'

'I like you,' says Bryn.

Thea looks uncomfortable, but says nothing.

'You don't have any other friends?' says Jamie. 'Apart from us?'

'No,' says Anne. 'I like being by myself.'

'Gosh,' says Jamie.

'It's my choice,' says Anne. 'I like it.'

'What's special about us?' asks Jamie.

'Nothing. I'm just stuck with you.'

'So are you going to pick one person?' says Emily.

'Like I said – either you, Paul or Jamie.'

'You have to choose one,' says Emily.

'Um ... you, then,' says Anne quickly.

'Cool,' says Emily. 'Thanks.' She wonders if that's really the truth, but doesn't want to challenge it.

It's Anne's turn. 'I pick ... um ...'

'Come on,' says Emily.

'All right. Bryn, then. Truth or dare?'

'Dare,' says Bryn.

'Dare,' repeats Anne. 'Are you sure?'

'Yeah.'

'All right. Um ...'

'Can't you think of one?' asks Emily.

'Hang on,' says Anne. 'All right, Bryn. You have to sing a Wham! song of your choice, in the style of an old woman on her deathbed.'

'What?' he says.

The others laugh.

'That's a cool one,' says Emily.

'Can't I have truth?' says Bryn.

'Nope. You have to do it now,' says Anne.

'And you have to stand up to do it,' says Emily.

'What, if he's an old woman on her deathbed?' says Thea.

'All right, then,' says Emily, getting up. 'You can lie on the sofa and do it.'

Bryn reclines on the sofa. 'Bollocks,' he says. 'Any Wham! song?'

'Yeah,' says Anne.

He thinks for a minute, looks a bit uncomfortable, then he starts.

'Da, da, da ...' he croaks really slowly. 'Woah woah yeah,' Emily recognises it as 'Freedom'. She starts giggling. So does Anne.

By the time he reaches the chorus, everyone's howling with laughter.

'Aren't you dead yet?' asks Thea.

'Girl all I want right now is—'

'Get him off,' shouts Emily through cupped hands.

Anne throws some carpet fluff at him.

He looks up. 'Have I done enough yet?' he asks in his normal voice.

'No,' says Paul. 'I think we want to hear to the end.'

'Please say he's done enough,' says Emily. 'I can't take any more.'

'OK,' says Anne. 'That's enough.'

Bryn sits up, coughs a lot and lights a cigarette. Emily sits back down beside him.

'Bryn's turn to choose,' says Anne, getting up and walking to the door.

'Where are you going?' demands Emily.

'Nowhere,' says Anne defensively, leaving the room.

'I pick Paul,' says Bryn.

'Truth,' says Paul.

'All right,' says Bryn. 'If you could choose between being stupid and happy, or clever and miserable, which would you choose?'

'That is *such* a cool question,' says Emily.

'Cheers,' he says. 'I heard it on TV once.'

'Hmm,' says Paul. 'Stupid and happy, I suppose.'

'I'd much rather be stupid and happy too,' says Emily. 'What about everyone else?'

'Stupid and happy,' says Thea.

'I'm not sure,' says Jamie. 'It's basically the two choices you have in life anyway, isn't it?' He looks thoughtful. 'Not that they are choices, strictly, but everyone falls into one category or the other.'

'Are you saying being clever makes you unhappy?' says Thea.

'Yeah,' he says. 'It does, if you think about it.'

'I suppose the more you know, the more there is to fear,' says Thea.

'Yeah,' says Emily. 'You understand how fucked up the world is.'

Anne returns with a big glass of strawberry milkshake.

'But all stupid people aren't happy,' Thea points out.

'Yeah,' says Paul. 'Look at the guests on Jerry Springer.'

'Mmm,' says Emily. 'But it wouldn't take much to make those people happy.'

'That's true,' says Paul. 'You could just give them all drugs and they'd be happy.'

'And stupid,' says Jamie.

'Maybe that's why people take drugs,' says Thea.

'What, to make them happy and stupid?' asks Emily.

'That's *exactly* why people take drugs,' says Bryn. 'And I should know.'

A couple of people nod. This makes sense.

'So you reckon it would be hard to make a clever person happy?' asks Paul.

'Yeah,' says Jamie.

'Exactly,' says Emily. 'Unless you count something like Prozac, but then that's the happy and stupid drug thing again.'

'That must be why we're all so unhappy then,' jokes Anne.

'What would make you happy?' Thea asks Paul.

'Being here,' he says enigmatically, in a kind of mumble.

'Anyway,' says Jamie, lighting another cigarette. 'It's your turn.'

'Oh, yeah,' says Paul. 'Bryn.'

'Truth,' says Bryn. 'I'm not going to make that mistake again.'

'What's the best drug you've ever done?' Paul asks.

'Crack,' says Bryn, without hesitation. 'Completely.'

'You've done crack?' says Emily.

'Sure,' he says. 'Best fucking buzz in the world. Totally.'

'Don't you get addicted to it really easily?' asks Jamie.

'Yeah,' says Bryn. 'I was lucky not to get too sucked in.'

'What happened?' asks Thea.

'What was it like?' asks Emily.

'It was amazing. The best feeling in the world.'

'Better than an orgasm?' says Jamie.

'Yeah, totally.'

'Better than winning the Lottery?' asks Emily.

'Probably,' he says. 'Although a crack-head would get a good feeling winning the Lottery, because he'd know he could spend all the money on rocks.' He licks his lips. 'It's hard to know how to describe what it's really like. It's completely intense, but not anything like heroin. It's a lot more like charlie, obviously, because it's the cocaine base that you're smoking anyway.'

'What?' says Jamie.

'Cocaine that you buy is actually cocaine hydrochloride,' explains Bryn. 'Plus whatever other shit the dealer cuts it with, and his dealer cuts it with, and his dealer, and so on. You can make a chemical reaction take place using ammonia or bicarb or whatever, where you make the hydrochloride part separate off and burn away along with all the other crap. You're left with rocks made of pure cocaine.'

'And that's all crack is?' says Jamie.

'Yeah,' says Bryn. 'So the buzz is kind of similar. But you don't have to wait for it, it's just completely instant. It makes you feel totally relaxed – like, the happiness and confidence of charlie without the nervousness and anxiety. You get this massive smile on your face. It's like that feeling you get when you sneeze, but it doesn't last for just one second. Mind you, it's not as rushy as a sneeze, it's more mellow, like just after you've come or something. In fact . . . you know when you laugh so hard that you think you're going to wet yourself? Well, it's just like that, but without the actual laughing or the pain in your stomach. It's like being really thirsty and then drinking a huge glass of Coca Cola, or having a dump when you've been waiting for ages to get into the loo, or sitting down after you've been on your feet all day, or having a bag of chips by the seaside, or a cream cake after you've been on a diet for ages. Just pure pleasure.'

'Sounds amazing,' says Paul.

'Totally,' says Emily.

'Why didn't you become addicted?' says Jamie.

'Oh, I did,' says Bryn. 'Imagine feeling like I just described. You'd get addicted to it after just one puff. But I didn't make it into what you'd call a habit, because I was lucky, and circumstances got in the way.'

'How?' asks Emily.

'I was hanging around with these two blokes in Westcliff at the time. They were brothers. One of them was really into the whole reggae scene, like I was at the time. The other one was a coke dealer, a real hardcore bloke. They had five other brothers – no sisters – and all of them were in prison. My mate, Winston, he was pretty straight compared to the rest of them. His brother Steve was a nutter, and had just got out of prison. I'd never met him before, but I'd heard all about him. Anyway, we all went through a bit of a charlie phase, which was pretty easy with Steve being a dealer. We used to sit around Steve's house before going out on a Friday night and just really cane it, doing line after line, while Steve saw all his Friday night customers. Then after that we'd usually go out to this club in Chelmsford that Steve's mate owned. Steve always kept a bottle of ammonia in the cupboard for what he called 'special occasions', although at first I didn't know what that meant.

'We were round his all the time, like I say, and as well as all the customers, he had a couple of flatmates and some friends who used to hang around there as well. It was a really nice little scene – it wasn't seedy or anything. It was pretty glamorous, in fact. We used to get really nice girls hanging about, although Steve always refused to sell them charlie. I don't know why, he just always refused to sell to women. Anyway, one time he got his bottle of ammonia out and started making rocks. I asked what he was doing and he invited me upstairs and we had a smoke together. Then later, Winston came up and joined in. It was our first time doing it. Steve always wanted to keep it a secret between us three, and we only really smoked with him at first.'

'Wow,' says Emily. 'So then what happened?'

Bryn shifts on the sofa. 'I'd been doing it for two weeks straight, and I could tell it was fucking with my head. I'd always just sold weed, but I was contemplating going into business sorting people out with charlie. There was a lot of money in it, and as I seemed to have all these contacts through Steve, it looked like it could be a good business venture. When I say contacts, though, I don't really mean blokes I could do business with, I just mean blokes who wouldn't shoot me for doing a bit of business on their patch. That whole scene is fucking mental, but I understood it pretty well, and I thought I wouldn't get into any trouble. So I'd already put in an order with Steve for half an ounce of charlie, which is a lot, and I was waiting for him to sort it out for me. But when he was on his way to see his man in London, him and Winston got picked up driving through Dagenham. When the police searched the car they found a load of charlie, plus some rocks that Steve had been dealing on the side, plus three firearms. They both got sent down.'

'What did you do?' asks Emily.

'Nothing. Everyone knew I was mates with Winston and Steve, and for a while no one would even sell me any weed because they were sure the police were on to me as well and were just waiting to pick me up. When the police get hold of someone like me, they're always trying to find the next bloke up in the chain. Since everyone thought I was going to get busted any minute, no one was prepared to be the next bloke up. I couldn't score any drugs for weeks. As far as charlie went, I didn't know any of the local blokes well enough to go to them direct for it. And in my heart I knew I wasn't going to sell any of it. I knew I would have just rocked it all up and then smoked it myself. So in the end, it wasn't my conscience that stopped me, or my common sense, just simple lack of availability.'

'You were so lucky,' says Thea. 'You could be an addict right now.'

'I know,' says Bryn. 'I'd probably be dead.'

'Were you actually a drug dealer, then?' says Jamie.

'Yeah, mate,' says Bryn. 'Although it's not such a big deal in Essex.'

'Why?'

'Everyone's a dealer there.'

'But it was just weed?' says Emily.

'Yeah. I hardly sold solid at all.'

'Why not?' asks Emily.

'I was on the reggae scene,' says Bryn, as if that explained it.

Emily stretches and pours another glass of wine.

'Looks like it's your turn then,' she says to Bryn.

'Right,' he says. 'Emily.'

'Truth,' she says.

'What's your biggest regret?'

'My biggest regret?' She thinks for a moment. 'I'm not sure I have any regrets.'

'Everyone says that,' says Paul. 'But it's always a lie.'

'You must have something,' says Jamie.

'Everyone regrets something,' agrees Thea.

'I don't,' says Anne.

'I'm not sure I do, either,' says Emily. 'Except . . .'

'What?' Jamie virtually pounces on her.

'It's a bit depressing,' she says.

Chapter Eighteen

Paul's on to his third glass of wine. Emily's telling some story about sleeping with a guy on holiday when she was sixteen, and some AIDS scare as a result of it. She doesn't seem thrilled to be talking about it, and quickly moves on.

'Anyway, it's my turn now,' she says, 'and I pick Thea.'

'Oh,' says Thea. 'Are you sure? I don't really want to—'

'You're in now, girl,' says Emily. 'Truth or dare?'

'Truth, I guess,' says Thea, looking completely uncertain.

'Who is the love of your life?' Emily asks.

'The love of my life?'

'Yeah. The One.'

'Have we just fallen into one of those city girl novels?' asks Thea.

'What?' says Emily.

'You know, all that crap about *The One*.'

'What's a city girl novel?' asks Jamie.

'You know,' says Anne. 'Bridget Jones.'

'Load of shit,' declares Paul. 'I hate all that stuff.'

'Most people do have a love of their life by the time they're in their twenties,' says Emily. 'They don't just make up all that stuff. It's pretty true to life.'

'Is it?' says Jamie. 'I haven't ever been in love. Oh, except once when I was eight.'

'That *so* doesn't count,' says Emily.

'I've been in love,' says Anne. 'But only with characters in plays.'

'OK, that doesn't count either.'

Emily looks at Bryn. He shrugs and shakes his head.

She looks at Paul. 'You?'

'No way,' he says. 'I don't even know what love is.'

'How do you know you don't know what love is?' says Jamie.

'All my girlfriends have told me. It's my biggest failing, apparently.'

'So who's the love of your life?' Anne asks Emily.

'I haven't got one either,' she says. 'But I just thought I was weird.'

'See,' says Thea. 'All that stuff's a load of shit.'

'So there's no big romance in your past?' says Emily.

'Nope,' says Thea

'Nothing we should know about?'

'No. A couple of blokes who didn't mean anything. One guy I thought I was in love with who turned out to be a twat. That's it.'

'God, you're boring,' says Paul. But he smiles, so she knows he doesn't mean it.

'Is it my turn to choose?' Thea asks.

'Yeah,' says Emily.

'Jamie. Truth or dare?'

'Truth,' says Jamie.

'Do you like it here?' asks Thea.

'Is that your question?' asks Jamie.

'Yeah. Do you like it here?'

'Yes. I think I do,' he says.

'Seriously?' says Thea.

'Yeah. It's quite nice. I've never been part of a group before.'

'He's got a point,' says Emily, smiling. 'It is quite nice to be in a gang like this.'

'It's like *Dawson's Creek*,' says Anne, giggling. 'Except there's no creek.'

The atmosphere in the room is changing. It's incredibly warm, and everyone's a bit drunk — except for Anne presumably, since she isn't drinking at all. The fear thing seems to have gone, or if it's still here it's that sexy, kids'-ghost-story way. It's McFear with fries, and it's even making Paul tingle.

'Anne,' says Jamie. 'Truth or dare?'

'Truth,' she says.

'Are you really a virgin?' he asks.

'Of course,' she says.

'For real?' says Thea.

'Yes. *God*. It's not that hard to believe, is it?'

'Anne,' says Emily, 'you're a babe.'

'She's right,' says Bryn.

Jamie nods. 'That's why we find it so hard to believe.'

'Well, it's true,' she says, looking flattered. 'Anyway. My turn.'

'Who's it going to be?' asks Jamie.

'Emily,' she says. 'Truth or dare?'

'Truth,' says Emily.

'OK,' says Anne. 'Do you masturbate, and if so, how often?'

This is the kind of question Paul likes. He's interested again now. Truth or Dare is supposed to really put people on the spot, not just encourage a group therapy session. And Emily strikes Paul as exactly the kind of girl who's at it all the time, but who never ever admits it.

'Do you?' Emily says back to Anne.

'She asked you,' says Paul.

'Um . . .' Emily goes a bit pink. 'Yeah.'

'How often?' asks Anne.

She cringes. 'Um, about once a week if I haven't got a boyfriend.'

'What if you have?'

'What? Got a boyfriend? I make him do it.'

'Is it the same?' asks Anne. 'I mean, with someone else doing it?'

'No,' says Emily. 'It's different. If they're good at it, it's better. If they're shit, then it's much much worse and you usually end up having to do it yourself anyway.'

'Do you masturbate?' Jamie asks Anne.

'Of course,' she says. 'Everyone does.'

'But you're a virgin,' he says.

'So?' says Anne. 'Doesn't mean I can't wank.'

'I don't masturbate,' says Thea.

'Yeah, right,' says Emily. 'Like we believe you.'

'I don't either,' says Bryn.

'You must,' says Jamie. 'I thought everyone ... I mean, all blokes ...'

'Nah. Not me,' says Bryn. 'That's what sex is for.'

'I agree,' says Thea.

'Have you ever tried it?' Emily asks Thea.

'No,' she says. 'I wouldn't know what to do.'

'You could always show her,' Paul says to Emily. 'We'll all help.'

Everyone's definitely a bit tipsy now.

Jamie doesn't seem as embarrassed as he usually appears to be.

'Yeah,' he giggles. 'We'll all help.'

'I don't think so,' says Thea, also giggling. 'But thanks for the offer.'

'You should try it some day, though,' says Anne. 'It's cool.'

'Anyway,' says Emily. 'My turn. I pick Thea.'

'Truth,' she says immediately.

'Are you sure you don't want dare?' says Emily playfully.

'No way,' she says. 'Not now I know what you'd all choose.'

'All right. How many people have you fucked?' asks Emily.

'What, how many different people?'

'Yeah. Animal, vegetable or mineral.'

'I'm going to have to add up,' says Thea. 'It's a while since I last counted.'

'Are there a lot?' asks Jamie.

'Quite a few,' says Thea. She thinks for a minute. 'Probably around seventy. Is that exact enough?'

'Seventy!' says Emily. 'Fucking hell, girl.'

'What's wrong with that?'

'I thought *I* was a slut.'

'You are,' says Paul.

'Stop it,' says Emily, hitting him on the arm. 'You're not funny.'

'How many have you slept with then?' Bryn asks Emily.

'About thirty,' she says. 'I thought that was loads.'

'Don't,' says Thea. 'You're making me feel bad.'

'Sorry,' says Emily. 'I didn't mean to. God. You've made me feel *better*.'

'Why is it a bad thing to have had sex with loads of people?' asks Jamie.

'It just is,' says Emily. 'If you're a girl.'

'According to *Cosmopolitan*, we're all freaks,' says Anne.

'Why?' says Jamie.

'We're all outside the average. I'm a virgin, and therefore frigid. They've slept with a lot of men, so they're automatically sluts. It's unattractive to be unaverage, whatever anyone says. We're freaks.' She mock-sobs. 'We'll never find husbands.'

'Is that really how it works?' asks Jamie. 'Are you all freaks?'

'Yeah. You're definitely not supposed to have slept with more than about five people by the time you're our age,' says Emily. 'Apparently men don't respect you if you're easy.'

'Five *was* the average number they said,' says Anne.

'I've slept with five people,' says Jamie. 'Does that mean I'm average?'

'No,' says Thea. 'You're a bloke. You're a freak too.'

'Yeah,' says Emily. 'Men are supposed to have slept with about twenty women by the time they're twenty-five or something.'

'That doesn't add up,' says Jamie, being mathematical.

'What?' says Emily.

'Well, if every man is supposed to have had sex with twenty women by the time they're in their mid-twenties, but all the women are supposed to have only slept with five men each, there wouldn't be enough women to go around. So that means that a huge proportion of them would have to go over the "average", at a ratio of three to one, with only one girl in every four actually sticking to the average. Which doesn't make it an average if you ask me.'

'So we're not freaks, then?' asks Emily.

'Not unless all men are as well. In which case, I don't know exactly who you would have been sleeping with at such a rate.'

'So maths does have a practical application,' says Emily.

'Whose turn is it now?' asks Jamie.

'Thea's,' says Emily. 'Go girl.'

'OK,' she says. 'Um . . . Paul.'

'Truth,' he says.

'You're all so boring,' says Emily. 'No one's choosing dare.'

'Truth,' Paul says again.

'What's the most important thing you own?' asks Thea.

'The most important thing I own?' he says.

'Yeah.'

'Thing?'

'Yeah.'

Paul thinks. What is it? Is it his computer? Paul mentally visits his flat and looks around at everything in it. There's the computer, a new Pentium III looming large in his sitting room. Apart from that, there's the pinball machine he bought for fifty quid and then customised; there's his oldest Atari, by far the most precious of all his console collection, with the original 'Space Invaders' and 'Pong' catridges; but while these are important objects, he guesses they are probably not the most important. In his mind, he returns to his computer. There's his modem, which is probably more important than the actual computer, but if he didn't have it, he'd just get another one. With things like that, it's not the object that's really important, more what the object does. There are a few books on the shelves next to his computer, they're pretty important. He's got an original first edition translation of *Seven Dada Manifestos* by Tristan Tzara. Then, all of a sudden, he realises what the most important thing he owns actually is. It's on the same shelf as his books. But should he tell the others about it?

'Come on,' says Thea. 'It can't be that hard.'

'I can't think of anything,' he says, pouring another glass of wine.

'There must be something,' says Emily.

'All right,' he says. 'It's a picture. A photograph.'

'A photograph?' says Thea. 'What of?'

'My father. He, um . . .'

'What?' says Emily.

'He died before I was born. It's no big deal or anything.'

'That is kind of a big deal,' says Emily.

'Do you want to talk about it?' says Thea.

'No,' says Paul. 'I think I want to pick who's next.'

'How did he die?' asks Anne.

'Anne!' says Emily.

'It's all right,' says Paul. 'He overdosed on heroin.'

'Shit,' says Emily. 'That's pretty fucked up.'

'I don't want to talk about it,' says Paul.

'Sure,' says Emily quickly. 'Who are you going to pick?'

'I think I'll pick . . . you,' says Paul.

'Me?' says Emily. 'All right. Um . . . Truth.'

'Who's boring now?' says Thea.

'I'm not ready for a dare yet,' she says. 'Come on. Truth.'

'Have you ever had anal sex?' he asks.

'Of course,' she says. 'Who hasn't?'

Jamie looks a bit shocked.

'Me,' says Anne. 'I haven't.'

'Not counting virgins,' says Emily.

'I haven't done it,' says Thea. 'Well, I tried it once, but it hurt.'

'Did it hurt when you did it?' Anne asks Emily.

'Yeah,' she says. 'But that's part of the fun.'

Emily draws her knees up to her chin and grins naughtily.

'Seriously?' says Jamie. 'Gosh.'

'Do you actually like it?' asks Thea.

'Yeah,' says Emily. 'It's really sexy.'

'Have you done it?' Jamie asks Bryn.

'What, fucked a girl up the arse?' he says. 'Yeah, sure.'

'Do you like it?'

'Of course. It's tighter. But you wouldn't do it with your girlfriend.'

'Why not?' asks Thea.

'It's dirty. You'd only do it on a one night stand.'

Emily looks a bit embarrassed.

'No offence,' he adds, offering her a B&H.

'Thanks,' she says, taking one.

Her ashtray is already overflowing, but then she is sharing it with Bryn.

'Does it feel different?' asks Anne.

'Yeah,' says Emily. 'It's more intense.'

'It is like that for blokes?' asks Thea.

'It's a fantasy thing,' explains Paul. 'It's not really the sensation that's different, it's more the feeling that this girl's letting you do *that*, and it probably means you can do things with her that most girls wouldn't let you do. And I guess for a lot of people that's a pretty big turn-on.'

'Oh, I did do anal once,' says Anne suddenly.

'Ha, so you're not a virgin,' says Emily. 'I knew it.'

'No, it was cyber, so I still am a virgin. Sorry.'

'Do you do cyber?' asks Paul.

'Yeah,' says Anne. 'Well, before I got bored with it.'

'What's *cyber*?' asks Thea.

'Cyber sex,' says Jamie immediately.

Paul laughs. 'You've done it too,' he says to Jamie. 'You pervert.'

'Oh yuck,' says Anne, poking the fire. 'I could have been cybering with Jamie.'

'Is *cybering* a word?' asks Emily.

'Yeah,' says Paul.

'On the net,' adds Jamie.

'You could have been cybering with me,' Paul says to Anne.

'Have you ever chatted with coolgirl?' she asks.

'Is that your login?' asks Jamie.

'One of them,' she says.

Paul shakes his head. 'Nope. Not coolgirl.'

'I never cyber as coolgirl anyway,' she says.

'Who do you cyber as?' asks Jamie.

'Abigail. Age fifteen.'

'Age fifteen?'

'Yeah. It's more fun when they think it's illegal. They feel really bad.'

'That's cruel,' says Jamie.

'Yeah. That's the point,' says Anne.

'How many times have you cybered?' asks Jamie.

'Only a couple, really,' says Anne. She thinks for a minute. 'Well, about twenty.'

Emily shrieks. 'She's as big a slut as we are,' she says.

'And still a virgin,' says Anne, smiling.

'I'm glad I didn't meet you in cyberspace,' says Jamie.

'I wish I had,' says Paul, laughing.

'Are you into all that, then?' Emily asks Paul. 'Do you like it?'

He shrugs. 'You can ask me when it's your turn.'

'It is my turn,' she says. 'So I choose you.'

'All right,' he says, smiling. 'Dare.'

'Dare?'

'That's what I said.'

'Oh, right. I've just got to think of one . . .'

'This is going to be a bad one,' says Jamie. 'I can feel it.'

While Emily thinks, Bryn gets up to put more coal on the fire. Anne gets out of his way and disappears into the kitchen, presumably for more milkshake. Paul's noticed that she never asks if anyone wants anything when she goes, she just scuttles out like a cute but determined beetle. He likes that. Thea tops up her glass with the bottle of Merlot that she's just opened, then passes the bottle around the room. It feels really late, but it must only be about ten. Paul yawns. He wonders what dare Emily's going to give him. He doesn't imagine that it will be anything to get worked up over. He never worries about dares. It's not like there's anything he won't do.

'All right, I've got one,' says Emily, once Anne's back with her milkshake.

'Well?' says Paul.

'You've got to kiss Anne for one minute.'

'What?' says Paul. Oh, shit. This isn't what he expected.

'Does that mean I won't be a virgin afterwards?' asks Anne sweetly.

'You have kissed men before, haven't you?' asks Thea.

'Um . . .' Anne pretends to think. 'No.'

'You have never kissed a man?' repeats Thea.

'No.'

'Have you ever kissed a woman?' asks Bryn.

'No.'

'Have you kissed on the Internet?' asks Thea.

'No,' says Anne. 'It's not like that.'

'So this is going to be your first kiss?' asks Emily.

'Hang on,' says Paul. 'I don't think—'

'You can't wuss out of the dare,' says Emily.

Paul desperately wants to kiss Anne. But surely not like this? And if he's going to be the lucky man who gets to give Anne her first ever kiss (imagine), he'd rather do it in private. Although she doesn't really seem to mind the idea of it now, she might feel differently afterwards.

'I'll do the forfeit,' he says quietly.

'What, rather than kiss the *babe*?' says Emily.

'Are you gay?' asks Thea.

'I'll do the forfeit,' he repeats.

Everyone gives each other looks. Anne says nothing.

'All right,' says Emily. 'You have to run around the island five times, naked.'

'Fine,' says Paul. 'I could do with some fresh air.'

'We'll all have to go outside with him,' says Emily.

'It's freezing,' says Thea.

'Don't you trust me to do it?' he says.

'We could always give him a different dare,' suggests Jamie.

'I think you should give him a different dare,' says Anne.

'Me too,' says Thea.

'But that's not the rules,' whines Emily.

'If anyone lies we'll send them outside,' says Jamie. 'How about that?'

'All right,' says Emily. She points at Paul. 'You have to show us your cock, then.'

'Is that my new dare?' asks Paul.

'Yeah,' says Emily.

'I don't want to see his cock,' says Bryn.

'I do,' says Thea.

'Get it out, get it out, get it out,' chants Emily.

'All right,' says Paul. 'Prepare yourselves.'

Chapter Nineteen

Anne's more disappointed than she thought she would be about not kissing Paul. She wonders why he'd rather have done the forfeit than kiss her. It's all very puzzling. It's probably because he doesn't want to, although after all that sexual tension between them before ... There's a chance he wanted to defend her honour, which, while not necessary, would have been incredibly sweet.

So now he's about to get his cock out.

Anne's excited. She's never seen a real penis before. She's seen loads in magazines and on porn sites on the Internet, but never in the flesh. She wonders how big it will seem, and whether the ones on the Internet were normal, or bigger than average, or what. She read somewhere that the average size of an erect penis is about six inches. That seems a bit small. She hopes it's bigger than that.

'Come on,' says Emily. 'We're waiting.'

Thea's waving her little finger around, obviously not expecting much.

In a way, Anne can't believe Paul's actually doing this, but then again, this game of Truth or Dare has become very relaxed indeed. Anne's sure she's not the only one caught up in the whole anything-could-happen feeling that's going on. Thea's calmed down a lot and seems to be — hold your breath — actually enjoying herself. Jamie's also letting his hair down, bless him, and even Paul's being a little less evasive and detached from everyone. No one seems scared any more either, which is cool.

'Paul's unbuttoning his trousers. Underneath, he's wearing boxer shorts.

'Is this some sort of strip tease?' asks Emily.

'Come on,' says Anne.

'Tell me when to open my eyes,' says Bryn.

Jamie also looks away.

'Fucking hell,' says Emily, when Paul eventually pulls it out.

'Why is it erect?' asks Thea.

'It's because he was thinking about kissing Anne,' says Emily.

'It's actually because I'm an exhibitionist,' he says, smiling.

'Are you?' says Thea.

'No,' he says. 'Can I put it away now?'

'No,' says Emily. 'I want a proper look.'

Anne can't take her eyes off it. She guesses its length at about nine inches.

'Is that big?' she asks Emily.

'I thought you looked at porn,' says Emily.

'I do, but it's not the same as real life.'

'It's big,' says Emily.

'Thank you,' says Paul.

He pulls his boxers up over it, making a kind of tent, and then does up his trousers.

'You can look again now,' Thea says to Bryn and Jamie.

'You all sounded pretty impressed,' says Jamie, jealously.

'You've either got it or you haven't,' says Paul.

'Time to move on,' says Thea. 'Who wants more wine?'

Everyone except for Anne says they do.

'Paul's turn,' says Anne.

'Jamie,' says Paul. 'Truth or Dare?'

'Truth,' says Jamie.

'Have you ever had a rape fantasy?' asks Paul.

'That's gross,' says Thea.

'What do you mean?' asks Jamie, going pink.

'Have you ever fantasised about raping someone?'

Jamie seems embarrassed. 'I, uh ...'

'It is a pretty normal fantasy,' says Emily.

'I kind of have,' says Jamie. 'I'm sure all blokes think about it sometimes.'

'We want more than *kind of*,' says Emily. 'We want details.'

'Within reason,' says Paul.

'I'm not sure I want to hear this,' says Thea.

'It was a particular person,' Jamie says. 'A celebrity.'

'You wanked about raping a celebrity?' says Anne. 'Which one?'

'Promise you won't think I'm disgusting,' he says.

'We already do,' says Paul. He sees Jamie's face. 'Joke,' he adds.

'All right. It was Princess Diana.'

'Eugggh,' says Thea.

'Before or after she died?' asks Paul.

'Before, of course. I'm not that sick.'

'Why Princess Diana?' asks Anne.

'It was something about all those clothes and gowns and tiaras and things,' says Jamie. 'And the fact that she was supposedly untouchable. The fantasy always had me working as a waiter at some function she was attending, and somehow cornering her outside by the bins. I liked thinking about pushing her up against the bins and pulling up all her long, satin skirts and petticoats—'

'She didn't wear satin skirts and petticoats,' says Emily.

'She obviously did in Jamie's fantasy,' says Thea.

'And she'd be getting all dirty and struggling ...'

'But she'd want it really, right?' says Paul.

'Yeah,' says Jamie. 'In the end. After I made her get down on her knees—'

'Was this one of your favourite wank fantasies?' interrupts Emily.

'Yeah,' says Jamie.

'I like this,' says Emily. 'Everyone's being really honest.'

'Lady Di,' says Bryn. 'Fucking hell.'

'My turn,' says Jamie.

'Who do you pick?' asks Thea.

'You,' he says. 'Truth or dare?'

'Truth,' she says.

'Right. What's the most embarrassing thing that's ever happened to you?'

'The most embarrassing thing?'

'Yeah. That's right. What is it?'

'Um ...' Thea looks like she's thinking hard. 'Oh, God.' She's obviously remembered something. 'I can't say this one.'

'You have to now,' says Emily.

'Or it's naked and around the island,' says Paul, pointing outside.

'Five times,' says Anne.

'Yeah, yeah, I get the picture,' says Thea.

Anne doesn't know too much about being drunk, but she can see that the wine is making Thea much more relaxed, and therefore much more likely to say something she will regret. Of course, Anne's more than familiar with the concept of embarrassment; it just doesn't bother her. She does embarrassing things all the time – either deliberately, or just by accident – and she never gives a fuck. One of her favourite hobbies is buying pop singles from her local 'cool' record shop. They really hate it when she gives them 911 or S Club 7 CDs to process. She enjoys telling jokes that other people don't find funny, saying inappropriate things, and singing badly when other people are listening. People hate uncomfortable silences; the moment when a conversation just stops because the people don't have anything else to say. Anne loves those moments.

'It was in Russia,' says Thea.

'This is going to be the *most* embarrassing thing, right?' says Emily.

'Yeah,' Thea says. 'But you will find it gross.'

'Cool,' says Paul. 'Carry on.'

'All right. I was twelve, and I was on a school trip to Russia.'

'You went on a school trip to Russia?' says Jamie.

'Yeah. We learnt Russian at school as well as French and German.'

'Do many schools do that?' asks Jamie.

'No,' says Thea. 'In fact, one of the funny things about the trip was that the other kids who were there at the same time as us were all from private schools. There were some boys from Marlborough and some girls from another posh fee-paying school in London. The boys were weird. They seemed to think chatting to grammar school kids like us was educational in some way. Anyway, we all spent the first half of the trip in Moscow, and then we were due to go by train to Leningrad for the second half of the trip. When I was twelve I didn't have very much confidence for various reasons, and although I wanted to hang around with the cool kids who were smoking and drinking cheap vodka in their rooms every night, I ended up going around with this girl called Gillian. She was fat and ugly and unpopular, but since she was the only person prepared to act like my best friend for the trip, I decided to stick with her. I really hated the food we got there, and being hassled by Russian kids all the time, wanting to buy our jeans – although, in truth, my jeans weren't cool enough for them to want; it was the kids who had Levi's who got all the hassle. In fact, all my clothes were completely unfashionable and everyone used to laugh at me. Anyway, so there I was with my crap friend and my unfashionable clothes, and I really wanted to go home, but my foster mother had paid loads for the trip and I was determined to enjoy it. But on the day before we were going to go to Leningrad, disaster struck.'

'What happened?' asks Jamie.

'This is so embarrassing. I've never actually told anyone this.'

'Go on,' says Emily. 'We won't laugh.'

'Oh, you will,' says Thea. 'We were all packed up to go to Leningrad on the night train. That morning, we had to get dressed, pack an overnight bag and then give our suitcases to the teachers. The teachers were really strict and said that we couldn't get anything out of our suitcases until we got to Leningrad. I don't know why all this was done so early in the day . . .'

'You probably had to check out of the hotel early,' says Emily. 'You know, they always kick you out at eleven or so if you're not booked for the next night.'

'Oh,' says Thea. 'I suppose so. Anyway, so this hotel we were staying in was about sixty stories high, and that evening I was on the ground floor, having just come back from some sight-seeing trip in the city, when I realised I wanted to go to the loo. This is totally embarrassing . . . Basically, I got that feeling that I had to, you know, shit really urgently. God, I hate talking about this. So anyway, I asked someone where there was a toilet, and they said it was on the fiftieth floor or something, so I had to go up there in the lift.'

'Wasn't there a closer loo?' asks Emily.

'No,' says Thea. 'Russia was a bit weird like that. Or at least, that's what I remember thinking. I mean, there was so much weird stuff there, from the food to the shops and everything else, that I just didn't question the fact that I'd have to travel fifty floors or so to get to a toilet. On reflection, maybe I'd misunderstood what the person said, or maybe they were even joking. Whatever. Anyway, when I got into the lift, I realised that the kids had been fucking around with it again. It was one of our favourite Moscow tricks. The lifts were so old and crap that we'd found that, say you punched in floors forty-nine, one, forty-seven, two, twenty-five, eighteen, in that order, the lift would travel to them in precisely that order. So if you wanted to get to floor eighteen, you'd have to wait while it went up and down to all these other floors first. Even I'd thought this was funny before, when we'd been messing around, but it's not so funny when you're dying for the loo and the lift just won't go to the floor you want.'

'What happened?' asks Emily.

'I shat myself,' says Thea.

'Unlucky,' says Bryn.

'Euugh,' says Paul. Emily kicks him. 'Ow,' he says instead.

'There's more to the story actually,' Thea says. 'The really embarrassing stuff's still to come. Do you want to hear?'

Everyone nods.

'All right. Well, it started, you know, *happening* in the lift. I tried so hard to stop it, but I couldn't. People were getting in and out the whole time, on all the floors the lift was stopping at on its way to the fiftieth. They were all giving me really funny looks and the lift was starting to smell. I mean, I was holding it in as much as I possibly could, but some was coming out. Then, once it was definitely coming out, it became a question of trying to keep it in my knickers and not let it slip down my jeans. When it got to be too much, I had to get out of the lift and try to walk up to the fiftieth floor. The other problem was that by this point, some of the other kids were hanging about. Our train was due to leave for Leningrad in about twenty minutes, and we were supposed to be meeting down on the third floor to be checked in by the teachers before going to the station. I needed to try to clean myself up, and fast. Eventually when I got to the toilet, it was engaged. I stood there waiting for five minutes, and while I was there, one of the Marlborough boys came to talk to me. I'd forgotten that their rooms were on that floor. I remember that there was a rumour going around that he had a crush on me, and I'd been waiting for him to talk to me for ages. But I certainly didn't want him to see me like that. First I tried to hide, and then when he found me and started chatting I must have acted like such a dickhead. I was blushing red and

I must have really smelt, too. As soon as the loo was free I just dived into it and left this bloke standing there. Of course, by the time I got inside, I didn't even want to shit any more. I'd been totally and completely caught short. So I set about trying to clean myself up. It was so horrible. I was only twelve, and I'd never had to do anything like that before. It was also the first time I'd stayed away from home and it all just made it a lot worse.'

'You poor thing,' says Jamie.

'I had to throw my knickers away,' says Thea. 'There was no way I could rinse them out or anything, and even if I did, they'd be wet and there was nowhere to put them. I washed my bum and my legs and tried to rinse out the brown stains on my jeans. I seem to remember that scrubbing at it only made it worse, though. Then I started crying, but I had to get back down to the third floor to meet the teachers. I knew if I hurried I could try to catch Gillian and see if she'd lend me her spare pair of knickers. I felt really embarrassed, because I hadn't actually packed a spare pair in my overnight bag – I'd been intending to sleep in the ones I had on. I was one of those kids who didn't change knickers and socks every day, if you know what I mean. I think a lot of kids are like that, but you sort of don't want to get found out. I didn't want to tell Gillian about what had happened in the lift, or admit that I didn't pack a fresh pair of knickers for that night, but I knew the teachers would go totally mad if I asked to unpack my suitcase. At best I'd make everyone miss the train, and at worst they'd make me explain what happened, and I would rather have died than done that.

'The thing is that Gillian got all sanctimonious about her spare pair of clean knickers, and although she agreed to lend them to me, she made it clear that she thought that borrowing someone else's knickers was disgusting. I also had to tell her exactly what had happened, and she made no secret of thinking I was stupid, and a baby. Meanwhile, I told everyone else that the brown stuff on my jeans was mud, and that I'd fallen over in some puddle or whatever. Some of the boys took the piss out of me for that, but I really didn't mind because it was so much better than the real story. I had to stay in my dirty jeans until it was time to go to sleep, and although we ended up in a sleeper next to these nice Marlborough boys – including the one who'd spoken to me before – I felt too mortified to even speak to them. Everyone else was using the train as an excuse to party and let their hair down, but I felt too ashamed. And when we got back to school, Gillian wouldn't stop asking me for her fucking knickers. Every day she'd come to my locker and ask me, but I'd lost them in the wash at home or something and she turned it into a really big deal. That's it. My most embarrassing thing.'

'That is seriously embarrassing,' agrees Emily. 'I don't understand why you needed knickers, though. Why couldn't you have worn your jeans without them?'

Thea laughs. 'I know. Stupid, isn't it? But those sensible grown up things don't really occur to you when you're a kid. It's more like, everyone wears knickers, you're a freak if you don't wear knickers, so you wear them. If you know what I mean.'

'Yeah. I do, actually,' says Emily. 'I didn't work out the knickers thing until I was about seventeen, and one of my friends pointed out that knickers ruin the line of your clothes. If she hadn't suggested it, I doubt I would have thought of it on my own. Mind you, after I realised she was right, I rarely wore them.'

'Are you wearing any now?' asks Jamie.

'Maybe,' she says, flirtatiously. 'Anyway, it's Thea's turn.'

'Paul,' says Thea. 'Truth or dare.'

'Truth,' he says.

'Ha!' says Emily. 'Wasn't there something we were going to ask you?'

'I know what I'm going to ask already,' says Thea.

'Oh,' says Emily, sounding disappointed. 'But what was it, though? The thing we were going to remember to ask Paul. I know it was something embarrassing.'

'I can't remember,' says Paul.

'You wouldn't remember, would you?' says Emily.

Anne can remember, but she's not saying anything.

'Anyway,' says Thea. 'My question is: what's your greatest ambition?'

'My greatest ambition?' he repeats.

'Yeah. Or your ultimate goal or dream, or whatever.'

'MoneyBaby,' he says. 'Although I never thought I'd talk about it with other people. In fact, maybe I should choose something else.'

'You can't now,' says Thea.

'What's MoneyBaby?' asks Anne.

'It sounds familiar,' says Jamie.

'Yeah,' says Emily. 'Money baby. Hmm. Money *baby*.'

'*Swingers*,' says Anne, suddenly. 'The Doug Liman film.'

'Oh yeah,' says Emily. 'Of course.'

For a few minutes, the people who've seen the film amuse themselves by saying things like *money* and *baby* and *you're money baby* and *it's money*, and so on.

'Don't you want to hear Paul's answer?' says Thea.

'Sure,' says Emily. 'Sorry.'

Everyone shuts up.

'This does not go off this island,' says Paul.

Everyone kind of nods and looks serious.

'Do you promise?' he says.

'What's the big deal?' asks Emily. 'Is it illegal?'

'Is stealing money from banks illegal?' he says.

'Is that what you're going to do?' asks Thea. 'Rob a bank?'

'Lots of banks,' says Paul. 'And then I'm going to give the money away.'

'To whom?' asks Jamie.

'Teenagers.'

'What, just random ones?' asks Emily.

'That's right,' says Paul. 'Random ones.'

'And how are you going to do this?' asks Thea.

'With a computer and a modem.'

'With your computer?' says Emily.

'It probably won't be my computer – they'd trace it back.'

'You know what I mean,' she says.

'Yeah. Just like I told you, a computer and a modem.'

'And you're going to hack into the banks?' says Thea.

'Already done it,' says Paul. 'Now I've just got to write the program to load on to their servers, and that'll be it. By the time the banks realise what's going on, billions of dollars will have just gone.'

'To random teenagers,' says Emily.

'Yeah,' says Paul 'Cool, huh?'

'Why don't you give the money to yourself?' asks Bryn.

'That's not the point of it.'

'Then what is?' says Thea. 'I don't understand.'

'I want to see how long the teen conspiracy will go on. How long they can, en masse, keep it a secret. Usually when people do this kind of thing they try to give the money to themselves, and that's how they get caught. By doing the illogical thing and giving it to people I've never even met, I should create a pretty interesting situation.'

'That will cause chaos,' says Jamie. 'It'll fuck the banks totally.'

'Exactly,' says Paul. 'That's the ultimate objective.'

'I see,' says Anne. 'The teen thing is just a gimmick.'

'Pretty much,' he says. 'I don't like teenagers that much.'

'Is it going to work?' asks Jamie.

'What do you mean?' says Paul.

'Well, don't people try that sort of thing all the time?'

'Yeah, I thought banks were pretty secure nowadays,' says Thea.

'I think I've found a loophole,' says Paul. 'But that's all I can say.'

'Wow,' says Thea. 'So when's this going to happen?'

'23rd January 2000. If we ever get out of this place.'

'Right. Paul's turn,' says Anne.

She's thinking about his plan. It sounds very, very cool.

'I choose Bryn,' says Paul.

'Go on, mate,' Bryn says. 'I'll have a dare.'

'You want a dare, huh?'

'Yeah. Shall I get my cock out?' He laughs.

'I'm flattered, but no,' says Paul. 'For your dare, you have to kiss Thea.'

'What if I don't want to be kissed?' says Thea immediately.

'Yeah,' says Emily. 'What if she doesn't want to?'

'She does,' says Paul. 'Trust me.'

Emily looks a bit huffy. She clearly wants Bryn for herself.

'Do you mind?' Bryn asks Thea.

'Make it a quick one,' she says.

He walks, or rather wobbles, over to her sofa and kisses her on the lips.

'Were there tongues?' asks Jamie.

'No,' says Thea.

'You're such a hypocrite,' Emily says to Paul.

'Why?' he says.

'You wouldn't kiss Anne!'

'It's hardly the same thing, is it?'

'Are you saying Thea's a slapper?' asks Emily.

'Does having more than zero kisses in your life make you a slapper?' asks Anne. 'I'd better watch out.'

'I don't think we should have any more of these physical dares,' says Emily.

'Dares are physical,' says Jamie. 'How can you have a non-physical dare?'

'All right. No sexual dares, then,' she says.

'You were the one who made Paul get his cock out,' says Thea.

'Showing's all right,' she concedes. 'But no more touching or kissing.'

'Sounds fine to me,' says Jamie.

'Fine,' says Thea.

'Boring,' says Paul, but Anne can tell he doesn't mean it.

'Is it my turn?' asks Bryn.

'Yeah,' says Thea.

'Right. I pick Emily.'

'Truth,' she says.

'What's the worst sexual experience you've ever had?' he asks.

'The night I was an escort,' she says, after a few moments' thought.

'You were an escort?' says Thea. 'God.'

'I ended up having sex with this guy for two hundred quid.'

'Fucking hell,' says Jamie. 'Didn't you, you know, *mind*?'

'I'm not embarrassed, if that's what you mean. It was shit, though.'

'Are you going to give us all the juicy details?' asks Paul.

'No,' she says. 'I'm not some phone sex line. Work it out for yourself.'

'Does that actually count as prostitution?' asks Thea.

'I guess so,' says Emily. 'I wouldn't do it again because of that, I suppose.'

'It's a lot of money, though,' says Bryn. 'And if it's only a fuck . . .'

'Would you let your girlfriend do it?' Emily asks him.

'I haven't got a girlfriend,' he says.

'But if you did have one.'

'Of course I wouldn't. No fucking way.'

'There you go then,' she says.

'It's your turn,' Thea says to Emily.

'Jamie,' she says. 'Truth or dare?'

Chapter Twenty

Jamie likes this game. He wasn't sure at first, but it is totally in keeping with all his campfire fantasies. Everyone's being so open. And it's just so cool. He's always dreamed of having this sort of conversation with some of his friends at Cambridge, but it never happened. He imagines trying to get Carla to talk about masturbation. It wouldn't be possible.

Emily's talking to him.

'Truth or dare?' she asks.

And Emily is something else altogether.

'Truth,' he says.

There's no way he's picking dare. Not yet.

'Truth,' repeats Emily. 'OK. Have you ever had a homosexual experience?'

'Me?' says Jamie.

'Duh,' she says. 'Yes, you.'

'Yes,' he says, without thinking about it. 'I, uh . . .'

'You *have*?' squeals Emily. 'When?'

'About a year ago,' he says, unable to lie. 'It was with my girlfriend's brother.'

'Your girlfriend's brother?' says Paul. 'Wow.'

Everyone seems pretty shocked.

'What happened?' says Anne.

'It was Boxing Day last year. We went to spend the day

with Carla's family at their house – or should I say mansion –
in Sussex.'

'Are they rich?' asks Emily.

'Oh yeah. Old money. Anyway, her brother Greg had come
out as gay to her about one or two years before, but her parents
still didn't know. Carla didn't approve at all, but was at least
trying to get to grips with the whole idea. There was no way
Mummy and Daddy would have accepted the idea, though.
They were total homophobes. So the whole of Boxing Day
was like some kind of farce, with us pretending everything was
fine, and Greg, who's really nice but totally camp, talking about
some made-up girlfriend called Julie the whole time. I thought
it was funny, but Carla found the whole thing distasteful.
Fairly early on in the evening, she put herself to bed with a
headache. Mummy and Daddy were settling in for a nice game
of Backgammon, so I went out into the local town with Greg.

'Although it was his home town, Greg didn't have any friends
there – something to do with boarding school, he said – and I
certainly didn't know anyone. We decided to just have a real
laugh, you know, get plastered and do karaoke or whatever, the
kind of things the rest of his family would loathe. In fact we
got completely into the whole anti-family idea as a theme for
the night. We went to McDonald's, because we knew they'd
hate the idea of it, then to the worst, most rough and dingy
bars we could find. Eventually we ended up at some gay club
at about one in the morning. I don't know what it is about gay
men, but they find it so easy to work out where the action is,
do you know what I mean?'

'It's called *gaydar*,' says Emily, pouring more wine.

Jamie laughs. 'Anyway, we had a good time dancing and
mincing around, still saying to each other, "Imagine what Carla
would say if she saw this," or "Imagine what Daddy would say
if he saw that," until eventually the club shut and we got a taxi
home. We ended up polishing off Daddy's Cognac by the fire
in the sitting room. Everyone had long since gone to bed, and

we were trying not to keep them awake with our giggling. It was really nice to be with a man who wasn't acting like, you know, well, like a *man*, for a change. I don't mean he wasn't masculine or anything, but when you're with a gay man, all the usual man-rules don't apply. We talked about things and joked, but none of it was crap about women and work. It was ... I don't know, stuff about pop music, or TV, and all about how Greg was going to decorate his house back in London. It was really nice gossiping about celebrities and talking about films and things. Carla had no interest in pop culture whatsoever, but her brother was the complete opposite. I can't remember how we ended up kissing, but I do remember I was *still* thinking, "What would Carla say if she saw this?" and feeling like it was just an extension of the game we'd been playing all night. I suppose in some way I was doing it to hurt her. She was being so boring and prudish. I liked the idea of doing things she didn't know about. So anyway, we kissed, and it was all right. He sucked me off. Then we had sex.'

'You actually had sex?' says Emily.

'Yeah.'

'Were you the giver or the taker?' asks Bryn, laughing.

'What?' says Jamie.

'Did you stick it in him or ... you know?' says Paul.

'Oh, I did the fucking,' says Jamie. 'Gosh, I wasn't ready to actually do *that*.'

'Was it like fucking a woman?' asks Anne.

'Any port in a storm,' jokes Bryn.

Everyone giggles.

'No way,' Jamie says. 'It was totally different.'

'Did you ever do it again?' asks Thea.

'No,' says Jamie. 'I don't find men attractive.'

'So why do it in the first place then?'

'I think because that family were so stuffy. Me and Greg were just acting like kids, you know, trying to be rebellious, doing things in secret. I think I actually liked that bit more than the sex. And we were both pretty drunk. Greg was chuffed that he'd managed to have it off with a straight bloke, and I was happy to have had a new experience. He was a really nice bloke as well, of course, which helped. I definitely wouldn't do it again, though.'

'Is it a common thing for men to have a homosexual experience?' asks Thea.

'I've never had one,' says Paul.

'Me neither,' says Bryn.

'I thought it was quite common,' says Emily. 'Maybe it's a London thing.'

Jamie can't believe that he told them about the Greg experience. That was something he had been sure he'd take to the grave with him. In a way he's slightly embarrassed that he's confessed everything, but in another way he's really pleased that he had something big to share. He's paranoid about people finding him boring, and this definitely takes him out of that category. In fact, so far, he and Emily have had the most risqué stories to tell. Thea's had the most disgusting, but it wasn't really what you would call risqué. Jamie's proud in a weird kind of way. And he likes having something in common with Emily.

'Did you split up with the girlfriend?' asks Emily.

Now he just wants to say yes. But he's too honest.

'No,' he says.

'Why not?' asks Anne. 'Doesn't sound like you love her.'

'I don't,' he says. 'But it's not as simple as that.'

'What do you mean?' asks Thea. 'How much more simple could it be?'

'She'd be upset,' he says.

'But you wouldn't care, right?' says Emily. 'I mean, she sounds like a nightmare.'

'I don't want to hurt her,' he says. 'Her whole world is about security and being secure. Mummy and Daddy expect that we'll get married one day. And they don't even disapprove of me. My mum thinks Carla's lovely, and they get on really well. The thing is, Carla thinks I'm someone I'm not, and I feel guilty about deceiving her, because the person she thinks I am probably would want to be with her forever.'

'And it is fun having a secret world,' says Paul.

'A secret world?' says Jamie. 'I don't understand.'

'Come on. Don't you think it's exciting that she doesn't know the real you?'

'I'm not sure,' he says. 'Maybe.'

'Sounds like you thought so when you were with Greg,' says Thea.

'I suppose,' says Jamie. 'Yeah, I do see what you mean. I like the privacy it gives me. For example, she doesn't know I'm on the Internet at home – she wouldn't know what a modem was if one fell on her head – so every time I look up porn it feels more exciting, because ... Gosh, now I think about it, I get turned on by betraying her.'

'Do *you* get turned on betraying people?' Thea asks Paul.

'Maybe,' he says.

'What about you?' Emily says to Bryn. 'Do you lie to women?'

'Of course. Every man does,' he says.

'Aren't you looking for a soulmate to share everything with?' asks Emily.

'No way,' says Jamie. 'At least, I *wasn't*.'

'Aha,' says Anne, picking up on this instantly. 'What does that mean?'

'Nothing,' says Jamie.

'Jamie's turn,' says Emily. 'Come on, sexy.'

Did she just call him sexy? God.

'It's your turn,' prompts Thea.

'Oh. OK. I pick Paul. Truth or dare?'

'Truth,' says Paul.

'Have you cried in the last year?' asks Jamie.

'Of course,' says Paul. 'What a weird question.'

'I never cry,' says Bryn.

'I bet you do,' says Emily. 'In secret.'

'What did you cry about?' asks Jamie.

'I think that's another question,' says Paul. 'Emily, truth or dare?'

'Truth,' says Emily.

'Wuss,' says Paul.

'Well, you wouldn't hesitate to make me strip or something, would you?' she says.

'Yeah, yeah,' says Paul. 'Anyway, your question. What's your greatest fear?'

'My greatest fear,' says Emily thoughtfully.

'Didn't they ask that on the application form for this job?' asks Thea.

'Yeah,' says Jamie. 'I thought that was weird.'

'That was the only bit I didn't lie about,' says Paul.

'Did you lie on the rest of it?' asks Jamie.

'The bits that were worth it, yeah. Of course.'

'I said I had a degree in Chemistry,' says Bryn, and laughs.

'I thought you did have a degree in Chemistry,' says Jamie.

'Yeah, right. And a rocket to fly to the moon,' says Bryn. Everyone else laughs.

'Didn't you lie?' Emily asks Jamie.

'Nope,' says Jamie. 'I've never lied on a form.'

'You've never lied on a form?' says Anne. 'Fucking hell.'

'So you really are a bright young thing, then,' says Thea.

'I wonder if we'll ever find out what that means,' says Emily.

'I think it means we're fucked,' says Bryn.

'No, seriously,' says Emily. 'Why kidnap people because they're clever? It doesn't make sense. If any old British citizens would do, then why advertise specifically for us? Otherwise, why not go all out and kidnap the Spice Girls or, I don't know, real VIPs at least. Why us?'

'You're assuming that the job interview people brought us here,' says Jamie.

'Well, they did drug our coffee,' says Thea.

'What if someone else drugged the coffee?' Jamie says.

'Seems a bit unlikely,' says Bryn. 'What would someone have to do to drug job-interviewees' coffee? The effort wouldn't be worth it. They'd have to have infiltrated the interview place and everything. Like Emily says, we're not important enough for someone to have done that. If we were totally random, then yeah, sure. But we obviously weren't, and it must be something to do with responding to that ad and what we put on the form.'

'Exactly. Why us in *particular*?' says Thea.

There's a few moments' silence. No one knows.

'Anyway, Emily hasn't answered her question,' says Paul. 'Emily?'

'I'm thinking,' she says. 'I suppose it's rape,' she admits eventually.

'Your greatest fear,' says Paul.

'Uh huh,' she says. 'Rape.'

'Is that what you put on the form?' asks Jamie.

'Yeah,' she says. 'Yeah. I put it on the form. What did you put?'

'Death.' He shudders. 'That's the biggest thing I'm scared of.'

'I put spiders,' says Thea. 'I'm fucking terrified of them.'

'Little furry spiders,' says Paul playfully. 'Ahhh.'

She grimaces. 'Euugh. Don't. What did everyone else put?'

'Needles,' says Bryn, frowning. 'Never been able to have an injection.'

'Imprisonment,' says Paul. 'Being locked up scares the fuck out of me.'

'Welcome to hell,' says Anne, gesturing at their current situation.

'No,' he says. Not like this. This is more like being trapped, and people are always trapped. I mean like behind a locked door, like in a prison cell or whatever. On my own.'

'What did you put, Anne?' asks Emily.

'I can't remember,' she says. 'I made something up.'

'Well, what's your greatest fear? Didn't you put that?'

'Nah.' Anne smiles. 'I don't have one.'

Chapter Twenty-One

It's getting late. Thea's been yawning every few minutes for about half an hour now. She's going to have to go to bed soon.

'Emily?' says Jamie.

'What?'

'How come your biggest fear is rape?'

'Hello?' she says. 'Have you never watched *Crimewatch*?'

'Yeah, I know it's frightening,' he says. 'But those things you were saying before . . . ?'

'What, about rape fantasies?' she says.

'Yeah. You said most people have them. But you don't.'

'Who said that?' she replies. 'Who said I don't?'

'Well, if it's your biggest fear . . .'

'Yeah?'

'Well, you wouldn't fantasise about it, surely?'

Jamie's looking increasingly uncomfortable as he speaks.

'There's a difference between non-consensual sex and rape,' says Emily.

'Is there?' says Thea. 'I'd like to see you tell that to a date-rape victim.'

'No, I mean that someone having sex with you when you don't want to is a bit different from being abducted and having your mouth duct-taped and your tits sawn off,' she says. 'And all I fantasise about is some guy forcing himself on me. Obviously I don't wank over some guy in a mask taking me to a dungeon to kill me. If you want to know the truth, I'm totally embarrassed that I fantasise about it at all.'

'So why *do* you fantasise about it?' asks Jamie.

'It's a guilt thing,' says Emily. 'I think. Help me out girls?'

'Sorry,' says Anne. 'I'm still a virgin.'

'I was raped once,' says Thea.

'Really?' says Jamie. 'God.'

'Well, it wasn't that bad,' she says. 'I sort of enjoyed it.'

'You enjoyed it?' says Emily.

'This is *so* Nancy Friday,' says Anne.

'What happened?' Emily asks Thea.

'It was a friend's brother,' she explains. 'I was staying over at my friend's house and sleeping in the spare room. Her mum was ill, and her dad was really worried about her. They were both in bed. The brother crept into my room and put his arm around me. We'd never liked each other, and he didn't get on with my friend either. Everyone knew he was a bit of a pervert. Anyway, he pushed me on to the bed and told me not to make any noise. He said no one would hear me scream. The thing is, if I had screamed, *everyone* would have heard. Because I knew that, I wasn't really scared. In fact, I was turned on.' She pauses. 'God, I can't believe I'm telling you this. I must be drunk. Anyway, I think we both knew we were acting out a fantasy. I had an orgasm almost immediately. He did too, then he just left the room. We never mentioned it again.'

'That is *so* not rape,' says Emily.

'So you fantasise about it as well?' Jamie says to Thea.

'Well, kind of,' says Thea. 'All women do. Like Emily said, it's a guilt thing.'

'I don't understand,' says Bryn.

'Well, if the guy's totally in control you don't feel like a slut,' she explains.

'Yeah,' agrees Emily. 'It's like if wanting it makes you a slut, then not wanting it sort of purifies you. You can enjoy the sex without the guilt of having initiated it. And you can do all these dirty things without having to admit you want to. In your fantasies at least,' she adds. 'Did you watch *Killer Net?*' she asks everyone.

'Yeah,' says Paul. 'That was pretty cool.'

'You know that bit where the virtual woman's in the alleyway?' asks Emily. Paul nods. 'Well, I got totally turned on at that bit. I imagined some guy pushing her up against the wall and having sex with her. But then all of a sudden she was getting her head bashed in with a hammer. I felt sick, because I'd been turned on and then *that* happened. I'm so scared that if it happens to me it will be because I've fantasised about it, and at the moment that he's sticking a knife into me I'll be thinking, *Well, girl, you got off on this, how does it feel now?* It's like all the guilt I thought I was saving by having the fantasy in the first place just comes back as fear. I won't walk down dark alleys, or go home on my own, or walk in empty parks,' she says. '*Ever.* But all those places are where my fantasies take place, and all the things that happen in my fantasies are things I'd do anything to avoid in real life.'

'Maybe it's like two poles of the same magnet,' says Bryn. 'The two can never meet.'

'Yeah, maybe,' says Emily.

'That's profound,' says Jamie.

Paul laughs. 'Are you sure you mean the same magnet?' he says.

'It's very Freudian,' comments Anne.

'What?' says Emily.

'The guilt not going away. Surfacing in your fears.'

'I bet it would go away if you liked yourself more,' says Jamie.

'Men can't understand,' Emily says to him angrily. 'It's hard to like yourself when you're a woman and you're surrounded by stuff telling you to hate yourself, or that you're not good enough or thin enough, and detailing the bad things that can happen to you just for being a woman. Imagine picking up *Men's Health* or *Playboy* or whatever and reading about penis mutilation? Don't you think that would fuck you up? It just doesn't happen, does it? All magazines are about screwing women up, even the women's magazines. What is it with all the diets and stories about rape and sudden death anyway? Like we need scaring more.'

Emily continues. 'The worst thing I ever read in a magazine was this feature on rape. You know, the kind with three case-studies? The first story was about some girl walking down a dark road and some guy jumping out and forcing her to have sex. I got off on that story. The next one was more of the same, but the third one was about some guy who talked his way into a girl's flat after he helped her with some groceries she'd dropped outside. She was a really cautious girl, but he saw her cat food and started chatting about it or something, saying he had a cat too, and being really friendly. I can't remember all the details, but he was really nice and made coming into the flat the most natural thing in the world. Next thing, the poor girl was being raped, which is bad enough. Then the guy left the room and put on some loud music. She thought the ordeal was over, but he'd actually gone into the kitchen to get a knife to kill her. He'd turned up the music so no one could hear her dying. She escaped somehow, but fucking *hell*. Imagine that. Being murdered with one of your own knives, with your own music playing, by some guy who'd been chatting to you about your cat? I had nightmares for weeks after reading that article. I hate women's magazines.'

'That's a horrible story,' says Paul. He looks genuinely upset.

Suddenly, there's a noise from the top of the house. Everyone jumps.

'Fucking hell,' says Jamie. 'Shit.'

'Hot Christ,' says Paul.

'What the hell was that?' says Bryn.

'Possums?' suggests Anne.

'*Possums?*' says Emily.

Anne shrugs. 'It's always possums in *Neighbours*.'

'Well this isn't fucking *Neighbours*,' says Thea.

There's no more noise from upstairs.

'That didn't sound like a bat or a bird,' says Emily.

'Or a possum,' says Paul.

'Maybe something fell off a shelf,' suggests Jamie.

'What, twice in one day?' asks Paul.

'Maybe it's a dodgy shelf,' says Emily.

They sit there waiting for more noises, but there are none.

'Maybe it's a ghost,' says Paul.

'Paul!' says Emily.

'What's scary about ghosts?' he enquires.

'Can we talk about something else?' asks Emily. 'I feel weird.'

'OK, well whose turn is it?' asks Jamie.

'I think I might go to bed,' says Thea, yawning. 'I'm pissed.'

'Party pooper,' says Emily.

'We can carry on without her,' says Jamie. 'Can't we?'

'I suppose,' says Emily.

'Aren't you scared of the ghost?' asks Paul.

'I don't believe in ghosts,' she replies.

'I'd be more scared in that case,' mumbles Bryn.

Thea ignores him. 'Anyway, goodnight,' she says.

Everyone says goodnight, but they seem more interested in the game.

'It's Anne's turn,' says Emily.

Thea walks out of the door and shuts it behind her.

It's much colder out in the hall. Freezing, in fact. Totally drunk, Thea finds it hard to maintain any kind of straight line while walking down the hall, and the stairs seem to be best tackled on all fours. Once in her room, she doesn't bother to get undressed, but climbs into bed fully clothed, giggling at nothing. She's still pissed off with whoever kidnapped her and made her come here, and she's worried about the odd noises. But for some reason – she expects it's the alcohol – all this just seems really funny. And another thing is making her laugh: suddenly it seems as if now's as good a time as any to give masturbation a try.

Under the covers, feeling like a kid reading after lights out, Thea reaches up under her skirt. It feels weird, slipping her hand under her knickers. This isn't something she does regularly for any reason other than maybe to take her knickers off. But even then, she would usually just yank them from the sides, rather than do what she's doing now. When she touches her vagina, it feels really odd. She's never touched it like this before. She's never really felt her pubic hair unless it's been wet (in the bath or shower). Not knowing what to do next, she investigates the area, looking for her clitoris. Several of her boyfriends have found it in the past, and she's definitely had orgasms before, but she's never had to find it herself.

Just as she's about to come, there's a noise from outside her door.

'Shhh. Thea's asleep,' says someone; it sounds like Bryn.

For fuck's sake. Thea removes her hands from her vagina and unspreads her legs. She can feel the sexy feeling leave her like a spirit leaving a dead body. Are they coming in here? She hopes she's not the target for some stupid dare. She can hear a whispered discussion, and Anne humming something which sounds familiar.

As they all burst in her door, she recognises it as the theme from *Ghostbusters*.

'Do you mind?' she says to them, pulling the covers over her head.

They seem pretty drunk.

'We're going ghostbusting,' says Emily. 'Do you wanna come?' She's slurring her words.

'No,' says Thea. 'Fuck off and let me go to sleep.'

'Suit yourself,' says Paul. 'Bye.'

✳   ✳   ✳

Ten minutes later they're all standing outside the attic room again.

'Thought you were tired,' Paul says to Thea.

'I was,' she says. 'Till you woke me up.'

'So who's breaking in?' asks Emily.

'Do you want me to pick the—' begins Bryn.

'No,' says Paul. 'I think we'll get in via traditional methods.'

'Huh?' says Jamie.

'It is his dare,' says Anne.

'Is this part of Truth or Dare?' says Thea. She sighs. 'For God's sake.'

'Stand back,' says Paul.

Everyone stands back. He kicks the door.

Chapter Twenty-Two

It's dark inside. Bryn takes a deep breath. His lungs fill with putrid air.

'It stinks up here,' says Emily. She waves her hand in front of her face.

'Yeah, this ghost really smells,' says Anne.

Paul ventures in first, feeling for a light switch.

'I don't like this,' says Thea.

Bryn suddenly shivers. He's scared by the tone in Thea's voice.

'What's wrong?' Emily asks Thea.

'That smell . . .' she begins.

Paul flicks on the light. Bryn grabs Emily's arm. She screams.

Anne, Jamie and Thea are standing behind Bryn and Emily. They all push forward.

'Oh fuck,' says Anne.

Paul's standing in the room, staring. 'Hot Christ,' he mumbles.

Thea takes a few steps into the room, then she screams too.

'Spider,' she shrieks, stepping behind Jamie.

There's a spider on the floor. It's about to crawl over the body of a dead man.

The spider is black, orange and furry. The man is blue. He looks frozen, lying in the pose he must have died in: hands on his chest, mouth in the shape of a scream.

'I think she's missed the dead guy,' mumbles Anne.

Thea's panicking. 'Fuck you. Of course I haven't missed it, I just . . .'

She runs down the stairs. Bryn hears a door slam.

Emily starts to cry. 'Fucking fucking fucking . . . *shit*,' she stammers.

Bryn's never seen a dead body before.

'This is bad,' breathes Paul. 'How long has he been dead?'

'Not long if he was the one making those noises,' says Jamie, surprisingly calm.

The spider moves.

'Oh, shit,' says Bryn.

Everyone except Paul moves back.

'Did it kill him?' asks Jamie.

'No,' says Paul. 'It's a tarantula. They're not deadly.'

The spider runs over to the far side of the room and disappears.

'I thought they were,' says Bryn uncertainly.

'Urban myth,' says Paul. 'Is the body warm?' he asks.

No one offers to find out.

'Hello?' he says, when there's no response.

'I'm not going near it,' says Bryn. 'You can if you want. I think we should just go.'

Everyone seems paralysed. Then, after a few seconds, Anne walks over to the body and touches it. Everyone seems to hold their breath, as if the dead guy is suddenly going to leer up at her or something. She seems calm as she touches his neck. 'He's stone cold,' she says.

The room seems more silent and cold than ever.

'I wonder what made the noises,' murmurs Jamie.

'Who the hell is he?' asks Bryn. 'What's he doing here?'

'I've seen him somewhere before,' says Paul.

'Oh f...fuck,' stammers Emily. 'It's the job interview guy.'

'Jesus,' says Jamie. 'This is horrible.'

'I agree,' says Paul. 'Let's go.'

Thea's at the bottom of the stairs, hopping from one foot to the other, sobbing.

'Has it gone?' she wails.

'What, the dead body?' asks Paul.

'No, you arsehole. The spider.'

'Settle down,' says Anne.

'Fuck you,' says Thea. 'You stupid, stupid ...'

Now Emily's crying again. She's wringing her hands.

'What's happened?' she pleads. 'Why is everyone being so mean?'

'Where's the spider?' begs Thea. 'You have to get rid of the spider.'

'Will you shut up about the spider,' says Jamie. 'It's only a—'

'What, only a spider?' shouts Thea. 'Maybe for you ... but I ... Oh, Jesus, I fucking hate you all. I've seen dead bodies *before*, for Christ's sake. I've sat by people's bedsides and watched them die. I wish you'd all grow up. Death is tragic and sad and a waste, but it's not fucking scary. You'll all be dead one day. Spiders are my greatest fear, remember, and although that poor dead guy's not going to hurt me, a fucking tarantula is.' She looks around her, like some sort of animal looking for a way out. 'I can't even get away from you all since we're stuck in this hell-hole. I wish I'd never filled in that stupid form and I wish I wasn't here. I want to go home.'

Emily's sitting on the bottom stair, her face in her hands.

'I want my mum,' she says. 'Please sort this out, someone.'

Thea is still looking for somewhere to go. Eventually she runs into the sitting room.

'What the hell are we going to do now?' asks Jamie.

'Please do something,' Emily says. 'Please, Jamie.'

'What do you want me to do?' he asks. 'What can I do?'

'Make it better,' she says.

Jamie sits down next to her. 'I don't know how to,' he says. 'Sorry.'

'Paul,' says Emily, looking at him with big teary eyes.

'What?' says Paul. 'What?'

'Can't you do something?' she pleads.

Everything has gone. No one's drunk any more. No one feels sexy.

'I can't bring him back to life,' he says gently.

'I don't want him brought back to life!'

'Well, what do you want me to do?' he asks.

'Just fix this. Somehow.'

'I'll make some tea,' says Anne.

'You know how to make tea?' asks Paul.

'In a crisis, yes,' she says, smiling. 'Sugar for everyone I guess?'

'Thank you,' says Emily, clutching Anne's hand as she walks past.

Thea's on the sofa, her knees clutched up to her chest.

'All right?' says Bryn, walking into the sitting room.

'I want to be by myself,' she says.

'Fine. I'll go then.'

'No. Don't. I just . . .' She starts sobbing again.

'It's shock,' Bryn explains. 'You'll be OK.'

She narrows her eyes. 'Will I?' she asks scathingly.

'Yeah, for sure. You just need to take some deep breaths or whatever.'

'*Deep breaths or whatever*. I'll keep that in mind.'

'I was only trying to help. What do you want me to do?'

'Get rid of the spider.'

'Seriously?'

'Yeah. Just get it out of this house. In fact, get it off this fucking island.'

'And then you'll feel better?'

'Please get rid of it,' Thea says softly. 'Please.'

She's rocking backwards and forwards now, like a mental person.

The real-life element of this has totally gone for Bryn. He feels like he's watching a film. He almost feels like laughing, not because this situation is funny, but because it's so bad. He wants to piss himself because the alternative is to shit himself. He wants to laugh at the movie character who's just decided to go up to an attic with a dead person in it, because he's nervous for them, and he knows something horrible is waiting if they do go up. He also wants to cry because that movie character is him.

No one's in the hall any more. They must all be in the kitchen.

Bryn stands at the bottom of the stairs. This is what he hates about being a man. He's as scared of going up there as any human being would be. His penis is not going to protect him from this. He starts walking up the stairs, not sure if he's ever going to have the guts to get there, and not really knowing what to do if he does. He wonders if the spider is already loose in the house. It was pretty big and furry, so it probably won't be too difficult to find, if it has stuck around, and not been scared off by Thea's screaming.

The others seem a long way away, even though they're only two floors below him.

The small staircase leading to the attic feels colder now. Bryn realises it's because there's a draft coming from the attic room, now the door's open. It's completely silent, and pretty dark. The light coming from the attic room is a hellish yellow glow, and Bryn imagines that some demon is whispering to him to come towards the light. He gulps. This is totally fucking stupid.

He can't help imagining the worst case scenario. He knows what it is, no competition. The worst case scenario would be if he walked into that room and the body wasn't there any more. Imagine that: the dead man risen, or maybe worse, never dead in the first place ... He just wanted to make them *think* he was.

Paranoia comes all too easily to Bryn. He knows people who made a mistake and ended up dead as a result. Like his dad, for example. Bryn sighs. He sweats. He sort of swears to himself, although this seems too theatrical. He wants to pace, but ditto. In the end there is no other option than to just enter the room.

The body is still there, lying on the floor in exactly the same position as when they left. Bryn tries not to look at it (in case it winks, or moves, or does that *Fatal Attraction* thing). Instead he looks at everything but the dead body. There is a bed on the far side of the room, which is made up with blankets (no duvet). There's a battered old brown suitcase propped up against the bed. Bryn's still too scared to move. He's been trying to tell himself that it's only a dead body, but his strategy is not working. It's not something he really practised as a child, not like *it's only a storm*. He wishes one of the others would come up, but no one does. He wishes there was something to listen to other than the howling wind outside. Howling wind, for fuck's sake. What next? Zombies?

The rest of the room is tidy but dusty. There's an old wash basin by the bed, and shaving things. On the far left-hand side of the room is a door which isn't quite closed. Bryn can see it's a toilet. There's a load of stuff that looks like junk stacked up next to it, again tidily. Bryn can't tell how long this guy's been up here, but he must have been here at least as long as they have. He's probably the person who brought them here. Bastard. Bryn's suddenly glad he's dead, and suppresses an urge to kick the body. His moment of aggression passes, and he goes back to being scared. Wanting to get out of there fast, he starts looking for the spider.

Almost as though it knows it's been bad, the spider is back in what must be its glass tank, looking, Bryn thinks, sorry and a bit frightened. Not wanting to hang around any longer, he secures the lid, picks up the tank and walks downstairs with it, hoping he doesn't bump into Thea.

'I think it's some sort of pet,' he says to the others in the kitchen.

He puts the glass tank down next to the kettle.

'Like we care right now,' says Emily. 'What is it with this fucking spider?'

'Have you been back up there?' asks Jamie.

'The guy's still dead,' says Bryn brightly, as if he's saying the weather's still fine.

'Thanks for letting us know,' says Paul, and laughs. 'You all right, mate?'

'Yeah, sweet,' says Bryn shakily. 'I just thought I'd better sort out the spider thing.'

Anne hands Bryn a cup of tea. It's too weak, but very sugary. He gulps it down all at once. He's not sure what time it is. Probably about two or three. He wonders if anyone's going to get to bed tonight.

Emily's holding a full cup of tea close to her chest. She's shaking like she's very, very cold, and a droplet of grey-brown liquid is working its way jerkily down her cup. No one says or does anything. Jamie, Anne and Paul are acting calm, although Bryn's pretty sure they're in shock. Jamie should be saying 'gosh' a lot and freaking out, but he's not. Anne should be acting all selfish, and definitely not making people cups of tea. Bryn's not sure what Paul should be doing in this situation. Probably nothing, which is what he is doing. Maybe he's not in shock. He must be. For fuck's sake, no one finds dead bodies in creepy attics. It just doesn't happen.

'It's quite cute,' says Paul, looking in the glass tank at the spider.

'Don't let Thea see it,' says Anne. 'She'll have a total spack-attack.'

'Let Thea see what?' says Thea, coming in to the kitchen. She sees the spider. 'Oh Jesus,' she shrieks.

Chapter Twenty-Three

All the voices — the shouting and swearing and through-clenched-teeth stuff — sound like echoes to Emily. She's never seen a dead person before. She hasn't even known anyone who's died before. That's all she can think: she's in a place of death — sudden, mysterious, horrible death. She's just spilt some milky tea in her lap and she doesn't care. The warm wet liquid feels like blood. She can't move, though. If she stays still then it's like she's not really here, and if she's not here then everything's OK. People die all the time in faraway places, and it's not like you have to care. So for Emily this is a faraway place right now, like somewhere you might see on TV but not be able to find on a map.

Every breath she takes is too long. She's holding each one, aware for the first time of exactly how she breathes — her chest moving, the air going in and then leaving. That's how simple life is. Could she just die like that man? Is she next? If she died right now, what pathetic thing would Thea find to freak out about? How much more nonplussed would Paul be? Emily's not sure who she's angrier with. But they're not here, right? They're simply not here. Those shapes, those voices all mean nothing to her. All she cares about is the air entering and leaving her body, and the tears running down her face. Being on this island was all right before she started feeling totally alone; now she just wants someone to hug her and love her and kiss it better. But it's not going to happen, is it? She's here with a load of strangers.

Emily's only just realised that this place is nothing like the outside world. In the outside world you'd be able to call an ambulance. In the outside world you can call people and they'll come and take the bad things away. If a fire starts, you call the fire brigade. If someone breaks into your house, you call the police. If you find a dead guy in the attic, you call a fucking ambulance. Emily suddenly understands that anyone could come and do anything to them here, and there'd be no one she could call. Someone could be careless with some matches and *whoosh*, that could be it. The house would go up in flames and there'd be no one to help. One of these people could lose it completely, and there'd be nothing anyone could do about it.

Chapter Twenty-Four

When Paul was six, his mum gave him a surprise. It wasn't something he'd expected. One evening in spring, somewhere between *Crackerjack* and *Grange Hill*, his mum told him to shut his eyes. He felt her put something warm and furry in his lap. When he opened his eyes there was a puppy sitting there, black and orange and brown. A Yorkshire Terrier.

Paul called his puppy Patch, even though he didn't really have any patches. He didn't ever give him bath or de-flea him or de-worm him or any of that stuff, but he loved Patch more than anything else in the world. Patch slept in his bed at night, and waited for him at the window when he got home from school. After school, Patch and Paul would go on elaborate adventures to the local dump or round the back of the shops. They explored the suburban Bristol wilderness at weekends, never doing ad-man things like romping through the woods, but always coming home dirty and smelly and full of super-hero thoughts.

Ever since he could read, Paul had been obsessed with manga comics from Japan. He didn't even know his dad had been Japanese until he was ten or so; his mum never found the time to tell him much about his father. The manga comics had been lying around the house for his whole childhood anyway, so he didn't see anything alien or exotic about them; they were just what lived in the cupboards. He certainly never thought to ask where they came from. When his classmates called him 'dirty-knees', he thought they just meant he had dirty knees, and he washed them more carefully during his weekly bath (which he shared with Patch).

When Paul was twelve and a half, Patch was run over by a van full of grinning men, going too fast to notice the little dog sitting tired in the road, or the little boy on the pavement pleading for the dog to come back. Patch spent a week at the vet's before dying, and Paul didn't wash the blood off his arm for a month.

After that, he could never imagine owning another pet, or loving another animal. Trouble is, Paul's one of those people whom animals naturally love, and he just can't help loving them back. Instead of owning another dog, or getting a cat, Paul joined the ALF and started setting innocent animals free and distributing anti-vivisection leaflets in Bristol town centre. He has been a vegetarian from age ten, and an environmental activist since he was about sixteen. He's never killed an animal, not even a fly.

Since he was about nineteen, all of his activism has taken place over computer networks. Paul got his first computer from his mother a few months after Patch died. At first he couldn't get into it; he just wanted his little dog back. But soon, Paul realised that he could take his mind off everything by constructing simple programs. He might even manage to impress his few friends, he thought. Most of Paul's friends were girls, though, and were of an age where they'd rather go to the cinema and kiss on the cheek than fiddle with electronics. Paul never had many male friends; they seemed suspicious of him for some reason – maybe his dirty knees. In his really lonely moments he'd cry for Patch and write another computer program, just to kill the hours before bed. Eventually he got over it, and got used to being alone.

✻   ✻   ✻

'Kill it,' says Thea. 'Will someone just kill it, please.'

'Will you calm down?' says Anne. 'It's in a tank, for fuck's sake.'

Paul's already bonded with the spider. He can't help it. He's trying to remember what he knows about spiders from his ALF adventures years ago. They did rescue a load of spiders once, he recalls. They were tarantulas, but not this brightly coloured. He remembers that the spiders dug holes in their tanks . . . they certainly liked to dig. He realises that there's no earth in this tank for the spider to dig in, and it doesn't have any food either.

'It needs some food,' he says.

'It needs to die,' says Thea.

'Are you normally this cruel to animals?' asks Paul.

'Of course not,' says Thea. 'But it's not an animal. It's a spider.'

Jamie sighs. 'Can't we forget about the spider?'

'We can if he kills it,' says Thea.

'We can if she stops asking me to kill it,' says Paul.

'What are we going to do about matey upstairs?' asks Bryn.

'Exactly,' says Jamie. 'That's rather closer to the point.'

'If you don't kill that spider,' declares Thea, 'I'm going to throw myself off the cliffs.'

'Be my guest,' says Jamie. 'Just do it calmly.'

There's a sudden silence.

Emily starts to wail; a low, howling sound, like she's giving birth.

Thea's gone bright red. She looks at everyone, waiting for them to do or say something. After a few moments, she unlocks the back door and runs out into the dark, crying.

'Now look what you've done,' says Anne.

'She'll be all right,' says Jamie.

'Are you sure?' says Paul.

'Do something,' wails Emily.

'I'll go,' says Anne.

She walks out of the door after Thea.

'Right,' says Jamie. 'What are we going to do about you-know-what?'

'You tell me,' says Paul. 'I don't know what to do with a dead body.'

'Did you cover it over?' Jamie asks Bryn.

'No,' he replies. 'It was too creepy. Do you think Thea will be all right?'

'She'll be fine,' says Jamie. 'Go after her if you're worried.'

'No thanks,' says Bryn. 'It's all too mental for me.'

'I didn't mean what I said,' says Jamie. 'I just wanted to shut her up.'

'As long as she's all right,' says Bryn.

Bryn looks tired. Paul finds it weird that he's not gone after her; weirder that Anne has. It's that sort of night, though, and no one's behaving normally any more.

'So he's still lying there like he was?' asks Paul. 'The guy upstairs, I mean.'

'Yeah,' says Bryn. 'So?'

'I don't know,' says Jamie. 'I don't know what you're supposed to do.'

'In a film,' says Bryn, 'they'd just chuck him over the cliffs or something.'

'I can really see us doing that,' says Paul.

'Did he bring us here?' asks Jamie.

'He must have done,' says Paul. 'He was definitely the job-interview guy.'

'Strange,' says Jamie, sounding slightly boy-detective. 'Why?'

'I guess we'll never know,' says Paul.

'What, we'll never know why?' asks Bryn.

'If he's dead, and he's the one that knows,' says Paul.

'Yeah, but there'd be something written down surely,' says Jamie.

'Probably,' says Paul. 'What do you think he died of?'

'Heart attack?' suggests Jamie. 'I've never seen anyone die before,' he adds.

'Me neither,' says Paul. 'Looked like the heart attacks on TV, though.'

'So what are we going to do now?' asks Bryn. 'I feel like we have to do something.'

'I wish Emily would snap out of it,' says Jamie. 'She'd know what to do.'

'Emily?' says Bryn, looking into her eyes.

Nothing happens.

'What's wrong with her?' asks Paul.

'Shock,' says Bryn. 'I've seen people in shock before. It's like this.'

'Why aren't we like that then?' asks Paul.

'Happens to everyone differently,' says Bryn.

'I don't feel anything,' says Paul. 'Not really.'

'Do you feel scared?' asks Bryn.

'Not really,' says Paul. 'I wish I did — it would be a bit more normal.'

'It doesn't feel real to me,' says Jamie. 'Nothing like this has ever happened to me.'

'Do you think he was just going to carry on hiding up there?' asks Bryn.

'Who knows?' says Paul. 'Bit of a weird thing to do.'

Jamie's up now and pacing around the table.

'Maybe now's a good time to think about escape,' he says.

Chapter Twenty-Five

It doesn't take long for Anne to find Thea. She's sitting up against the back of the house around the corner from the kitchen. It's not that dark, with the light from the hall window.

Anne laughs. 'When I used to run away from home,' she begins, sitting down next to Thea, 'I never used to go further than the end of the driveway. I used to sit there like this, waiting for someone to come out and find me. The one time my parents called my bluff and refused to come after me, I didn't know what to do. I didn't know what extra thing I could do to get their attention. It was the first time I thought about suicide. I must have been about ten.'

'Did you really think about it?' asks Thea.

'No,' says Anne. 'Not really. I just wanted to turn myself inside out or something. It was like I'd done the worst thing I knew to get their attention and it hadn't worked. I was just stuck I suppose.'

'Are you saying I'm doing this to get attention?'

'Yeah. But not in a nasty way. You needed to get their attention.'

'Didn't exactly work, though.'

'Well, not everyone's scared of spiders. Not everyone understands what it feels like.'

257

'And you *do* understand, I suppose?'

'I'm terrified of wasps,' says Anne. 'I act the same way.'

'But not when there's a dead body around, I bet,' says Thea.

'I wouldn't know,' says Anne. 'I don't know how I'd react.'

'You don't seem very freaked out,' Thea observes.

Anne thinks for a moment. 'I don't know why that is,' she admits. 'I've always been pretty good at blocking things out. People say I'm cold. Maybe I am.'

'Maybe.' Thea picks up a stone from the ground and starts turning it over in her hands. 'Anne, why are you being nice to me?'

'Sorry?'

'Why are you being nice to me? I've been horrible to you ever since we got here.'

Anne shrugs. 'When you put it like that I guess I don't really know.'

'Well, thanks anyway,' says Thea. 'It's nice.'

'So are you going to throw yourself off the cliffs then?' says Anne.

'Probably not,' says Thea. 'You could go in and say I had, though.'

'I could,' laughs Anne. 'But they *would* believe me. I'm very believable.'

'Serve them right,' says Thea. 'Fucking men.'

'I can see why Paul wouldn't want to kill the spider,' says Anne diplomatically.

'Hmm,' says Thea. 'Maybe.'

'I mean, if it was a wasp ... But I couldn't kill an animal I liked, could you?'

Thea shakes her head. 'I suppose not. But to spare someone's feelings ...?'

'I don't know,' says Anne. 'But it can't get you now, though. It's in the tank'

'That's not how it feels,' says Thea with a shudder.

'What about the dead guy?' says Anne. 'What do you think happened to him?'

'Heart attack?' suggests Thea. 'I've only ever seen people die of old age,' she adds.

'He was up there all that time. What do you think he was going to do?'

'Murder us? Who knows? Good job he's dead, really.'

'Don't you feel sorry for him?'

'Not if he's our kidnapper, no. Why, do you?'

Anne shrugs. 'Not really, but I thought that was just me.'

'It's not that weird,' says Thea. 'We didn't know him.'

Anne reaches down beside her. 'Do you want a fag?' she asks Thea. 'I brought you some.'

'Cheers,' says Thea, taking one. 'Thanks again for coming out here. I am sorry about all the things I said about you.'

'It doesn't really matter, does it?' says Anne. 'I mean, we'd hardly be friends outside of here anyway. We didn't ask to be here together, did we?'

'Maybe we would have become friends outside,' suggests Thea.

'You hated me on sight,' laughs Anne. 'So I don't think so.'

Thea laughs too. 'You've got a point.'

'I'm used to people hating me,' says Anne. 'It's no big deal.'

'People shouldn't hate you. You're nice.'

'You hated me.'

'Yeah, but only because I was jealous of you.'

This has gone all weird. They're bonding because of some dead guy and a spider.

'Jealous of me?' says Anne incredulously. 'Please.'

'You always manage to be centre of attention.'

'Me? That's rich coming from Miss I'm-Going-To-Throw-Myself-Off-The-Cliffs.'

Thea laughs. 'Well, you manage to be so blasé about everything. The guys adore you.'

'I wish I wasn't so blasé about things. And guys do not usually *adore* me.'

'They must do. You're all girly and innocent.'

'Me? Girly and innocent? You must have the wrong person.'

'All that virginity and stuff about soap operas. It's girly and innocent.'

'No,' Anne corrects. 'It's weird. I'm not innocent, any-way.'

'You're a virgin.'

'It's not the same thing. Anyway, you're more innocent than me. You've never ...'

'What, wanked?' says Thea. She laughs. 'Not till tonight.'

'What?' Anne giggles. 'You mean ...?'

'Well, I was in the middle of it when you all disturbed me.'

'Whoops,' says Anne. 'Sorry.'

The more relaxed Anne gets, the more she realises she's freezing out here.

'I'm cold,' she says to Thea.

'Me too,' says Thea. 'But it feels safe out here.'

'Mmm. What are we going to do about Mr Dead?'

'I don't know.'

'What would you do if this happened to you at home?'

'I don't keep guys in my attic at home.'

'No, but ... You know what I mean.'

'I don't know. Call an ambulance. Call my foster mum. I don't know.'

'We need a telephone,' says Anne.

'Yeah. And a council and the emergency services and everything, really.'

They listen to the waves for a few minutes, while Thea finishes smoking.

'I don't want to sleep in there,' admits Anne.

'No, neither do I,' says Thea. 'Silly, isn't it?'

Chapter Twenty-Six

Everyone goes to sleep at dawn, just as the first light blue patches of sky are emerging outside. For some reason it feels safer this way, all going to sleep together in the sitting room again, with the light coming in and the birds starting to wake up. It's as if daybreak marks the end of the horror-film setting; the end of danger and death and vampires and ghosts and all the other nightmare things. Jamie's aware that they still have a nightmare thing upstairs in the attic, and that this problem is not going to get smaller, but by about six o' clock he doesn't care any more and drops off.

Emily is the first up at about twelve, cooking breakfast for everyone as though nothing has happened. Jamie can hear her singing on his way to the kitchen; some old Smiths song he thought no one remembered.

'Morning,' he says, entering the kitchen and yawning.

'Afternoon,' she says. 'Heavy night, huh?' She hands him a cup of tea. 'Breakfast won't be long. Are the others up?'

'They're awake,' says Jamie. He smiles. 'You seem better this morning.'

'Yeah, well, I bounce back,' she says. 'Sorry I freaked so badly.'

'It was totally understandable,' he says. 'We all lost it a bit.'

'It's only a dead guy. Don't know what all the drama was about, really.'

'It is pretty major,' Jamie points out. He can't believe this transformation.

'People die all the time, Jamie. It's natural.'

'Didn't seem very natural last night,' he says huffily.

'Lighten up,' she says. 'Look, we'll escape and it'll be cool. OK?'

He's not convinced it's going to be that simple. 'OK,' he says anyway.

'I'm fucked,' says Bryn, staggering into the kitchen. 'Did I dream all that stuff?'

'What stuff?' says Emily brightly.

'You didn't dream it,' says Jamie. 'It's real.'

'Fuck. This hangover's real,' he says. 'Any aspirin any-where?'

Super-efficient, Emily hands him a glass of water and two tablets.

'Oh, cheers,' he says.

Bleary-eyed and unhealthy-looking, the others appear through the door.

Emily serves breakfast, cheerfully informing everyone that lunch will be at three.

'Are you OK?' asks Anne, but Emily says nothing.

'This is worse than last night, I think,' whispers Paul.

'Escape plans please everyone,' says Emily. 'To discuss at lunch.'

No one seems sure what to do when breakfast's over. It seems kind of obscene to behave normally with a dead body upstairs. On the other hand, no one offers to do anything about the dead body. There's a group paralysis; no one has any idea of their next move. Eventually, Bryn and Thea decide to help Emily with the washing up, and Anne goes off outside with Paul to search for food for the spider, who's now living in one of the cupboards in his (Paul's sure it's a he) tank. Thea hasn't demanded its death again, and everyone seems to be keeping quiet about it.

Jamie's in the kitchen obsessing about the attic room. He knows there must be some clue in there as to why everyone was brought here in the first place. There was some brief discussion about this last night and this morning. No one's prepared to admit that the knowledge died with the man, but equally, no one's prepared to actually go upstairs and look for evidence either way. Before long, Jamie's in the middle of a fantasy about being the brave one who really does venture into the attic. In his fantasy, the others are all totally impressed because not only has he ventured up there alone, but he has also brought the secret down with him. In a few seconds he's become Indiana Jones, searching for the Lost Arc. And the moment he sees it like that, he realises that all he has to do to make the fantasy real is to actually go up there.

Swallowing his fear (Indiana wasn't scared), Jamie excuses himself from the kitchen and starts running up the stairs, two at a time, in case he loses his nerve. By the time he reaches the very top he's already covered in a thin layer of sweat. What he could really do with is a glass of cold lemonade and a nice breeze. What he actually gets is the smell of death, and several flies. This really is horrible. Before he does anything else, Jamie pulls a sheet off the bed and drapes it over the man. He finds a can of air freshener in the small toilet and sprays it around the room until it smells of spring meadows and death, rather than just death.

He goes through the room like he imagines an FBI team might, ruthlessly sifting through piles of papers and documents, making as much mess as possible. Once he's fully involved with his task, he doesn't really notice the large lump on the floor. Instead of being afraid up here alone, Jamie finds himself feeling territorial and important, not wanting anyone to join him in case he is forced to share the victory when it comes. Not that it's coming very easily. There are loads of documents in here, mainly obscure academic articles, but none which seem to relate to the kidnapping.

Half an hour after Jamie begins his task, he finally finds something important — a folder containing all the application forms and interview letters corresponding to the six people here. Apart from these documents, there is only one other sheet of paper in the folder.

It's a letter, dated 10 August 1999. It is addressed to Mr Smith.

It's from a helicopter hire company and details Mr Smith's requirements for what is described as his 'last trip' with them. It confirms that he will be taking a 'smaller cargo' this time, that he will provide the container and that the container will carry 'Fragile' labels. It also mentions that Mr Smith will be liable for the container and for ensuring air holes for his 'pets'. The company states that they understand the cargo to be more books (*more* books — so the contents of the library must have been brought here too) and supplies as well as the pets. This last journey will take place, the letter goes on to confirm, on Monday 6 September 1999. The day they came here. Jamie gulps. *They* must have been in that container. Fuck. He has to pause for a few moments and take some deep breaths before he realises the other unnerving implication of the letter — that the trip in the helicopter was to be the last, and that there were no arrangements made for the collection of 'Mr Smith' or his 'pets'.

So the man — 'Mr Smith' — is definitely the job-interview man, and he did indeed bring them here deliberately. Trouble is, there's nothing in the folder or this room to suggest why. Why would he get a helicopter to drop them all off here? Why wouldn't he arrange transport back? At least it seems that no terrorists are coming to murder them, which is something.

Jamie almost overlooks the brown suitcase. It is only when he's pulled the whole of the rest of the room apart that he decides to open it. He almost doesn't even bother; it's only a suitcase, after all. Jamie knows that whenever he travels he unpacks as soon as he reaches his destination. If this was Jamie's suitcase, it would be empty, but the man is clearly not like Jamie. There are some items he didn't unpack.

Chapter Twenty-Seven

'So you're all right now, then?' Thea asks Emily, who has insisted on washing, not drying.

'Me? Oh yes. Fine. Why?'

'You were virtually catatonic last night.'

'Yes, well. Do you want tea?'

Emily's voice seems higher pitched today. Thea wonders if she's on the verge of panicking again, and gets a strong urge to be gentle with her; to talk to her like she speaks to the elderly men and women at the residential home. She used to work nights occasionally, when the home was short-staffed. The home was a different place at night, with residents often 'wandering', haunting the corridors like almost-ghosts, sometimes making it as far as the road outside or the local park. Whenever a member of the local community returned a resident, it was like they were returning a stray dog. Matron even slapped one resident on the bottom after one such return, in front of the lady who'd returned him. Before they escaped, or went madder or attacked one another, the residents' voices would always become more high pitched. And when she was about to abuse one of the residents, Matron was the same.

Outside it's another sunny day, although the sky is slightly darker and there are clouds in the distance. At least people are talking

269

about escape now. Bizarre that it took a dead man to get people to actually think about taking action. Thea wonders what would have happened if he hadn't been here. Would these people ever have considered escape? She thinks about what Paul said, about what she has to go back to. Maybe even she would have stopped thinking about escape eventually.

Emily makes better tea than Anne. They sit and sip it as if they're cleaners on a tea-break. Bryn has gone to chop more wood for the fire, even though Emily says they'll need it for the boat. Thea's not sure where Paul and Anne have gone, or Jamie, come to that.

'What do you make of Paul?' asks Thea.

'He's a geek, isn't he?' says Emily. 'A good-looking one, but definitely a geek.'

'Hmmm.'

'Some sort of animal activist or whatever.'

'Yeah, I guessed that.'

Emily smiles at Thea. 'I'm glad you didn't throw yourself off the cliffs last night.'

'Me too,' says Thea. She thinks for a moment. 'Were you aware of that, then?'

'What?'

'Well, everything really. You looked totally blank.'

'Yeah, it was weird,' says Emily. 'All the sounds were like being under water. You know you hear these stories about people who wake up from their anaesthetic during an operation, and they can feel everything, but they're paralysed from the other drugs? It was a bit like that. I was aware of everything, but I couldn't do anything. Silly really.' She grins. 'Anyway, let's not talk about last night. It depresses me. Let's have a girly chat.'

'A girly chat?'

'Yeah. Let's stop stressing about everything.'

Thea gets that old-person feeling again. She must humour Emily.

'Did you know that Paul hasn't had sex for six years?' says Emily, conversationally.

'Seriously?'

It's like Emily's on some kind of weird prescription that only allows her to talk about the cheerful, the inane or the trivial. She'd make a great subject for a documentary right now, although Thea would want her to talk more about last night.

'Uh huh,' says Emily. 'Six years.'

'Why hasn't he had sex for that long?' Thea asks.

'I can't remember exactly why, but apparently he always tells women he's a member of True Love Waits, and then if that doesn't put them off, he goes out with them, but never actually sleeps with them.'

'How do you know this?'

'It was one of the truths last night after you went to bed.'

'How old is Paul?' asks Thea.

'Twenty-five, I think,' says Emily. 'Yeah. That's right. Twenty-five.'

'So he last had sex when he was nineteen. I wonder what she did to him.'

'Or *he*,' says Emily, raising an eyebrow.

'I thought only Jamie had done it with a bloke.'

'That's true. That was a cool story, don't you think?'

'I thought it was a bit gross.'

'I found it sexy,' says Emily. 'I'd love to ... you know.'

'With Jamie?'

'Yeah. Shocking, huh?'

'Wouldn't you be worried about disease? You know, after ...'

'*Duh*. He probably used a condom with whatshisname, silly.'

'If he didn't he was a complete moron,' says Thea. 'Where is he, by the way?'

'Dunno,' says Emily. 'Upstairs?'

'On his own?'

'Maybe he went outside.'

'I'll go and look for him,' says Thea.

He's not outside. Paul and Anne look like they're doing some sort of school nature project, hovering around the trees with jam jars. It's started raining, and the sky has stopped being blue. Thea smiles at Anne and goes back inside. Emily's humming something and putting pasta on the stove. She hardly seems to notice as Thea walks past her and out of the kitchen.

On the way upstairs there's a noise which Thea can't place. It intrigues her. It sounds like a baby, or even a baby animal, left alone without its mother.

As soon as the enters the attic room she can see it's coming from Jamie. He's sitting by the bed with his knees drawn up, a file in his hand and an open suitcase by his feet. He's crying.

Chapter Twenty-Eight

Because of the dwindling light outside, the electric light is on.
Suddenly, it goes off.

'That's the battery flat,' says Paul.

'I thought the power came directly into the house,' says
Anne.

Paul shrugs. 'Maybe it was connected wrong. Maybe it's
been coming off the battery.'

There's still enough light to see the spider eat the cricket
Paul found.

'Better put that away before Thea gets back,' says Bryn.

'Where is Thea?' asks Emily.

'And Jamie,' says Bryn. 'They both know how the batteries work.' Bryn gets up and stretches. 'I'll go and look for
them,' he says.

'Jamie's been gone for ages,' says Emily.

Her pasta's boiling over. She looks like she might cry.

Anne's spooning earth into the spider's tank.

'Can someone make a start carrying them logs through?'
Bryn says as he leaves.

Five minutes later he's back in the kitchen. Emily's about to
serve lunch.

'Paul,' he says, breathlessly. 'Anne.'

They both look at him. He knows he sounds freaked out. He has to sound casual. 'I ... just need your help for a second.'

They can tell something's wrong. They both get up immediately.

Emily turns and smiles at them. 'Hurry back,' she says. 'Before it gets cold.'

'What is it?' asks Paul, as soon as they are out of the kitchen.

'You've got to come upstairs,' says Bryn.

'Why?' asks Anne.

Bryn shakes his head. 'I can't explain. It's totally fucked up. Jamie's in a mess.'

'Jamie?' says Paul. 'What's happened to him?'

'He found something. Hurry up.'

They all run up the stairs and into the attic room.

Thea's sitting with her arm around Jamie, who is crying softly.

'I couldn't get him to move,' she says to Bryn. 'Hi guys.'

'What's happened?' asks Paul, stepping over the lump on the floor.

'He found this,' says Bryn, kicking the suitcase open.

Paul and Anne look inside. They see what Bryn has already seen: a single key, a knife, a syringe, a mask, three dildos, a blindfold and a sewing kit.

'What is all this?' asks Anne.

Paul stares at the items. 'No way,' he says eventually.

'Do you see?' says Bryn.

Paul nods slowly. 'I feel a bit sick,' he says, holding his stomach.

'I don't get it,' says Anne. 'What is all this stuff for?'

'The spider was part of it,' prompts Bryn. 'Just not in the suitcase.'

Thea passes the folder over to Bryn. 'Show her this,' she says.

Anne takes the folder and starts reading.

'I'd look at the greatest fears section of the application forms if I were you,' says Paul. He looks at Bryn. 'That's right, isn't it? These are supposed to represent our greatest fears?'

'Yeah, mate,' says Bryn. 'That's exactly right.'

'Rather more than just *represent*, I think,' says Thea.

'He was going to rape her,' sobs Jamie. 'And lock Paul up, and ... and ...'

'Oh Christ,' says Anne, realising. 'This is disgusting.'

'And look what else we found,' says Thea.

She hands Anne a sheet of card. Bryn's already seen this. It's a floor plan of the six bedrooms with a key sellotaped to each room.

'Fucking hell,' says Anne. 'This gets worse.'

'We can't tell Emily,' says Bryn. 'She'll freak.'

'He definitely put most thought into hers,' says Thea. 'Mask, dildos, blindfold.'

'The blindfold's for me, though,' says Anne. 'I said I was scared of going blind.'

'But you lied, though, right?' says Paul.

'Well, it was just something to put,' she says.

She looks even paler than usual, and slightly green.

'What's the sewing kit for, then?' asks Thea.

'And the knife,' says Paul.

'The knife could have been part of the rape thing,' says Bryn.

'It was to kill me,' says Jamie. 'I'm scared of death, remember.'

He's stopped crying, but his eyes are red and puffy.

'Maybe the sewing kit's just for sewing,' says Paul, but no one looks convinced.

'I'm fucking glad he's dead,' says Bryn.

This time he can't suppress the urge to kick the body, so he does.

'Stop it,' says Anne quietly.

'No, kick it hard,' says Jamie. 'Fucking cunt,' he shouts at the dead man.

'We're not like him,' says Anne softly. 'Come on. Let's just go.'

'What are we going to say to Emily?' asks Paul.

'Nothing,' says Anne. 'We can't tell her. Bryn's right.'

'Are you all right to go downstairs?' Thea asks Jamie.

'No,' he says. 'I want to go home.'

'We all want to go home,' says Thea. 'But you've got to be brave.'

'Can't we just tell Emily?' says Paul.

'No way,' says Jamie.

'Yeah,' says Bryn. 'Her fear is the worst one. We can't let her see this stuff.'

'I find her fear scarier than mine, seeing it like this,' says Thea.

'Yeah,' says Anne. 'I don't find the syringe scary, or the key, or the spider ... But these other things are so horrible. And the fact that he was going to lock us in our rooms ...'

'Which room is the single key for?' asks Paul. 'I wonder where I was going to be imprisoned. I wonder why my bedroom wasn't enough.'

He picks up the key and puts it in his pocket.

'We'd better go down for lunch,' Bryn says.

'Not a word to Emily,' warns Thea.

'Agreed,' says Paul.

Everyone else nods.

'I'm not going to be able to eat anything' says Anne.

'I'm going to be sick,' says Jamie.

'Come on,' says Thea. 'Let's go.'

Emily's sitting by herself at the table. In front of her is a plate of pasta and tomato sauce. Everyone else's plates are untouched.

'Sorry,' says Paul.

They sit down. No one says anything.

'It's got cold,' says Emily. It looks like she's been crying again.

'Are you OK?' asks Anne.

'Me? I'm fine, silly,' she says sadly. 'I just wish your lunches hadn't got cold.'

No one's touched their food yet. Bryn tastes some.

'It's perfect,' he says, looking like he's going to be sick.

'Mmm,' says Thea. 'Just right.'

'Yum,' says Anne, forgetting to taste any at all.

Chapter Twenty-Nine

'So. Escape,' says Emily, once everyone's tucking in to their lunch.

'We need to know where we are,' says Jamie blankly.

'We're in the UK somewhere,' says Paul.

Has someone given this lot tranquillisers or something? They're all acting weird. Emily's not sure what's going on.

'We do need to know more specifically, though,' says Thea tiredly.

'Anne can research that,' says Emily. 'And then check the tides.'

'I'll try to cut a path down the cliff,' says Thea, looking at her plate.

'Will you be all right doing that?' asks Bryn.

'Of course,' she says. 'Why wouldn't I be? There's a scythe around the back.'

'Maybe Death left it there,' mutters Anne.

'Paul can design the boat,' says Emily.

'No, Jamie can do that bit,' Paul says. 'I'm shit at boats.'

Jamie's eyes look all red. Maybe he's got hayfever.

'OK,' he agrees, smiling weakly. 'I'll have a go.'

'What are you going to do?' Thea asks Paul.

'Design the motor, of course.'

'We don't need a motor, do we?' says Emily. 'Can't we just have oars?'

'Have you ever rowed a boat?' says Paul. 'Anyway, it'll be fun.'

'This *is* real, you know,' says Emily sternly.

'So?' he says.

'I don't think you understand. This isn't a game.'

There's silence for a few moments.

'We all know that, Emily,' says Thea eventually.

'What about me?' asks Bryn quickly. 'What shall I do?'

'Um . . .' says Emily.

'Materials research,' says Jamie.

'And buoyancy,' adds Paul.

'For the boat?' asks Bryn.

'Of course for the boat,' says Emily. 'God.'

'What are you going to do, Emily?' asks Jamie.

'She's going to pack the sandwiches,' jokes Bryn.

'I'll help Jamie,' she says, hitting Bryn on the leg playfully.

Thea glares at Emily. Emily doesn't know why. What's she done wrong now?

Emily can feel something beginning to happen. Last night everyone was friends but now there's some tension creeping back in. Maybe the friends thing was a bit optimistic. As Thea pointed out early on, they haven't got much in common. Except, Emily thinks, they have got loads of things in common. Much more than you would have thought. And they all discovered that dead guy, which should have made them bond even more. Maybe everyone's just tense about escaping. Everyone was fine this morning, so that's probably it. She gets the feeling that perhaps everyone's being funny around her because of last night, because they're worried about another psychotic episode. She wishes they'd all just chill out.

'Why are we doing this outside?' Emily asks Jamie.

The sky is still dark grey, and spots of rain are falling on Emily's cheeks.

'Because we can see all the sources of wood,' he says. 'It'll help us plan.'

'Oh. I thought Bryn was doing materials research?'

'Yeah, but he's looking at furniture.'

'Why can't we look at the furniture too, then?'

'Because I wanted to clear my head. I thought you would too.'

'What?'

'I thought you'd want to clear your head.'

'Why? There's nothing wrong with me.'

'Are you sure?'

Emily's fucked off with everyone saying things like this today.

'Why?' she says. 'God, I have one moment of weirdness and you all think I'm, like, totally cuckoo or something.'

'We're just trying to be nice. We are your friends . . .'

'I know,' she says. 'Just stop treating me like I'm mental.'

'Sorry,' says Jamie.

'Hey,' she says, giggling. 'Who do you think is most likely to drown first?'

Jamie doesn't say anything.

'Jamie?' she says, after he's just stood there for a couple of minutes.

'Leave me alone,' he says.

She puts on her smallest girly voice. 'I was only joking.'

He won't look at her.

'Jamie?'

She touches his shoulder, but he shrugs her off.

'You're not crying are you?'

He looks up. There are tears in his eyes.

'Leave me alone,' he says.

'What's wrong? It was only a joke, for God's sake.'

'Everything's gone wrong,' he says. 'You don't even know how fucked up everything is. You've got no idea. It's all gone wrong.'

'It was only a dead body,' she says.

'Yeah, whatever.'

Still crying, Jamie gets up and goes inside.

Emily's been thinking a lot about drowning this afternoon. It makes her laugh, the idea of drowning. She's not sure why, because it scares her more than anything else. Well, anything except rape and torture. She remembers someone saying that death is the worst think that can happen to you. How stupid is that? Being tortured would be worse than being killed. But on the general pain/death-ometer, drowning would be pretty bad. She imagines her lungs filling with water; that time when you're drowning when you are actually breathing water in and out, like an artificial lung.

Her piece of paper is blank. Suddenly inspired, she draws a comic-book boat, a sort of floating banana on a wavy-line wave, with a stick-and-triangle mast. Then, not really knowing why, she draws the remains of five stick people in the water, with air bubbles above them to show that they're drowning. The one person left in the boat is just watching, but if you look carefully you can see that she is about to throw herself overboard as well.

Chapter Thirty

Paul's washing up again, trying to sort out the kitchen after lunch.

He doesn't see Jamie coming in, but he hears him muttering something.

'What?' he says.

'Nothing,' says Jamie. 'It doesn't matter.' He sits down at the table and puts his head in his hands. His hair's wet from the rain.

'What is it?' asks Paul.

'Maybe we should tell Emily,' says Jamie.

'We agreed not to, though,' Paul reminds him.

'Yes, but now she thinks we think she's mad. And now she's driving me mad being overnormal while we all pussyfoot around her. And the more we pussyfoot, the more normal she tries to be, because she thinks we're doing it because of how she was last night. It doesn't seem fair. You know, we're trying to protect her and she gives us a hard time for being weird.'

'Was she giving you a hard time?'

'Oh, she was making tasteless jokes about drowning.'

'She's probably scared,' says Paul. 'We all take the piss when we're scared.'

Jamie folds his arms petulantly. 'I don't.'

Paul laughs. 'Well, maybe you should try harder.'

'Where's your spider?' asks Jamie.

'He's in his cupboard. He's scared of Thea.'

Jamie manages a smile. 'Where is she?'

'Down by the cliffs. She didn't want anyone to go with her.'

'Why?'

'Who knows? So what do you make of that helicopter letter?'

Jamie takes it out of his pocket and unfolds it. Everyone read it upstairs.

'Well, no one's coming,' he says, looking over it.

'No,' says Paul. 'No one's coming to kill us.'

'Or set us free,' says Jamie.

Paul finishes the washing up and sits at the table playing 'Snake' with Jamie for long enough to take his mind off the Emily problem. Paul's having trouble thinking about motors and boats and escape. He's too fixated on the key in his pocket and the parallel universe in which he's a prisoner somewhere in this house, more of a prisoner than he is now, actually imprisoned in a room; his greatest, greatest fear.

Why the hell did he tell the truth on that form? It's not as if he'd usually tell the truth about something like that. Maybe he just found the question interesting, and that compelled him to be honest, as if to reward whoever had constructed the form for asking such good questions. Or maybe he was just caught off guard, like with those trick-series questions where you end up saying green traffic lights mean stop, or whatever. *Name: Paul Farrar; Age: 25; Place of birth: Bristol; Degree: Art; Greatest fear: Imprisonment.* You just get used to filling in the boxes, don't you?

Predictably, the key ends up fitting the basement door. Paul accepts this with a small lump of fear in his throat. It didn't *actually* happen, he tells himself. Everything's all right. He never did get locked in this room, and his captor is dead. He forces himself to take one, then two steps into the room, unable to shake off the irrational fear that someone could still come and lock him in. His breathing is short and shallow as he tries and fails to take a third step.

It's funny the way prisons only become prisons when there's a chance you could be locked in them. Paul tries to remember how unthreatening this space was when he first came in here. It was horrible, sure, but it wasn't his prison then. Unable to take any more steps, he retreats from the room and locks the door. But the act of locking the door suddenly frightens him. He imagines locking himself in there by accident and then losing the key, or locking himself in and then having an urge to swallow it. Stupid, he knows, but terrifying. It's like that fear people have of throwing themselves from high places, or jumping in front of a train. Paul once knew someone who couldn't wait on a train platform because she thought there was a risk that one day her body would just throw itself in front of the train, independently of her mind. She couldn't trust her own body, and now Paul knows how that feels. He unlocks the door and puts the key back in his pocket. He needs to find Anne.

She's in the library.

'How's it going?' he asks her.

'Not so well. I don't understand these tidal charts.'

She's blissfully normal. Thank God.

'Do you know where we are, then?' he asks her.

'Not exactly.'

'Then how can you work out the tidal charts?'

'Well, since they're the only ones here, I assume they're the right ones.'

'Cool. Let's have a look.'

'OK, here,' she says, giving them to him.

He looks at them for a few seconds.

'I think everyone's in crisis,' he says, putting the charts to one side.

'It's this whole fear thing,' says Anne. 'It's upsetting people.'

'Hmm. The escape thing isn't helping. It's that neither-here-nor-there feeling.'

'Are people afraid of escaping?'

'Yeah. Shitting themselves. I mean, we weren't exactly rushing to escape before.'

'Why do you think that is?'

'It's scary,' he says. 'Cold water, big waves, high cliffs.'

'Do you think we were supposed to?' asks Anne.

'What? Escape?'

'Yeah.'

He thinks. 'I'm not sure. I do wonder if that guy was studying us, you know, like, *Can they switch on the electricity? Can they keep warm? Can they handle their greatest fears? Can they escape?*'

'I thought that. But why would he leave all that food for us?'

'Maybe it was more a fear thing than a survival thing.'

'But then why the electricity?' says Anne. 'And the logs?'

'Well, he got here at the same time as us. Maybe he wanted to stash himself in his attic before we came to. Maybe he just didn't have time to switch on the power or organise heating.'

'Who knows?' says Anne.

'Maybe he didn't mean to actually hurt us,' suggests Paul uncertainly.

'What, you mean he was going to cure us of our fears or something?'

Paul laughs. Anne's said this in such a cynical way.

'You never know,' he says. 'We'll never know now, will we?'

'Isn't that weird?' she says. 'Not ever knowing.'

'Maybe it's best we didn't find out,' he says.

There's a noise coming from one of the other rooms. Paul

can hear someone calling for him. It sounds like Bryn.

'I'll see you later,' he says to Anne.

When Paul gets to the kitchen, Bryn's co-ordinating a rescue party.

'Thea's slipped and hurt herself,' he says, soldier-style.

'We need to get down to help her, and lift her back up to the top,' says Jamie.

'OK,' says Paul. 'Lead the way.'

'Come on,' says Bryn urgently.

They all march efficiently out of the door.

Chapter Thirty-One

Anne knows Paul's right about people being afraid of escaping. You only have to go and look over the cliffs to realise what a stupid idea the boat thing is. But what are their other choices? Are they all really such slackers that they wouldn't even bother trying to escape? Maybe before, but not now, with all this dead body and greatest fear stuff. The trouble with this whole situation is that it's just way too real. If this was a videogame, you'd just find the preprogrammed way out. And it probably would turn out to be down the cliffs in a boat. But if this was a videogame, you'd probably die a few times before you got it right. As far as Anne knows, no one here is into extreme sports, or white-water rafting, or anything like that. Not in real life. And when you look down those cliffs and think about actually dying in that freezing grey water, it's actually real. It's not a game or a book or a film. It's something that she and everyone else here have to really do. And the thought makes her feel sick.

The escape is the first real thing about being here. Coming here didn't feel real, in the sense that they didn't really come here as such, they just woke up here. Even discovering the man and the suitcase didn't feel totally real. It's not like they actually saw him die or anything. They will never know what his plans were, why he brought them here, or what those horrible fear-props were all about. Their experience of him will only ever be second-hand or

289

made up. The only real thing about the man is the gaps he left, the gaps which people have to fill in with their imaginations, with guesswork and with bits from old horror films and urban myths. In reality, nothing about him or the threat he posed can ever exist outside everyone's imaginations, and that's the way Anne likes it.

Anne's whole life has been about avoiding the real, and she doesn't want that to end now. She doesn't believe in anything; she doesn't subscribe to anything. From an early age she rejected what was normal, not by doing really wild or wacky or different things, but by doing nothing. She didn't attend her classes at school because she didn't want to. She didn't feel that learning all that crap was actually going to do anything for her. And she was right; it didn't. And when she did learn stuff, it was the cool stuff. Studies on suicide, bizarre conspiracy theories, existentialism, nothingness, postmodernism. When you're born into a world where everything is false, and in which you are never going to make a difference, what other alternative is there than to just skate around on the surface, making pretty patterns?

Games are cool because they are so meaningless. You play, you win or lose, and it doesn't matter at all. And you may as well play games in which life is important, because in the real world, it just isn't. Anne's knows that most videogames have nicer environments than the real world, better moral structures, and certainly a value on life, even if it is just one hundred coins. If you want morals, you'd better look to fiction, because they're not there in the real world. Life's cheap, but as long as death is cheaper, death will always win. The safety record of any privatised transport company will tell you that.

Knowing this from an early age didn't make Anne resort to a life of irony; it just made her stay a child, enjoying the moment and pretending that all the bad stuff in the world is just the trick stuff they put on before they wheel out the really cool parts. Like everyone pretending to have forgotten your birthday when all along they've planned a surprise party for you.

The moment at which Anne decided that the world sucked was when she was about five or so. *Blue Peter* did a report on Pol Pot, and described the way he killed people's mummies and daddies. At the time, Anne's mother was still interested in her, and spent a long time trying to explain the whole thing to little Anne, who had always been a very sensitive child, and who demanded to know how this could be allowed to happen. All the usual questions were asked: *If God exists, how can He do this? Why can't our government stop this?* and so on. Anne's mother gave fairly honest answers to these questions, hard though they must have been to answer, and suggested that if Anne felt that strongly about Pol Pot, she should draw a picture to send to *Blue Peter*.

Anne drew a picture of a circle. And on it she drew, and then coloured in, the words: KILL POL POT. She sent it off, but it was never displayed on the programme, or even mentioned by the presenters. It was the first time Anne had really been ignored – and over such an important issue as well. It hurt.

At five, Anne was already an advanced child, although no one had really noticed yet, because it was demonstrated in such eccentric ways. She'd already been in trouble at infant school for her experiment: *Can snails distinguish colour?* because the teacher didn't understand it. It was such a cool experiment as well. Anne always put the snails' food through the same colour door in their little tank, and created all sorts of data to try to work out whether they'd try the same colour door for their food, even though the position of the door was changed. In the end, the teacher wrote to her mother, and Anne ended up growing a sunflower instead.

The Pol Pot thing was what really rocked Anne's boat, though. Her most advanced area had always been logic, which is what had led to the snail experiment. From about three or four, Anne had always been able to project various possible outcomes from an event in order to work out either what might happen if she did something, or, more frequently as she got older, why it wasn't worth doing something. So once she was aware of Pol Pot, she wondered what would happen if someone killed him. Would that get rid of all evil in the world? No. So what if someone killed all evil people? That would be good, except for one problem: who would decide who was evil? Anne had watched a programme on TV about people who were wrongly accused of things. What if someone decided she was evil – or her mummy or daddy – and came to kill them? If she thought it was right for Pol Pot to be killed, maybe one day someone would think it was all right for her to be killed, and what logic could stop them? So maybe it was right for Pol Pot to be left alone. Perhaps everything he did was just his responsibility, and not Anne's problem.

As soon as Anne stumbled on this solution – that the world's problems were not *her* problems, she felt much, much better. But something had gone to sleep in her over the months she'd agonised over Pol Pot. She'd thought about other things as well, and at the age of five had decided that it was probably best if she tried not to love her parents so much, since they were going to die someday, and that it would probably be best for her not to have any babies herself, because she'd die and make them sad; or worse, they'd die and make her sad. She also decided not to have a boyfriend, or any friends.

All the fun she had from that point on didn't involve anything real. She loved novels with happy endings, and Hollywood films and, of course, soap operas. In these fictions she knew she would find true love and friendship and gossip and excitement, and she could absolutely guarantee that she would get a happy ending. For Anne it was simple. If life wasn't going to be like a Hollywood film, there was only one option: fuck life and rent the film instead.

Anne always makes sure that she never watches war films, never reads a book with a sad ending, never tunes in to charity events (Live Aid was the worst), and hardly ever watches the news. When her aunt got cancer, she just tuned her out. She enjoys illness only if it is abstracted; if it happens to a stranger or a minor character on TV. Good characters always recover from illnesses anyway, and even if the worst does happen, characters on TV can be given beautiful deaths which they can more or less choreograph themselves. They can say the right last words, leave the right will, and make everyone they leave behind happy. And if someone dies in a soap, you usually get a new character to replace them.

Having said that, Anne was too upset to watch either Helen Daniels or Bobby Simpson (she still can't call her Bobby Fisher) die. They had both become really old friends, and there was no way she could have handled it. But when she saw her own grandmother die in a hospital bed right in front of her, she felt absolutely nothing. Recently, when there have been great tragedies or disasters on TV, she's tried to feel sad for the people involved – sometimes she has even tried to cry, because that's what people do. But that part of her is now as dead as Princess Diana, whose actual death Anne just found farcical, and whose funeral she found vulgar. She tried to understand the idea of a condolence book, but just couldn't. Why would people stand in a queue for hours just to sign a book? It's totally pointless. Sentimental and pointless.

Although Anne has no problem with other people's deaths, she has a great problem with her own. When she was fifteen, she had her first panic attack. She had just completed her best ever poem – her last ever poem, because no other could better it – and she was lying in bed trying to fall asleep. Lying there in the dark she was struck by the lack of sound in her room and in the usually busy street outside. Soon she started listening to her heartbeat. At first it sounded regular and comforting. And until that moment, Anne had never actually thought about her heart stopping, or becoming irregular. But the second she started thinking about it, she suddenly realised how fragile her life was. This lump of tissue, veins and flesh in her body was the thing that kept her alive. It could go wrong, surely? Or just stop? What about heart attacks? Anne had read about heart attacks, and she knew that one of the symptoms was a pain in your left arm.

Within five minutes, Anne had a pain in her left arm, and an irregular heartbeat.

Within fifteen minutes, she'd gone to casualty.

In the next four years, she visited the local casualty department so many times that they virtually banned her, and after that it didn't take too long for her to develop a Boy-Who-Cried-Wolf complex. She believed that each time she caused a false alarm by believing she was dying, she was actually reducing the chances of them taking her seriously when she *was* dying – which was going to be soon, considering the condition of her heart. She stopped going to casualty, but the attacks didn't go away. And once she realised that her heart was probably not going to just give up on her, she focused on other diseases instead: meningitis, MS, BSE; she was secretly incubating all of them. But she never told anyone about the way she was feeling, because she didn't want to make them sad.

When she was very small, the family had owned a black cat called Sascha. One day, after being quite ill, Sascha ran away. Anne's mother explained to her that Sascha was going to die, and that she was going to go away and do it in secret, because she didn't want everyone to be sad. Anne knew that was what she would do in the end as well. She'd die like a cat, in secret, in private, and without hurting anyone's feelings.

Anne doesn't drink. She doesn't smoke. She doesn't ever want to rely on these things, or feel like she might ever have to do without them. For this reason, she has avoided any addictive substance, and she has avoided sex. She knows if she had sex she'd miss it if it wasn't there, and that she wouldn't be able to help forming emotional attachments to the men she had sex with. So she just hasn't done it.

The idea of having a down-to-earth part-time job has never appealed to Anne. In fact, until her mother threatened to cut off her allowance, she wasn't at all interested in working. Apart from the cleaning job in her year of existentialism, she has never had a job. Why work for people? Why go out – out of choice – and get exploited? The maths has never added up for Anne. If you sell someone your service, and then they make a profit, you must be selling yourself for a price that's too low. But here's the really stupid bit: you can't up your price because it's a buyers' market, even to the extent that your employer decides what to pay you. And since all employers are in the business of making money, they are always going to pay you less than you're worth. So Anne doesn't believe in working for other people. Why bother? She's no good with responsibility, even if she did want to be exploited. The only real possibility for Anne career-wise would be to go into screenwriting or romantic fiction, and she doesn't even need to try to do these things because her parents are rich enough to support her.

She only applied for this job because it sounded so stupid.

Chapter Thirty-Two

The sea looks fucking cold.

Jamie and the others have almost reached Thea. She's about twenty or so metres from where the waves are breaking, sitting on a rock, clutching her ankle. It doesn't seem very safe down here, and Jamie's still not sure how the hell they're actually going to get her back up the cliffs. It hasn't exactly been that easy getting down this far, especially carrying the weight of his awful discovery.

'What is this, Mountain Rescue?' she asks when she sees the boys.

Jamie's not in the mood for this.

Bryn seems nervous for some reason. He's shivering.

Paul reaches down and takes Thea's hand.

'Can you stand up?' he asks.

'Yeah,' she says, standing up. 'But I've definitely twisted my ankle.'

'So you can't walk?' says Paul.

'Not really,' she says.

Jamie's ears feel like they're going to drop off. It's so horribly cold. Spray from the sea hits his face every time a wave breaks, and in between there are droplets of rain and a few bursts of hailstones. This turn in the weather is not good. From the tops of the cliffs the sea looked pretty rough, but from here it looks totally monstrous. No one with a brain would go anywhere near it right now, Jamie's certain. Probably not even experienced seamen. He hopes it calms down for when they escape, although he doesn't remember it being that calm at any point since they arrived.

Thea's saying something, but her voice is lost in the wind, spray and rain. Jamie realises that he's wandered a bit in front of the others. He's not very good at rescuing. Wondering what he is actually good at, he watches the waves smashing against the rock for a couple more minutes, before making his way back to Thea and the others.

Bryn has hitched Thea up on to his back and started retracing his steps. Jamie and Paul scramble up behind him. At every step this mission seems precarious, and it is unlikely that Bryn will be able to support Thea all the way to the top. Jamie knows he will blame himself if anyone gets hurt. He should be doing the rescuing. *He* should be a hero. He's lost a lot of opportunities to be a hero over the last couple of days, and as he struggles uphill through the half-cut-down weeds and mud he makes a vow to himself: he's not going to lose the next one.

'At least it is possible to get down there,' Paul says, when they reach the top.

Bryn gently lowers Thea on to the grass. He did make it, after all.

'Thanks,' she says.

'Can you walk?' asks Bryn.

She limps a few steps. 'Not really,' she says. 'I think it might be sprained.'

'I'll carry you inside,' says Paul. But Bryn wants to, so he does.

When they get in the house, the kitchen's empty.

'Where's Emily?' asks Thea.

Jamie shrugs. He's lost track of everything.

Paul's cooking.

It's already dark. The rain hasn't stopped, and there's the odd rumble of thunder in the distance. Emily still hasn't reappeared. Jamie and Paul are the only ones in the kitchen.

'What are you making?' asks Jamie.

'Bean stew and mash,' says Paul.

'Good,' says Jamie sadly. 'Something comforting.'

'Are you sure you're OK?' asks Paul.

'What are you going to do if I say no?' asks Jamie. 'Call a doctor? Take me to the pub? Hire me a video? I'm not OK, but I will be. I mean, I'll have to be. Don't worry about me, I'll survive.'

'Has anyone lit the fire?'

'Bryn's doing it now,' says Jamie. 'He said he didn't need any help.' He yawns. He's tired from all the upset.

'How's the boat-design going?' asks Paul.

Jamie's been dreading this. He can't design a boat, for fuck's sake. And even if he could, what with lying to Emily and worrying about the knife and the mask and everything in the suitcase, and then rescuing Thea, he just hasn't had time. Yet again, Jamie's fucked up being a hero. Yet again, he's fucked up being a survivor. On the plus side, neither Bryn nor Paul seem to have achieved their tasks either, but this is cold comfort. Jamie wanted to design the best boat in the world, and he can't.

'It's not,' he says weakly. 'I fucked it up.'

'Is this it?' asks Paul, laughing.

He shows Jamie a small piece of paper with a crude drawing of a boat on it. Several people are drowning in the water, while one person looks at them smugly from the safety of the boat. Jamie screws it up and throws it in the bin.

'Very funny,' he says.

'Do you want to peel some potatoes?' asks Paul.

'I thought you didn't do this kind of thing,' says Jamie. 'Cooking and everything.'

'I don't if I can help it,' says Paul.

'Well, I suppose Emily's not going to do it,' says Jamie, sadly.

'What is the matter with you?' asks Paul.

'I don't want to talk about it,' says Jamie.

'Fine,' says Paul.

When Anne walks in, the room is silent.

'Who died this time?' she asks.

'Thea twisted her ankle,' says Paul.

'What did you learn about the tides?' asks Jamie.

'Not much,' says Anne. 'They happen.'

'Great,' says Jamie. 'And do you know where we are?'

'Sorry, there was no tourist map with a *You Are Here* sign in the library.'

'So we really are fucked, then,' says Jamie.

'You're cheerful,' says Anne.

'Leave me alone,' says Jamie. 'Please. I've had a really shit day.'

'Every day's shit when you're kidnapped,' she says cheerfully. 'Oh my God,' she says to Paul. 'You're cooking.'

'Don't tell everyone,' he says, smiling.

'Why are you cooking?' she says.

'Didn't you hear? We're having a dinner party.'

'Who said?' asks Jamie.

'Me,' says Paul. 'To celebrate not being raped and mutilated. Just don't tell Emily.'

Anne laughs. They exchange a look. Jamie doesn't know if they're joking.

'Are you messing about?' he says.

'No, I'm serious,' says Paul.

'Where are we eating?' asks Anne.

'At the kitchen table,' says Paul.

'Why?' asks Jamie. 'It was nice in the sitting room last night.'

'But tonight there's sauce,' says Paul.

Chapter Thirty-Three

No one's saying very much over dinner.

Thea's ankle is killing her. It's already swollen to twice its original size, and it's red and throbbing. She knows from old school hockey games that it's only a matter of time before it goes purple. She could do with some Ibuprofen cream and one of those ankle supports, but there isn't a casualty department around here. Earlier on today, and last night, all Thea felt was fear. The dead man scared the shit out of her. Now she doesn't feel scared at all, just angry. How dare he bring them here like this? How dare he bring them to a place with no medical help or experts of any kind? One of them could have become seriously ill; had he considered that? Thea knows he was probably going to kill them all, or at least try to scare them to death, but still.

After about five minutes of pure silence, Emily starts sniffing.

When Thea looks at her, she can see a tear rolling down her face.

In a few minutes, everyone's noticed.

'What's wrong?' asks Paul.

'Everyone hates me,' she sobs.

'Who hates you?' says Paul. 'I don't.'

'Everyone thinks I'm mad.'

'We don't,' says Thea.

'So what's your problem, then?'

Thea looks down at the table. 'We just ... Look, it doesn't matter.'

Bryn gets up.

'Where are you going?' asks Emily.

'To check the fire,' he says.

'Me too,' says Thea. 'I'll come and help you.'

'I wish everyone would stop avoiding me,' says Emily. 'I'm *not* mental.'

Thea gets up and limps after Bryn into the sitting room.

When they get back, Emily's still sniffling and the others are talking about the Dreamcast being out soon. Anne and Paul are saying they're going to preorder them.

'Is there any dessert?' asks Thea.

'Tinned fruit and condensed milk?' suggests Paul.

'God, this is so 1950s,' says Anne.

Thea doesn't see her say no when Paul dishes it up, though.

'I wish there was some Coke,' says Anne.

'So do I,' says Bryn.

'She doesn't mean that sort of coke,' says Paul.

'Neither do I,' he says. He looks at Anne. 'Coke or Pepsi? Which do you prefer?'

'Coke,' she says.

'Same,' he says.

'Pepsi,' says Paul.

'Blonde or brunette?' Anne asks.

'Brunette,' Bryn says.

'Same,' says Paul.

'Same,' says Anne.

'Blond,' murmurs Emily.

'Is this some sort of game?' asks Thea.

Some of the tension has been suddenly diffused.

'It is now,' says Paul.

'All right,' she says. 'Fascist or communist?'

'What?' says Anne.

'I don't think she gets this game,' says Paul.

'No, I do,' says Thea. 'Dictators. Fascist or communist?'

'What, which are better?' asks Bryn.

'That is the game, right?' she says.

'I guess,' says Paul.

'Communist,' says Anne.

'Communist,' says Paul.

'Communist,' says Bryn.

'This is fun,' says Paul. 'Nintendo or Sega?'

'Nintendo,' says Anne.

'Snap,' says Paul.

'Sega,' says Bryn.

'Sega' says Thea.

'What do you know about games?' asks Anne.

'I've been addicted to arcade games since I was a teenager,' she says.

Everyone shuts up.

'Seriously?' says Bryn.

'I didn't think you were the type—' starts Paul.

'Why?' says Thea.

'I'm not sure, to be honest,' he says. 'You seem too sensible.'

'Yeah, well, I'm not,' she says.

'Is it a problem?' says Anne. 'I mean, like a serious addiction?'

'Kind of,' says Thea, looking down at the table. 'I don't really know.'

'Why didn't you talk about this before?' asks Bryn.

'I didn't know you very well,' she says.

'What's your favourite game?' asks Anne.

'I quite like "House of the Dead II".'

'God,' says Paul. 'Who would have thought?'

'This must be "House of the Dead I",' comments Anne quietly.

'We're all pretty fucked up,' says Emily. She's stopped crying, finally.

'What's fucked up about you?' asks Thea. 'You've got everything.'

'Oh, please,' says Emily. 'You've got no idea about my problems.'

'You did lose it a lot yesterday,' says Paul.

'That was nothing,' says Emily. 'It's been a lot worse. The same kind of thing. The blanking out. One time I couldn't even remember where I lived.'

'Why?' asks Jamie. 'What happened to make you like that?'

'I wasn't sure for ages,' she says. 'But I've been in therapy for a while, and my therapist's convinced about what started it all.'

'What?' says Anne.

'An abortion that went wrong,' she says. 'When I was sixteen.'

'You were pregnant at sixteen?' says Anne.

'Yep,' says Emily. 'Pregnant at sixteen. I was normal before that.'

She looks like she might cry again.

'I don't usually talk about this,' she says. 'Has anyone got a cigarette?'

Jamie lights one for her.

'What went wrong with the abortion?' asks Anne.

'They gave me these pessaries the day before,' she says, 'which they inserted up near my cervix to try to make it open enough to make the operation easier or whatever. Apparently, they had to do it because I was so young – I didn't really under-stand it. Anyway, it was about an hour after they gave me the first one that I realised something was badly wrong. I was having the most intense period pains of my life, and I had started to bleed. I later realised that it was actually labour pains I was having.'

'Labour pains?' says Thea.

'Oh, God,' says Jamie quietly.

'They were labour-inducing pessaries,' says Emily. 'Or at least I found out later that's what they were. Anyway, when it was time for them to insert the second one, I made a real fuss and said I didn't want it. I knew they were fucking up my insides, and I was in so much pain I couldn't even walk down the corridor. After I'd refused it for about the third time, the nurse made me talk to this doctor. He didn't even come to see me. I got dragged, in pain, down to see him in his horrible little office. He basically told me that if I didn't have this second pessary, and if the operation went wrong because of it, then I would probably become infertile. I still believed he was wrong, but I didn't want to become infertile, so I let them insert it. The pains got worse, then I vomited about three times – the nurses got really cross with me, I don't know if they thought I was doing it deliberately – and then finally, in the morning, I had a miscarriage.'

'You poor thing,' says Jamie, putting his hand on her shoulder.

A tear runs down her cheek. 'I always pretended it didn't bother me. I mean, it was the most horrible thing I've ever seen in my life. You know, it actually looked like those pictures of developing babies you see sometimes on TV. But I was so determined to be grown up and put it behind me that I just walked out of the hospital the next day and decided I would move on. At the time I believed that coping with a trauma was just mind over matter. Like, if you don't actually count something as a trauma then it doesn't have to be one. After all, loads of people have abortions. My friend Lucy had one in her lunch break. I just decided it wouldn't be a big deal.'

'Sounds like a fucking big deal to me,' says Thea.

'Yeah, I guess it was,' says Emily. 'Anyway, now you know.'

'Do you just blank out with stress?' asks Anne. 'Or is it more random?'

'I thought it was random for a while,' she explains. 'But then when I looked at it with my therapist, I realised there was a kind of pattern. Often it would be when I was really anxious about something, but I wasn't admitting it. You know the kind of thing. My conscious self would think everything was totally cool, but my unconscious self would know better. I've never been able to stay with a boyfriend I didn't love — which is, like, all of them — because I'd start blanking out all the time, like my unconscious telling me he was wrong for me.'

'I get panic attacks,' says Anne.

'What for?' says Jamie. 'There's nothing wrong with your life, surely?'

'It's not my life that's the problem,' says Anne. 'It's everything else.'

'Is there any cure?' Bryn asks Emily. 'For the blankness, I mean.'

She laughs. 'No, probably not. You see, it *is* my life that's the problem, and I can't run away from myself. Of course, the world doesn't exactly help. All the pressure: trying to find a decent job, a flat in a cool place, a bloke, a good friend, the right food, worrying about your parents dying and planes crashing on London and IRA bombs and tube disasters and hijackings and radiation from mobile phones and GM food and psychopaths and muggers and corrupt policemen and date-rape drugs and carbon-monoxide poisoning and toxic-shock syndrome and road accidents and drive-by shooting and war and people being horrible to refugees and debt and prison and horrible bank managers. Maybe Anne's right. Life totally sucks.'

Paul's laughing. 'When you put it like that . . .' he says.

'If it wasn't so horrible and there wasn't a dead person here . . .' begins Emily.

'What?' says Jamie.

'Well, this would be a great place to . . . I don't know. *Heal.*'

'Heal?' says Bryn. 'That sounds a bit new-age.'

308

'Well I'm only saying,' says Emily. 'It would just be nice to not have all that stuff any more. If I could escape from the world, then I reckon I'd probably be all right. Then I wouldn't need to escape from myself, because it's the way I react to the world that's a problem.'

'It's like we've overdosed,' says Thea thoughtfully.

'Overdosed?' says Jamie.

'Yeah. We're only in our twenties, but we've already overdosed on the world.'

'Heal,' says Jamie thoughtfully, like he's meditating.

'Shall we go through to the sitting room?' says Paul. 'I'll make coffee.'

Chapter Thirty-Four

In the sitting room, people are talking about escape.

'How soon do you think we can do it?' asks Thea.

'There's your ankle to consider,' says Jamie.

'It'll be all right tomorrow, I'm sure.'

'And if it's not?' he says.

'Then I'll take my chances and go in the boat with you lot.'

'What boat?' says Jamie. 'I don't remember making one.'

'We'll sort something out,' says Paul.

Bryn ends up making the coffee, since Paul cooked. He places dripping mugs on the floor next to each person and then sits down on the sofa next to Thea. Everyone's here, except Emily, who's still in the kitchen.

'We fucked up pretty bad today, didn't we?' says Bryn.

'We suck at escaping,' says Anne.

'It's not like any of us have been in this situation before,' says Jamie.

'Makes you realise you should have joined the Scouts after all,' says Paul.

'I was a Brownie for a day,' says Anne.

'What happened?' asks Jamie.

'I got expelled for saying fuck.'

'Were none of us in the Scouts or the Guides or anything?' asks Jamie.

'You must have been in the Scouts,' says Anne. 'Weren't you?'

'No,' he says. 'It was on a Monday night and my mum had to work.'

'But you wanted to be, though, I bet?'

'Yeah.'

'You know,' says Anne. 'It is funny, don't you think?'

'What?' says Thea.

'Well, we're all so useless,' she says. 'We're the perfect kidnappees.'

'Did the dead guy know that?' asks Jamie. 'Do you think it's significant?'

'I think it's an accident,' says Anne.

'How did it happen?' asks Paul.

'What?' asks Emily, walking in with a tea towel.

'We're just wondering how come we're all so incompetent,' says Anne.

Emily laughs. 'I see.'

'Paul isn't incompetent,' says Thea. 'He could design some system to get us out.'

'What, a teleport system?' he says. 'Get real.'

'See,' says Anne, laughing. 'We all suck.'

'Well, we're all urban young people,' says Emily defensively. 'We're not exactly geared up for survival in the fucking wilderness.'

'It's ironic, isn't it?' says Jamie.

'What?' says Emily.

'Well, that we got here by claiming to be Bright Young Things.'

'We are Bright Young Things,' says Paul. 'We're just not very practical.'

'But we are going to do it,' says Jamie.

'Yeah,' says Emily. 'We'll prove ourselves wrong.'

'They always escaped on *The A Team*,' says Bryn.

'Yeah, and when we get out of here, we can go on *Trisha*,' says Emily.

'What's *Trisha*?' asks Thea.

'Never mind,' says Emily.

'So much for healing,' says Bryn.

Bryn's got a headache.

'Does anyone want anything from the medicine cabinet?' he asks.

'He just can't help drug-dealing,' jokes Paul.

'Yeah, you're funny mate,' he says. 'Anyway, I'm going to give all that up.'

'Seriously?' says Thea.

'Yeah. I'm going to sort my life out when we get home.'

'Cool,' says Emily. 'I think we could all do something like that.'

'Not the life-change thing, please,' groans Anne.

The cold air out in the hall clears Bryn's head almost instantly. Nevertheless, he could do with one of the Tamazepams he saw in the medicine cabinet up in the dead guy's room. The stuff up there is far superior to the medical supplies in the kitchen. In the kitchen there's paracetamol; upstairs there's co-proxamol. In the kitchen there are some plastic plasters; up here there are proper bandages. He must remember to take an ankle support down for Thea. He wonders why he didn't think of it before. Anyway, he doesn't know why someone would have sleeping pills on a desert island, but it's cool, because jellies are Bryn's favourite. Of course, he's going to give up drugs and all that one day; it's just not going to be today.

Bryn's already been up here exploring once. The room's full of fucked up but interesting things (apart from the fear stuff and the body, that is): loads more seeds, fertiliser, hosepipes, funny tubes, some kind of air pump, supplies of paper, pens and notebooks, water-purifying tablets, rolls of material, wool, and about fifty bars of soap.

He necks a couple of jellies and goes to leave. There are some planks of wood and old bookshelves stacked against the wall just by the small toilet. He didn't do a very thorough job of materials research or whatever the hell it was earlier on, but now he wonders if you could make a boat out of all these bits of wood. Of course he'd have to test their buoyancy, but they could be just the thing. He starts pulling the planks away from the wall, examining each one. They seem to be the top, bottom and sides of a large crate. Soon, without even really noticing, he's shifted all the junk away from the wall, and it's only then that he realises there's another small room behind it.

When he goes downstairs, he's carrying an inflatable boat and an outboard motor.

'Fucking hell,' says Paul, when Bryn walks back into the sitting room.

'Is that a boat?' says Emily.

'Shit,' says Jamie. 'Where did you get that?'

'Upstairs,' says Bryn, putting it, and the motor, down in the middle of the floor.

'Cool,' squeals Emily. 'This is *so* cool. Does the motor work?'

Paul pokes at it a bit and then pulls its string. Nothing happens.

'No,' he says.

'Why would there be a boat upstairs?' muses Jamie.

'It was behind a load of crap,' says Bryn.

'But still,' says Emily. 'You'd think that the dead guy wouldn't just leave a boat lying around. I mean, we're just going to fuck off now, first thing tomorrow, right?'

'I suppose he didn't know he was going to be dead and that we'd have carte blanche to search through everything in his room,' Anne points out.

'Maybe the boat was for him to get away in,' suggests

Thea. 'Since he didn't have the helicopter coming back for him.'

'The motor doesn't work,' Paul points out. 'It won't get very far.'

'Do you know what's wrong with it?' asks Thea.

'No,' he says.

'Can you mend it?' asks Jamie.

'Don't know,' he says. 'Probably.'

Chapter Thirty-Five

Paul makes a start on the motor immediately. Anne's helping him and talking about some weird holiday in California. The fire's still hot, but seems to be dying. The rain has almost stopped, although the wind's still strong. Emily imagines all the power from the wind going through the turbine and being stored in the batteries. It's a comforting thought, that the elements are providing power for the house. All the noises soon become hypnotic and Emily yawns.

'Where are we all sleeping tonight?' she asks.

'Down here again?' suggests Bryn.

Paul groans. 'No way. My back won't take it.'

'Or mine,' says Thea. 'That floor's too hard.'

'It'll be cold upstairs, though,' says Bryn. 'On our own in those rooms.'

'The fire warms the whole house,' Jamie points out.

'But not enough,' says Bryn. 'And I'm not sleeping on my own with a dead body one floor above me. No way.'

'We could all sleep together in one of the beds,' suggests Emily.

'What, in a single bed?' says Thea. 'Get real.'

'We could double up,' suggests Bryn.

Emily gets the impression he doesn't want to be alone tonight.

'I'm going to be doing this for a while,' says Paul.

'Do you mind if we go to bed?' says Thea.

'No,' says Paul. 'You need to rest for tomorrow.'

'I'll go with Jamie,' says Emily.

Jamie looks astonished. Happy but astonished.

'Are you sure?' he asks, slightly breathlessly.

'Don't get excited,' she says. 'I only want your body heat.'

Jamie looks like he can't get up fast enough. Emily winks and smiles at Thea.

'Right, then,' she says, getting up. 'Is everyone else going to be OK?'

'I'm going to stay and help Paul,' says Anne.

'That leaves me and you then,' Bryn says to Thea.

'Needs must,' she says, getting up and yawning.

'I haven't changed my socks for three days,' he warns her.

'Don't worry, you won't be getting undressed,' she says.

'Oh,' says Bryn. 'Right.'

The four of them go upstairs.

At most, Emily's spent a total of half an hour in 'her' room since she arrived on this island, but she's still managed to spread her stuff around everywhere. There's an empty tampon-holder on one of the pillows (romantic, huh?), and the chest of drawers is covered with bits of tissue, two lipsticks (she brought four), some loose face powder (spilled), a comb, some hairspray, a small pocket mirror, her tweezers and some old receipts that were at the bottom of her bag. Her original knickers are on the floor and the spare pair, which she wore yesterday, are soaking in the sink.

'Sorry about the mess,' she says to Jamie.

He looks nervous. 'Are you sure about this?' he asks.

'About what?' she says teasingly.

'This,' he says. 'You know.'

'Have you never shared a bed with a girl before?' she asks.

318

'Yes, of course. But only with, you know ...'

'Girlfriends.'

'Yes.'

She sits on the bed and takes off her trainers.

'It's no big deal,' she assures him. 'Everyone does it.'

He's still standing by the door, shaking slightly. Emily gets under the covers fully clothed, and after a few seconds Jamie does the same, stopping first to take off his shoes and socks. Emily notes that his feet don't smell. Well, that's good.

Once in bed, he won't stop fidgeting.

'What's wrong?' Emily asks him eventually.

'My trousers are itchy,' he complains.

'Take them off then,' she says. 'You are wearing boxers, aren't you?'

'Of course,' he says, and wriggles out of his trousers.

'Is that better?'

'Yes, thanks. Emily?'

'What?'

'What you said about healing before ...'

'Mmm.'

'Did you mean it?'

She sighs. 'Of course I did.'

'So, in theory, you would like to stay here for a while?'

'Yeah, in theory,' she says. 'But not now. I mean, there's a dead body here.'

'Hmm. The island's nice, though, isn't it?'

'Yeah, I guess the island's all right. Just right for six,' she jokes.

'Yeah,' laughs Jamie. 'Just right for six.'

Emily picks up her white notebook and a pen from the bedside table and starts writing her journal entry for today.

'What are you writing?' asks Jamie.

'Just stuff,' she says. 'I'm keeping a journal.'

'That's such a good idea,' says Jamie.

'Yeah, well.'

'Did you write about last night?'

'Yeah. Bits.'

'Did it make you feel better?' he asks.

'It did, actually.' She looks at him. 'Sorry I was so mental.'

'I'm sorry I was so weird today,' says Jamie. 'I had things on my mind.'

'That's OK. I've been trying to feel normal all day. It's hard.'

'I know.'

'Jamie?'

'Mmm?'

'Are you scared of drowning?'

'I haven't really thought about it.'

'I can't stop thinking about it,' she confesses. 'Sorry, but I had to say.'

'You can tell me anything,' says Jamie. 'Please tell me anything that upsets you.'

'Really?'

'Yes. Really.'

'I could go on forever, though,' she says, laughing. 'You'd get bored.'

'I promise you I wouldn't.'

'You're so sweet,' she says.

'It's not because I'm sweet,' he says. 'I care about you. I want you to get better.'

Emily laughs again. 'You make it sound like I'm ill.'

'I think you are. And I think talking will make you better.'

'The therapy didn't cure me. It made it a bit better, but—'

'Yes, but you need to talk to someone who cares about you.'

'Maybe. Well, where do you want me to start?'

'At the beginning,' he suggests. 'Tell me your earliest memory.'

It's a bit cramped in the single bed, but Emily likes the feeling of Jamie next to her.

'You're not too cramped in here are you?' she asks him suddenly.

'Are you?' he says.

'I'm fine.'

'Yeah. Me too. So tell me your earliest memory.'

'OK.'

Hours later, Emily is still holding the notebook. Her face is wet with tears, and her throat hurts from talking so much. She puts the book back on the bedside table and switches off the light.

'Goodnight,' she says, turning away from Jamie.

'Night,' he says, turning to face her back.

They lie there for about ten minutes, not moving, hardly breathing.

'Can I put my arm around you?' Jamie asks eventually.

'Sure,' says Emily.

Chapter Thirty-Six

Paul's tinkering with the outboard motor, trying to make it work by tomorrow. Everyone except him and Anne are in bed now, 'doubling up', whatever that involves. Anne's looking serene, reading in front of the fire. He can't help but stare at her, but every time she looks up, he pretends to be concentrating on the motor.

'Do you want something to drink?' he asks her eventually.

'Coke,' she says hopefully.

'Milkshake?' he offers.

'Cool.'

When he gets back, she appears to have given up reading and is lying on the sofa.

'How did you get into computer hacking?' she asks him.

'Messing about with e-mail,' he says. 'What about you?'

'I never said I was a hacker,' says Anne.

'Oh, come on. You've got it written all over you.'

'What?'

'The attitude, the disrespect for authority, the junk food stuff.'

'I've only done a little bit,' she admits. 'I'm more into games.'

'What, programming?'

'Yeah.'

'Didn't you create a game at university or something?'

'That's right.'

'What is it called?'

'"Life".'

'What's it about?'

She smiles. 'Life. It's a life sim.'

'A *life* sim?'

'Yeah. You know "Sim City" and "Theme Park" and everything?'

'Yeah, of course.'

'Well, it's like that, but it has life as its theme. Instead of creating a world or a business and running it successfully, the object of the game is to take a human character through their life. You have to decide what the person will eat and drink, at what age they will lose their virginity and with which other character it will take place. There are over five hundred characters in the game, all with artificial intelligence developed to a level where the main character can interact with them. You have the same bank of characters – five hundred – to choose from at the start. The opening level is a load of babies all about to be born, and you can look at the characteristics of the parents and choose which baby you want to "be". Then for the first few "years" – in game time – you only have to decide when to cry or smile. Then you have to learn how to use the potty you get, which is quite complicated. When you're a kid, you can earn pocket money, which you can spend on sweets or comics or whatever. If you eat too many sweets, though, you end up spending a load of money at the dentist when you're an adult.'

'Does the character work when he or she grows up?' asks Paul.

'If they learn the skills to get a job, then yes. All through the game you have the option to go to places and learn particular skills. For example, if you befriend the video shop owner, he'll eventually offer you a Saturday job and train you to use the till – unless you've already taken up skateboarding, in which case you might turn him down to enter a series of competitions which are all on a Saturday. If you spend most of your time at school, you get the chance to take academic qualifications. Your character can open bank accounts, get mortgages, loans, and so on. They can also visit the hospital if they're ill – although the NHS hospital is shit, so it's a good idea to invest in private health insurance when you're quite young. You receive money, which you keep in the bank – unless you decide to keep it under your mattress, in which case you encourage burglars – favours, which you keep in the form of greetings cards on your mantelpiece, and feuds, which come in the form of bricks through your window.'

'What happens if you run out of money?' asks Paul.

'You get a loan. But if you can't pay it off, you'll have to start selling things.'

'What if you sell everything and you still don't have any money?'

'You have to cut your costs. And if you're still fucked, you can either try to get a better job, go to a loan shark, or beg on the streets. If you beg on the streets, it helps if you have a skill you can trade on, for example if you learned to play the guitar as a child, you can do that to earn money. I programmed elements into the game where, for example, if you've learnt an instrument at home, befriended a particular set of people, bought a pet goldfish, and then ended up busking on the streets for money, you'll get approached by a scout for a new boy or girl band. I didn't actually write these bits for my project, but I'm working on them now. The idea is that there are hidden "celebrity" levels in the game that you try and get to. Then you basically get to live the life of a celebrity.'

'It sounds so cool,' says Paul. 'How do you win the game?'

'By making your character live to a hundred.'

'What if your character dies before that?' he asks.

'Game over,' she says. 'It's quite hard. Even I find it difficult.'

'I bet it's totally addictive,' he says.

'Mmm. I was quite inspired by playing games like "Final Fantasy VII", where you do almost feel like your character has a real life, and you're able to earn money and then spend it on things. One of the problems in the real world right now is that a lot of the time you can't earn money even if you want to. So a game like mine allows a person to have a normal life, even if it's just in a game, which is basically — except for a few random elements — fair and makes sense. Real life *so* isn't like that. That's why I thought the game would work. Plus, people can have fun experimenting with different characters. You can set yourself challenges, like you could choose to be a baby from really poor DSS parents, and try to turn the character into the prime minister or something.'

'And this is a comment on what you think about the world?' asks Paul.

'No,' she says defensively. 'It's just a game.'

'Yeah, right,' he says, smiling. 'Whatever you say.'

She smiles back. 'Yeah.'

'I've often thought about designing a game,' says Paul.

'You should. It's fun.'

'Hmm. It's not really going to change anything if I do, though.'

'Change what?'

'The world.'

'The world? Anne starts laughing. 'You want to change the world? How?'

'By fucking things up. Making people aware. Why are you laughing?'

'You can't change the world. You have no control over it.'

'You do, though. Especially now.'

'Why now? Why not before?'

'Computers. You must know what you can do with computer systems.'

She frowns. 'Yeah, I do, but . . .'

'What?'

'So you fuck up the system, which eventually fucks up the company . . .'

'It's like the "Horseshoe Nail" poem,' he says. 'If you can fuck up a nail . . .'

'I loved that poem when I was a kid. How did it go? Oh, I remember: *Because of the nail the shoe was lost, because of the shoe the horse was lost, because of the horse the battle was lost, because of the battle the kingdom was lost, and all for the want of a horseshoe nail.* Something like that, anyway.'

'Well, then, you can see what I mean.'

'But no one ever won a battle by tampering with a horse's hoof, Paul. The poem's just a metaphor for what could happen if that particular horse was crucial to winning the battle. It doesn't mean that if it happened to any horse the battle would be lost.'

'So maybe I'm just trying to find the right nail, or the right horse.'

'Do you think MoneyBaby does that? Do you think the horse is the banks?'

Paul loves this girl. She thinks like him. 'Yeah,' he says.

'So you really want to change the world, then?'

'Of course,' he says, smiling at her.

'Do you think people want that?' she asks.

'Sorry?'

'Normal people. Your mother, your friends, whoever. Do they want the world changed?'

'They . . . I don't know,' says Paul. 'Probably not.'

Anne pulls a face. 'They've been *brain*washed,' she says, in a film-trailer voice.

They both laugh.

'They have, though,' says Paul. 'They just want to buy stuff. Be entertained.'

'Exactly,' says Anne. 'They want to be entertained.'

'I don't get what you're saying.'

'Why not just let people watch their TVs and play their games and stuff?'

'Because there's more to life than that. More than just capitalism.'

'Who says?'

'You know it's true,' he says. 'Come on.'

'Yeah, but if these people don't believe that, who's going to convince them?'

'People like me, I guess.'

'What, by force?' she says.

'No, of course not. By educating people. Shocking them. Pranks.'

'So you dress up as a rabbit and people throw away their TVs?'

'You know it's not as simple as that.'

'The only way to have any effect on people is through entertainment.'

'In what way?' he asks.

Anne looks like she's about to say something profound.

Then her expression changes.

'Give them fun stuff to do. Make them nice games. Nice books. Nice films.'

'Why?' he says.

'Because it makes life *nice*. No one wants to live in a time of revolution. Not when we've been lucky enough to be born into a time of luxury and wealth and quilted loo roll and chocolate-covered pretzels and a McDonald's on every high street. What people don't ever consider is that maybe McDonald's isn't an evil capitalist icon taking over the world; that maybe it's just a convenient way of eating in a hurry, and people like it so much it's everywhere. Maybe the power of the consumer is more valid than the power of the people. Or maybe there's no difference any more.'

'Do you believe all that crap?' asks Paul.

She shrugs. 'Maybe.'

'For someone who doesn't care, you've sure given this a lot of thought,' he says.

'Maybe I have,' she says, smiling.

'Seriously,' he says. 'What you were saying about games and books and stuff . . .'

'What about it?'

'You were going to say something else, weren't you?'

'No,' she says.

'You were.'

'Why do you care?' she asks.

He moves closer to her.

'Look, Anne, I'm being really honest with you right now. I'm not making jokes or messing around like I do with the others. You're the first person who's ever made me want to be totally honest, and, believe it or not, I actually care what you think.'

'You care what I think?'

'Why is that such a surprise?'

'No one cares what I think.'

'I do.'

'Why, though? Why me?'

'You're clever. And . . .'

'And what?'

'Nothing,' he says. 'It doesn't matter.'

'Well tell me more, then,' she says. 'Do you actually go on protests and everything?'

'Fucking hell, no,' he says, laughing.

'Why not?'

'You don't change anything that way.'

'So all the stuff you do is computer-based?'

'Yeah. I break into systems and do damage.'

'And is this because you want to save the world, or just because you enjoy it?'

'If I'm really, really honest? Both, I guess.'

'Aha! I knew it.'

'What?'

'All this political stuff is just entertainment for you. I win.'

'Is this a game?'

'It is now.'

'Well then tell me this: is your game just a game?'

She smiles. 'I think you know the answer to that.'

'You're not as cold as you make out, are you?' he says.

'Maybe. Maybe not. I'm just living in a way that makes sense to me.'

Paul unscrews something on the motor.

'So what are you going to do now you've got friends?' he asks Anne.

She shrugs. 'I don't really know.'

'Why didn't you have any friends before?'

'Didn't need any.'

'Are you sure that's why?'

'I prefer being on my own.' She pauses. 'It's less ... painful.'

'I see,' he says, looking at her. 'Now I think I understand.'

'Understand what?'

'What drives you.'

'Why would you want to understand what drives me?'

'Because I'm in love with you.'

Anne hasn't said anything for about ten minutes. She looks confused.

'Anne?' Paul says eventually.

'What?' she says.

'Aren't you going to say anything?'

'I, uh ...'

'I take it you don't love me back?'

She still looks vacant, like she doesn't understand the question.

Paul's not sure whether he should have told her. But, you know, this whole experience just has spill-your-guts written all over it. There's something about discovering dead bodies and planning escapes and then talking about important things with the only person you've ever really cared about that makes a person want to be totally honest. And there won't be time for any of this tomorrow. Paul can't bear to think that they could all drown, and he'd have never told this person what he thinks of her.

'Why do you love me?' she asks eventually.

'Why?'

'Yeah. Why.'

'Because you're clever and funny and sharp and sweet and—'

'But I don't think the same things you do,' she says.

'I think maybe we've got more in common than we're making out.'

'Hmm. Maybe. But you hardly know me.'

'I know you like strawberry milkshake.'

'That's a good start. I prefer Coke, though.'

'I also know that inside you're a very emotional person.'

'Am I?'

'Yeah. I know you care about a lot of things. That's why you don't do anything.'

'That's why I don't do anything?'

'Yeah. Because you care too much. You'd always be disappointed.'

She looks down at her knees. 'Maybe,' she says.

'I'm not going to ask you to change,' he says.

'I thought that was what came next?'

'No. I love you the way you are.'

'Well I'm not going to change, so that's good, I suppose.'

'So?'

'Will you kiss me?' she asks eventually.

'Now?'

'Yes, now.'

Chapter Thirty-Seven

Anne wakes up at about seven. Paul's lying beside her.

'Go back to sleep,' he mumbles, when she sits up.

'Shhh,' she says. 'Sorry I disturbed you.'

This is the earliest Anne's woken up in the last ten years. Rain is tapping at the window and it's cold. She snuggles closer to Paul, watching the raindrops hit the glass pane and then trickle down it. The wind occasionally makes a sharp whistling sound, and when it does there are suddenly more raindrops on the window.

It's 9 September 1999, and Anne's not a virgin any more.

'I can't believe I lost my virginity in a house with a dead guy in the attic,' she says.

'You said you wanted to do it Jerry Springer-style,' he mumbles.

'I did, didn't I?'

'Anyway, I'm not that bothered about the dead guy any more,' says Paul.

'No, me neither,' says Anne. 'It's like having a weird pet.'

'The others don't agree,' says Paul, laughing sleepily.

'No. Well, he is rotting. It's a shame we can't stay here now.'

'Maybe we could,' says Paul thoughtfully. 'You know, if the dead guy goes.'

'Everyone wants to go home, though, don't they?'

'Emily wants to *heal*.'

'She thinks she does,' says Anne. She yawns. 'What time are we going?'

'Well, the motor works now.'

'So?'

'When everyone's up, I suppose. When it stops raining.'

By midday, everyone's standing by the cliffs. The boat is now fully inflated with the air pump Bryn found in the attic room. The motor works, which Paul demonstrates while everyone oohs and ahhs over how clever he is.

The sky's still grey, and the rain has turned to drizzle.

'Right,' Paul says, after killing the motor. 'Who's going, then?'

It was obvious when the boat was inflated that it would only take two people at most.

'Remind me of the plan again,' says Anne.

He grins at her. 'Two people go. Or one, but two's better. Get help. That's it.'

Emily's shivering like a child who's been in the sea too long. 'Count me out,' she says.

'I want to stay and look after Emily,' says Jamie.

'And I've got a sprained ankle,' says Thea.

'I'm not going,' says Anne.

'Me neither,' says Paul.

Everyone looks at Bryn.

'Don't fucking look at me,' he says.

'Jesus,' says Thea. 'Someone has to go.'

'I thought someone would want to,' says Paul.

'I'm epileptic,' says Jamie.

'Have you got any medication with you?' asks Paul.

'I don't need it,' says Jamie. 'Unless I'm stressed.'

'Oh, so the stress of being here has just been mild, then?' asks Thea.

'Yes, if you must know,' says Jamie. 'I've quite enjoyed it.'

'All right,' says Paul, sighing. 'Do we have a plan B?'

'*We* sort of had a plan B, didn't we?' Anne says to him.

'Not a very good one,' says Paul.

'Spill,' says Thea.

'Just that we could send the dead guy instead of us. But that doesn't—'

'Cool,' says Bryn. 'Top idea, mate.'

'Yes, but it doesn't help us escape, does it?' says Paul.

'It might,' says Thea. 'If he was, what would you call it . . . a message in a bottle.'

'A message in a bottle?' says Jamie.

Emily's sitting cross-legged on the floor, ignoring everyone.

'*Message in a bottle*,' she sings.

'Go on, Thea,' says Paul. 'Explain.'

'Well, we could strap him to the boat and send him off to sea. He'd wash up somewhere, and whoever found him would be like, *whoa, dead body*, the same as we were, and then they'd tell someone because they'd actually be able to, and we'll have left a note in the dead guy's pocket, or stuck to him or whatever, that says: *I've kidnapped six people and they're on the island I've just floated from*. Then someone will come and rescue us.'

'That's the most stupid thing I've ever heard,' says Paul, smiling.

'I love it,' says Anne. 'It's totally ridiculous.'

'Can't we just send the boat and the note?' says Bryn, frowning.

'There'll be no weight,' says Jamie. 'The boat won't float.'

Anne laughs. 'Does this all have to rhyme?'

'Boat, note, float,' says Emily, beginning to sway.

'She can't handle this any more,' says Jamie. 'Let's just do it.'

'Is everyone sure they don't want to go in the boat themselves?' says Paul.

'We're sure,' says Anne.

Paul smiles at her. *I love you*, he mouths, when no one else is looking.

'I'm not touching the dead guy,' says Jamie.

'For fuck's sake,' says Paul. 'I'll do it.'

'I'll help,' says Thea.

'What about your ankle?' says Bryn.

'Oh, good point. You'd better go then,' she says to Bryn, flashing a grin at Anne.

'Go on, Jamie,' says Anne. 'You go as well. We'll look after Emily.'

Jamie turns a bit green, then a bit pink. 'OK,' he says.

'Use a sheet,' Thea shouts after them. 'Like a hammock.'

'OK,' Paul calls back.

'Do they know what they're doing?' asks Anne.

'Who knows?' says Thea. 'Anyway. Tell me about last night . . .'

'You could compose the note,' Bryn shouts to them.

Jamie says something to Bryn that the girls can't hear.

'Oh, don't worry,' calls Bryn. 'Jamie says he's going to do it.'

'Cool,' says Anne. 'We'll just sit here, then.'

Thea smiles at her. They both look at Emily. She's totally vacant.

'Emily?' says Anne. 'Are you OK?'

'Oh, fine,' she says, snapping out of it. 'I just didn't want to go on the boat.'

'Oh. We thought you were having an episode.'

'I will be when they bring that *thing* down here,' she says.

The grey sky gets darker, and it begins to rain hard again.

'Maybe I'll wait in the kitchen,' says Emily, looking at the sky.

'I'll go with you,' says Thea. 'Anne?'

'No. I like the rain. I'll stay here and help the others when they come.'

'Are you sure?' says Thea.

'Yeah. It'll probably take four of us.'

'OK.' Thea smiles. 'I'll put the kettle on.'

After five minutes, there's no sign of the boys and Anne's totally wet. There's something about standing in the rain, though. Something different from standing in a cold shower, which it basically is. Anne loves the rain. You never get wasps when it rains, and children aren't out playing, and people don't lie in parks. She wonders where they go in winter, those hedgehog-people you only ever see in London parks in spring and summer, gulping Diet Pepsi in their lunch breaks in their short-sleeved work shirts.

Sunshine always ruins Anne's walks in London. It's too hot, there are too many people, and you just can't feel properly alone in the sunshine. She wonders whether she'll ever feel properly alone again now she has Paul. She smiles. She doesn't mind, as long as he lets her walk in the rain on her own from time to time. She suddenly wonders where she'll be taking these walks, and if they'll ever take place off this island. The escape plan, after all, isn't going very well.

Anne imagines never seeing another Tango commercial or Levi's campaign. She imagines not drinking Coke again, or going to McDonalds. She imagines not paying council tax and rent (soon, her parents have threatened), and not buying travel cards and magazines and videogames. She imagines not living in a world with stupid people and racism and violence and big corporations. She imagines living in a world in which people don't travel, all energy is renewable, and nature is just, well, natural. Whatever she said to Paul last night, it would be pretty cool.

'Hey,' says Paul, walking towards her, carrying the brown suitcase and some twine.

'Hey,' she says back. 'Where's the dead body?'

He kisses her wet forehead. 'On its way.'

Soon, Jamie and Bryn emerge from the house. They have done what Thea said and used a sheet to transport the body, which is itself covered by another sheet. They all walk to the cliff edge. The waves below are at least five metres high. Each one smashes at the cliff face as if attacking it.

'Glad I'm not going out in that,' says Bryn.

'Me too,' says Anne.

Bryn and Jamie lower the sheet on to the ground.

'Aren't you going to put him into the boat?' asks Paul.

'Maybe we should put him in the boat when we get down there,' suggests Bryn.

'No,' says Paul. 'If we tie him strongly to the boat up here, then it'll be easier.'

'I think so too,' says Anne.

'It's going to be really slippery going down the cliff,' says Jamie.

'Then we'll have to be careful,' says Paul. 'Come on, get him in the boat.'

Bryn and Jamie pick up two corners of the sheet each and lift the body off the ground. They start swinging it horizontally like a hammock, aiming at the boat.

'Don't be stupid,' says Anne. 'Just slide him in vertically.'

In the end the procedure looks like something Anne saw on the in-flight safety manual on the way to California. The dead man slips off the sheet and into the boat as if he is alive and has just been rescued from a plane. He lands there with a thwack, lying in the exact same position as he was in upstairs when they first discovered him.

Paul starts unravelling some twine.

'Anyone know any good knots?' he asks.

No one does, so he just improvises. Once he's finished, the man looks quite secure. Paul has looped the twine around his arms and legs and then through the ropes on the sides of the rubber boat. Then he's made a few more loops around the dead guy's middle and tied several more knots to secure him.

'He's not coming out of that,' says Jamie, smiling.

'The water'll tighten the ropes as well,' says Bryn.

'What?' says Anne.

'When the rope gets wet, the knots will become tighter,' he explains.

'Oh,' she says. 'Cool.'

'What about his horrible suitcase?' says Paul. 'I thought it could go too.'

'You should have tied it on with him,' says Jamie.

'No,' says Paul. 'I had a better idea.'

He opens the suitcase and takes out the mask.

'Are you going to put it on him?' asks Bryn, laughing.

'Let me do it,' says Jamie, taking the mask.

He pulls it over the man's head. 'This is for Emily,' he mumbles.

'We'd better not give him the knife,' says Anne. 'It'll deflate the boat.'

Paul takes it and throws it over the cliff into the sea.

Bryn's pulled the syringe out of the suitcase. He looks uncomfortable.

'I've never touched one of these,' he says.

'What are you going to—' begins Jamie, but Bryn's already stuck the syringe through the mask and into the man's forehead.

'Have we gone mad?' asks Anne, laughing and shivering in the cold.

'No,' says Paul. 'We're just making him easier to spot.'

'Oh. Well in that case . . .' Anne takes one of the dildos and sticks it in his open mouth.

The others laugh.

'Cool,' says Jamie. 'Where shall we put the other two?'

'Don't even go there,' says Anne, and throws them over the cliff into the water below. She also throws the blindfold and the sewing kit. The suitcase is now empty, so she throws that, too.

'What about that spider?' asks Bryn.

'What, Sebastian?' says Paul.

'You called it Sebastian?' says Jamie.

'Yeah. Well, Anne did. What about him?'

'Shall we send him away too?'

'No!' wails Anne. 'He'll drown.'

'It would be a bit cruel,' says Paul.

'But we're sending our fears away with him,' says Bryn.

'Not that one,' says Paul firmly. 'It's not sinister like the others. It'll be all right.'

'Did you write the note?' Anne asks Jamie.

'Yep,' he says, waving it around.

'What does it say?' asks Bryn.

'Just what Thea said.'

Anne takes it from Jamie and looks at it. He's written it on a piece of blue paper. It says: *I've kidnapped six people and they're on the island I've just floated from. Please rescue them. They are the 'Bright Young Things' you probably know about. The ones who went missing on 6 September 1999.*

'Cool,' she says, giving it back to him.

'Where's it going to go?' asks Paul.

'In a plastic bag in his pocket,' says Jamie. 'I'll do it now.'

He seems to take ages fiddling with the bag and sticking it in the man's pocket.

'Let's go, then,' says Bryn.

Getting the boat down the cliff path is an inch-by-inch process, which is slow and cold and wet. They could have slid it down the mud, but there are too many prickly plants and sharp rock edges. No one wants to burst the boat. Anne is at the back with Paul, walking forwards. Jamie and Bryn are at the front going backwards, constantly looking over their shoulders for edges and things they might slip on. Now Thea's cut this path, there are no big plants or stinging nettles to get in their way. And it's not too treacherous in itself, going down here — there are no vertical drops or anything — but no one wants to fall or slip and risk losing the boat over the edge. Paul explains all the way down that it has to launch properly, and that they have to make it land the right way up. Bryn says it would be easier if they could switch on the outboard motor, but they've left it at the top. There'd be no safe way of turning it on without being in the water, and no one's getting into this stormy sea and coming out alive.

If they can just get the boat almost to the bottom, and then give it a good shove, it should land just beyond where the waves are breaking. Anne knows there's a good chance it'll get cut to pieces on the cliff face, but at least they're taking the chance with a dead man and not with themselves.

Eventually they reach a ledge.

'This is as far as we can go,' says Paul.

The waves are breaking only a few metres below them, licking up the cliff face.

'So what do we do?' says Bryn.

'We have to throw it just after a wave has broken,' says Paul, raising his voice over the wind and the spray. 'Aim for the calm bit.' He points at a patch of navy blue beyond all the froth and gush of the waves. 'Hopefully the pull-back effect will take the boat clear of the island. The tide is going out in theory, so ...'

'How do you know the tide's going out?' shouts Anne, pushing wet bits of hair out of her eyes.

'The charts,' Paul shouts back.

So he could read them.

'OK,' he shouts. 'Everyone ready?'

'Yeah,' shouts Bryn.

'Yes,' calls Jamie.

'Yeah,' says Anne, her fingers slipping slightly from the ropes on the boat.

'On three,' shouts Paul. 'One, two ... three.'

On *one* and *two* they swing the boat. On *three*, they let it go.

At first it seems as if the boat will be destroyed; it instantly catches an incoming wave and just misses some jagged-looking rocks. Almost vertical, the little boat bounces on the sea like a stray beach ball. But gradually it seems to move away from the island, rising and falling dangerously as it goes. Anne and the others stand there for about ten minutes until it's safely on its way.

'We did it,' laughs Jamie.

'Cool,' says Anne.

'Goodbye, Psycho,' says Paul.

'Yeah, bye,' calls Bryn, waving to the yellow shape in the mist.

'Better get back,' says Anne.

They turn to walk back up to the house.

At the top, the house suddenly looks warm and inviting; it's so incredibly wet outside. As they walk towards it, the rain suddenly turns to a drizzle and then stops. The sun comes out. Feeling like a little girl, Anne instantly turns to see if there's a rainbow. And there's Jamie, standing on the cliff-edge, screwing up a piece of blue paper and throwing it into the sea.